THE ENFIELD GANG MASSACRE

IMAGE COMICS, INC. • Robert Kirkman: Chief Operating Officer • Erik Larsen: Chief Financial
Officer • Todd McFarlane: President • Marc Silvestri: Chief Executive Officer • Jim Valentino: Vice
President • Eric Stephenson: Publisher / Chief Creative Officer • Nicole Lapalme: Vice President
of Finance • Leanna Caunter: Accounting Analyst • Sue Korpela: Accounting & HR Manager •
Lorelei Bunjes: Vice President of Digital Strategy • Emilio Bautista: Digital Sales Coordinator •
Dirk Wood: Vice President of International Sales & Licensing • Ryan Brewer: International Sales &
Licensing Manager • Alex Cox: Director of Direct Market Sales • Jon Schlaffman: Specialty
Sales Coordinator • Margot Wood: Vice President of Book Market Sales • Chloe Ramos: Book
Market & Library Sales Manager • Kat Salazar: Vice President of PR & Marketing • Deanna Phelps:
Marketing Design Manager Drew Fitzgerald: Marketing Content Associate • Heather Doornink:
Vice President of Production • Ian Baldessari: Print Manager • Drew Gill: Art Director • Tricia
Ramos: Traffic Manager • Melissa Gifford: Content Manager • Erika Schnatz: Senior Production
Artist • Wesley Griffith: Production Artist • Rich Fowlks: Production Artist • IMAGECOMICS.COM

THE ENFIELD GANG MASSACRE

Chris Condon
Jacob Phillips

Color Assists by Pip Martin

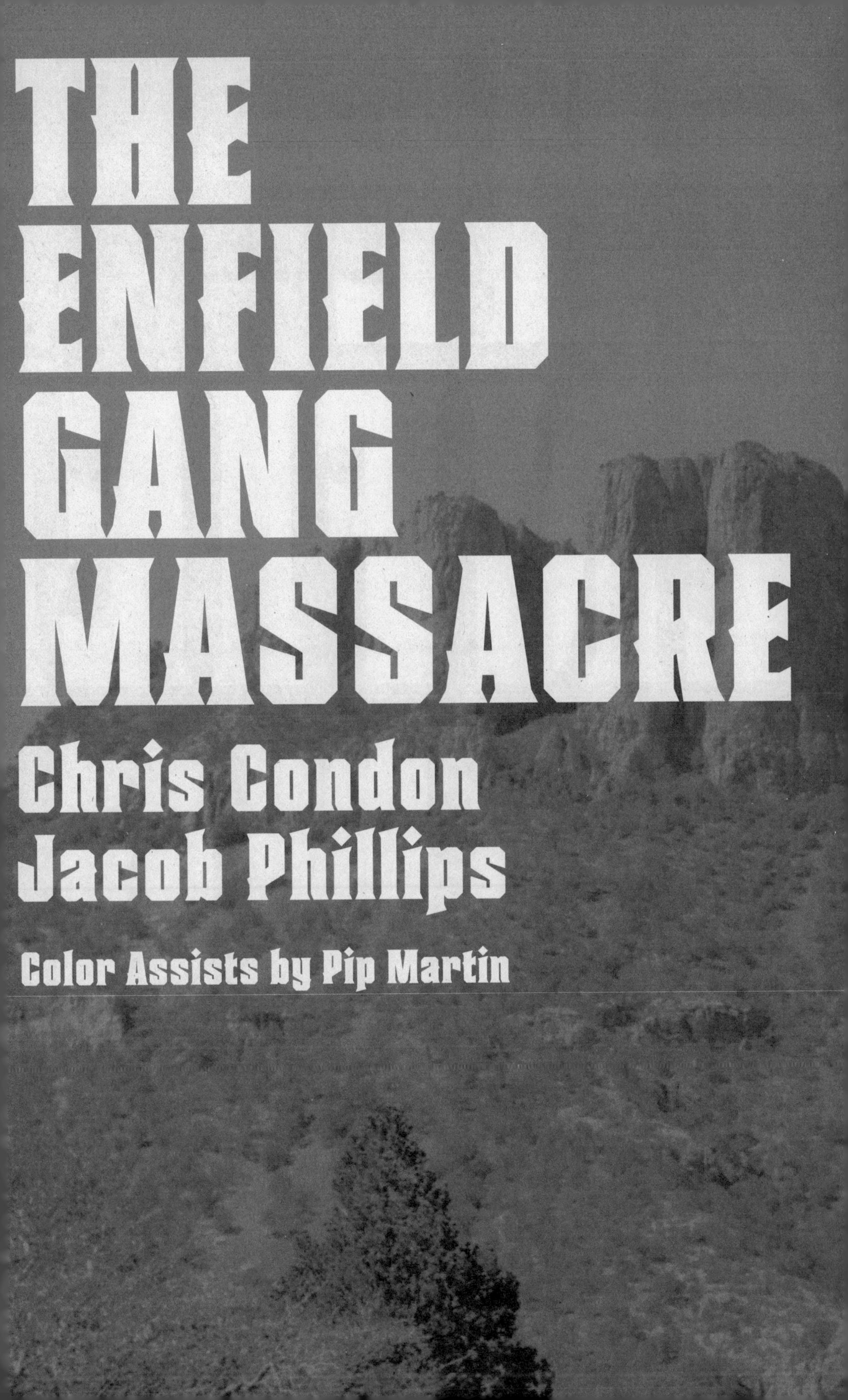

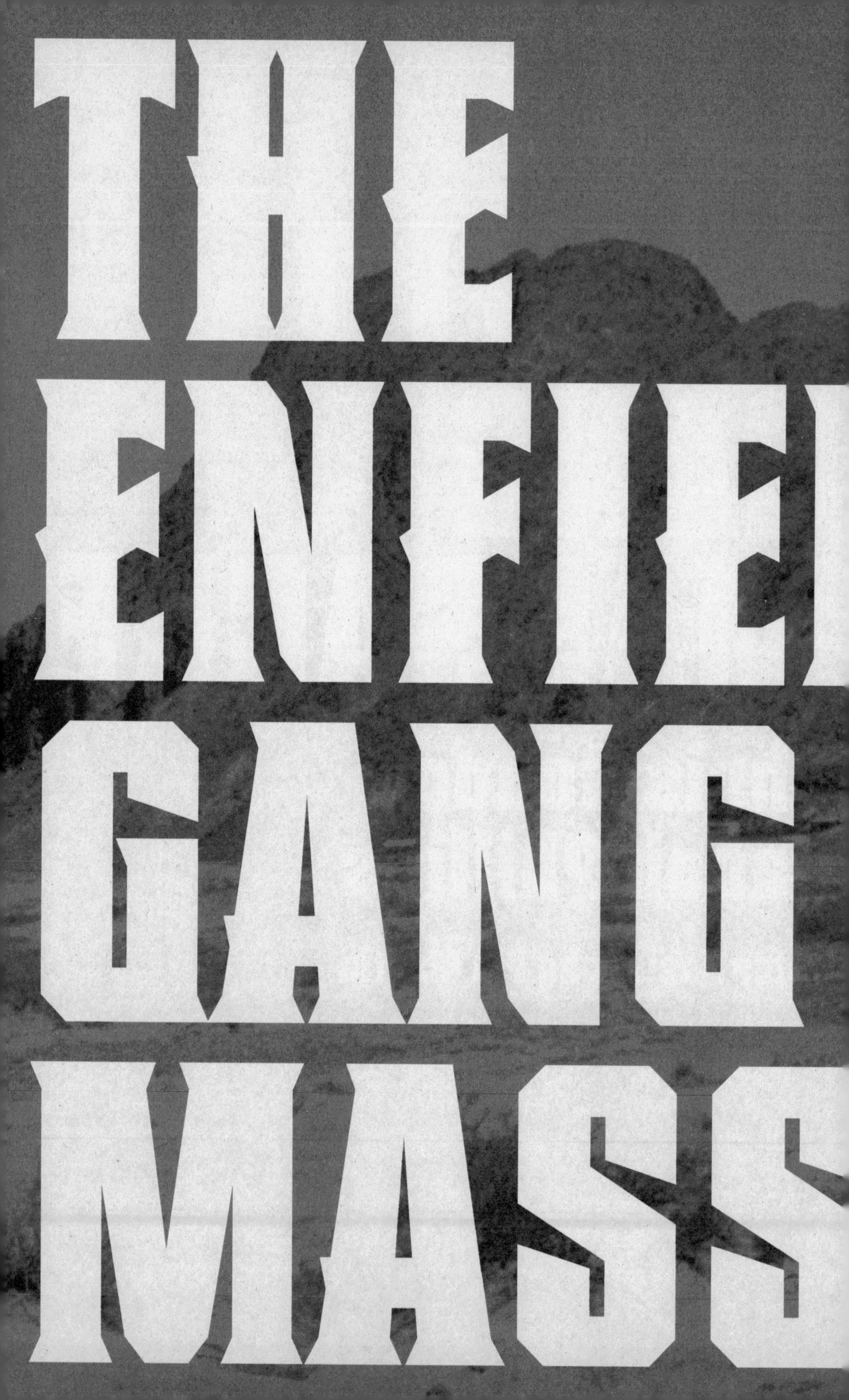

THE ENFIELD GANG MASS

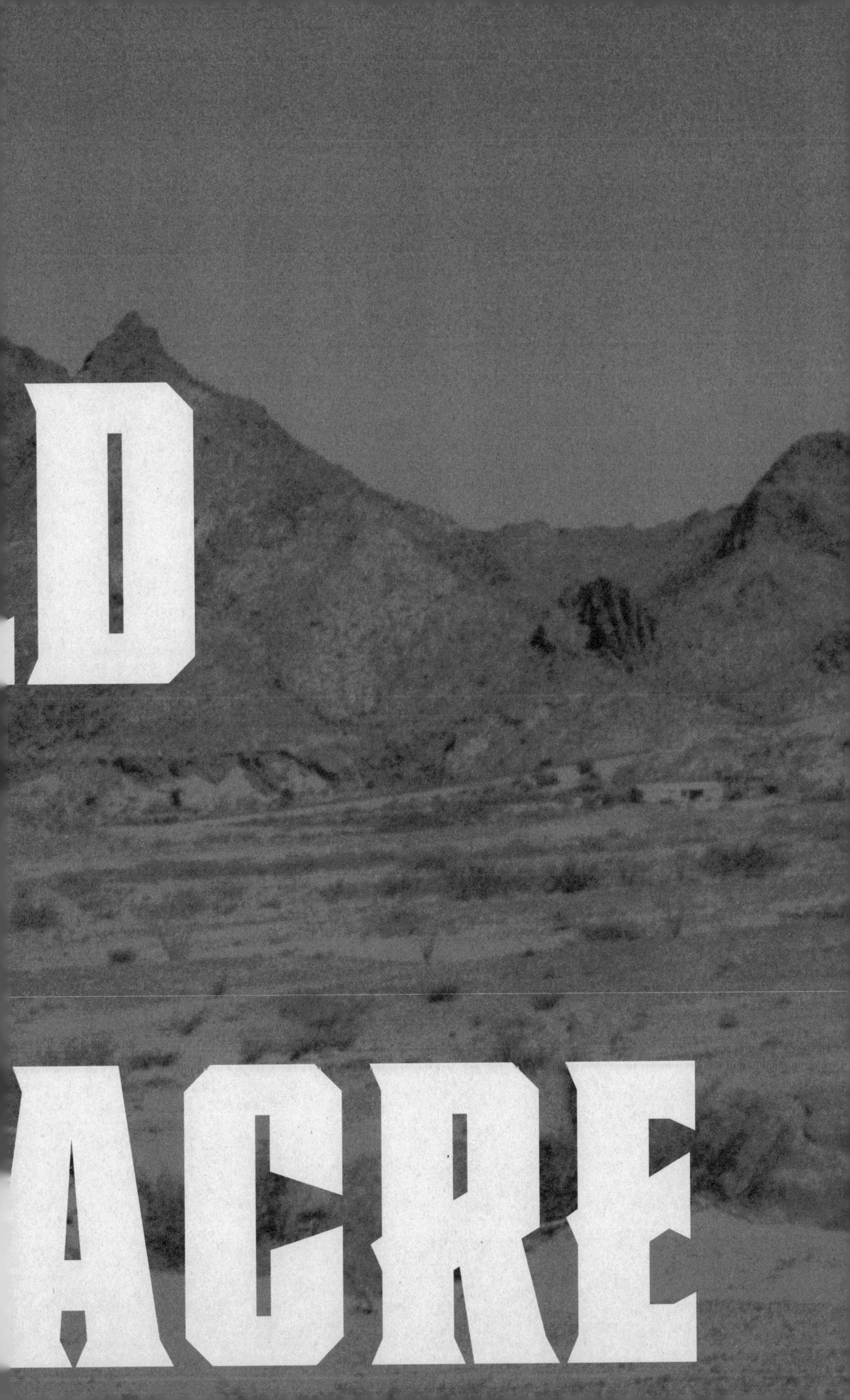
D
ACRE

CHAPTER ONE

THE BAD DEATH OF BILL BARLEY

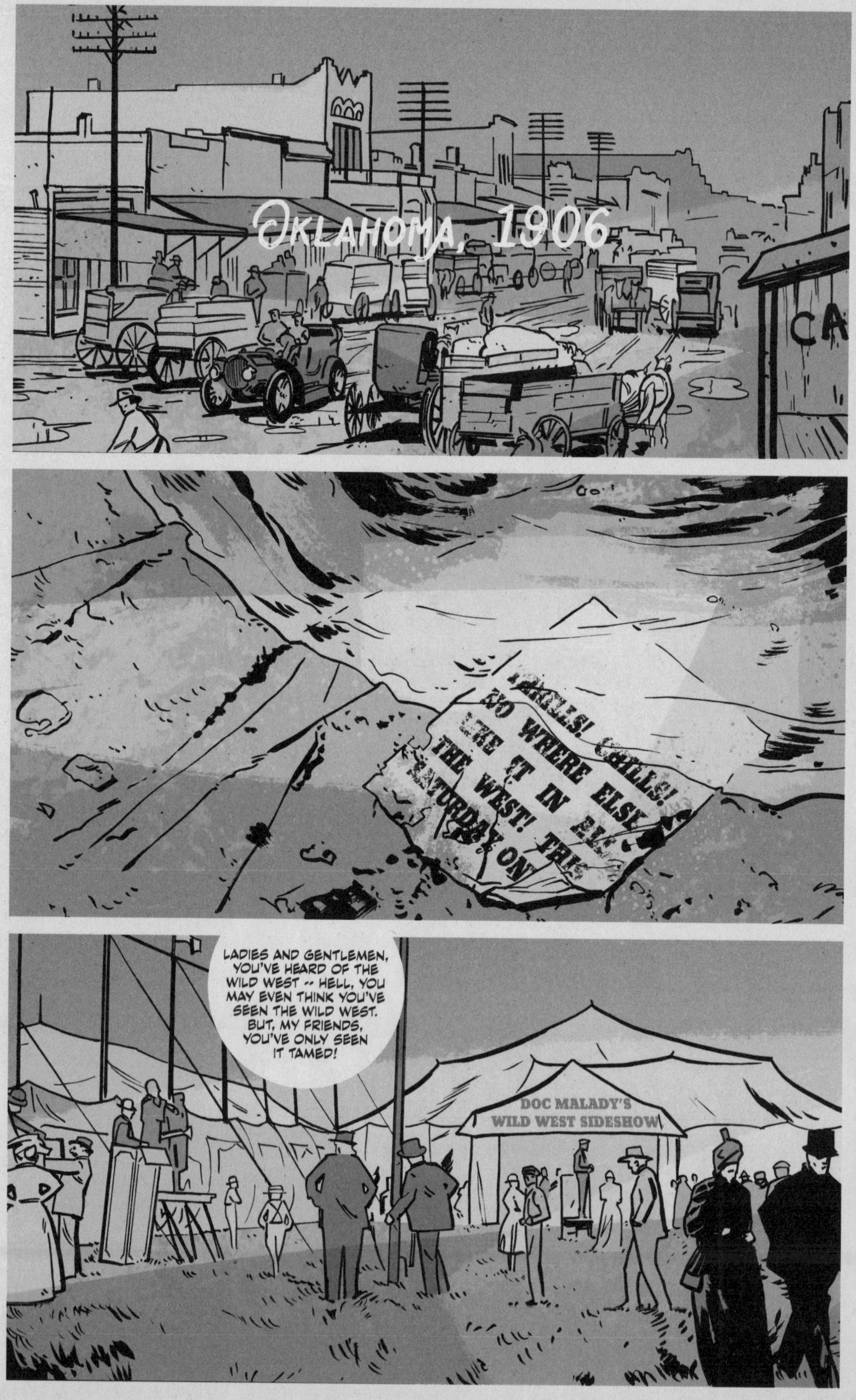
OKLAHOMA, 1906
CHILLS!
NO WHERE ELSE
IT IN
THE WEST!
LADIES AND GENTLEMEN, YOU'VE HEARD OF THE WILD WEST -- HELL, YOU MAY EVEN THINK YOU'VE SEEN THE WILD WEST. BUT, MY FRIENDS, YOU'VE ONLY SEEN IT TAMED!
DOC MALADY'S
WILD WEST SIDESHOW

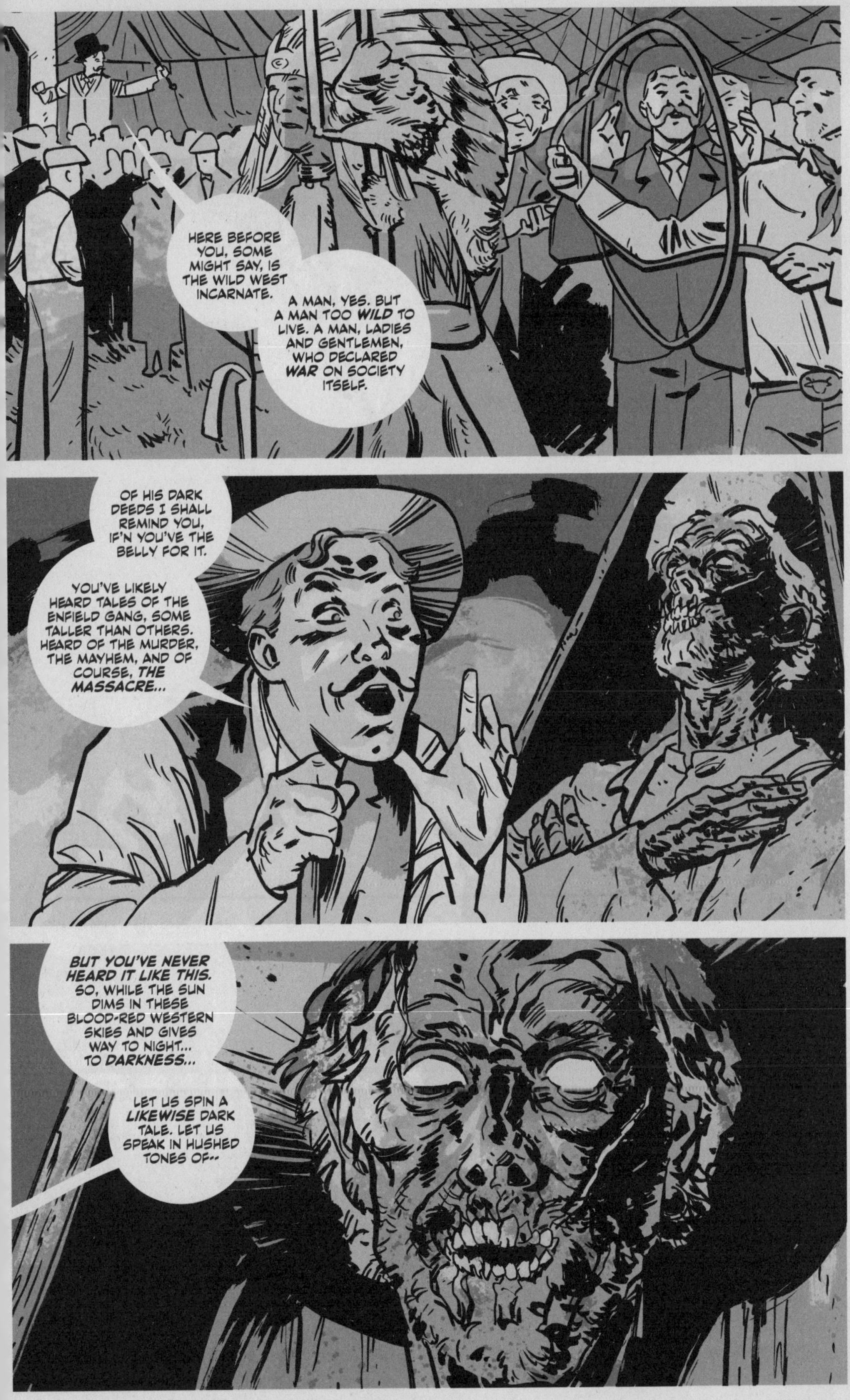

HERE BEFORE YOU, SOME MIGHT SAY, IS THE WILD WEST INCARNATE.
A MAN, YES. BUT A MAN TOO *WILD* TO LIVE. A MAN, LADIES AND GENTLEMEN, WHO DECLARED *WAR* ON SOCIETY ITSELF.
OF HIS DARK DEEDS I SHALL REMIND YOU, IF'N YOU'VE THE BELLY FOR IT.
YOU'VE LIKELY HEARD TALES OF THE ENFIELD GANG, SOME TALLER THAN OTHERS. HEARD OF THE MURDER, THE MAYHEM, AND OF COURSE, *THE MASSACRE...*
BUT YOU'VE NEVER HEARD IT LIKE THIS. SO, WHILE THE SUN DIMS IN THESE BLOOD-RED WESTERN SKIES AND GIVES WAY TO NIGHT... TO *DARKNESS...*
LET US SPIN A *LIKEWISE* DARK TALE. LET US SPEAK IN HUSHED TONES OF--

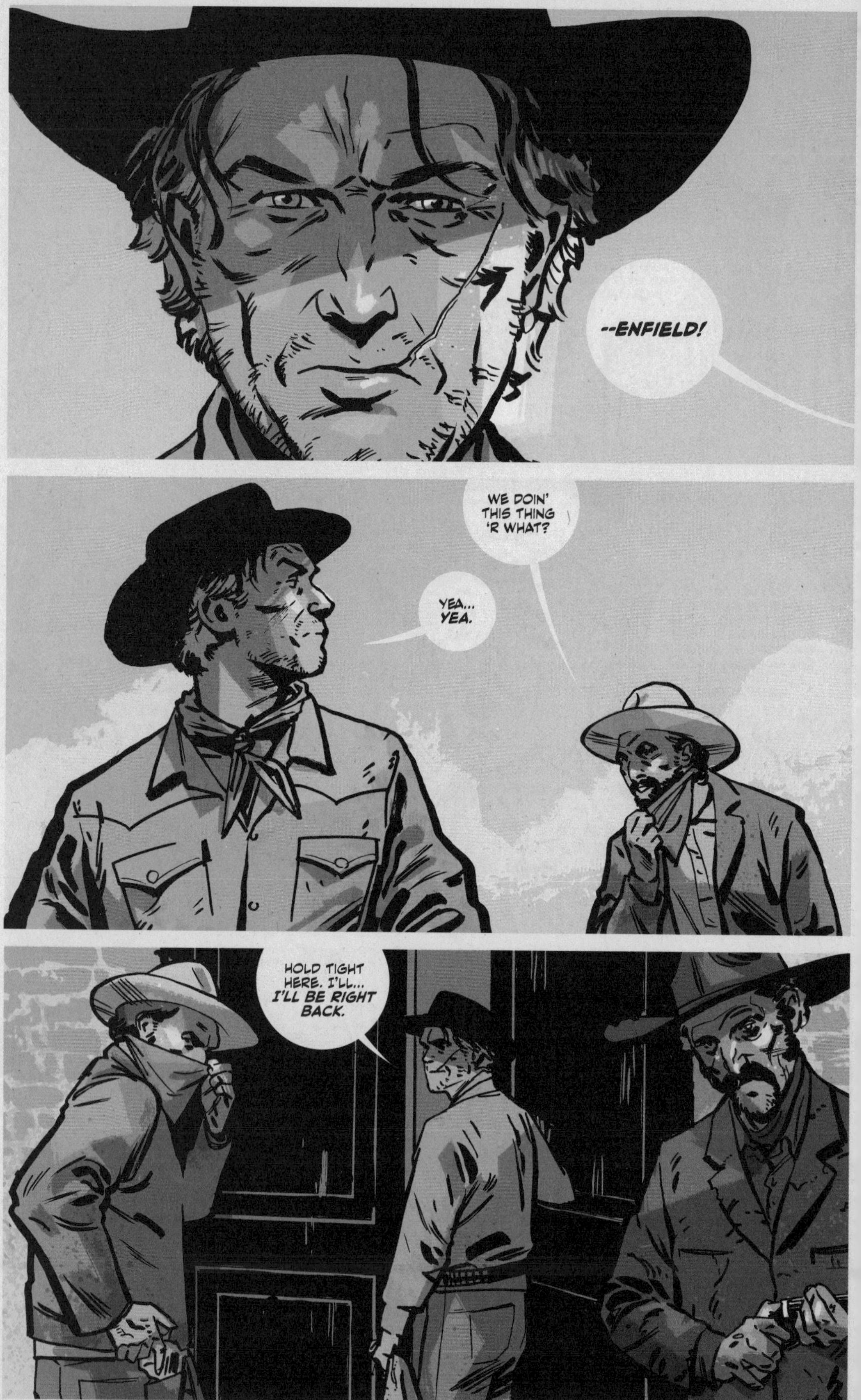
--ENFIELD!
WE DOIN' THIS THING 'R WHAT?
YEA... YEA.
HOLD TIGHT HERE. I'LL... I'LL BE RIGHT BACK.

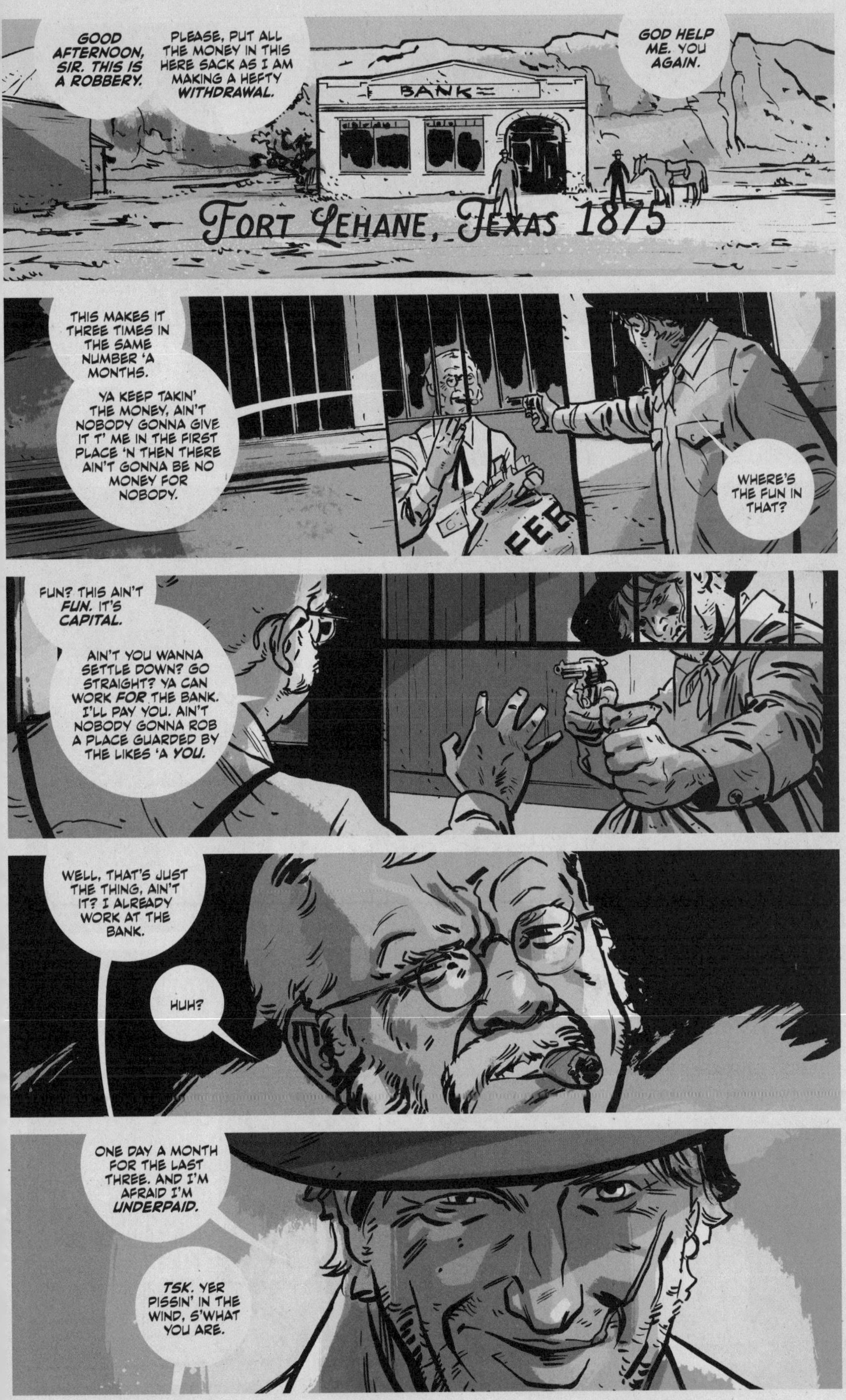
GOOD AFTERNOON, SIR. THIS IS A ROBBERY.
PLEASE, PUT ALL THE MONEY IN THIS HERE SACK AS I AM MAKING A HEFTY WITHDRAWAL.
GOD HELP ME. YOU AGAIN.
BANK
FORT LEHANE, TEXAS 1875
THIS MAKES IT THREE TIMES IN THE SAME NUMBER 'A MONTHS.
YA KEEP TAKIN' THE MONEY, AIN'T NOBODY GONNA GIVE IT T' ME IN THE FIRST PLACE 'N THEN THERE AIN'T GONNA BE NO MONEY FOR NOBODY.
WHERE'S THE FUN IN THAT?
FUN? THIS AIN'T FUN. IT'S CAPITAL.
AIN'T YOU WANNA SETTLE DOWN? GO STRAIGHT? YA CAN WORK FOR THE BANK. I'LL PAY YOU. AIN'T NOBODY GONNA ROB A PLACE GUARDED BY THE LIKES 'A YOU.
WELL, THAT'S JUST THE THING, AIN'T IT? I ALREADY WORK AT THE BANK.
HUH?
ONE DAY A MONTH FOR THE LAST THREE. AND I'M AFRAID I'M UNDERPAID.
TSK. YER PISSIN' IN THE WIND, S'WHAT YOU ARE.

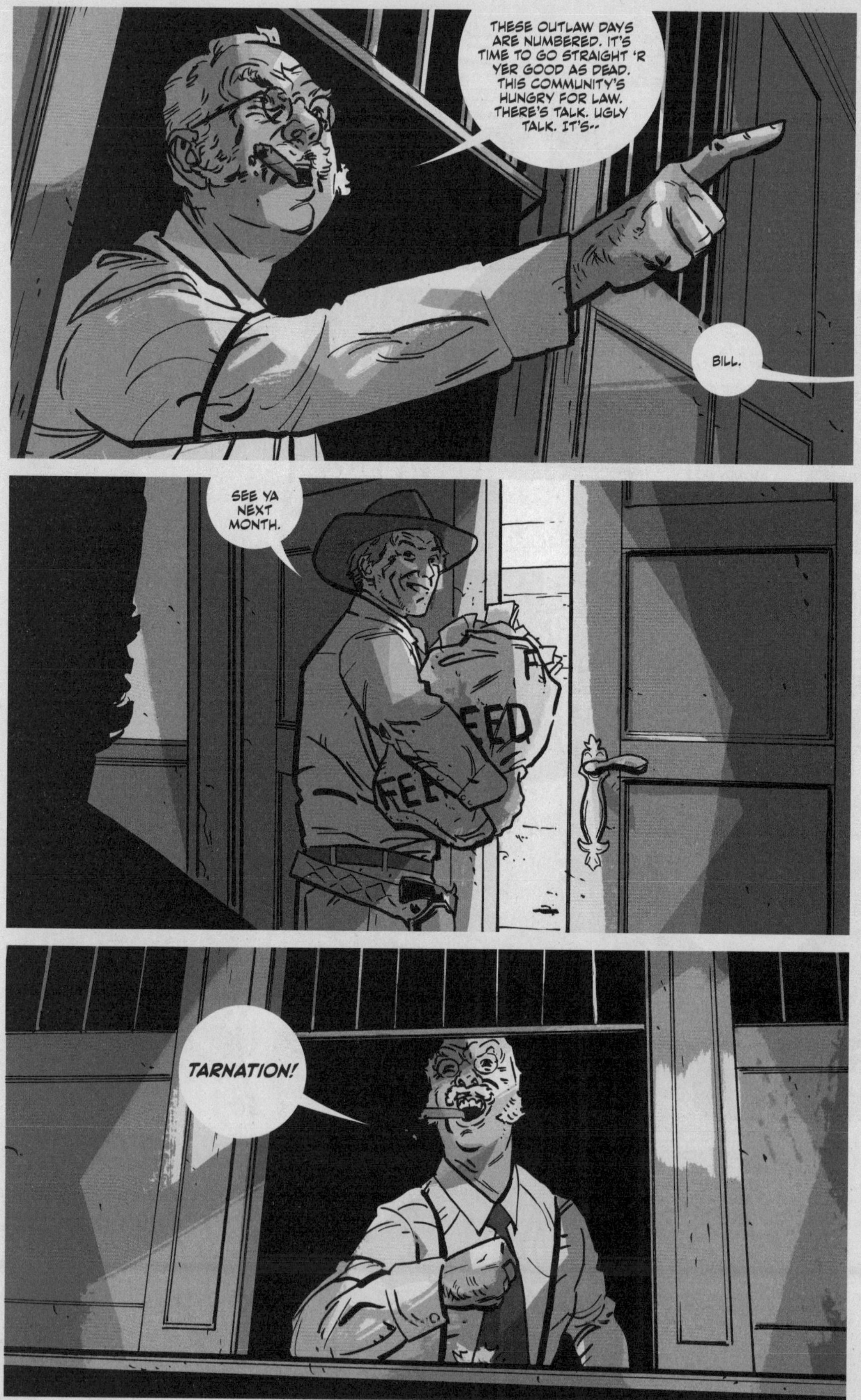
THESE OUTLAW DAYS ARE NUMBERED. IT'S TIME TO GO STRAIGHT 'R YER GOOD AS DEAD. THIS COMMUNITY'S HUNGRY FOR LAW. THERE'S TALK. UGLY TALK. IT'S--
BILL.
SEE YA NEXT MONTH.
FEED
FEED
F
TARNATION!

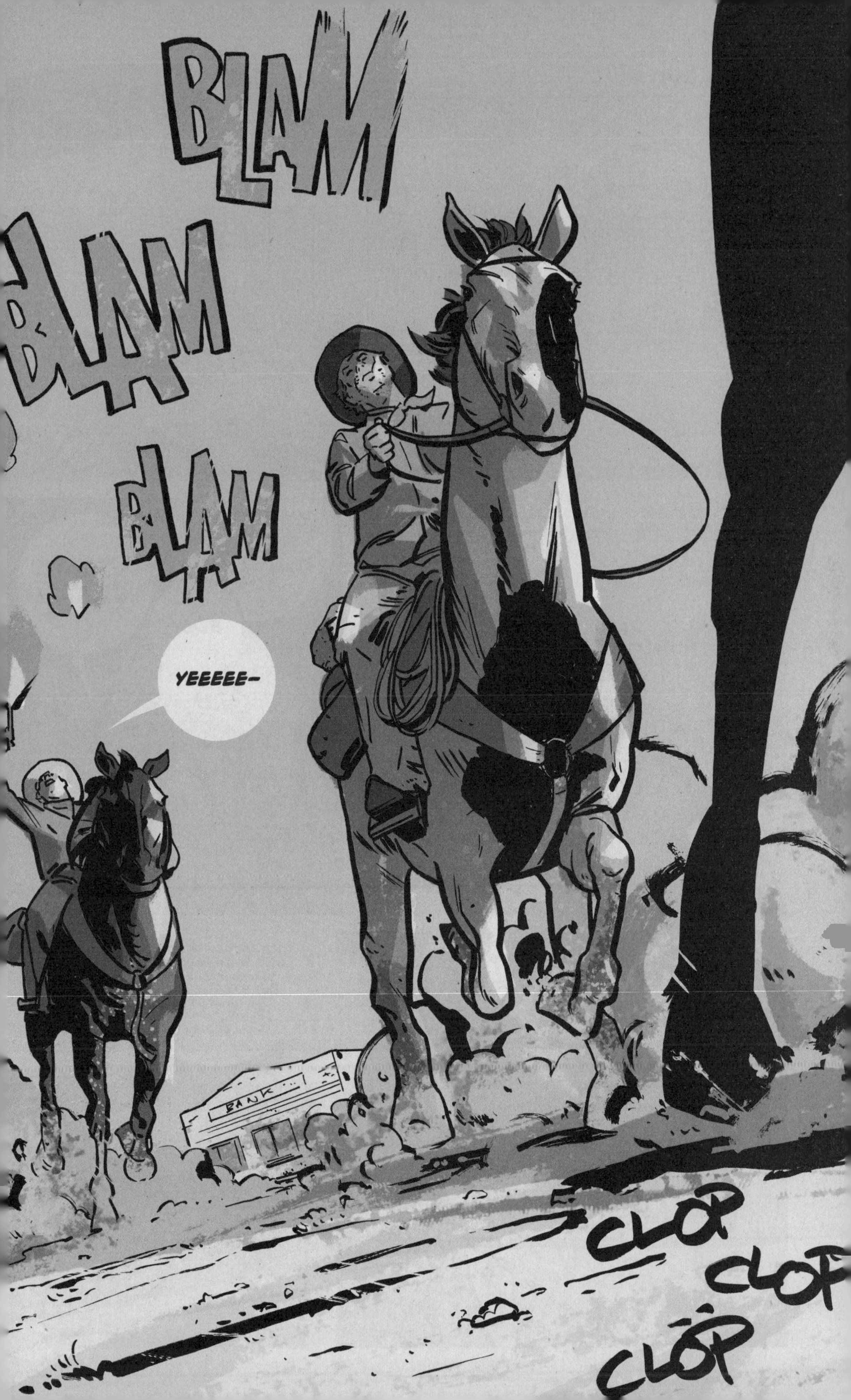
BLAM
BLAM
BLAM
YEEEEE–
BANK
CLOP
CLOP
CLOP

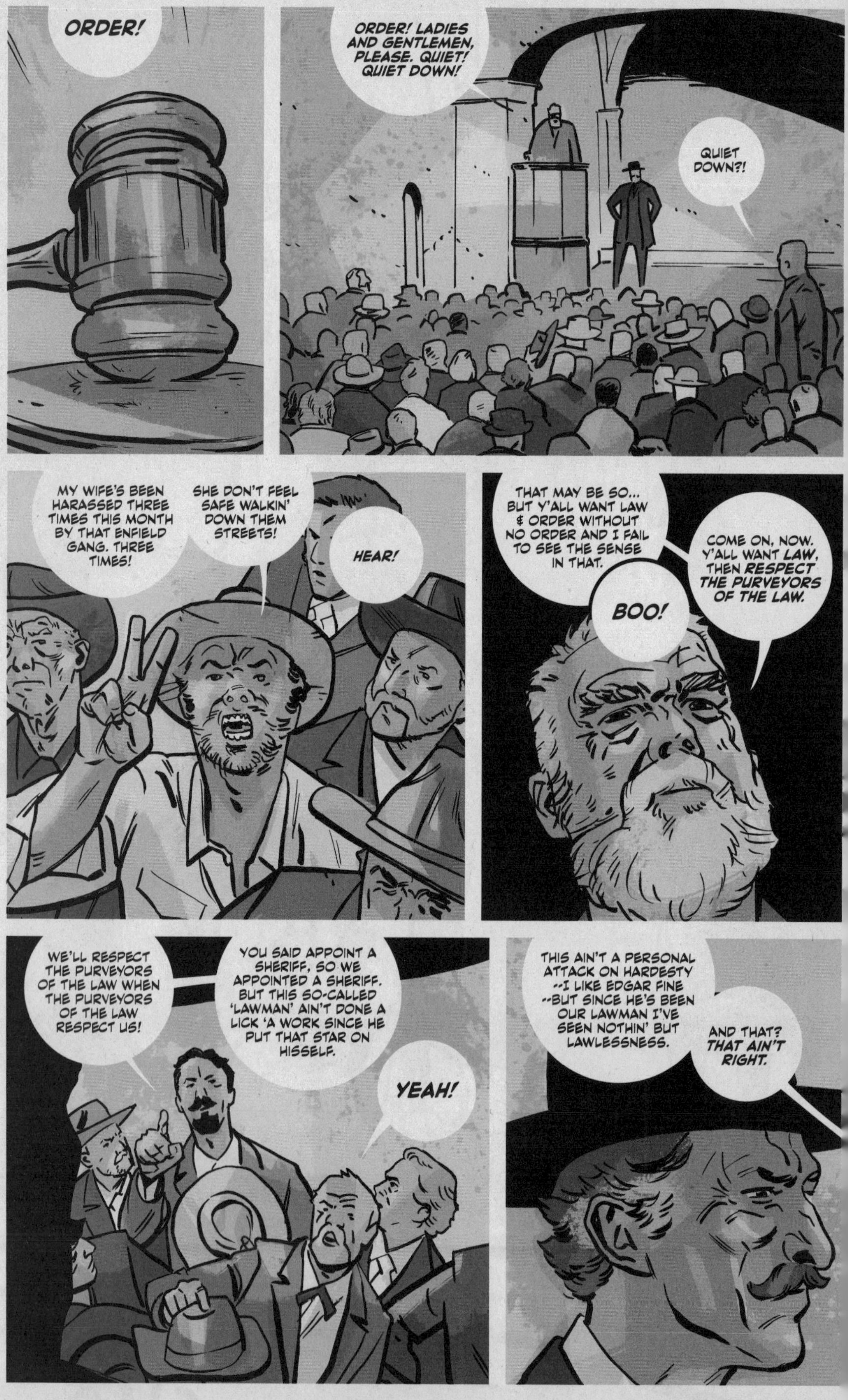
ORDER!
ORDER! LADIES AND GENTLEMEN, PLEASE. QUIET! QUIET DOWN!
QUIET DOWN?!
MY WIFE'S BEEN HARASSED THREE TIMES THIS MONTH BY THAT ENFIELD GANG. THREE TIMES!
SHE DON'T FEEL SAFE WALKIN' DOWN THEM STREETS!
HEAR!
THAT MAY BE SO... BUT Y'ALL WANT LAW & ORDER WITHOUT NO ORDER AND I FAIL TO SEE THE SENSE IN THAT.
COME ON, NOW. Y'ALL WANT *LAW*, THEN *RESPECT THE PURVEYORS OF THE LAW.*
BOO!
WE'LL RESPECT THE PURVEYORS OF THE LAW WHEN THE PURVEYORS OF THE LAW RESPECT US!
YOU SAID APPOINT A SHERIFF, SO WE APPOINTED A SHERIFF. BUT THIS SO-CALLED 'LAWMAN' AIN'T DONE A LICK 'A WORK SINCE HE PUT THAT STAR ON HISSELF.
YEAH!
THIS AIN'T A PERSONAL ATTACK ON HARDESTY --I LIKE EDGAR FINE --BUT SINCE HE'S BEEN OUR LAWMAN I'VE SEEN NOTHIN' BUT LAWLESSNESS.
AND THAT? *THAT AIN'T RIGHT.*

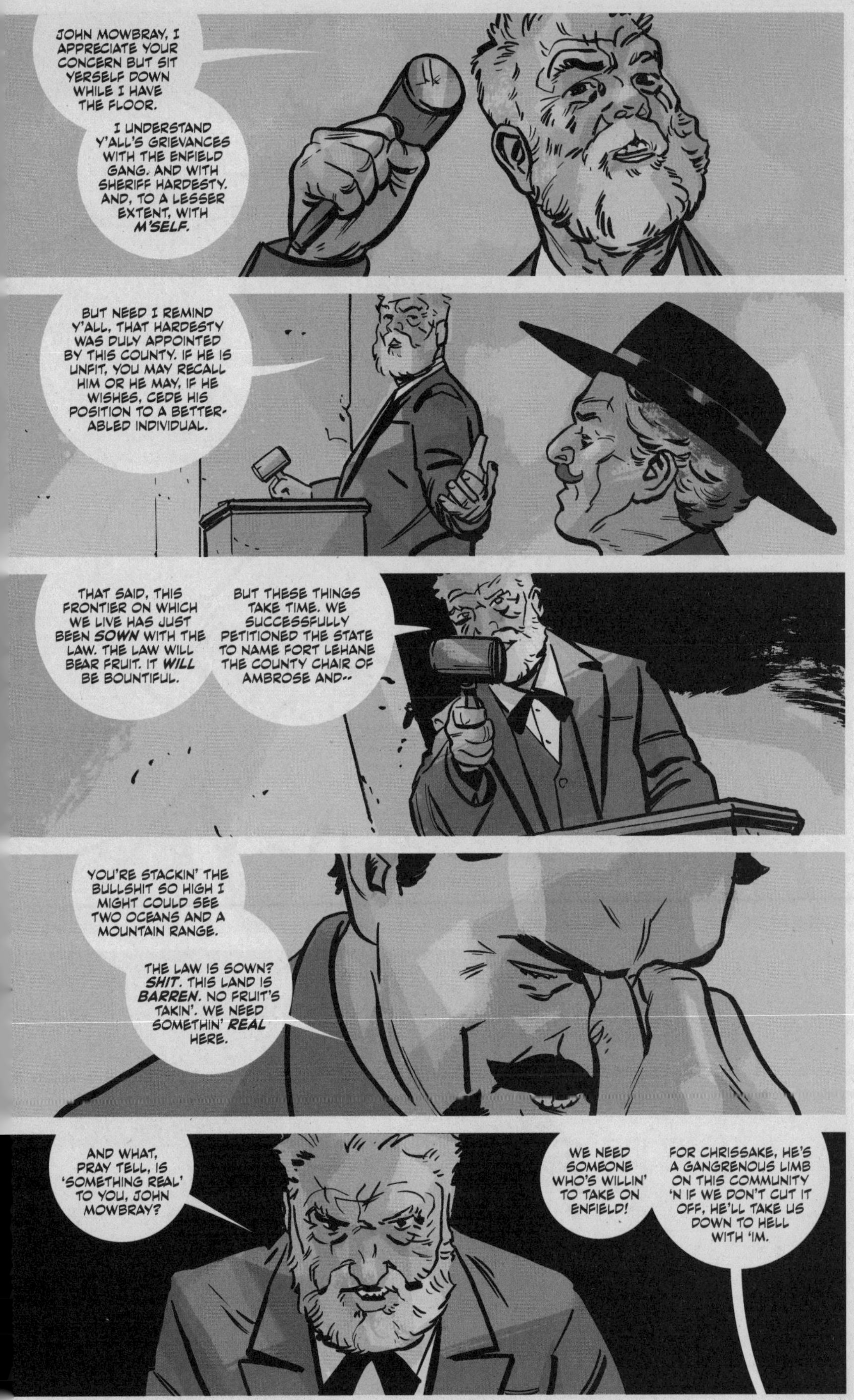
JOHN MOWBRAY, I APPRECIATE YOUR CONCERN BUT SIT YERSELF DOWN WHILE I HAVE THE FLOOR.
I UNDERSTAND Y'ALL'S GRIEVANCES WITH THE ENFIELD GANG. AND WITH SHERIFF HARDESTY. AND, TO A LESSER EXTENT, WITH *M'SELF.*
BUT NEED I REMIND Y'ALL, THAT HARDESTY WAS DULY APPOINTED BY THIS COUNTY. IF HE IS UNFIT, YOU MAY RECALL HIM OR HE MAY, IF HE WISHES, CEDE HIS POSITION TO A BETTER-ABLED INDIVIDUAL.
THAT SAID, THIS FRONTIER ON WHICH WE LIVE HAS JUST BEEN *SOWN* WITH THE LAW. THE LAW WILL BEAR FRUIT. IT *WILL* BE BOUNTIFUL.
BUT THESE THINGS TAKE TIME. WE SUCCESSFULLY PETITIONED THE STATE TO NAME FORT LEHANE THE COUNTY CHAIR OF AMBROSE AND--
YOU'RE STACKIN' THE BULLSHIT SO HIGH I MIGHT COULD SEE TWO OCEANS AND A MOUNTAIN RANGE.
THE LAW IS SOWN? *SHIT*. THIS LAND IS *BARREN*. NO FRUIT'S TAKIN'. WE NEED SOMETHIN' *REAL* HERE.
AND WHAT, PRAY TELL, IS 'SOMETHING REAL' TO YOU, JOHN MOWBRAY?
WE NEED SOMEONE WHO'S WILLIN' TO TAKE ON ENFIELD!
FOR CHRISSAKE, HE'S A GANGRENOUS LIMB ON THIS COMMUNITY 'N IF WE DON'T CUT IT OFF, HE'LL TAKE US DOWN TO HELL WITH 'IM.

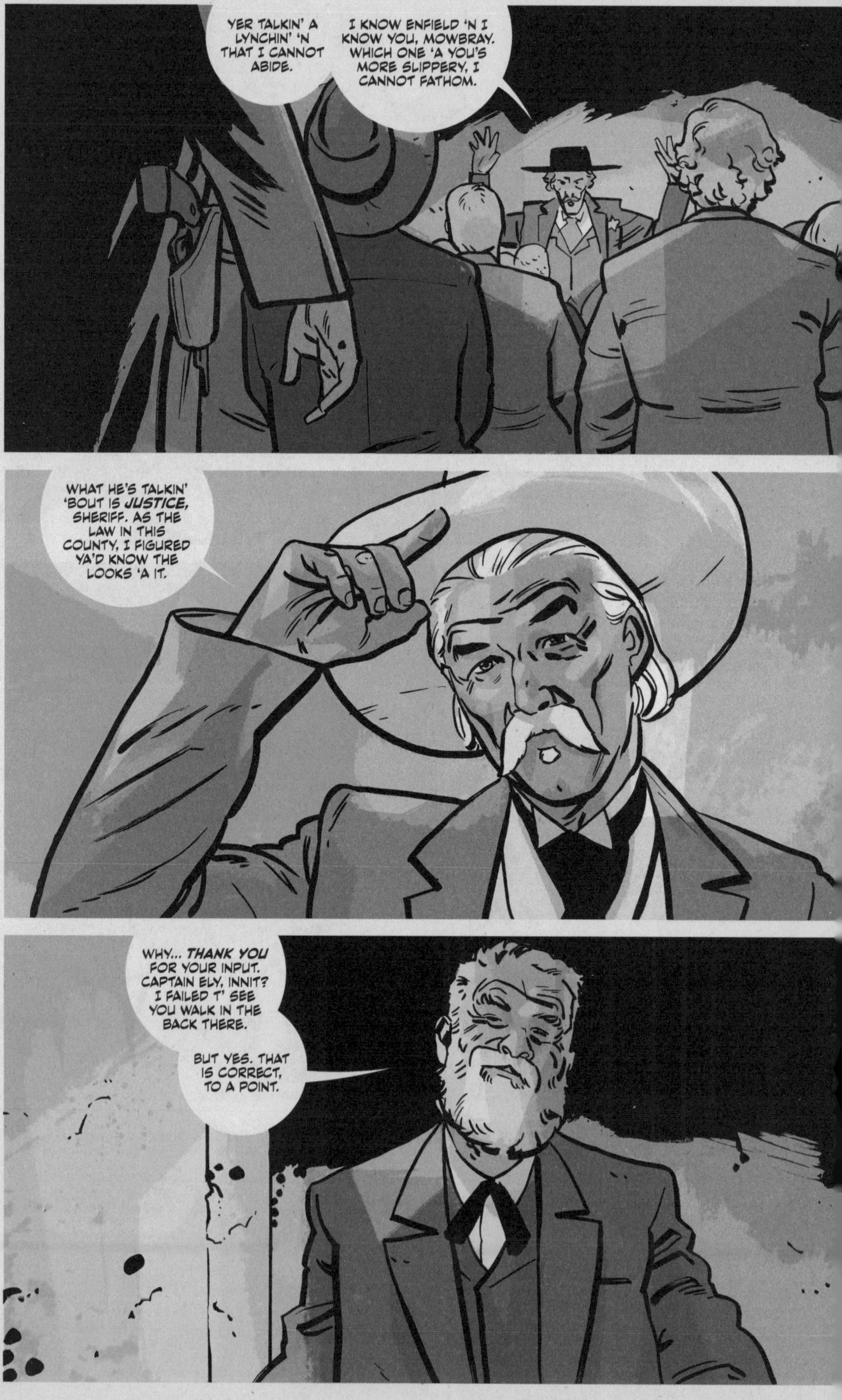
YER TALKIN' A LYNCHIN' 'N THAT I CANNOT ABIDE.
I KNOW ENFIELD 'N I KNOW YOU, MOWBRAY. WHICH ONE 'A YOU'S MORE SLIPPERY, I CANNOT FATHOM.
WHAT HE'S TALKIN' 'BOUT IS JUSTICE, SHERIFF. AS THE LAW IN THIS COUNTY, I FIGURED YA'D KNOW THE LOOKS 'A IT.
WHY... THANK YOU FOR YOUR INPUT. CAPTAIN ELY, INNIT? I FAILED T' SEE YOU WALK IN THE BACK THERE.
BUT YES. THAT IS CORRECT, TO A POINT.

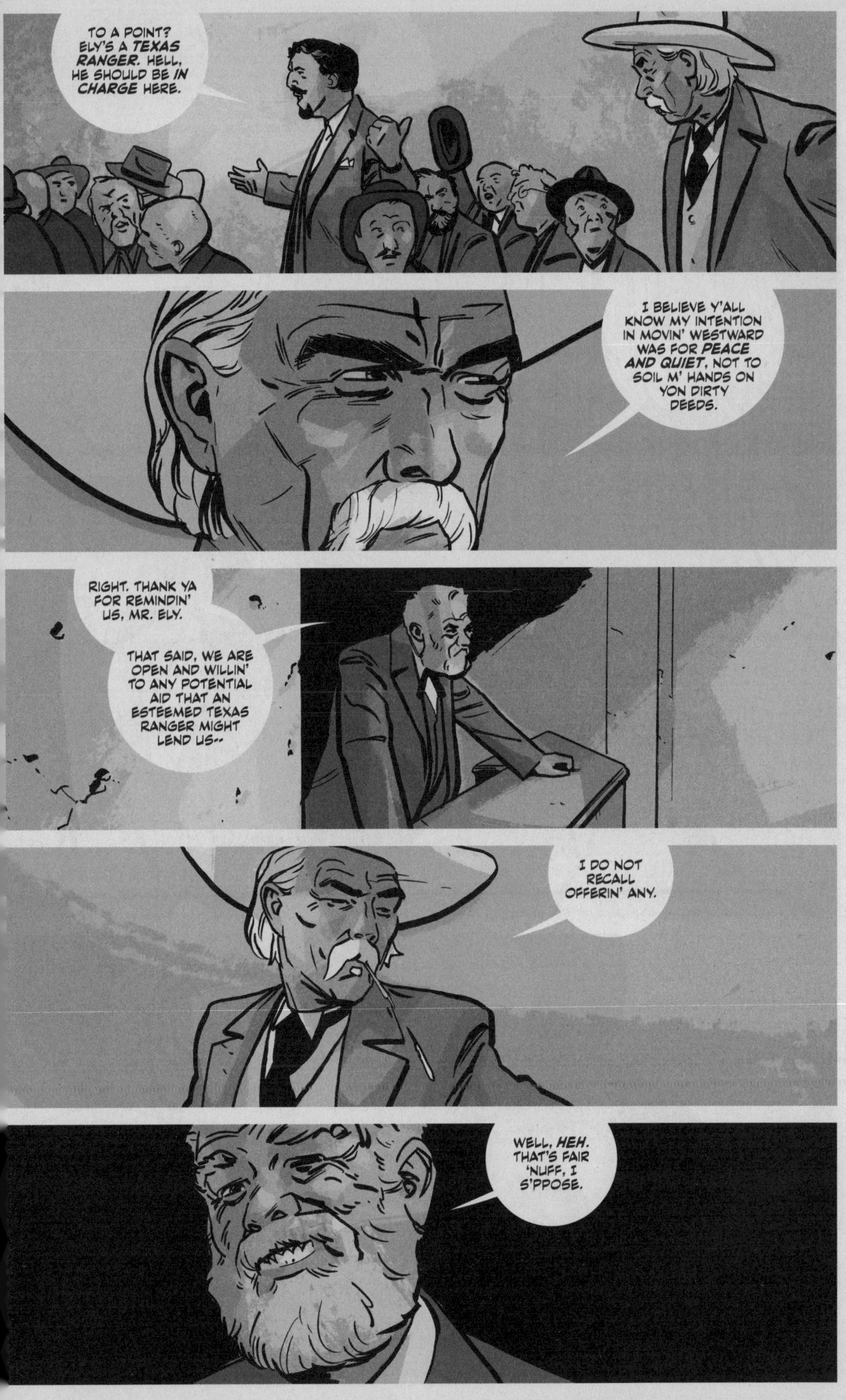
TO A POINT? ELY'S A TEXAS RANGER. HELL, HE SHOULD BE IN CHARGE HERE.
I BELIEVE Y'ALL KNOW MY INTENTION IN MOVIN' WESTWARD WAS FOR PEACE AND QUIET, NOT TO SOIL M' HANDS ON YON DIRTY DEEDS.
RIGHT. THANK YA FOR REMINDIN' US, MR. ELY.
THAT SAID, WE ARE OPEN AND WILLIN' TO ANY POTENTIAL AID THAT AN ESTEEMED TEXAS RANGER MIGHT LEND US--
I DO NOT RECALL OFFERIN' ANY.
WELL, HEH. THAT'S FAIR 'NUFF, I S'PPOSE.

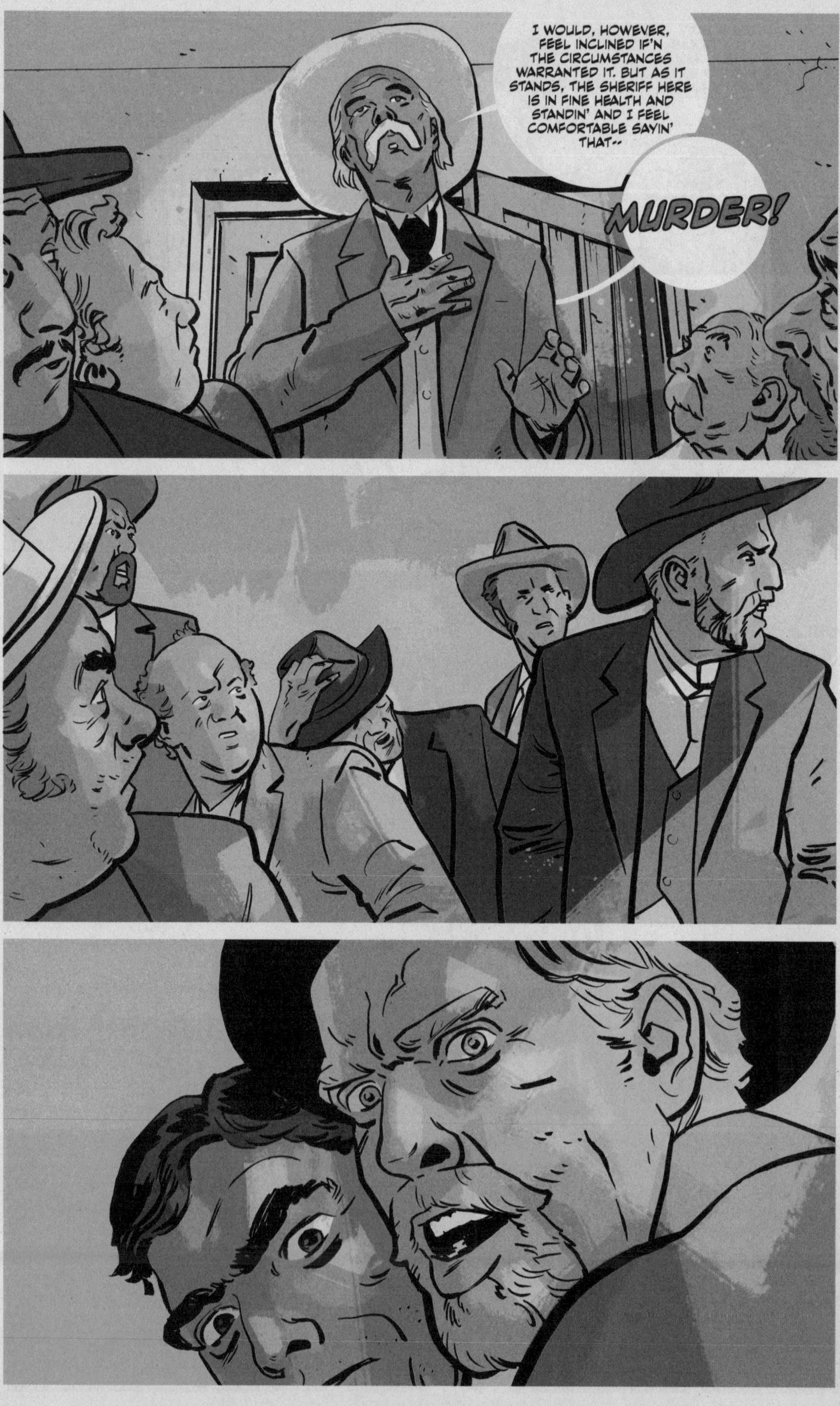
I WOULD, HOWEVER, FEEL INCLINED IF'N THE CIRCUMSTANCES WARRANTED IT. BUT AS IT STANDS, THE SHERIFF HERE IS IN FINE HEALTH AND STANDIN' AND I FEEL COMFORTABLE SAYIN' THAT--
MURDER!

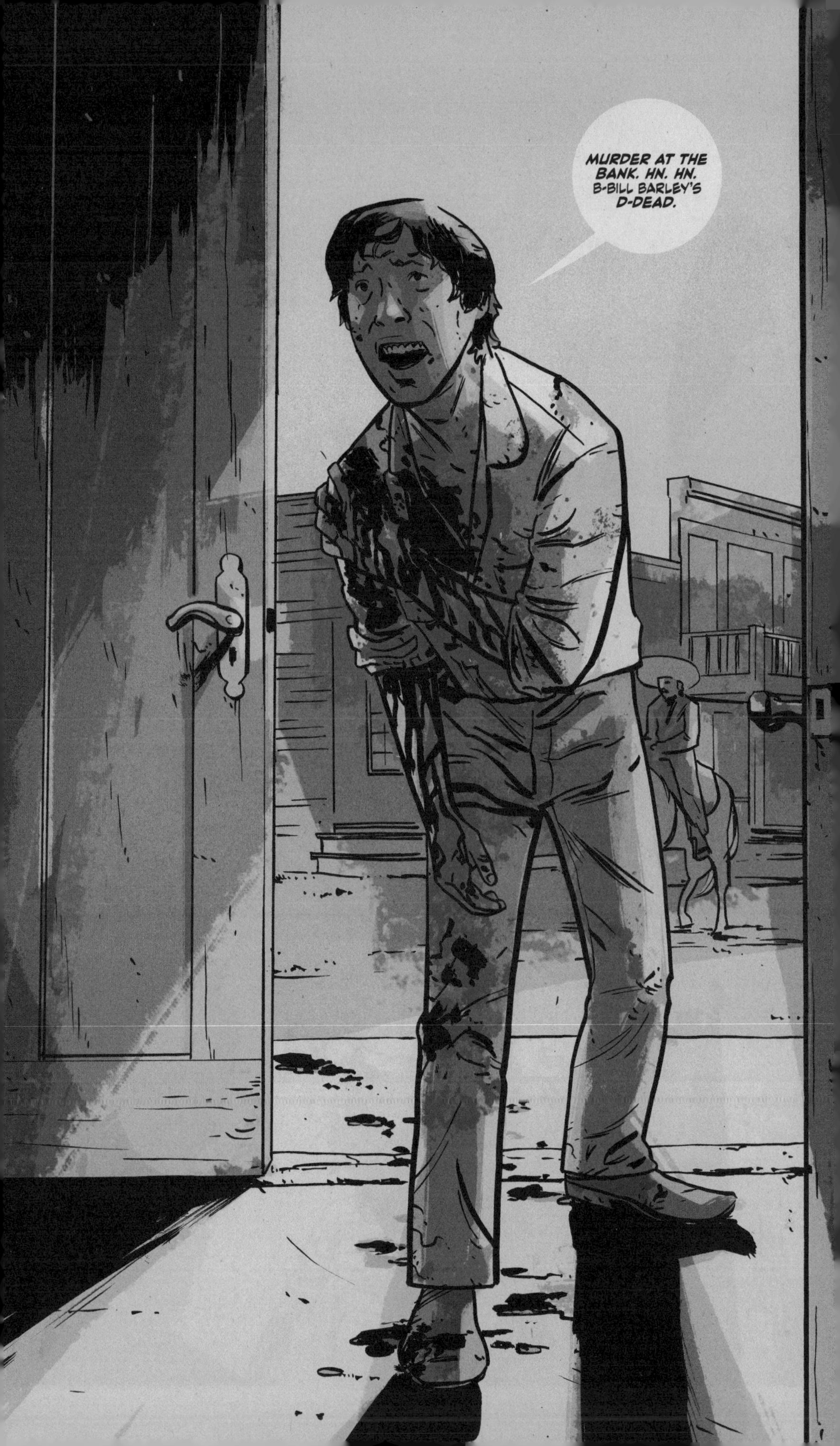
MURDER AT THE BANK. HN. HN. B-BILL BARLEY'S D-DEAD.

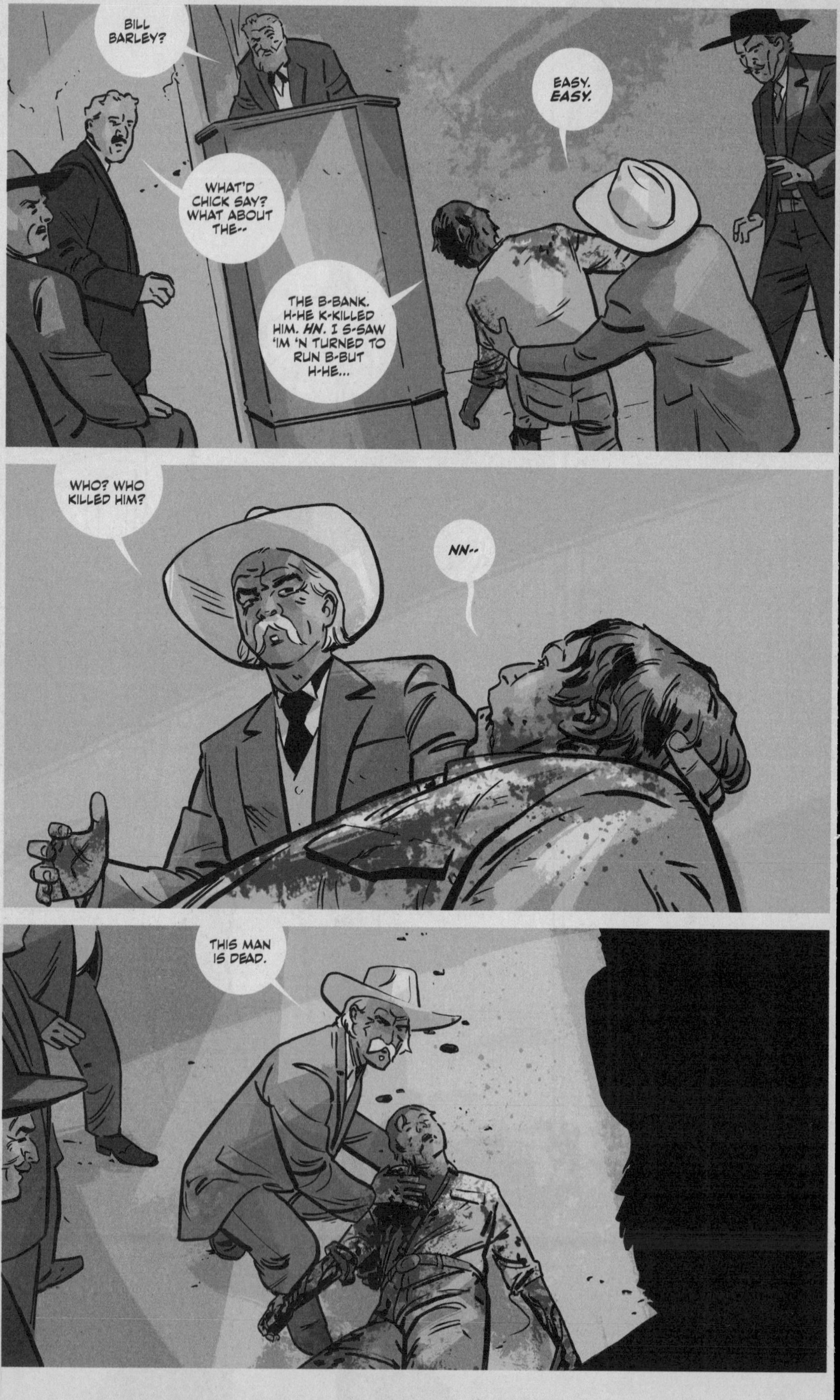
BILL BARLEY?
WHAT'D CHICK SAY? WHAT ABOUT THE--
EASY. EASY.
THE B-BANK. H-HE K-KILLED HIM. HN. I S-SAW 'IM 'N TURNED TO RUN B-BUT H-HE...
WHO? WHO KILLED HIM?
NN--
THIS MAN IS DEAD.

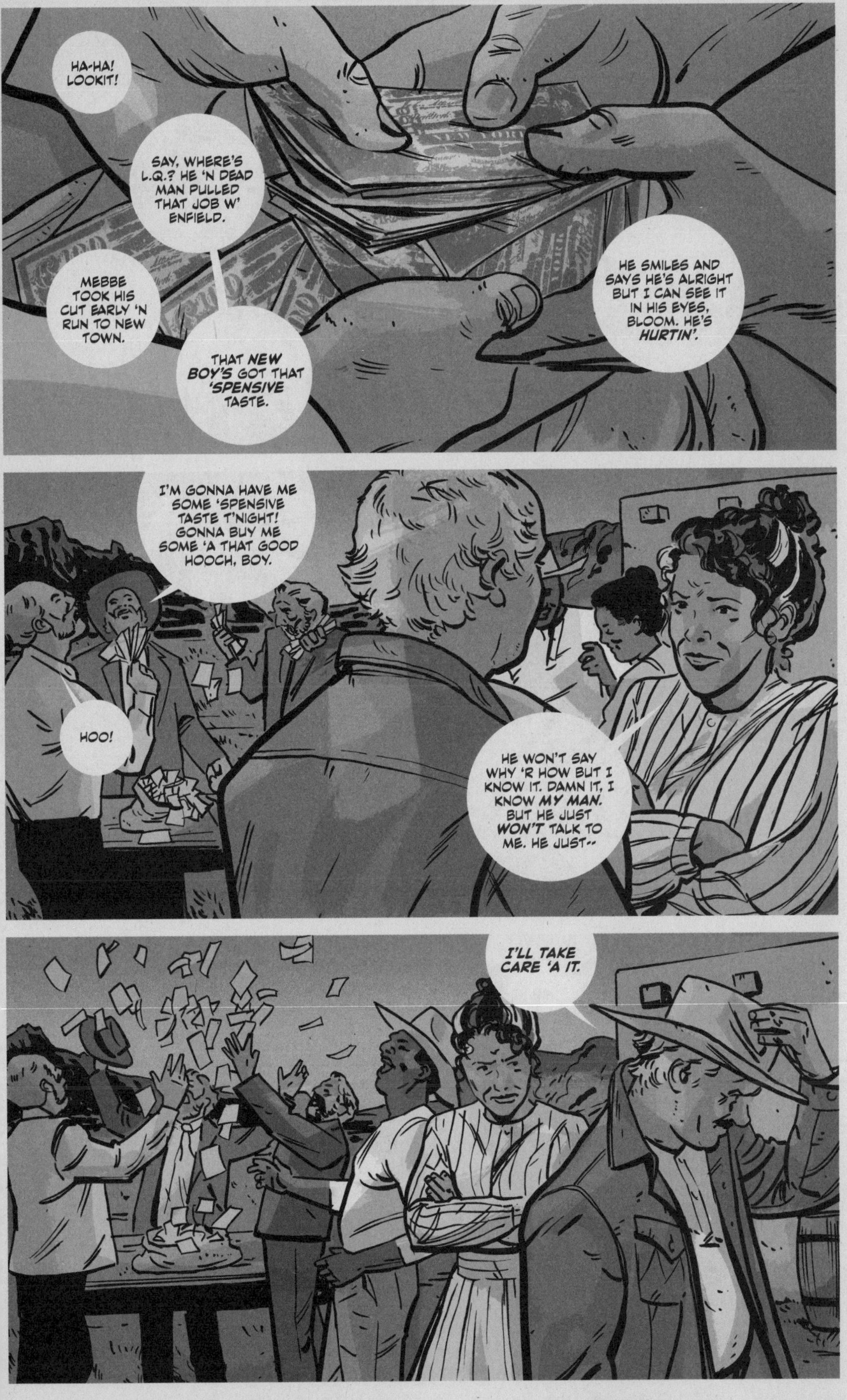
HA-HA! LOOKIT!
SAY, WHERE'S L.Q.? HE 'N DEAD MAN PULLED THAT JOB W' ENFIELD.
MEBBE TOOK HIS CUT EARLY 'N RUN TO NEW TOWN.
THAT NEW BOY'S GOT THAT 'SPENSIVE TASTE.
HE SMILES AND SAYS HE'S ALRIGHT BUT I CAN SEE IT IN HIS EYES, BLOOM. HE'S HURTIN'.
I'M GONNA HAVE ME SOME 'SPENSIVE TASTE T'NIGHT! GONNA BUY ME SOME 'A THAT GOOD HOOCH, BOY.
HOO!
HE WON'T SAY WHY 'R HOW BUT I KNOW IT. DAMN IT, I KNOW MY MAN. BUT HE JUST WON'T TALK TO ME. HE JUST--
I'LL TAKE CARE 'A IT.

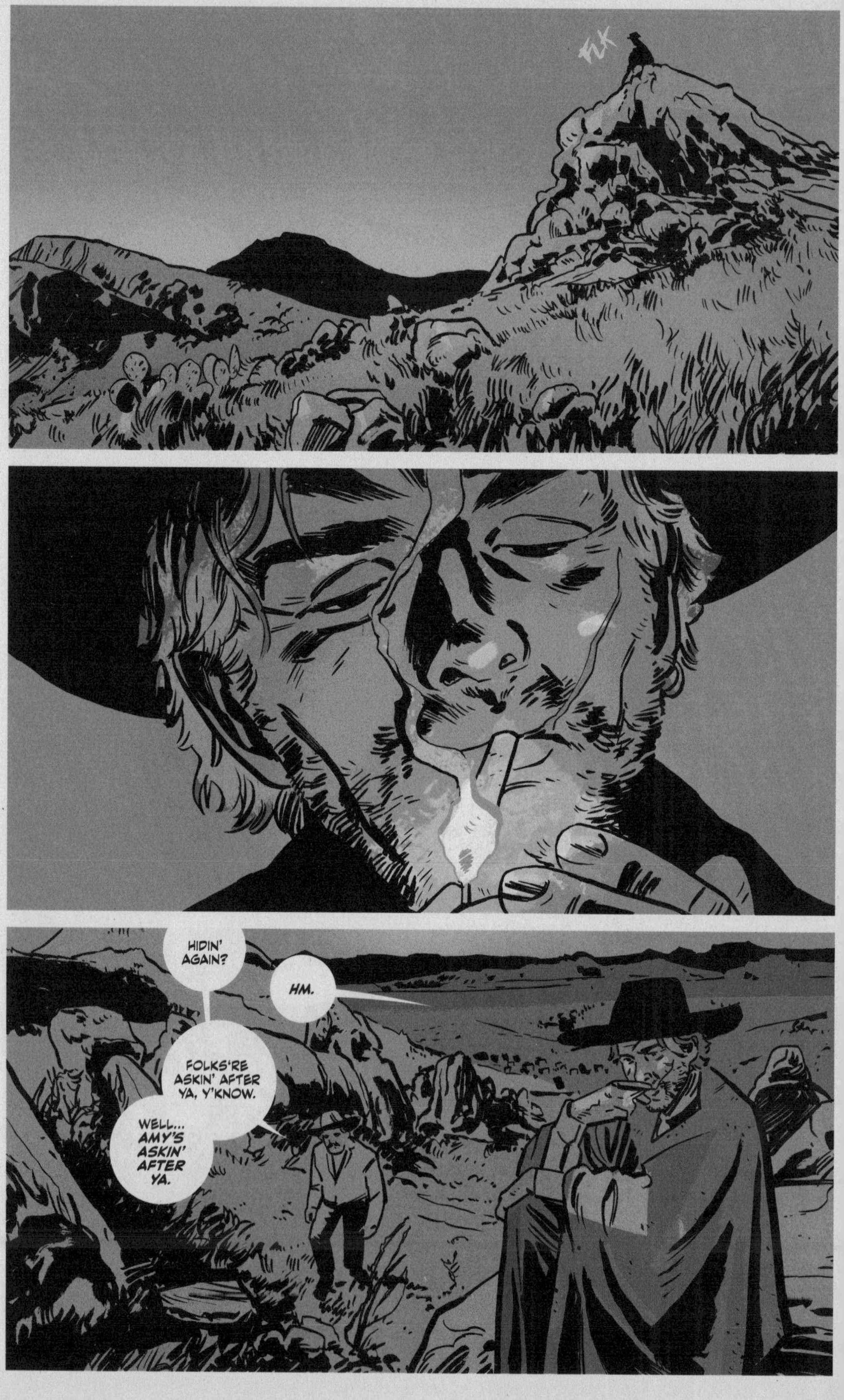
FLK
HIDIN' AGAIN?
HM.
FOLKS'RE ASKIN' AFTER YA, Y'KNOW.
WELL... AMY'S ASKIN' AFTER YA.

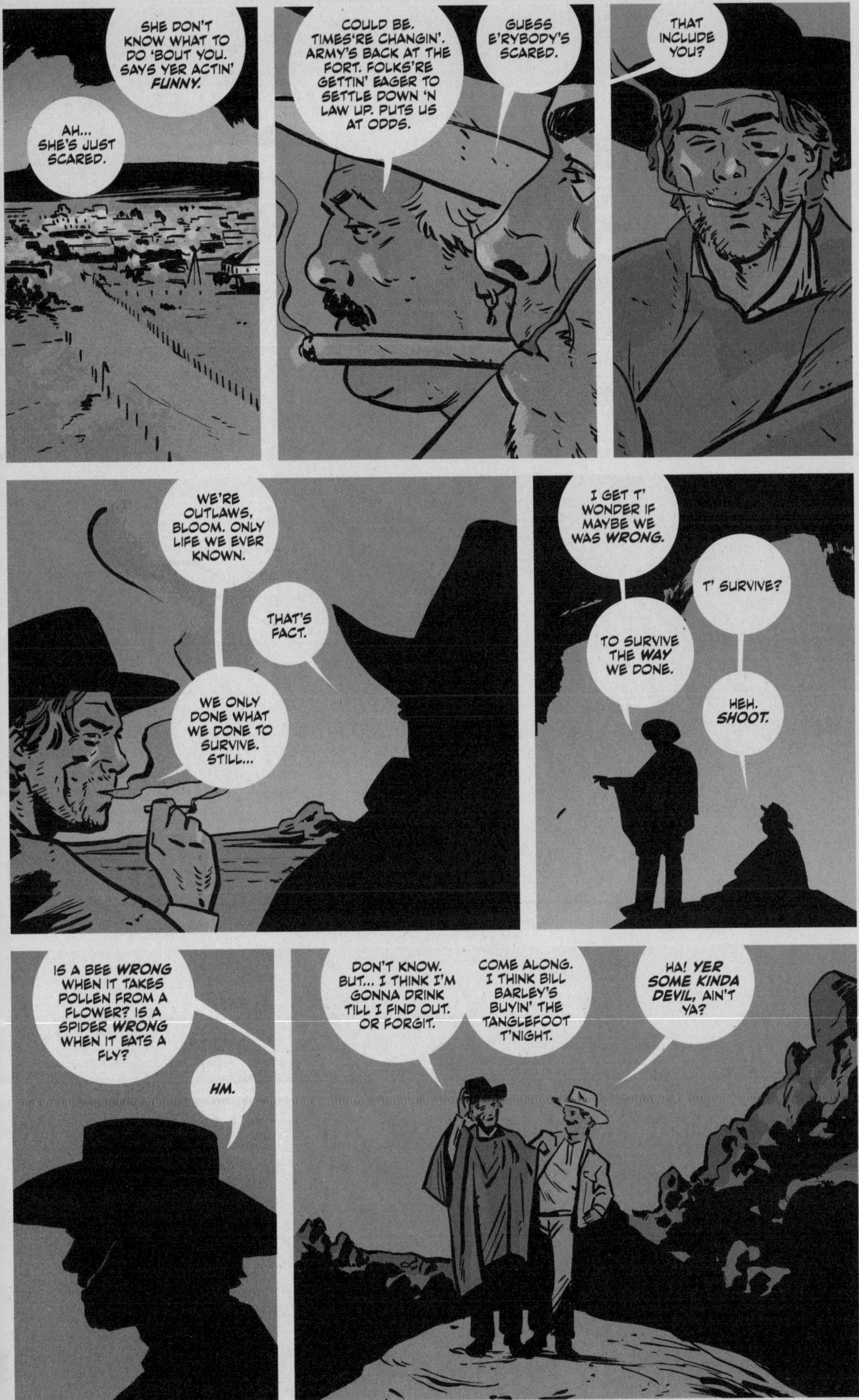
SHE DON'T KNOW WHAT TO DO 'BOUT YOU. SAYS YER ACTIN' FUNNY.
AH... SHE'S JUST SCARED.
COULD BE. TIMES'RE CHANGIN'. ARMY'S BACK AT THE FORT. FOLKS'RE GETTIN' EAGER TO SETTLE DOWN 'N LAW UP. PUTS US AT ODDS.
GUESS E'RYBODY'S SCARED.
THAT INCLUDE YOU?
WE'RE OUTLAWS, BLOOM. ONLY LIFE WE EVER KNOWN.
THAT'S FACT.
WE ONLY DONE WHAT WE DONE TO SURVIVE. STILL...
I GET T' WONDER IF MAYBE WE WAS WRONG.
T' SURVIVE?
TO SURVIVE THE WAY WE DONE.
HEH. SHOOT.
IS A BEE WRONG WHEN IT TAKES POLLEN FROM A FLOWER? IS A SPIDER WRONG WHEN IT EATS A FLY?
HM.
DON'T KNOW. BUT... I THINK I'M GONNA DRINK TILL I FIND OUT. OR FORGIT.
COME ALONG. I THINK BILL BARLEY'S BUYIN' THE TANGLEFOOT T'NIGHT.
HA! YER SOME KINDA DEVIL, AIN'T YA?

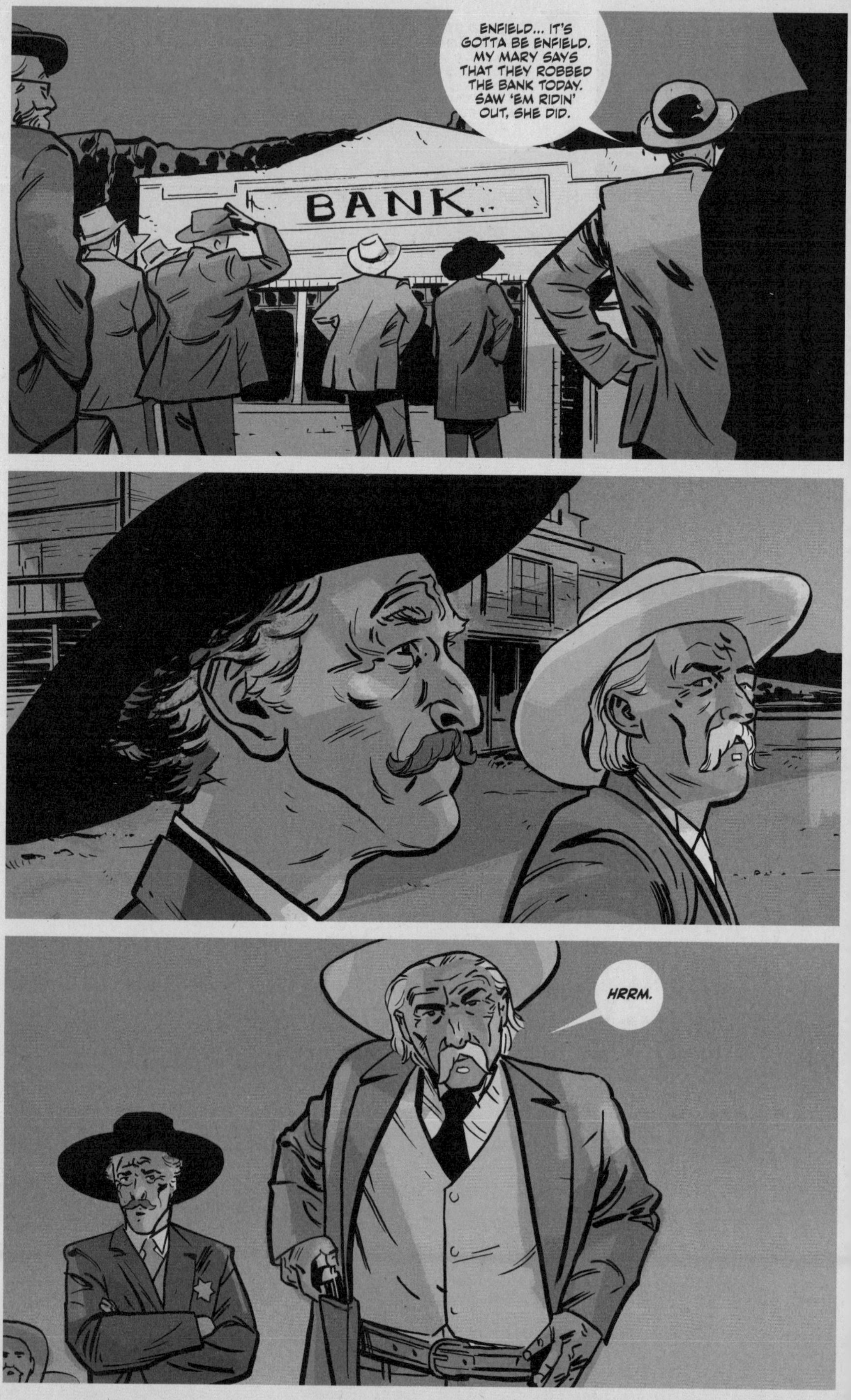
ENFIELD... IT'S GOTTA BE ENFIELD. MY MARY SAYS THAT THEY ROBBED THE BANK TODAY. SAW 'EM RIDIN' OUT, SHE DID.
BANK
HRRM.

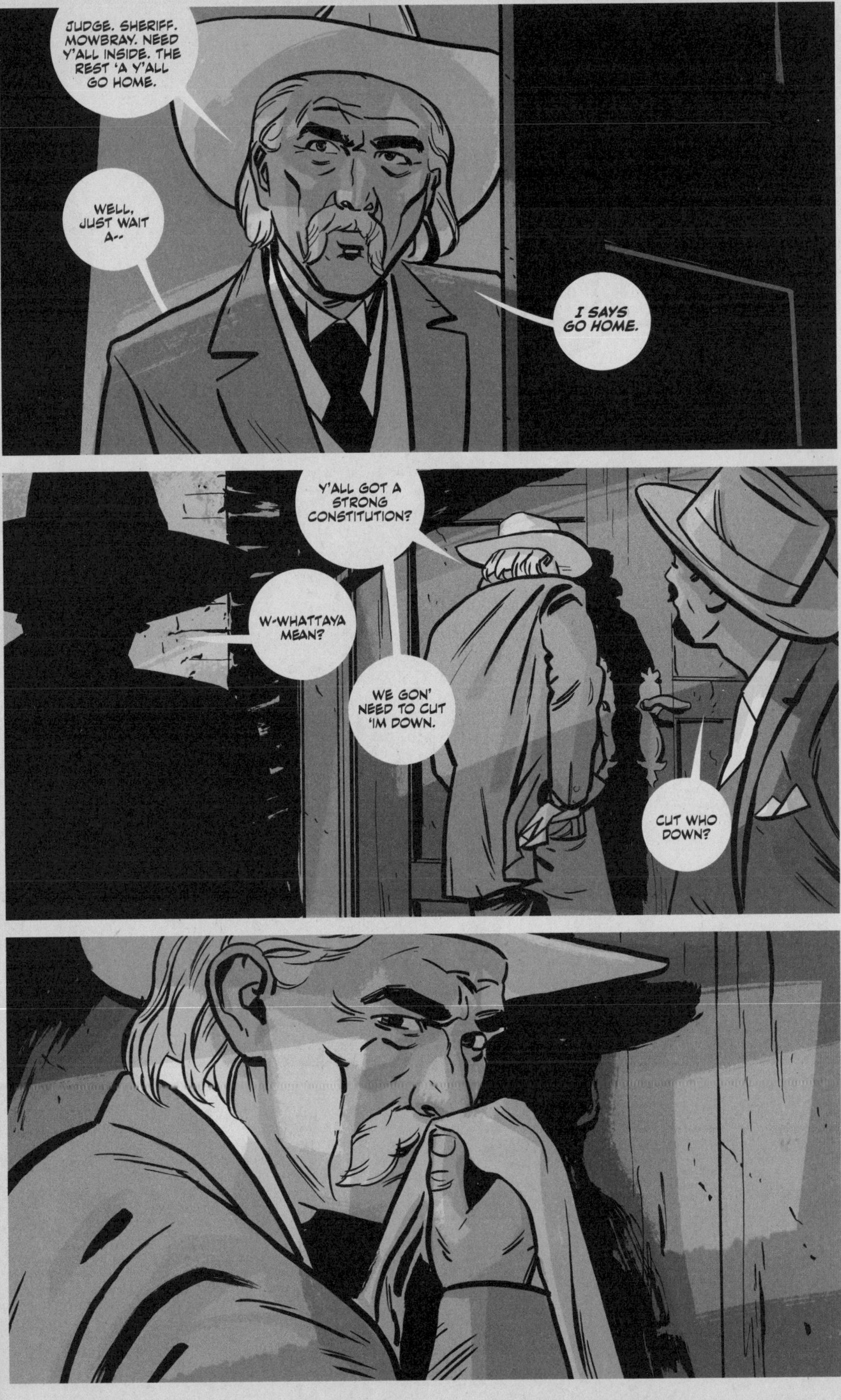
JUDGE. SHERIFF. MOWBRAY. NEED Y'ALL INSIDE. THE REST 'A Y'ALL GO HOME.
WELL, JUST WAIT A--
I SAYS GO HOME.
Y'ALL GOT A STRONG CONSTITUTION?
W-WHATTAYA MEAN?
WE GON' NEED TO CUT 'IM DOWN.
CUT WHO DOWN?

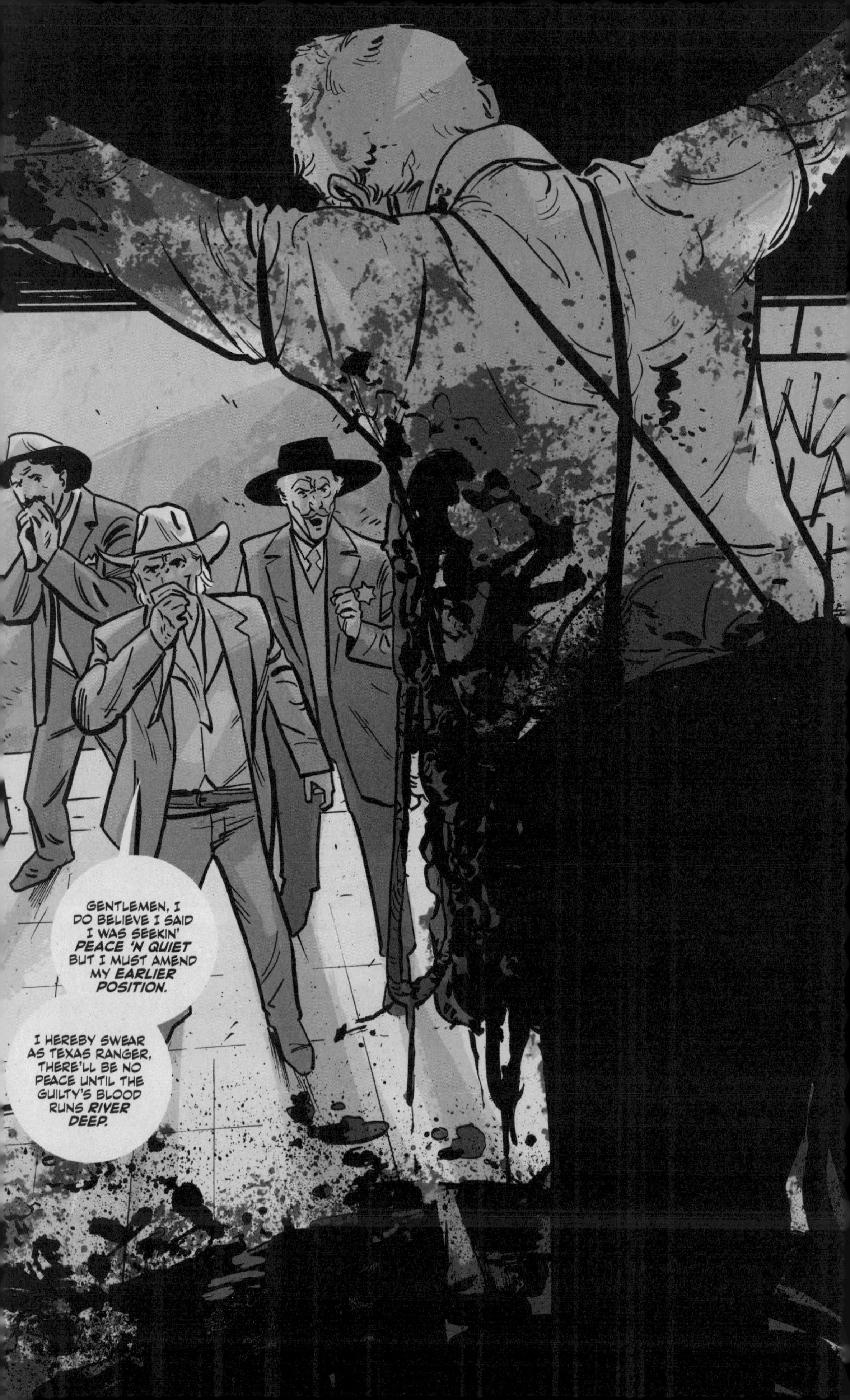
GENTLEMEN, I DO BELIEVE I SAID I WAS SEEKIN' PEACE 'N QUIET BUT I MUST AMEND MY EARLIER POSITION.
I HEREBY SWEAR AS TEXAS RANGER, THERE'LL BE NO PEACE UNTIL THE GUILTY'S BLOOD RUNS RIVER DEEP.

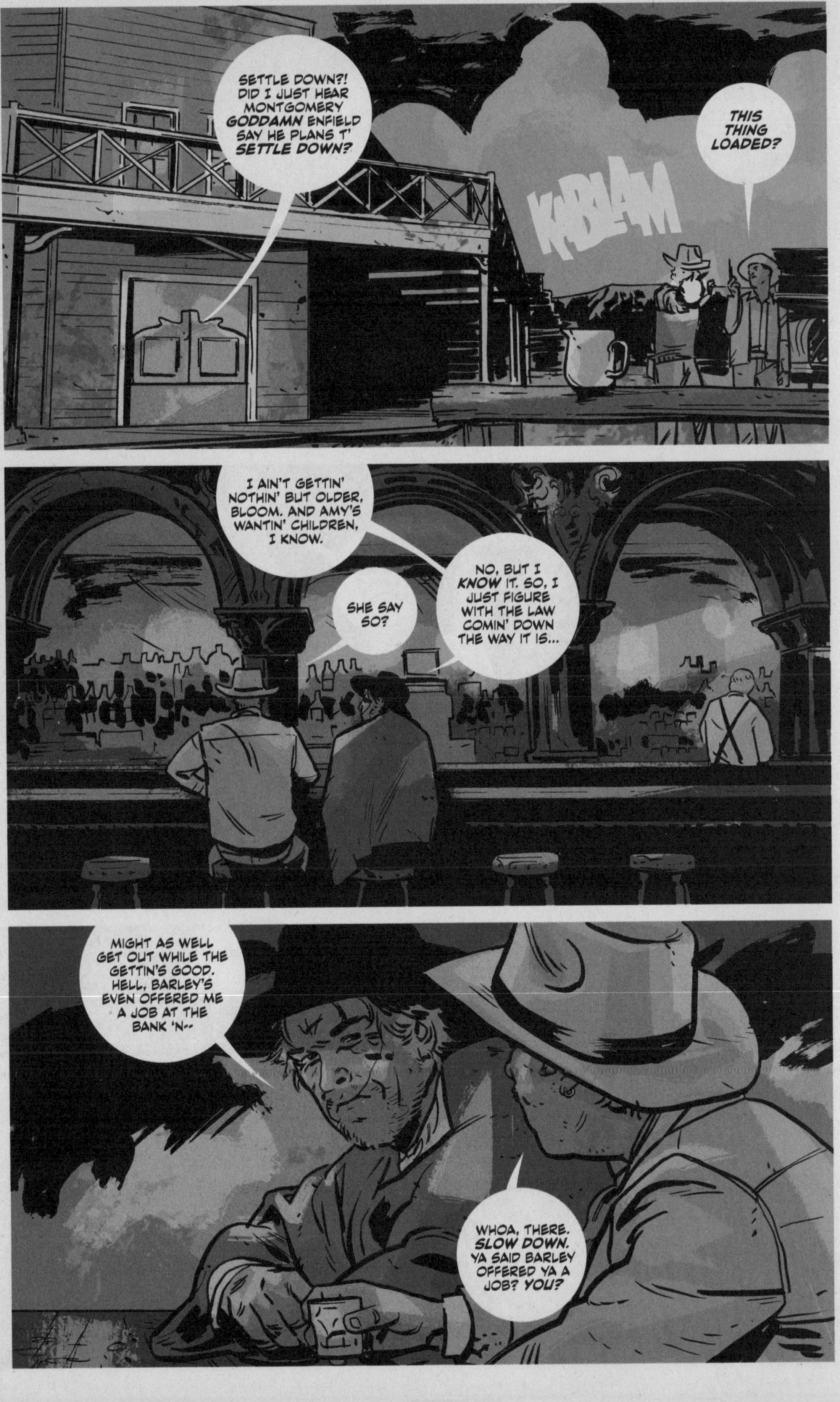
SETTLE DOWN?! DID I JUST HEAR MONTGOMERY GODDAMN ENFIELD SAY HE PLANS T' SETTLE DOWN?
KABLAM
THIS THING LOADED?
I AIN'T GETTIN' NOTHIN' BUT OLDER, BLOOM. AND AMY'S WANTIN' CHILDREN, I KNOW.
SHE SAY SO?
NO, BUT I KNOW IT. SO, I JUST FIGURE WITH THE LAW COMIN' DOWN THE WAY IT IS...
MIGHT AS WELL GET OUT WHILE THE GETTIN'S GOOD. HELL, BARLEY'S EVEN OFFERED ME A JOB AT THE BANK 'N--
WHOA, THERE. SLOW DOWN. YA SAID BARLEY OFFERED YA A JOB? YOU?

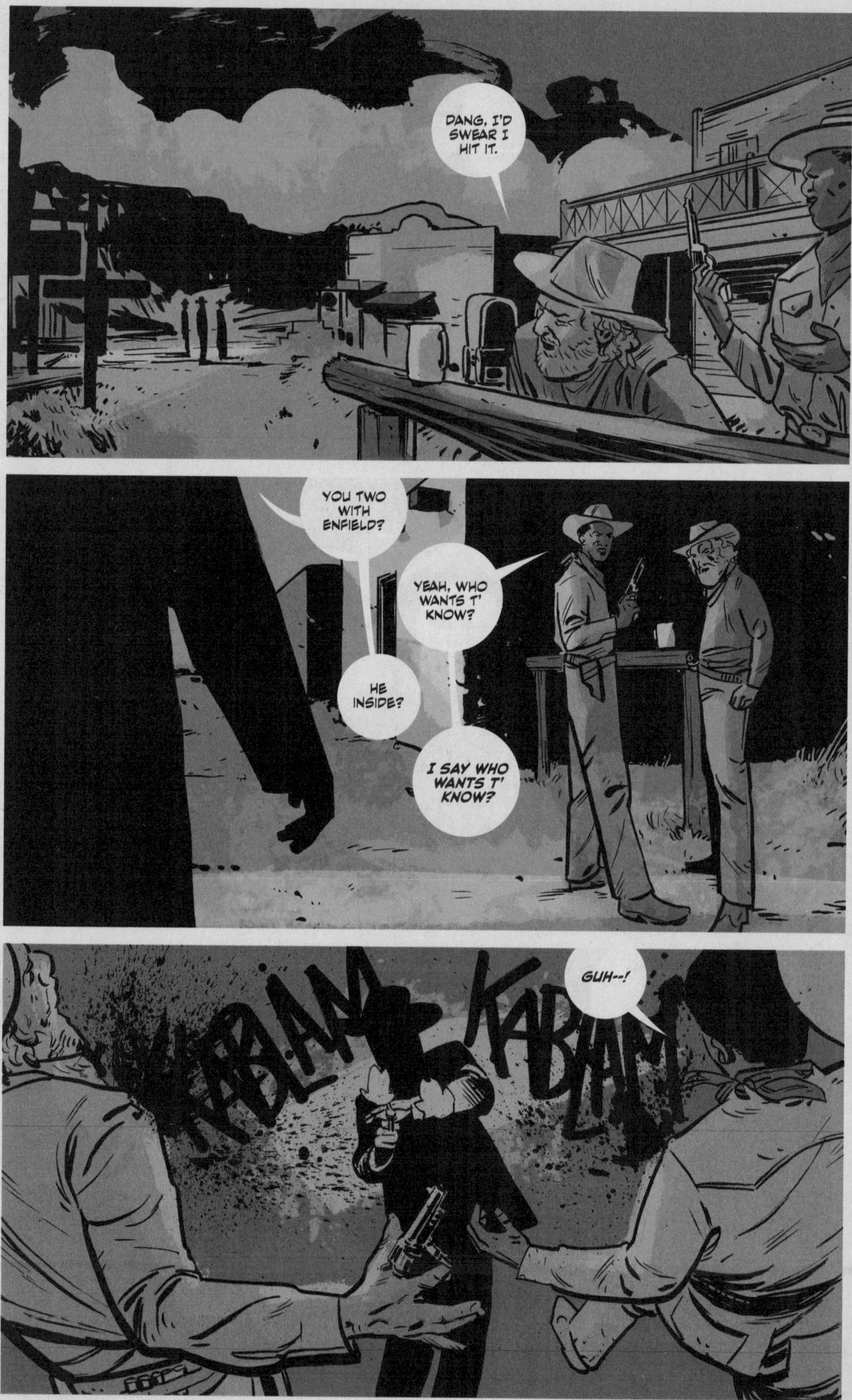
DANG, I'D SWEAR I HIT IT.
YOU TWO WITH ENFIELD?
YEAH, WHO WANTS T' KNOW?
HE INSIDE?
I SAY WHO WANTS T' KNOW?
KABLAM
KABLAM
GUH--!

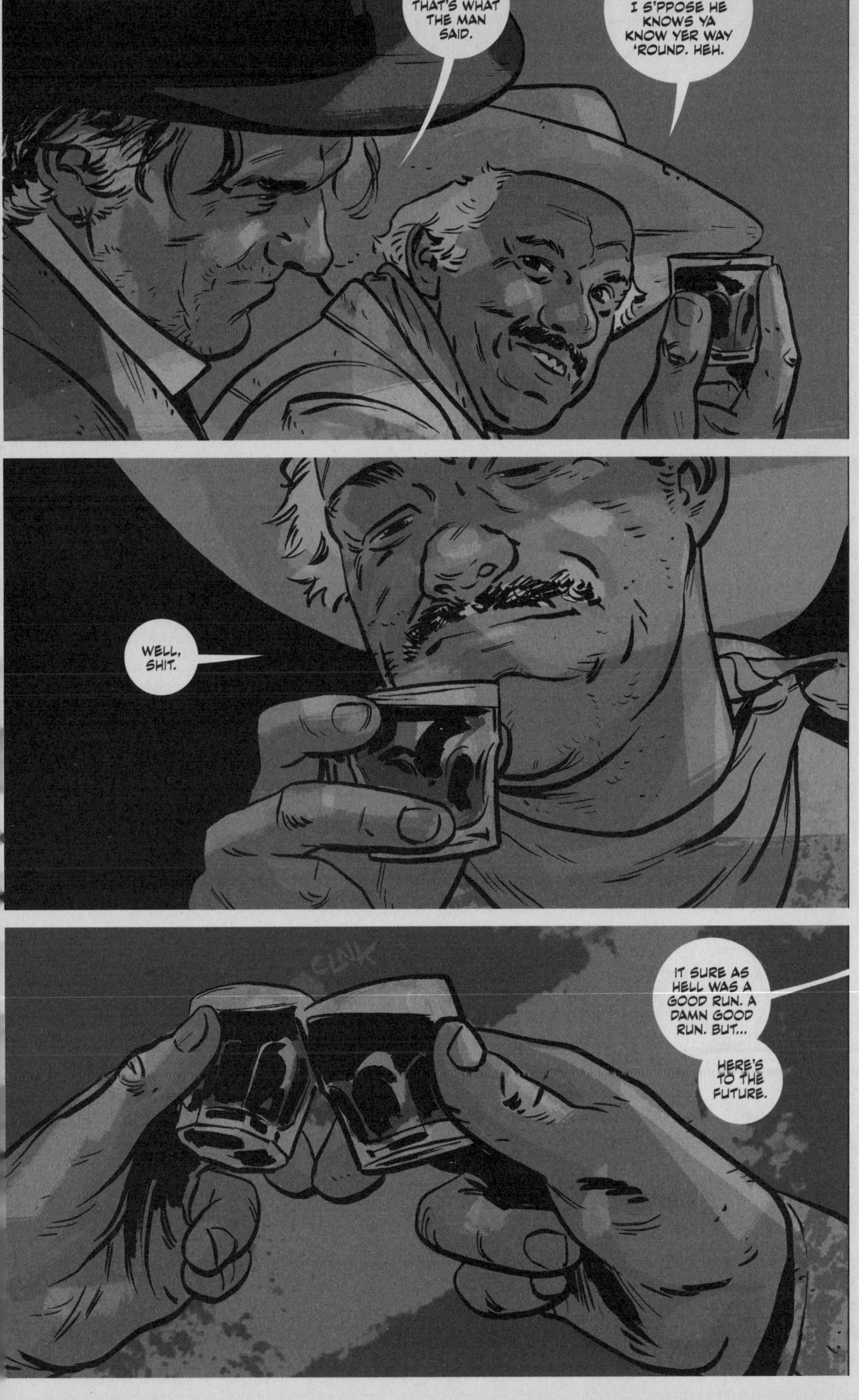
THAT'S WHAT THE MAN SAID.
I S'PPOSE HE KNOWS YA KNOW YER WAY 'ROUND. HEH.
WELL, SHIT.
IT SURE AS HELL WAS A GOOD RUN. A DAMN GOOD RUN. BUT...
HERE'S TO THE FUTURE.

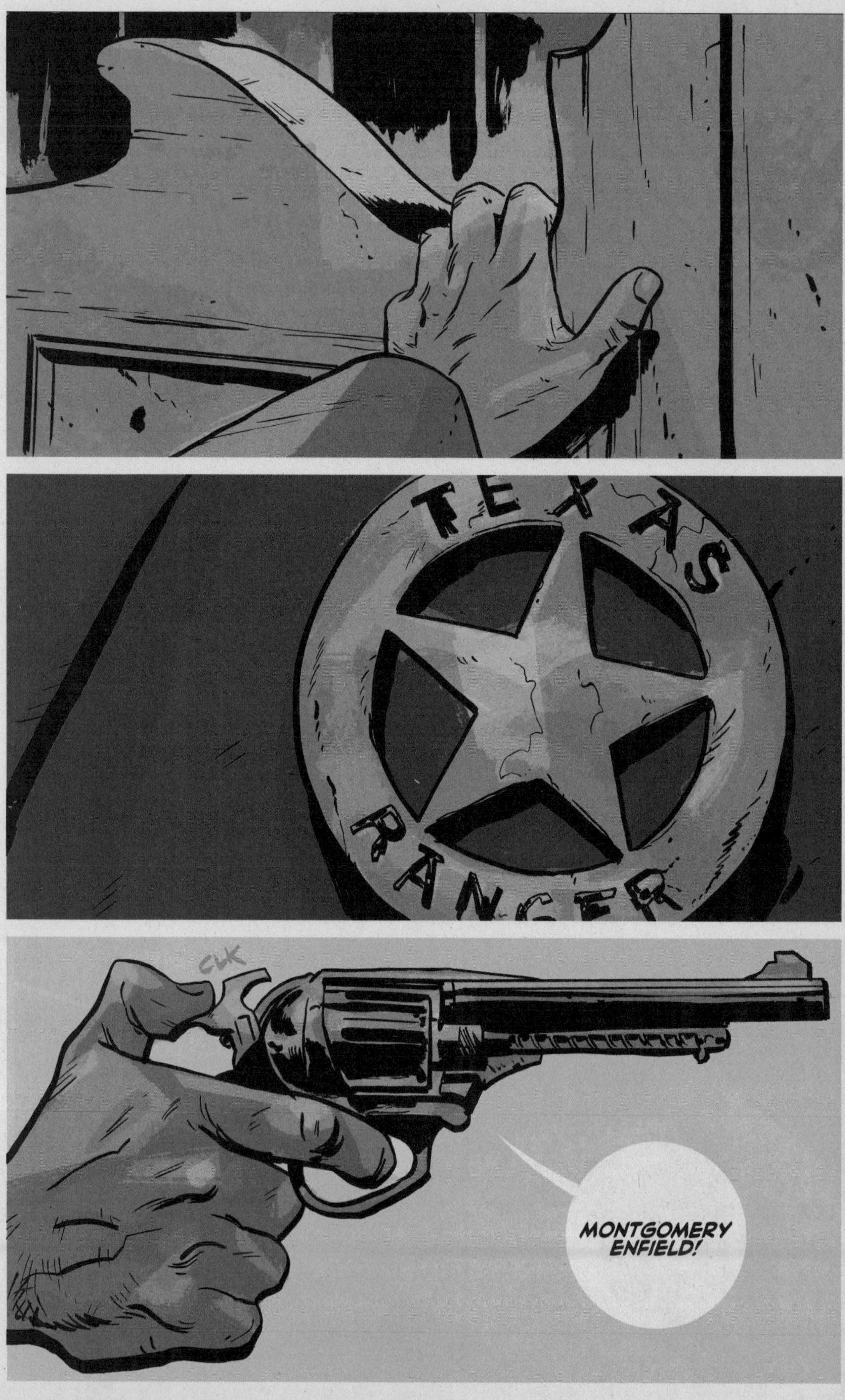

TEXAS
RANGER
CLK
MONTGOMERY ENFIELD!

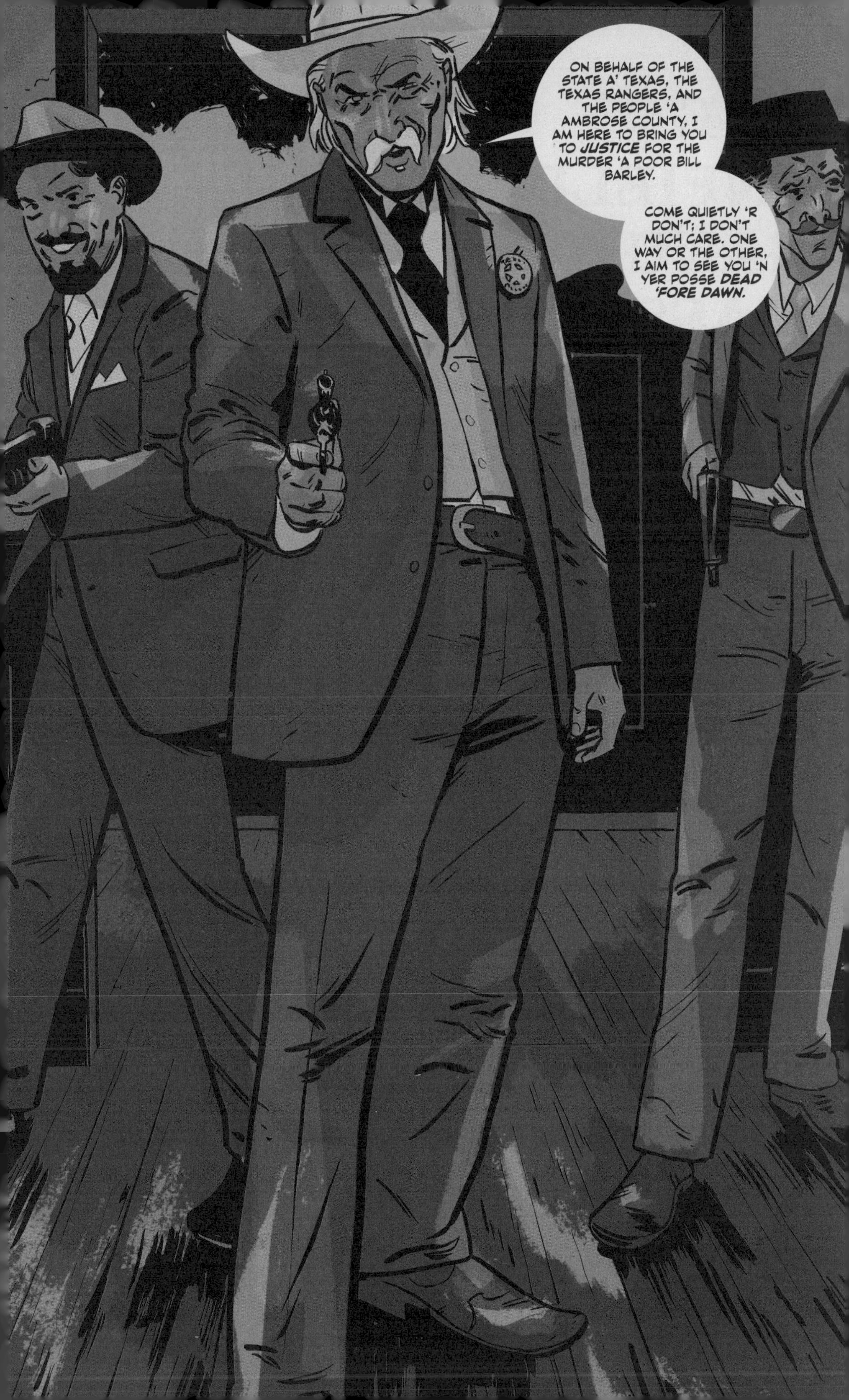
ON BEHALF OF THE STATE A' TEXAS, THE TEXAS RANGERS, AND THE PEOPLE 'A AMBROSE COUNTY, I AM HERE TO BRING YOU TO *JUSTICE* FOR THE MURDER 'A POOR BILL BARLEY.
COME QUIETLY 'R DON'T; I DON'T MUCH CARE. ONE WAY OR THE OTHER, I AIM TO SEE YOU 'N YER POSSE *DEAD 'FORE DAWN.*

THE ENFIELD GANG MASSACRE

Ambrose County's 'Day of Justice' May Be More Fiction Than Fact

If there is one thing Texans know, it's Texas history. It's ingrained in us from youth, hammered into our heads at school like a horseshoe into a hoof. Not every state flies their flag in unison with that of the Union's, or sometimes, in favor of the Union's, but that's Texas. We know of its battles as we were taught them - good guys versus bad, cowboys versus Indians, the civilized versus the savage. In these stories there is always a well-defined line between who is right and who is wrong. And a Texan? He is never wrong.

There's that classic line of dialogue in John Ford's likewise classic 1962 film, The Man Who Shot Liberty Valance, that goes like this: "This is the West, sir. When the legend becomes fact, print the legend." One might think that this is a bit of hyperbole, after all, this quote comes from a motion picture and motion pictures are built on dramatization and fabrication. However, we find in our own West Texas history an egregious effort by historians and Western fanatics alike to rewrite history from a certain point of view. While true that history is written by the victors, as a born and bred Ambrose Countian, I feel it is not only morally right but downright necessary to examine the facts and to tell the story of our past in the most accurate ways we can without the aid of a time machine. It brings me no joy to tell you, dear reader, that others have deceived you about one of Ambrose County's most celebrated stories, however, that seems to be the case. I do not claim to know whether this deception was done maliciously or if it was merely an example of bad facts and lack of evidence. But what I do know is that The Enfield Gang Massacre – a defining moment in the history of Ambrose County that many consider to be the birth of the county itself – has been painted as a classic 'Western' story featuring those tried-and-true Good Guys versus those no-good Bad Guys, and to the surprise of nobody, the Bad Guys lose. Even more popular is the story that followed when the Wild West Sideshow run by the now-notorious confidence man, Franklin Docker AKA Doc Malady, mummified Enfield's corpse and traipsed it around like an ice-skating monkey. The advertisements of the day all noted the "Evil Eyes" of Montgomery Enfield, promising dark fortunes i you peered into them for any length of time. It wa all bull, of course, but the sentiment has stuck: th Enfield Gang were the villains and they were, b all accounts, evil. But what the historical evidenc suggests is something different entirely. The so called Bad Guys were outlaws, yes, and they were in fact, called The Enfield Gang. However, the trut of who this gang was is far more nuanced than t paint them with such a broad brush. But the inac curacies don't end at who The Enfield Gang actuall was. Dates, locations, the length of the massacr itself – all have been misrepresented, even in th March 1979 issue of The Texas Record (yes, the ver magazine you hold in your hands) in an article writ ten by my friend and colleague, W.H. Walton (sorr Willy).

Here's what we've been told: The Enfiel Gang Massacre was a three-day long shootout tha took place in 1875 at The Grady Inn. I couldn't fin any mention of how many members of the gan were killed, but it was many, including both Mont gomery Enfield himself and his criminal cohor Willard Bloom. The massacre followed the murde of an innocent banker, William Barley, who wa killed by The Enfield Gang. Texas Ranger Quenti Ely led the charge alongside the army which wer stationed nearby at the fort (which gives the tow Fort Lehane its name, of course).

There are certainly grains of truth in th previous paragraph. William Barley was murdere and he was, by all accounts, innocent. However, th shootout lasted not three days but five and range from Grady's Inn to the gang's stables and ende it seems, in the cemetery. While there is no defini tive accounting of the number of dead, by my coun

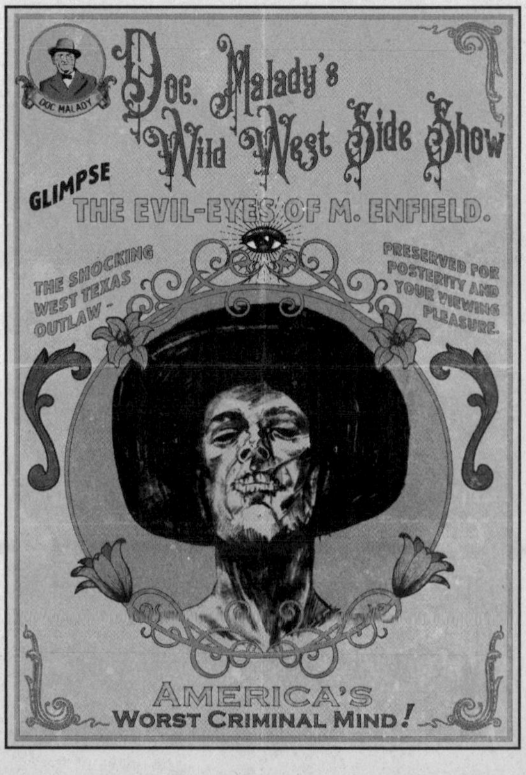
DOC MALADY
Doc. Malady's
Wild West Side Show
GLIMPSE
THE EVIL-EYES OF M. ENFIELD.
THE SHOCKING WEST TEXAS OUTLAW -
PRESERVED FOR POSTERITY AND YOUR VIEWING PLEASURE.
AMERICA'S
WORST CRIMINAL MIND!

Poster for Doc. Malady's Wild West Side Show

ıere were at least thirteen members of the gang illed, though some may have slipped through the racks of history. That number, large as it is, doesn't ıclude the bystanders killed in the shootout, mong them women and children. There is a reason ıat this event was dubbed a massacre and not a attle.

The only written account that I can find as written in the later years of one L.Q. West, the nly surviving member of the Enfield Gang. If you aven't heard of him, you're not alone. For his part, e should have faced prison time and, perhaps, a ıte far worse. Instead, he was afforded years that ıe rest of his gang had stolen from them as a result f his cowardly actions. He died a poor man in his ıid-seventies, about 100-miles south of Ambrose ounty in sparse Terlingua. He was said to have een a broken man whose primary companion was bottle of cheap whisky. The journal he left behind as written in broken English and soaked through ith alcohol, but it reads well enough to tell us hat happened. The massacre wasn't the justifia- ly violent end to a murderous gang. It was, in fact, setup.

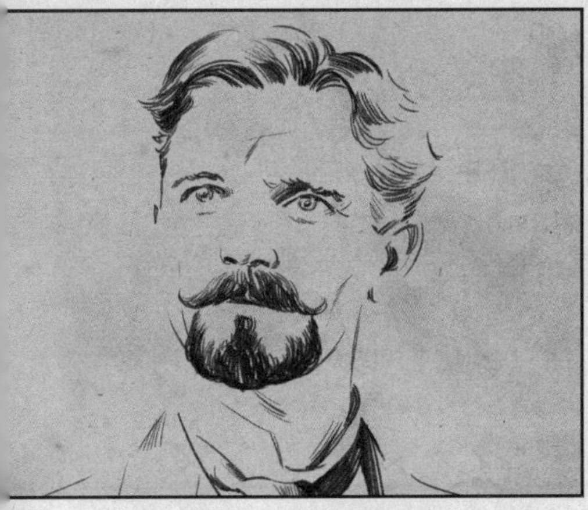

Portrait of John Mowbray

If that's so, then how did we get here? here and when did the legend stray from the uth? To find the answer to that question, we must g through our county records to turn up informa- on on one man, forgotten to time: Mr. John Ruther- rd Mowbray.

John Mowbray was one of the founding embers of Ambrose County, and was one of the ıitial signatures to petition the state to name the ounty after General I.W. Ambrose, who fought for ıe Confederate States in the Civil War. The gen- al died a year after the Confederacy surrendered some affliction or other, so he never knew that a nall West Texas county was commemorating him such a way, but his ruthless tactics and penchant r dehumanization really spoke to the citizens that ad come to inhabit the area around Fort Lehane. hen I asked Ambrose County historian and librar- n, Nancy Gibbons, about the name (and why the ounty has yet to change it) she merely shrugged r shoulders. "They just can't seem to get together do it, that's all," she told me. "Most folks admit

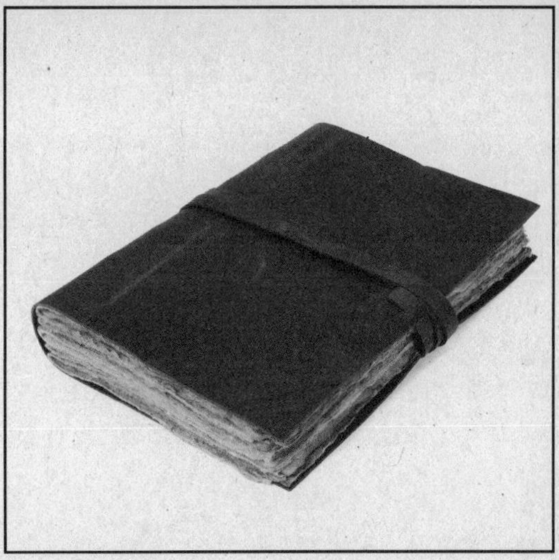

L.Q. West's Journal

that Ambrose was a cur, one who tortured, mutilated, and killed soldiers on both sides of the war. A lot of historians miss that part - it was on both sides. He tortured his own men if they refused orders or if they needed, in his eyes, 'discipline.' What the first settlers here liked about him was his gumption and independent spirit. They thought it embodied what they were trying to do out west on the frontier."

Mowbray owned a shop in what had become known as "New Town," a thriving local area that positioned itself as the bedrock of Fort Lehane and, thus, Ambrose County. New Town was home to a small hotel, saloon, bank, and a few other shops. It was described as 'quaint' in contemporary correspondence and every word I've read about it seems to imply that the town was trying to establish itself as some sort of normalcy in a largely untamed land.

Across town, on the southeastern edge, sat what was, and still is, known as "Chihuahua," named for the Chihuahua desert in which it resides. Chihuahua was a largely segregated area of Fort Lehane that was home to the people that Mowbray described as "undesirables" in a letter he had sent to the Texas legislature seeking their expulsion from the state. These "undesirables" included members of the Enfield Gang, including Montgomery Enfield himself, along with indigenous peoples, freed slaves, and immigrants from Central and South America, Europe, and beyond.

But unknown until recently - in fact, until my research for this article unearthed it - it was Mowbray's insidious desire to wipe Chihuahua off of the face of the earth entirely that led directly to the ruthless death and destruction that has become known far and wide as The Enfield Gang Massacre, the event Texas history students are taught is a "Day of Justice." But there was no justice to be had that day in 1875. It was quite the opposite. In this author's opinion, the whole ordeal should be remembered instead as "The John Mowbray Massacre."

TO BE CONTINUED

CHAPTER TWO

PINNED DOWN

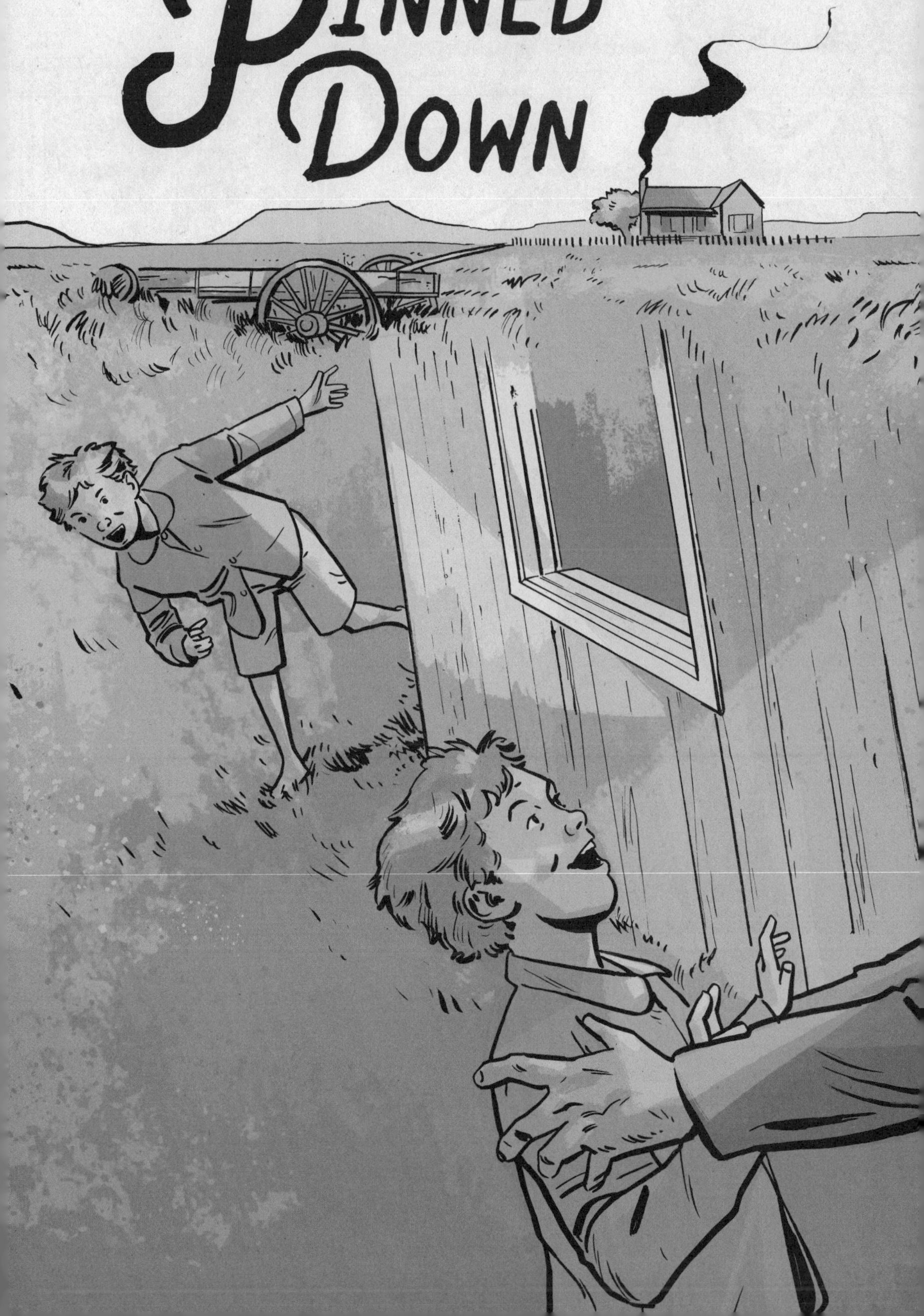

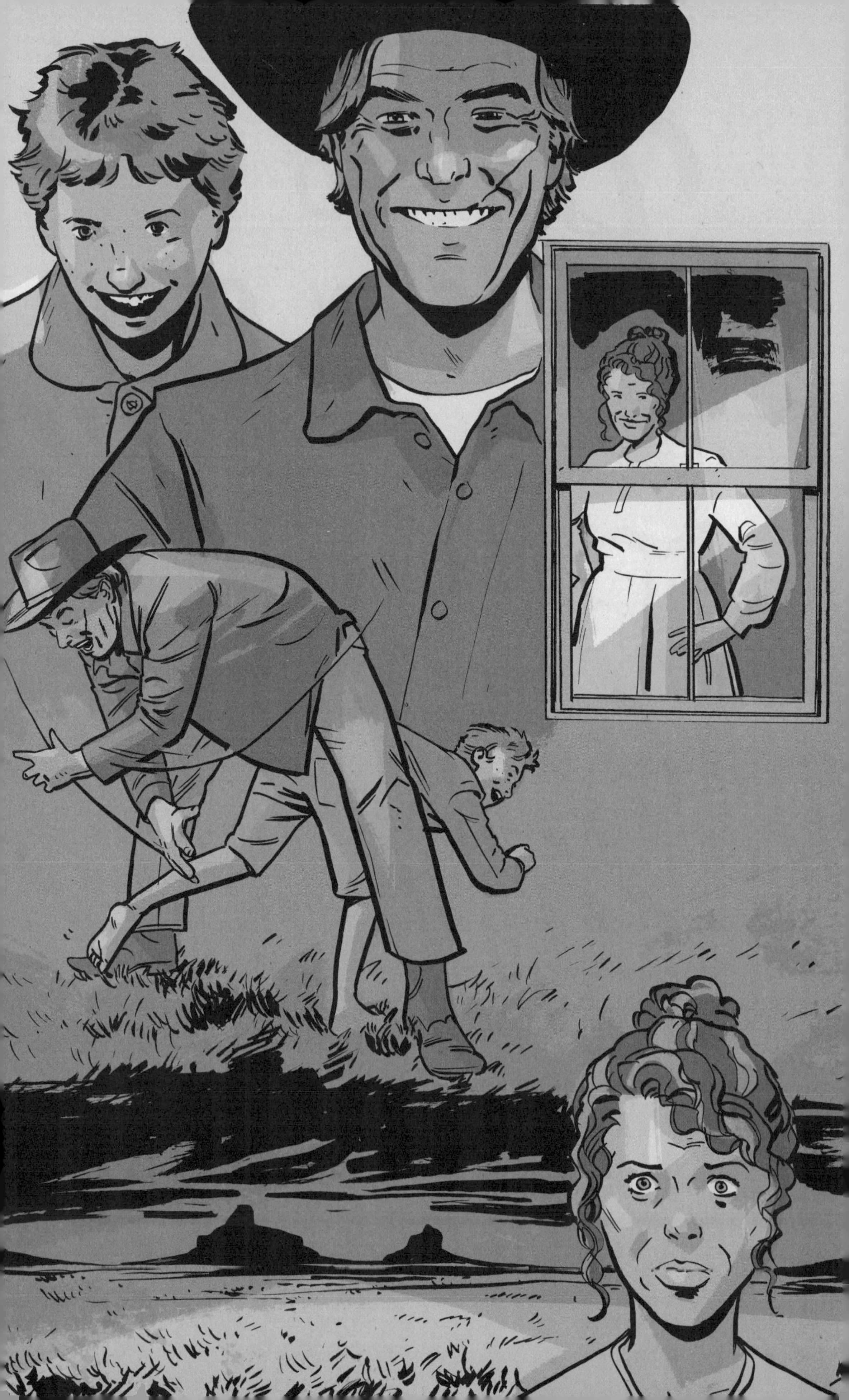

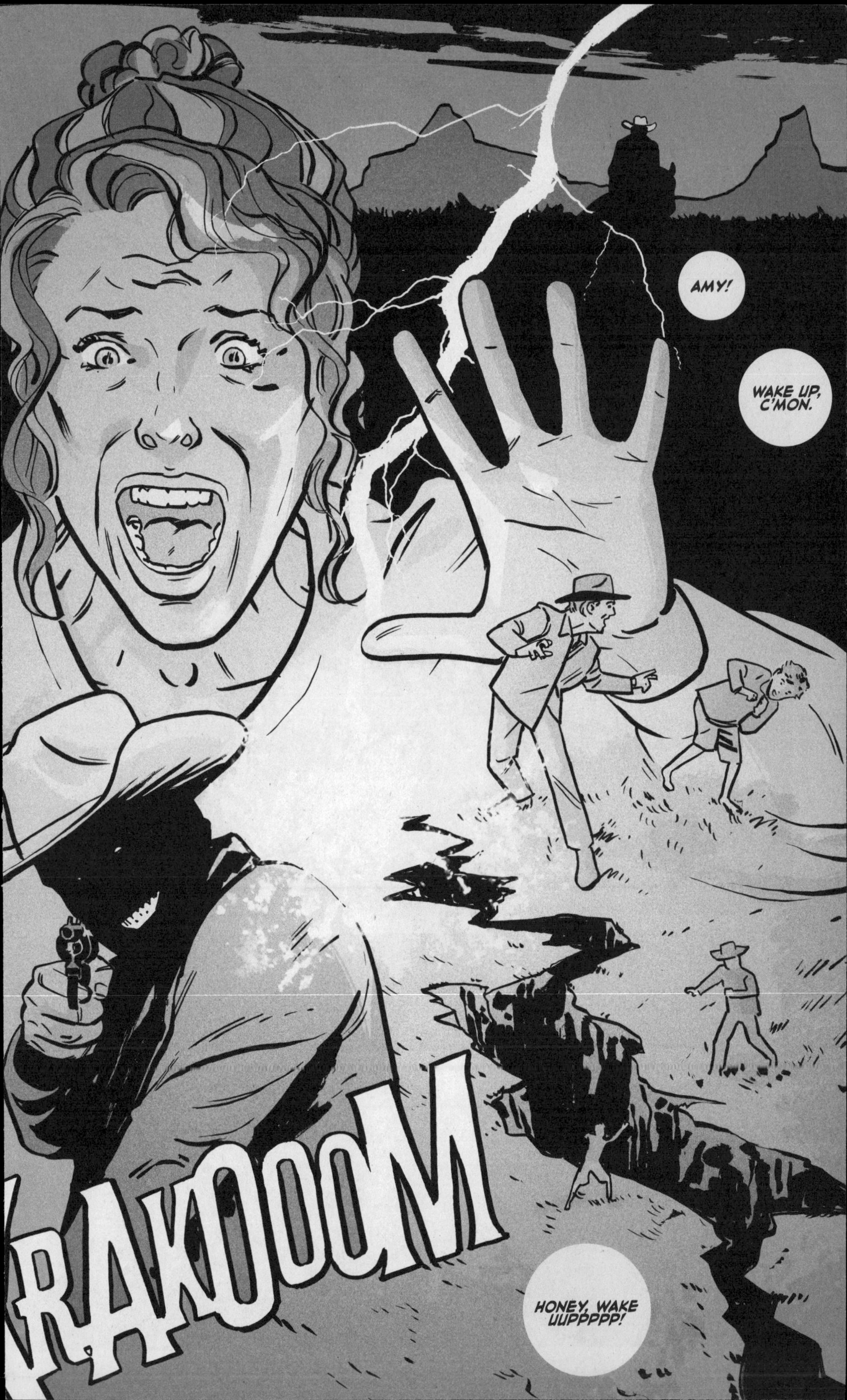
AMY!
WAKE UP, C'MON.
RAKOOOM
HONEY, WAKE UUPPPPP!

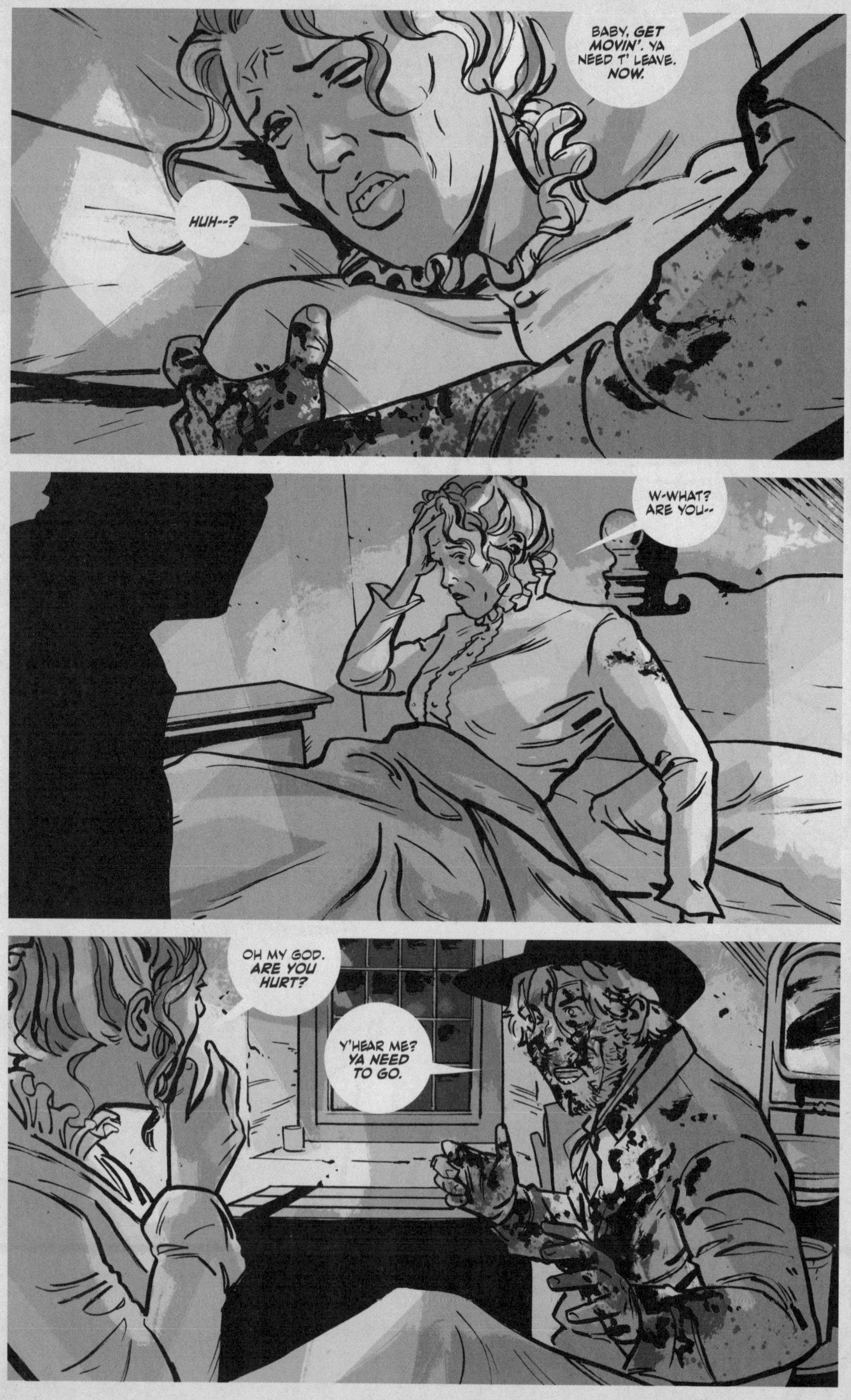
BABY, GET MOVIN'. YA NEED T' LEAVE. NOW.
HUH--?
W-WHAT? ARE YOU--
OH MY GOD. ARE YOU HURT?
Y'HEAR ME? YA NEED TO GO.

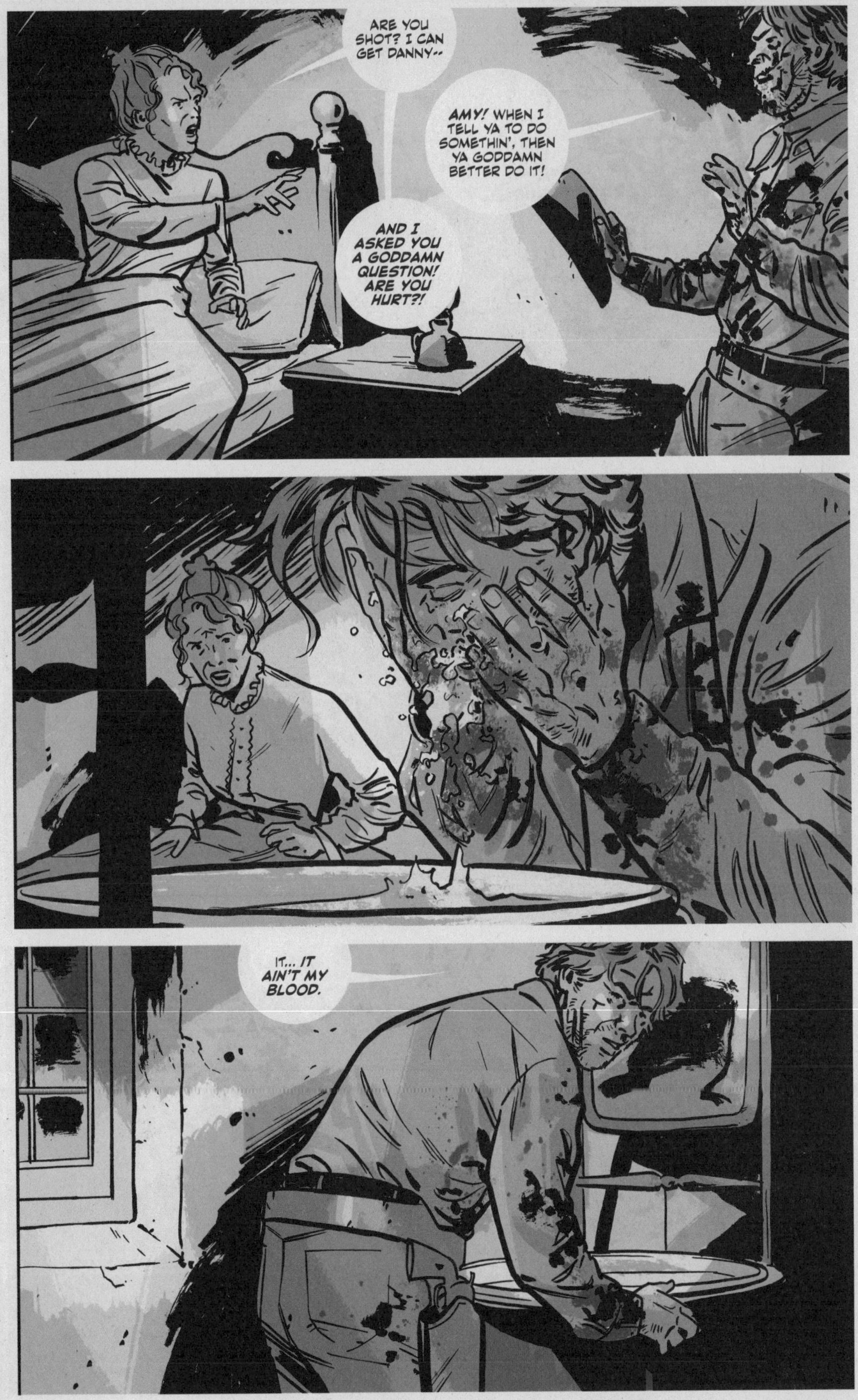
ARE YOU SHOT? I CAN GET DANNY--
AMY! WHEN I TELL YA TO DO SOMETHIN', THEN YA GODDAMN BETTER DO IT!
AND I ASKED YOU A GODDAMN QUESTION! ARE YOU HURT?!
IT... IT AIN'T MY BLOOD.

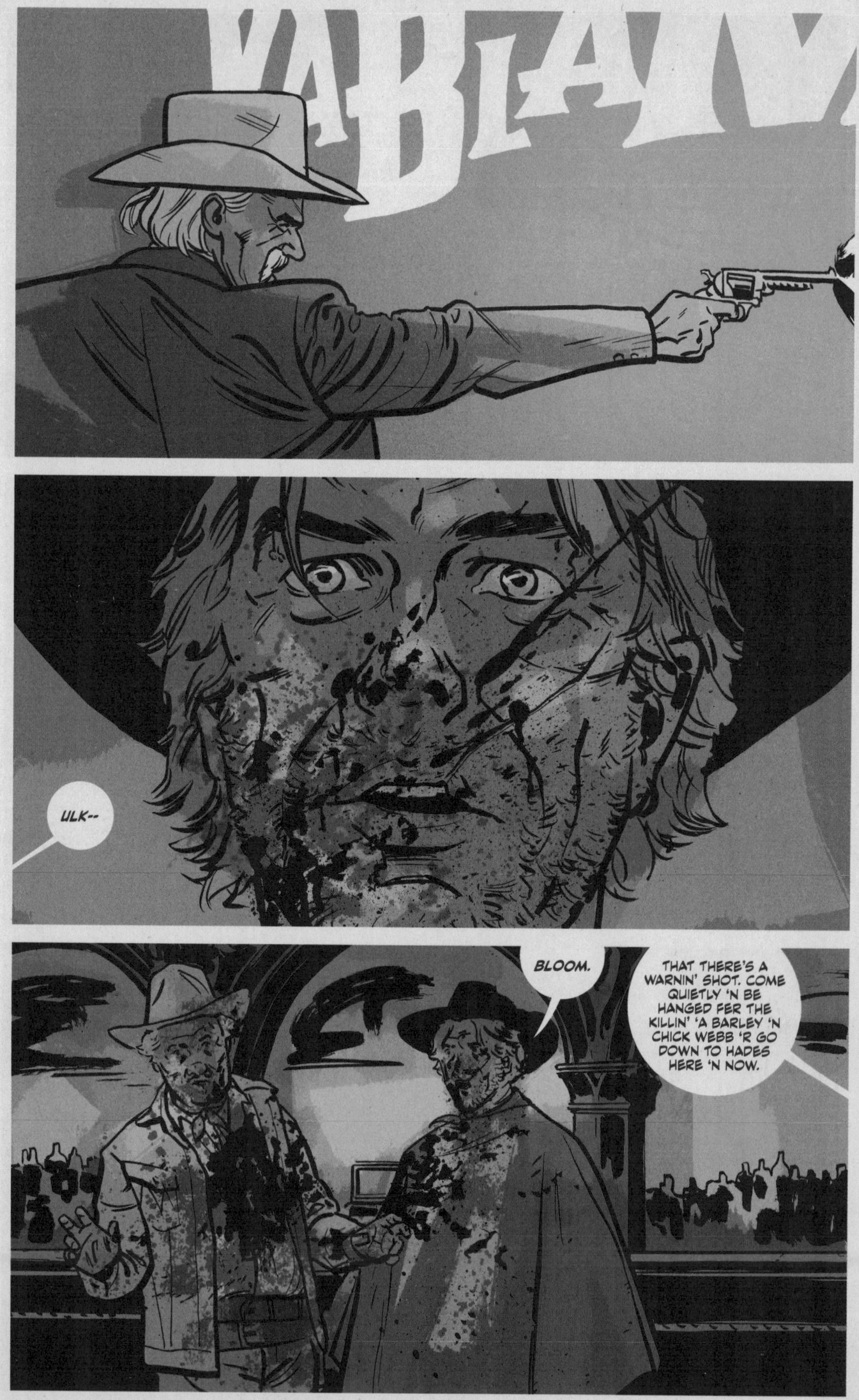
ULK--
BLOOM.
THAT THERE'S A WARNIN' SHOT. COME QUIETLY 'N BE HANGED FER THE KILLIN' 'A BARLEY 'N CHICK WEBB 'R GO DOWN TO HADES HERE 'N NOW.

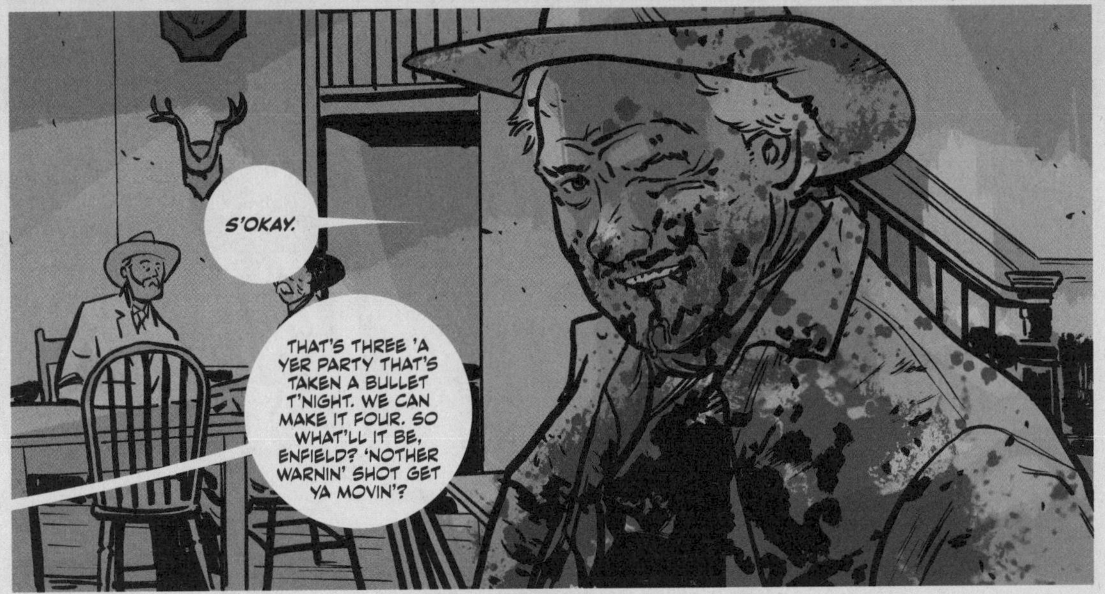
S'OKAY.
THAT'S THREE 'A YER PARTY THAT'S TAKEN A BULLET T'NIGHT. WE CAN MAKE IT FOUR. SO WHAT'LL IT BE, ENFIELD? 'NOTHER WARNIN' SHOT GET YA MOVIN'?

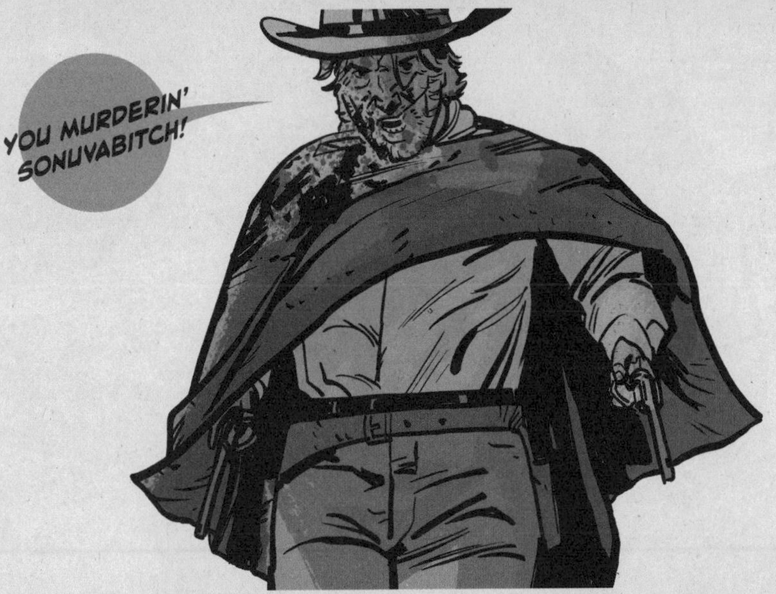
YOU MURDERIN' SONUVABITCH!

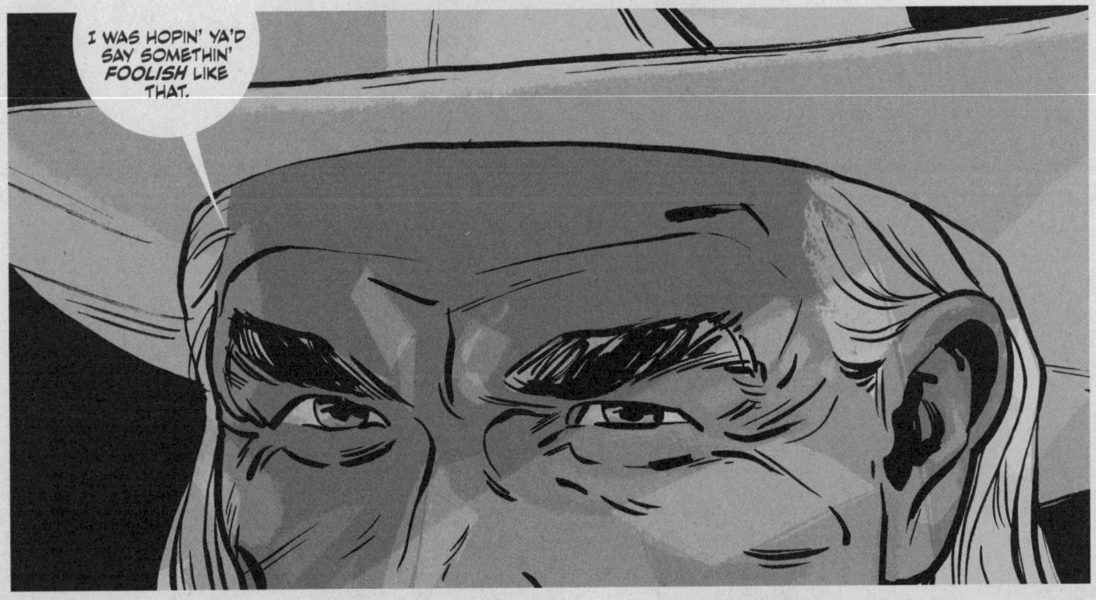
I WAS HOPIN' YA'D SAY SOMETHIN' FOOLISH LIKE THAT.

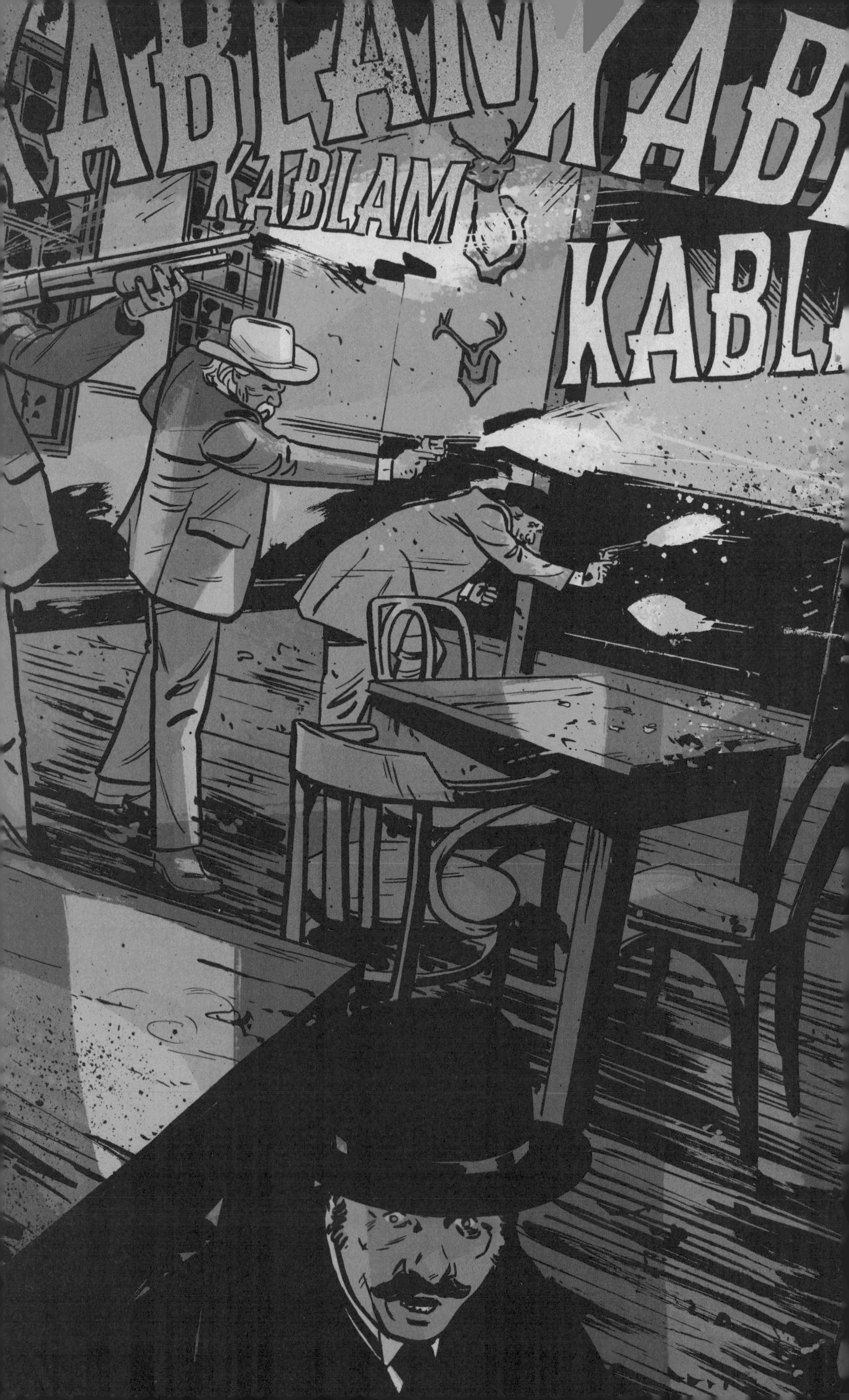
ABLAM KAB
KABLAM
KABL

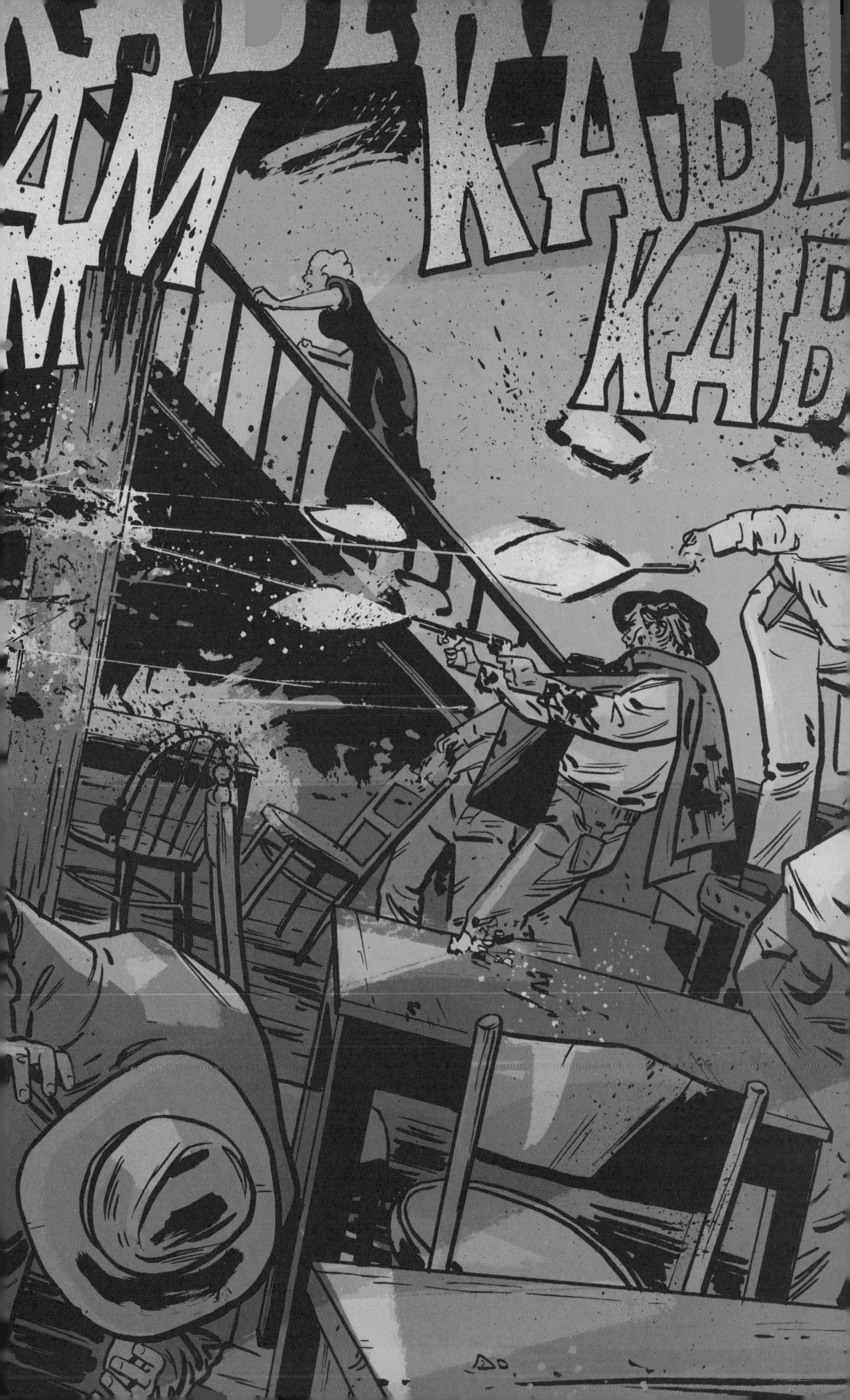
KABL
KAB

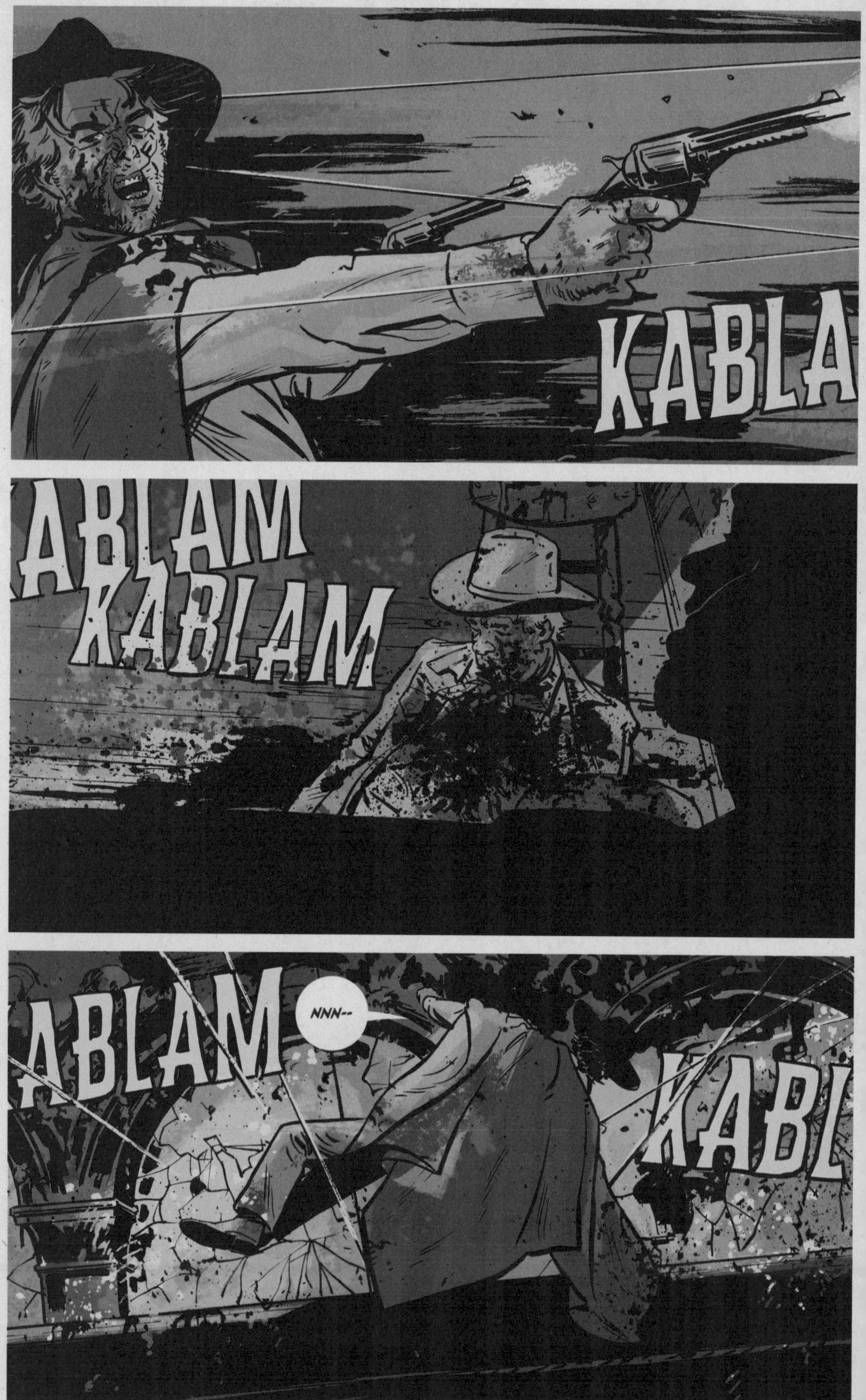
KABLA
ABLAM
KABLAM
ABLAM
NNN--
KABL

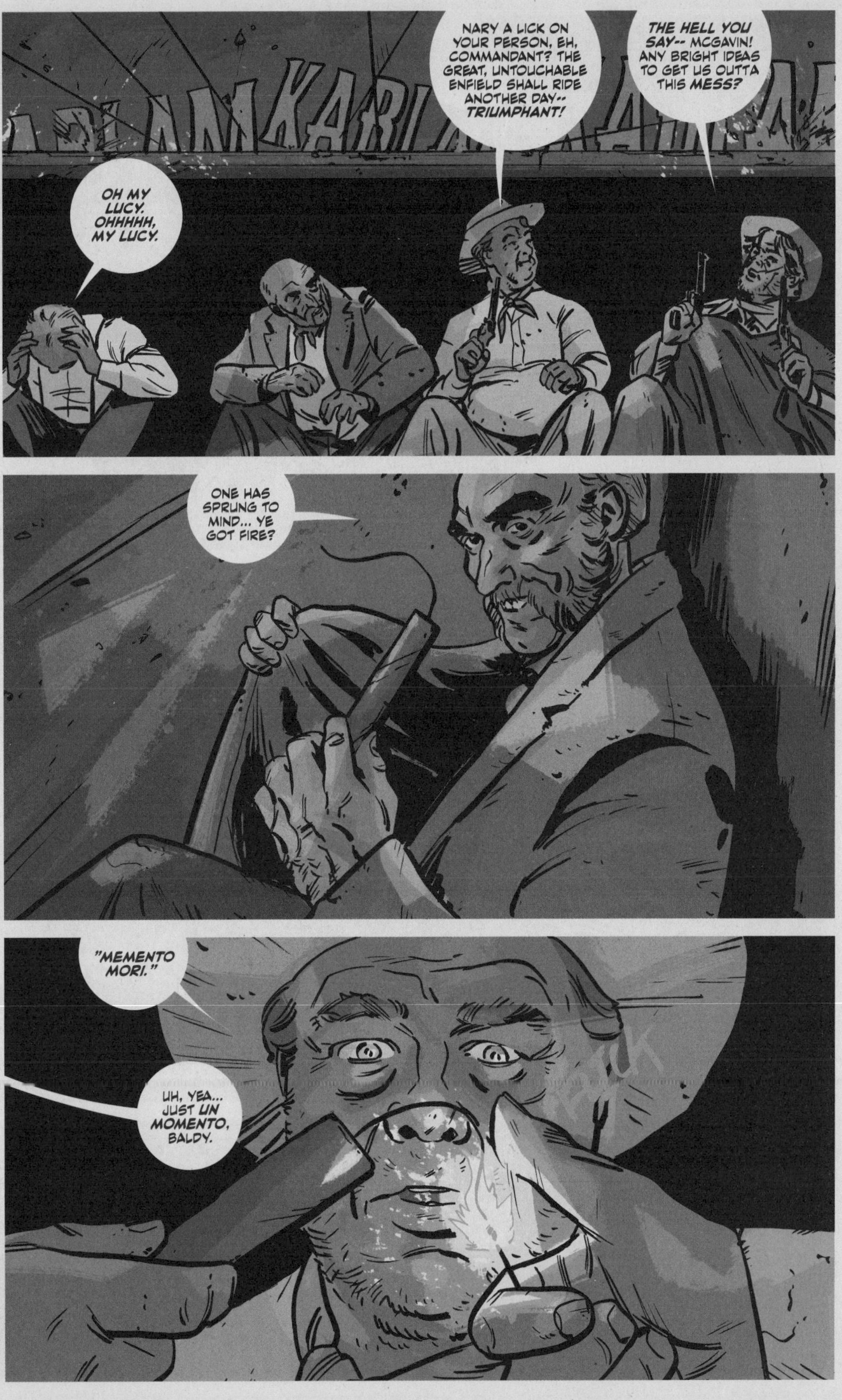
NARY A LICK ON YOUR PERSON, EH, COMMANDANT? THE GREAT, UNTOUCHABLE ENFIELD SHALL RIDE ANOTHER DAY-- *TRIUMPHANT!*
THE HELL YOU SAY-- MCGAVIN! ANY BRIGHT IDEAS TO GET US OUTTA THIS *MESS?*
OH MY LUCY. OHHHHH, MY LUCY.
ONE HAS SPRUNG TO MIND... YE GOT FIRE?
"MEMENTO MORI."
UH, YEA... JUST *UN MOMENTO,* BALDY.

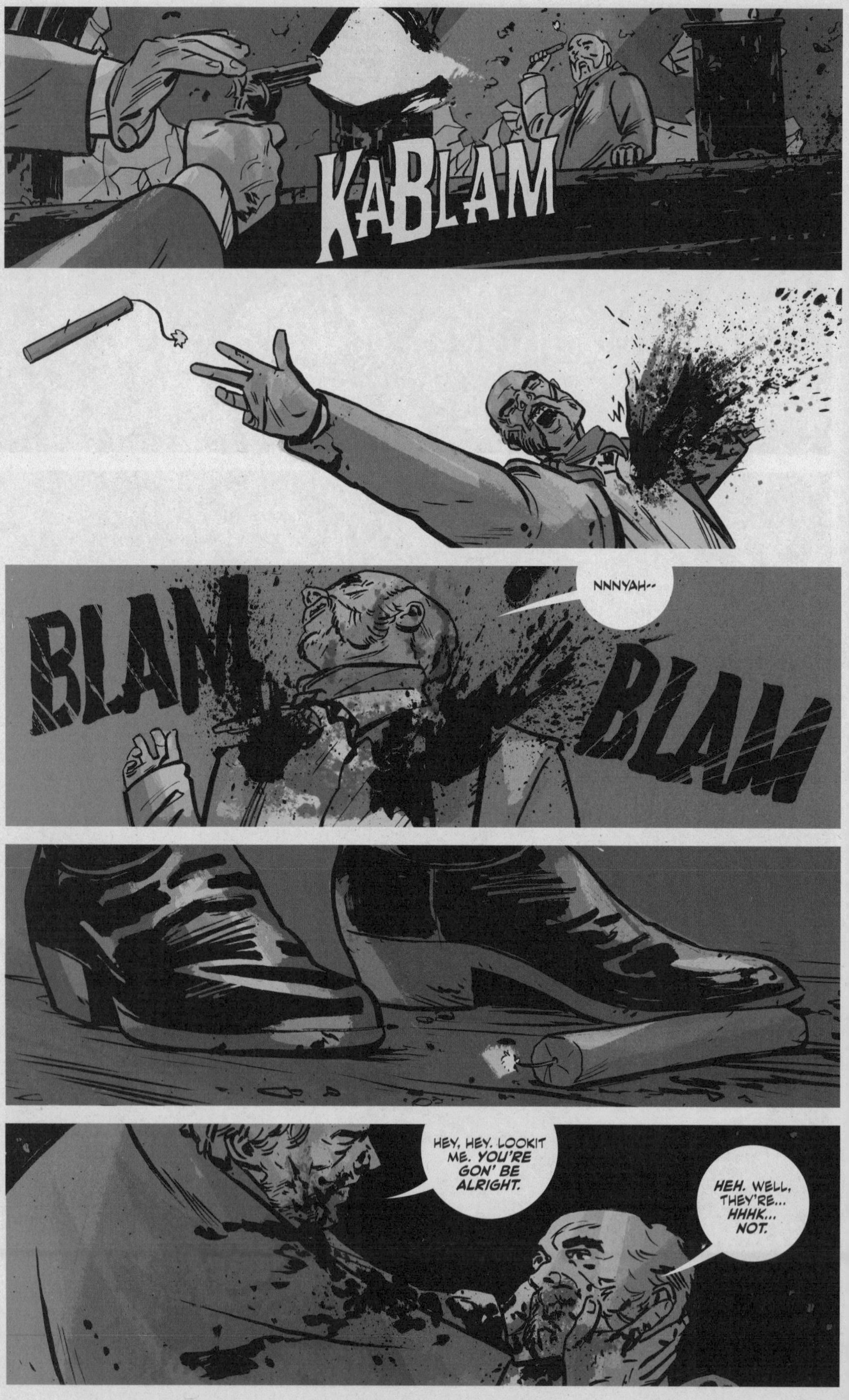
KABLAM
NNNYAH--
BLAM
BLAM
HEY, HEY. LOOKIT ME. YOU'RE GON' BE ALRIGHT.
HEH. WELL, THEY'RE... HHHK... NOT.

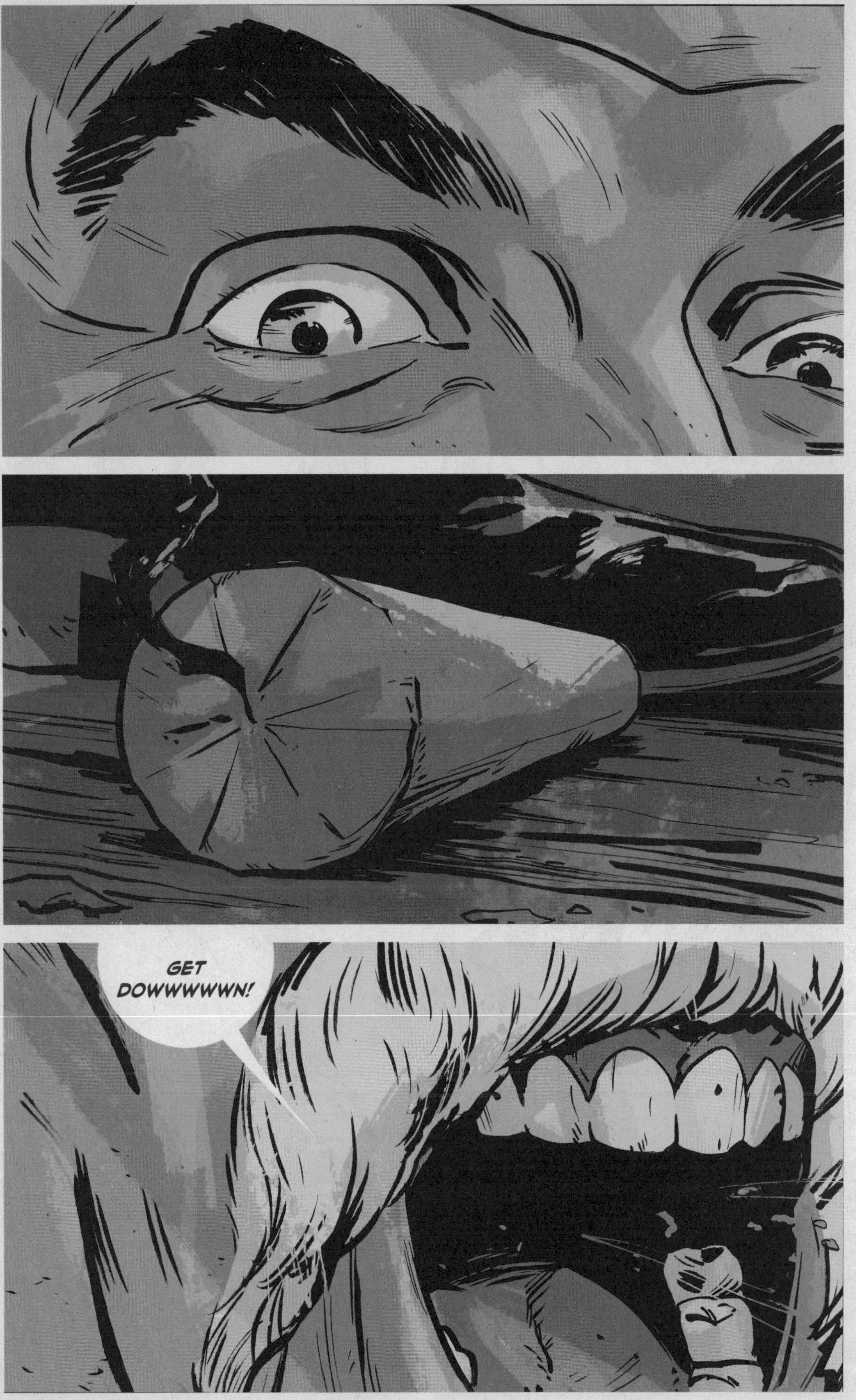
GET DOWWWWWN!

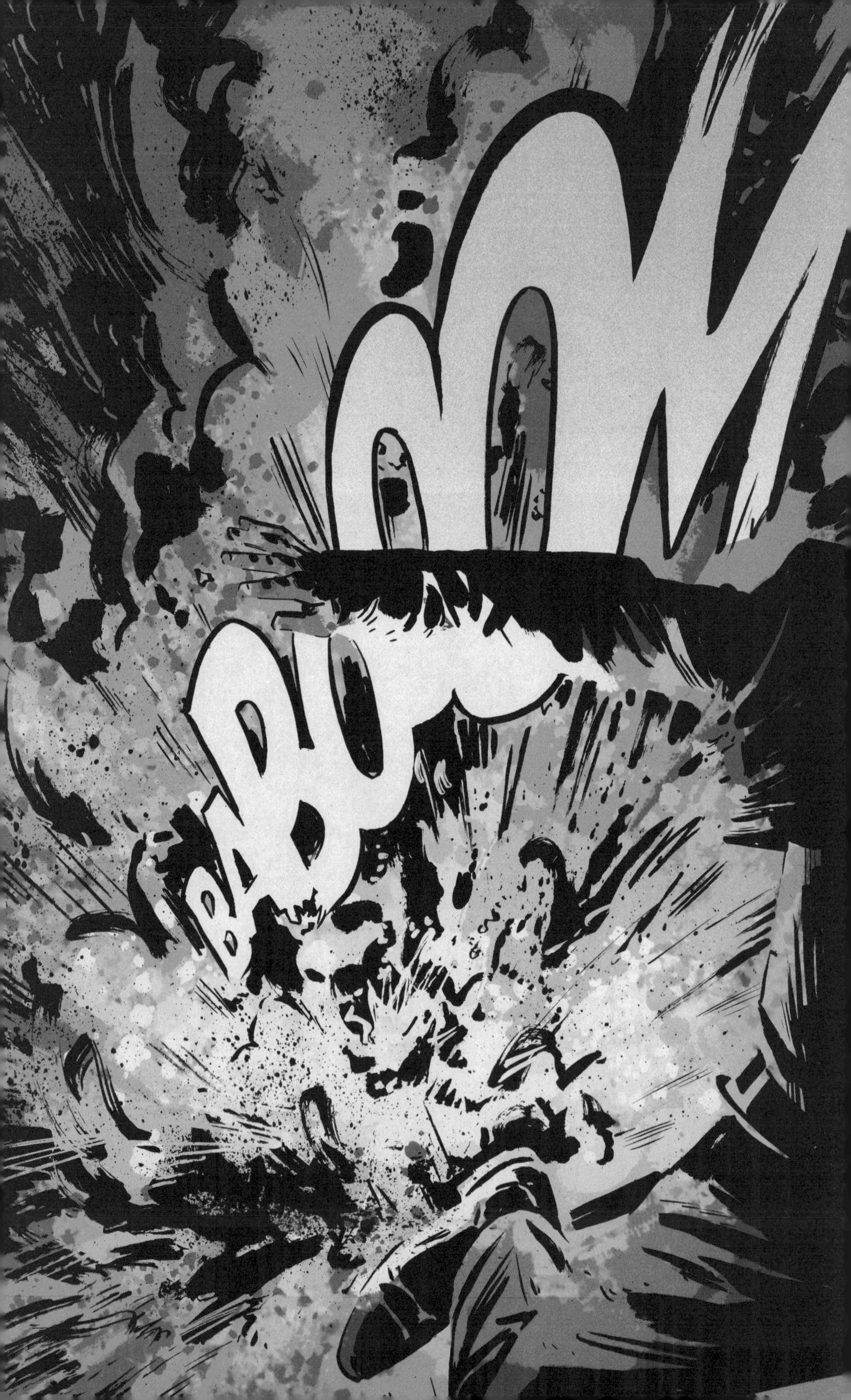

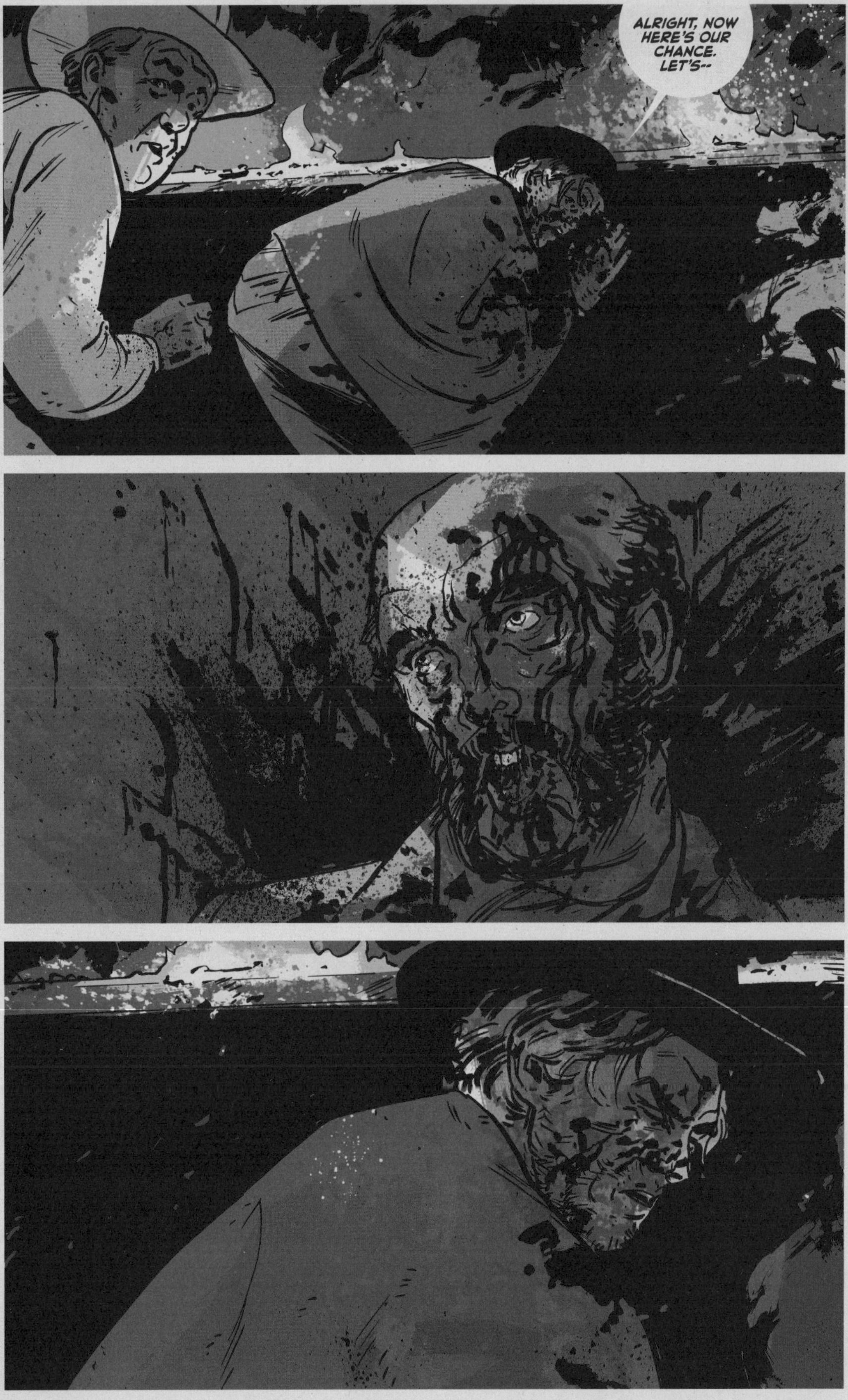
ALRIGHT, NOW HERE'S OUR CHANCE. LET'S--

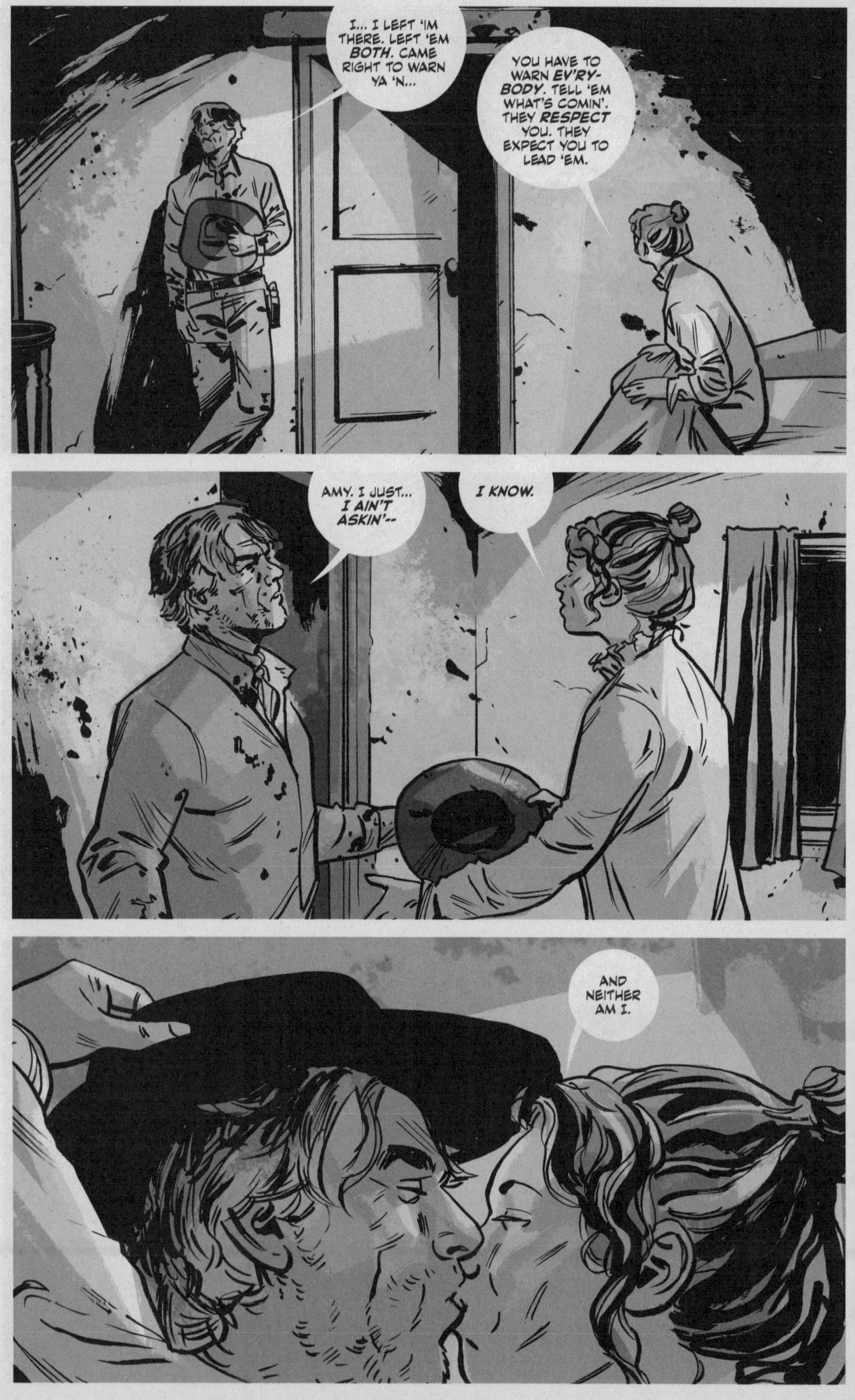
I... I LEFT 'IM THERE. LEFT 'EM BOTH. CAME RIGHT TO WARN YA 'N...
YOU HAVE TO WARN EV'RY-BODY. TELL 'EM WHAT'S COMIN'. THEY RESPECT YOU. THEY EXPECT YOU TO LEAD 'EM.
AMY. I JUST... I AIN'T ASKIN'--
I KNOW.
AND NEITHER AM I.

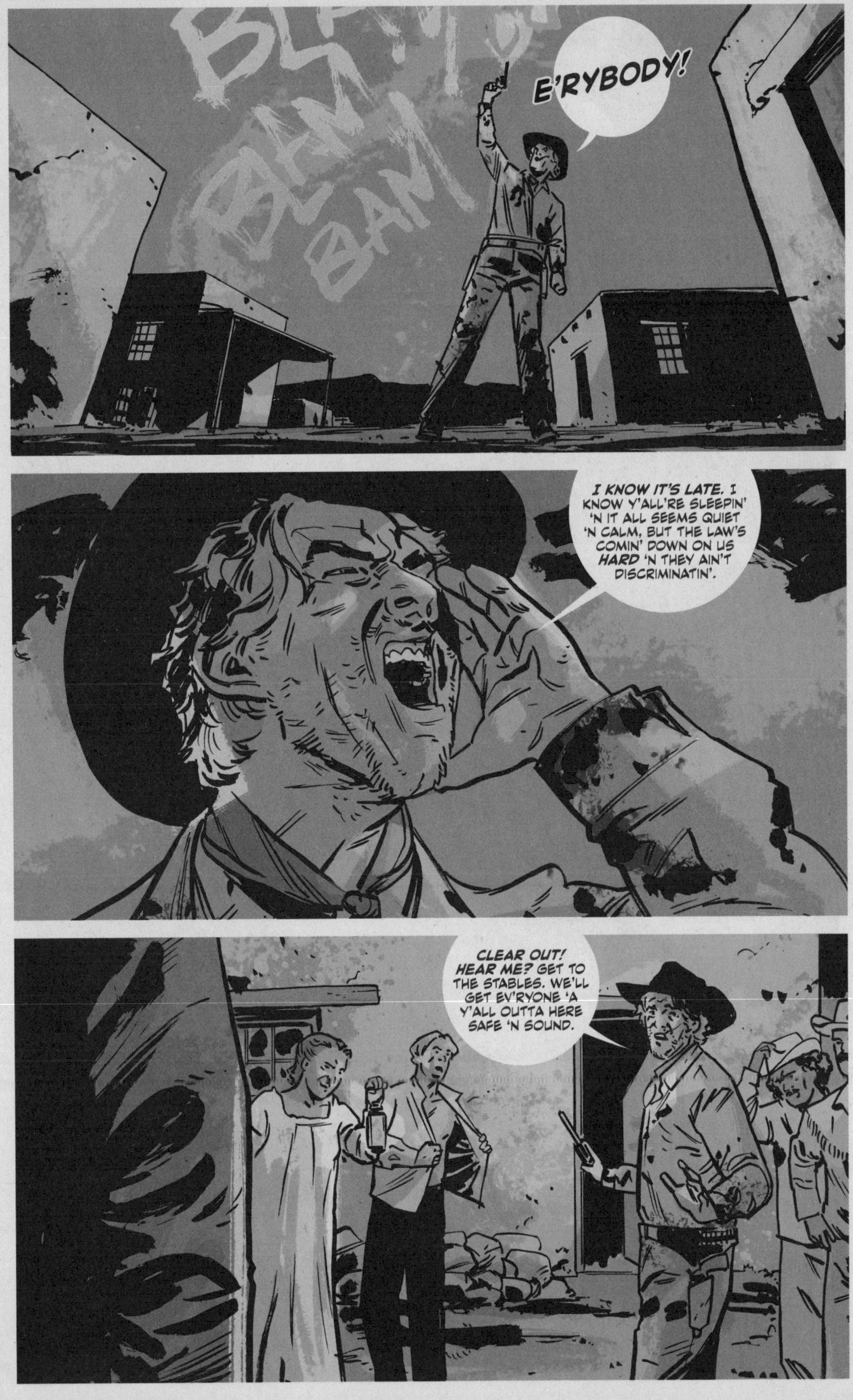
E'RYBODY!
I KNOW IT'S LATE. I KNOW Y'ALL'RE SLEEPIN' 'N IT ALL SEEMS QUIET 'N CALM, BUT THE LAW'S COMIN' DOWN ON US HARD 'N THEY AIN'T DISCRIMINATIN'.
CLEAR OUT! HEAR ME? GET TO THE STABLES. WE'LL GET EV'RYONE 'A Y'ALL OUTTA HERE SAFE 'N SOUND.

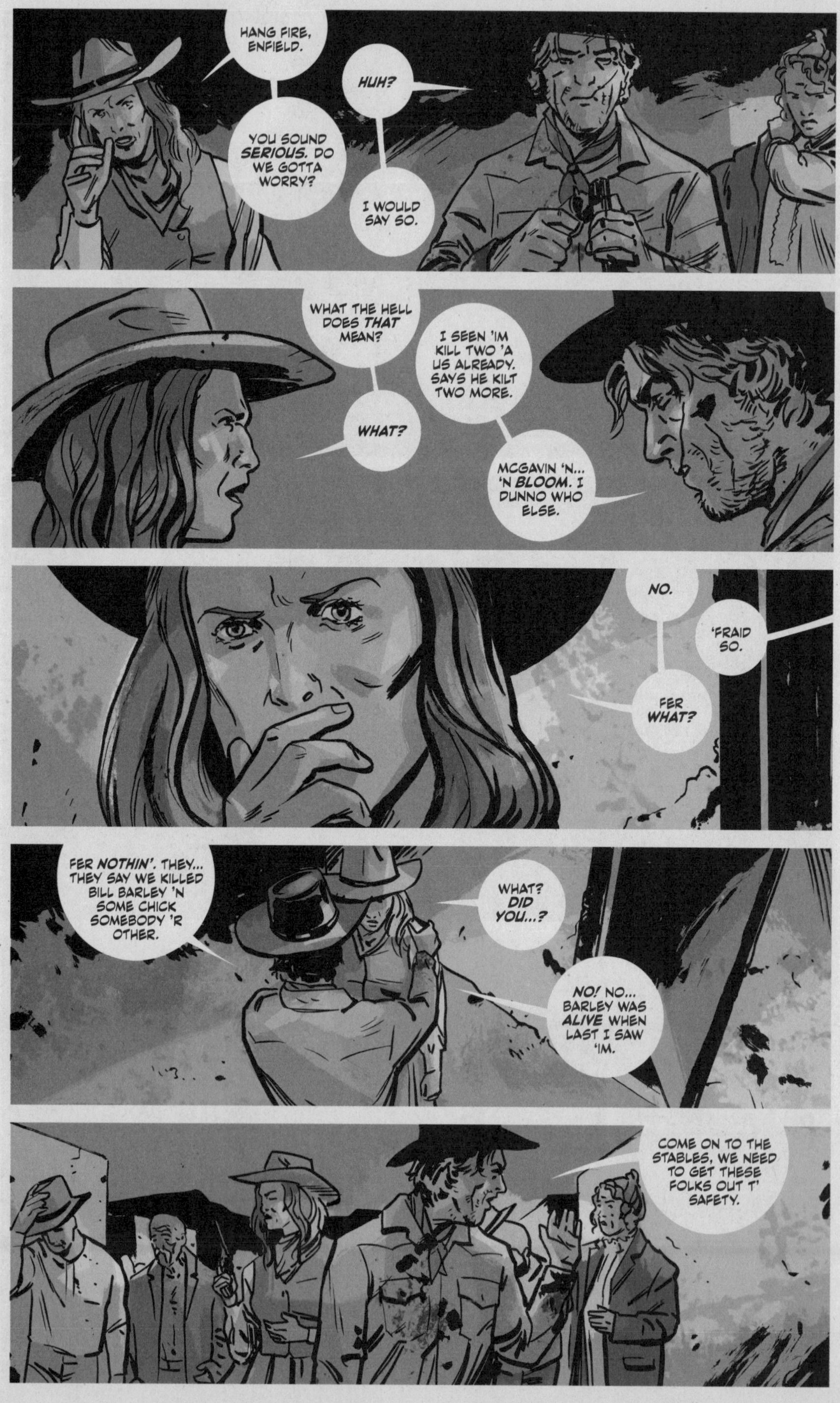
HANG FIRE, ENFIELD.
HUH?
YOU SOUND SERIOUS. DO WE GOTTA WORRY?
I WOULD SAY SO.
WHAT THE HELL DOES THAT MEAN?
I SEEN 'IM KILL TWO 'A US ALREADY. SAYS HE KILT TWO MORE.
WHAT?
MCGAVIN 'N... 'N BLOOM. I DUNNO WHO ELSE.
NO.
'FRAID SO.
FER WHAT?
FER NOTHIN'. THEY... THEY SAY WE KILLED BILL BARLEY 'N SOME CHICK SOMEBODY 'R OTHER.
WHAT? DID YOU...?
NO! NO... BARLEY WAS ALIVE WHEN LAST I SAW 'IM.
COME ON TO THE STABLES, WE NEED TO GET THESE FOLKS OUT T' SAFETY.

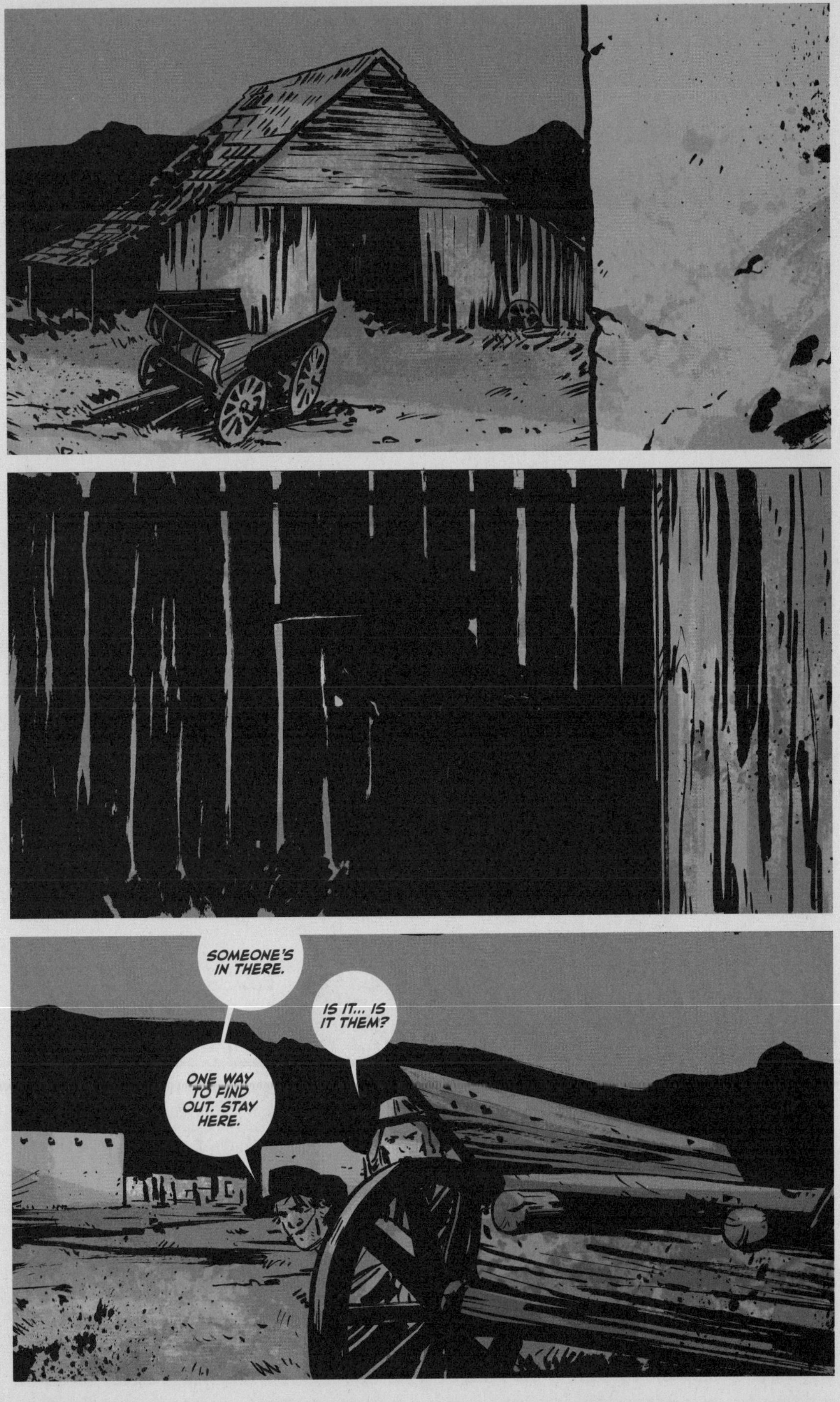
SOMEONE'S IN THERE.
IS IT... IS IT THEM?
ONE WAY TO FIND OUT. STAY HERE.

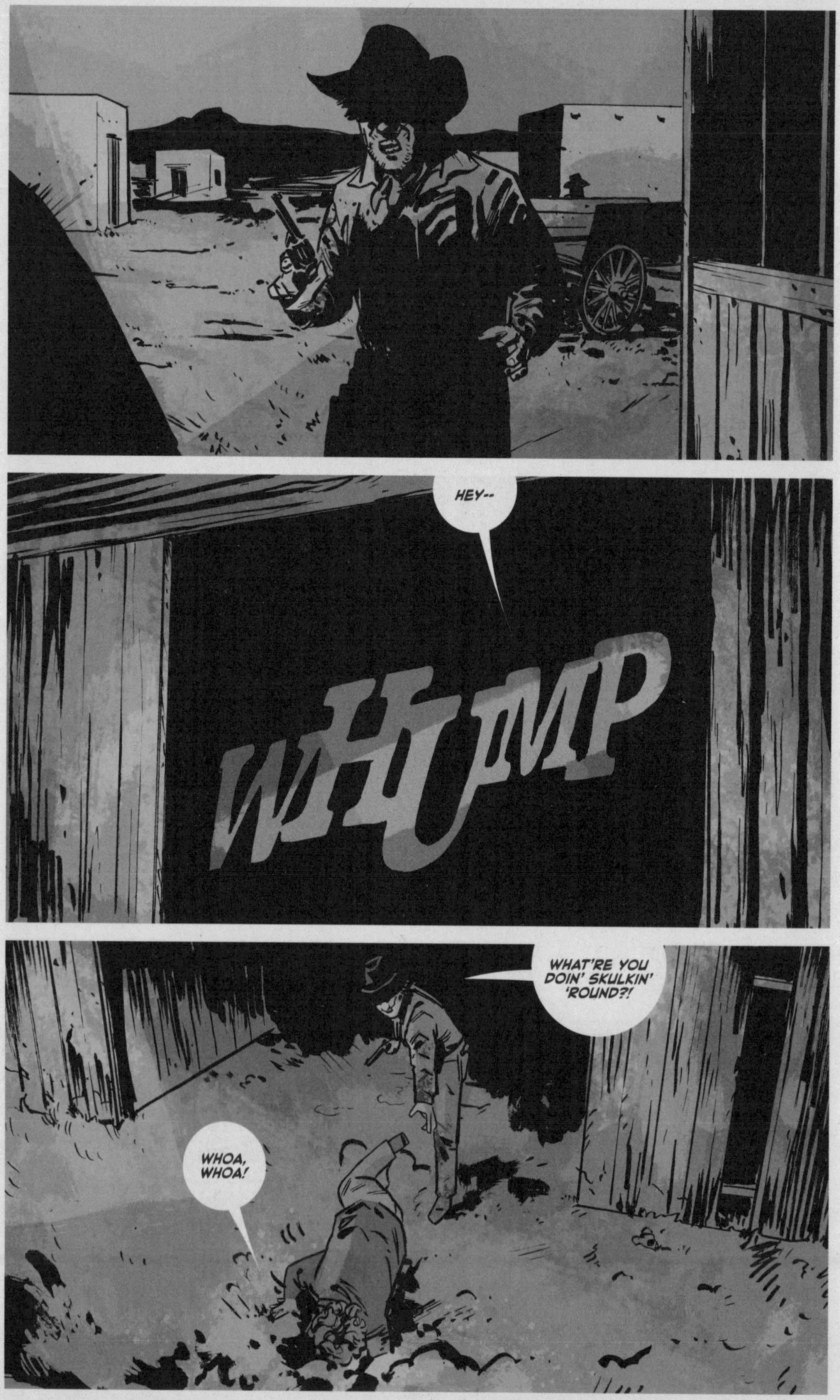
HEY--
WHUMP
WHAT'RE YOU DOIN' SKULKIN' 'ROUND?!
WHOA, WHOA!

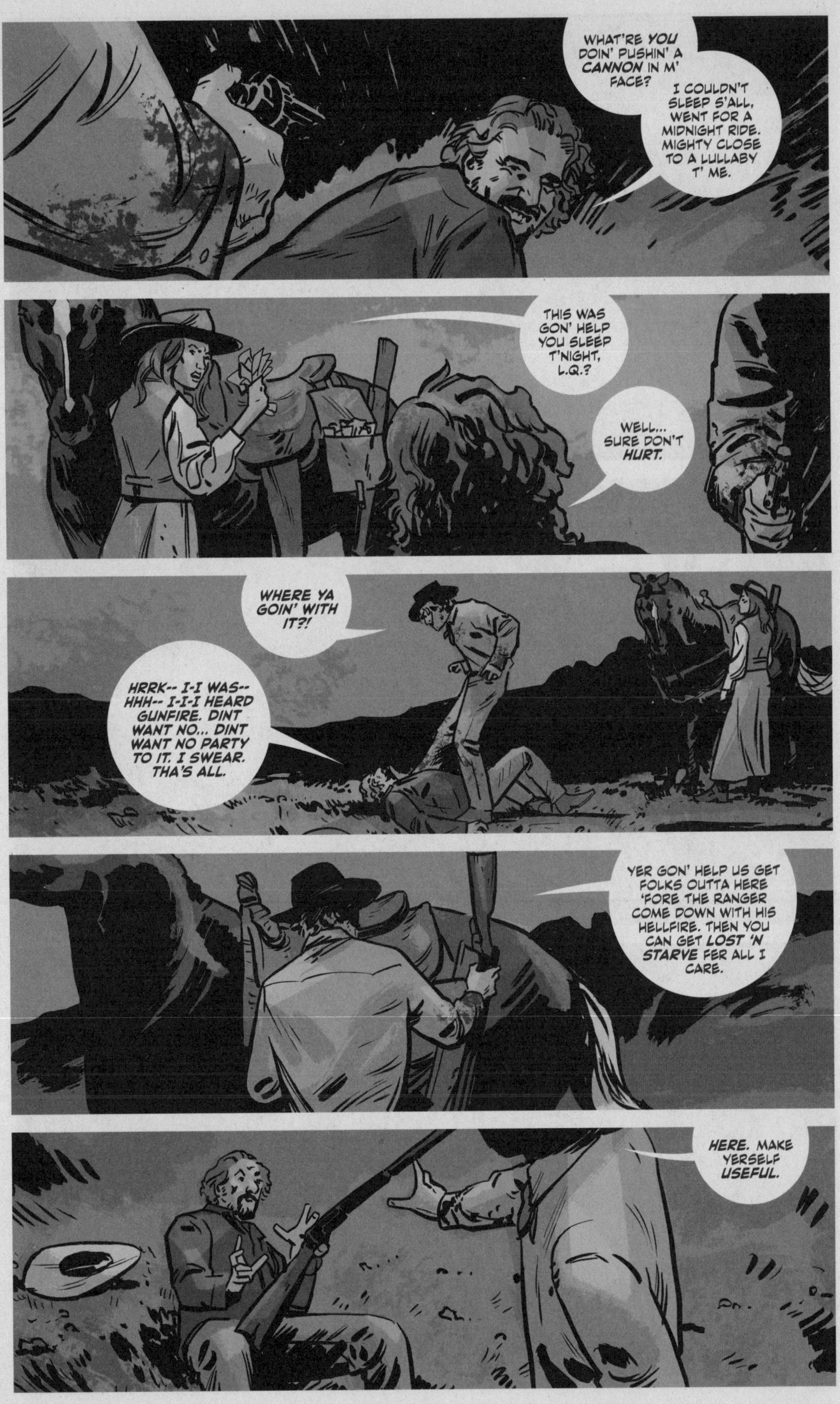
WHAT'RE YOU DOIN' PUSHIN' A CANNON IN M' FACE?
I COULDN'T SLEEP S'ALL, WENT FOR A MIDNIGHT RIDE. MIGHTY CLOSE TO A LULLABY T' ME.
THIS WAS GON' HELP YOU SLEEP T'NIGHT, L.Q.?
WELL... SURE DON'T HURT.
WHERE YA GOIN' WITH IT?!
HRRK-- I-I WAS-- HHH-- I-I-I HEARD GUNFIRE. DINT WANT NO... DINT WANT NO PARTY TO IT. I SWEAR. THA'S ALL.
YER GON' HELP US GET FOLKS OUTTA HERE 'FORE THE RANGER COME DOWN WITH HIS HELLFIRE. THEN YOU CAN GET LOST 'N STARVE FER ALL I CARE.
HERE. MAKE YERSELF USEFUL.

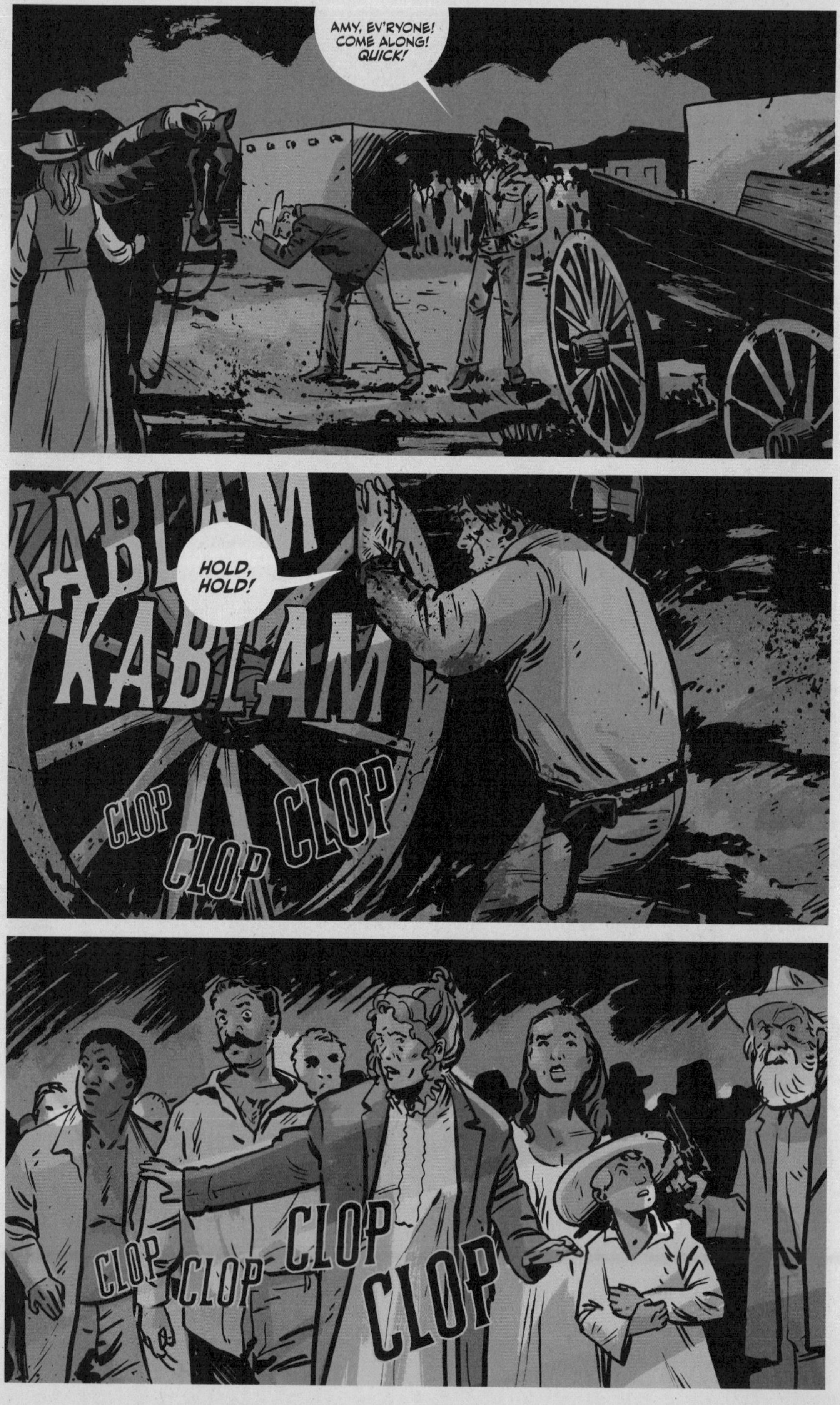
AMY, EV'RYONE! COME ALONG! QUICK!
KABLAM
KABLAM
HOLD, HOLD!
CLOP
CLOP
CLOP
CLOP
CLOP
CLOP
CLOP

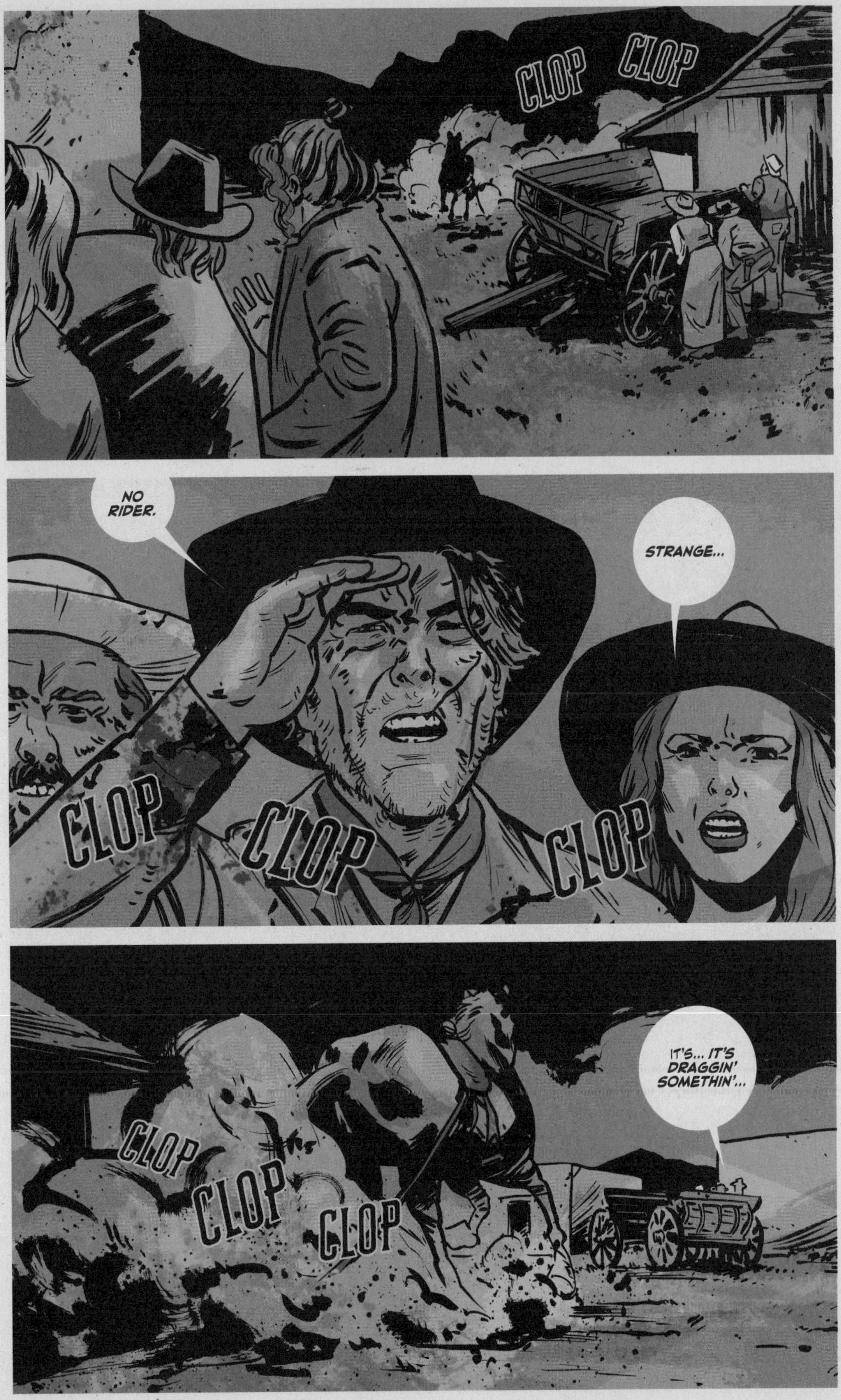
CLOP CLOP
NO RIDER.
STRANGE...
CLOP
CLOP
CLOP
IT'S... IT'S DRAGGIN' SOMETHIN'...
CLOP
CLOP
CLOP

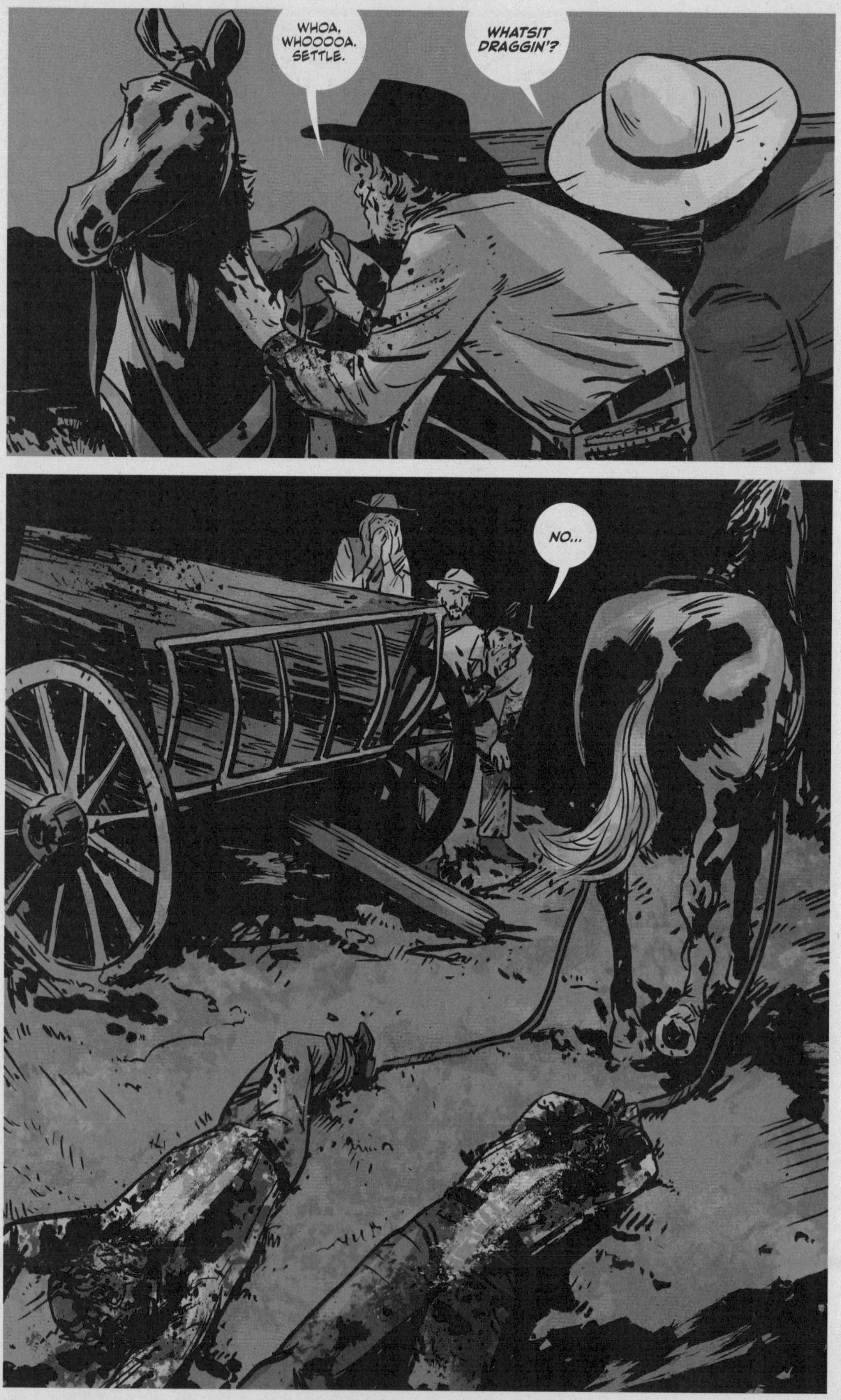
WHOA, WHOOOOA. SETTLE.
WHATSIT DRAGGIN'?
NO...

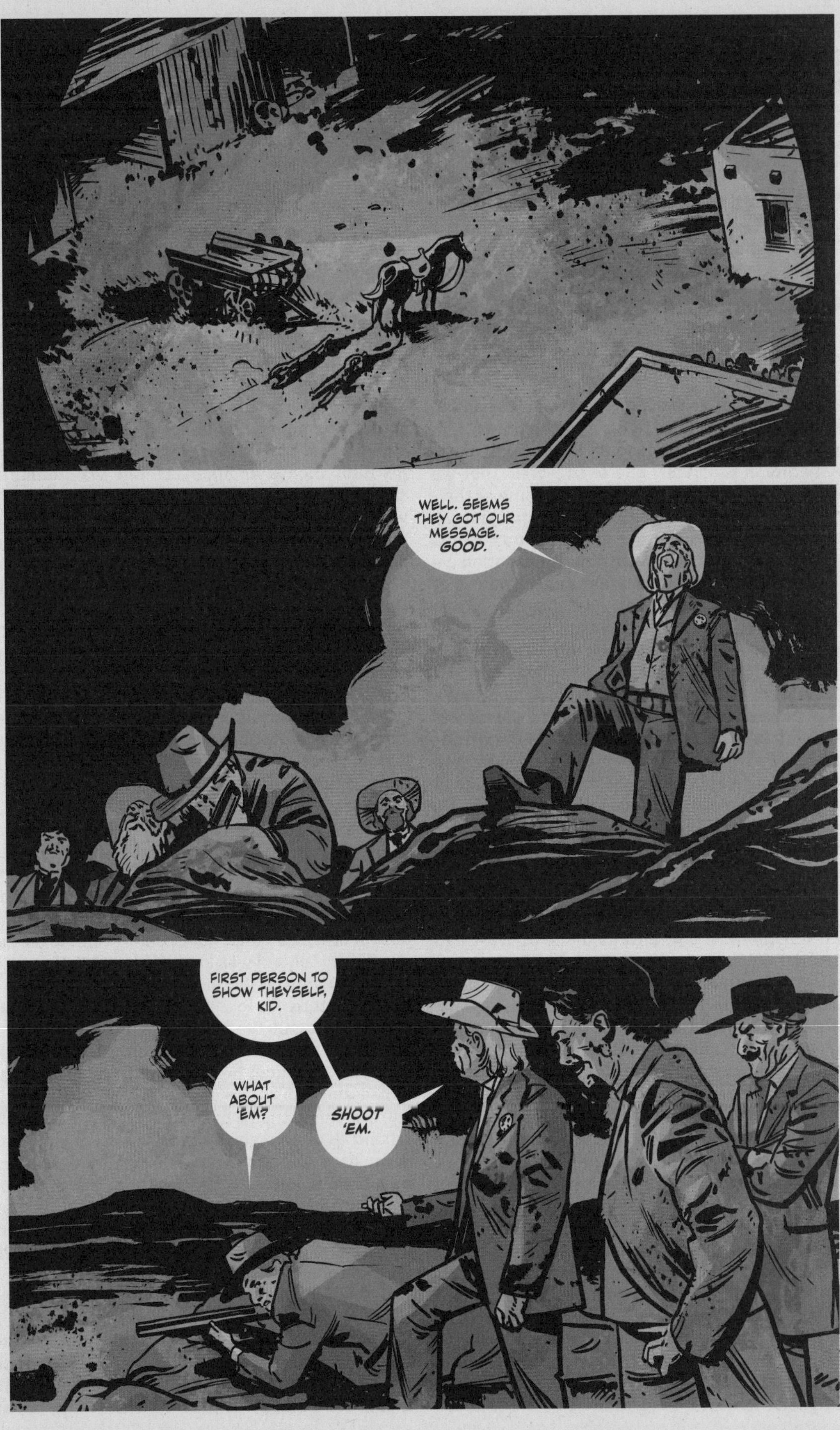
WELL. SEEMS THEY GOT OUR MESSAGE. GOOD.
FIRST PERSON TO SHOW THEYSELF, KID.
WHAT ABOUT 'EM?
SHOOT 'EM.

THE ENFIELD GANG MASSACRE

cont'd.

Knowing this, let us backtrack a bit and examine the gang itself before we delve into the horrid and, frankly, sad details of their end. Despite his unsavory nature, it is actually due to L.Q. West that we know the names of the members and some of their background, which he chronicled in his journal. How accurate his accounting was remains unclear, but when cross-referenced with the information we do have about the gang, it seems to check out.

Lynton Quayle West, born Lynton Quayle O'Connor, was born on the shores of Ireland sometime around 1840 to parents Jack and Elizabeth. He was the youngest of six children and was barely a year old when the family set sail across the Atlantic Ocean for New York City. Growing up on the streets of Manhattan, Lynton was, seemingly, a born troublemaker. On his seventeenth birthday, he assaulted a police officer and lit fire to a textile factory, evaded capture, and wound up in Ohio where he bought his first six-shooter, a Colt of some kind or other, according to his journal. He was a small-time crook with a thirst for violence who worked alone until he met a partner, a man that went by the name Jefferson Colgate. This man—Jefferson Colgate—did not exist. Whether this was a trade name or West had concocted the individual entirely from his deviously imaginative mind, we do not know. There is no mention of Jefferson Colgate anywhere; no arrests, no warrants, no nothing. There is one photo that exists of West with another gentleman, similarly clad and sporting identical facial hair, but the identity of that individual remains unknown. There is an inscription on this mysterious photograph but all it says is "L & G." Whether that's indicative of the subjects or a signature of the photographer on his work remains unknown (I would be inclined to believe the latter). In fact, a lot is unknown about L.Q. West, which is quite a funny thing considering his lengthy (though poorly written) journal entries. Still, we do know that he apparently joined up with the Enfield Gang in June of 1875 in Fort Lehane, Texas, a mere month before the massacre. This would make West a new recruit and, thus, not as ride-or-die loyal to the outfit as so many of the other members were. This is not to excuse his actions, merely to understand them. The other thing that we do know about

him is that he walked with a substantial limp afte he was fired upon while committing a robbery ir Louisiana. Reading through his journal, he tended to blame the bullet lodged in his leg for his myriad troubles, including his violent temper and hard drinking ways.

While we're left guessing when it comes to West's past, we do know quite a bit about Enfield's origins. Edward Montgomery Enfield (yes, his true name was Edward) was born in January of 1838 to widowed mother Jane Enfield in Chicago, Illinois Young Edward's father, Julian, was killed in a factory accident just two months before he was born Julian's death had a traumatic impact on Jane, who died in February of 1839 after "succumbing to a broken heart," according to contemporary reports Whether this means hers was a death of despair or some other ailment, I cannot decipher. What we do know is that Enfield was shipped away to stay with his Aunt Glenys in Arkansas. She was unmarried and by all accounts treated young Enfield well. He was a good student and contributed to the household. It was in his lust for adventure, though, where he was led astray. He read obsessively, specifically a copy of The Count of Monte Cristo by Alexandre Dumas that he had borrowed from a school teacher His teenage years were rough, as they usually are and he began to experiment with how far he could push himself and the law. He refused to join the Confederacy when war broke out in 1861, and instead found himself on the run. As he was an outlaw from an early age, it was difficult to hold steady legitimate work, though there is record of him working as a ranch hand in Texas for a time. But the majority of his time was spent committing some crime or other– whether it was robbing a bank, a wagon train, or, well, any train. He was wanted in several states, including Missouri, Arkansas, Mississippi and, eventually, Texas. He first came to Fort Lehane in 1868 following a train robbery gone wrong (the details of which could fill an entire volume on their own). Fort Lehane was sparsely populated and distant enough from the incident that he managed to evade capture. He found, however, that he enjoyed the climate and the environment and decided to return for permanent residency in 1872, alongside Amy Martin, whom he met in 1867 in El Paso. They dillied and dallied, as lovers do, and finally decided to commit themselves to each other sometime around 1872, though the precise date is unknown Some have said they were married, though there is no official record of this. Perhaps it was a personal engagement made under the West Texas stars While we may not know the legitimacy of their romantic partnership under the law, we do know that they loved each other—right to the bitter end.

Willard Tobias Bloom, often referred to solely as 'Bloom,' was considered by many to be Enfield's premiere partner. They first encountered each other in Arkansas in 1864, both of them on the run from the Confederacy and the Union alike. What that first meeting was like, we don't know, but anecdotal evidence seems to indicate that Bloom and Enfield got themselves a bottle of whisky and robbed a courthouse of some confiscated gold pieces. I have tried my darndest to uncover some more information about this supposed robbery, but I can only find brief mentions of an altercation between two "unsavory" individuals at the Yell County courthouse that resulted in the "loss of valuables." The dates lead me to believe that these individuals were, in fact, Bloom and Enfield and that the "valuables" were the confiscated gold. Whatever the truth, these two stuck together from then on. Bloom never married.

Not much is known about James McGavin, but according to West's journal, he had a particular talent for explosives. It was said that McGavin didn't leave the house without a stick of dynamite in his coat pocket, a fact substantiated by West's description of his death. He had a wife, Cora, but we don't know much about her either, unfortunately. What little information I can find contradicts the other bits I've read. Some accounts say he came from St. Louis, others say he was from the Carolinas. Whatever the truth, he called Ambrose County's Fort Le-ane home.

If James McGavin seems a bit mysterious, meet the man known solely as 'Dead Man' or 'El Muerto' – names that West used interchangeably throughout his writings. Nobody in the gang knew his real name or where he came from and he never uttered a single word of explanation. West seemed to indicate that Dead Man was a Mexican individual who had pulled odd jobs across Texas before finally finding a sufficient home with the Enfield Gang. He was known for his one dead eye that had gone eerily milky-white and his jet-black apparel and six-shooters which promised death to any who got in his way. That was the legend, anyway. Interestingly, West theorized that Dead Man's signature silence was not by choice. He believed that the man had his tongue cut out after some ordeal or other and that was why he never uttered a word. While there are no records to back up this claim, the explanation seems likely, if not probable. While I can find minimal records attributed to a 'Dead Man,' I have, however, found some that report on a Mexican gunfighter named Germán Gallego who fought in the Mexican-American War. Gallego's description, and the few photographs in which he appears, seems to correspond with those of Enfield's silent Dead Man. Even more intriguing, there were rumors from around 1848 or 1849 that Gallego had bedded a married woman and had his tongue cut from his mouth in retribution. While I am no detective, I find it extremely unlikely that Dead Man and Germán Gallego are not one and the same.

The knife-wielding Rose Dellford had made a name for herself in the Wild West as "Pretty Poison" long before her association with Enfield. She kept her true origins to herself but had floated around from state to state and territory to territory. She was famous for her refusal to wear a gun belt and instead elected to use a collection of deadly knives that she had collected. Her most famous, and oft repeated, exploit involved a duel with famed gunman "Killer" Jack Jones wherein she entered the duel without aid of a pistol and–remarkably–won. West describes her as 'feisty' but 'fair' in his journal but doesn't go into detail about her beyond that.

The man called "Gibraltar" is an interesting case. An escaped slave from Mississippi, he discarded the name given to him (which has been lost to time) and embraced the nickname that had been given to him due to his height. According to West's journal, Gibraltar was a sweet man who was a friend to all, especially the underprivileged children of Chihuahua. Sweet or not, Gibraltar was also deadly when push came to shove. West notes that he carried a stolen Union Army gatling gun with him at all times and it, unsurprisingly, came in handy during the shootout that preceded the massacre. Gibraltar had joined with Enfield sometime in 1870 as they both appeared on a wanted poster issued in Missouri around that time.

"Blood-Red" Danny Cannon was a Union Army sawbones (slang for surgeon) who provided his services to the gang following the war, curing ailments as defuse as a stroke to a vicious hangover. Due to his wartime service, there is a trove of documents that cover this particular member of the gang, though the details get sparse once he settled in Ambrose County. He served his country admirably, according to the reports that I've read, and even took a bullet to the leg while defending a wounded soldier. One interesting note about his wartime service is that his skills with a knife did not end with his medical prowess. Cannon was also adept at throwing knives, a trick he had picked up to win bets and entertain. In his later years, he carried a six-shooter but preferred not to use it. According to West, Cannon saw the gun on his hip as a last resort for defense. West wasn't completely sure he even knew how to fire the thing.

There were others too, of course. There is mention of a man named Baldwin who was an actor who fell in with the gang. He didn't seem to provide much aside from his skills at oration, according to accounts. There is likewise mention of an Aaron Gather, who West nicknames "Teacher," and a man he refers to as "The Reverend." Whether this Reverend character was actually a man of God or was merely given the nickname for some reason or other remains unknown. There are also the two unidentified individuals who were the first victims of the massacre, killed outside of the Grady Inn prior to the intense shootout within its walls. Aside from the scant information West provides and blurry appearances in photographs, there isn't anything known about these individuals.

But we do know one thing: aside from L.Q. West, none of these people survived July 1875.

TO BE CONTINUED.

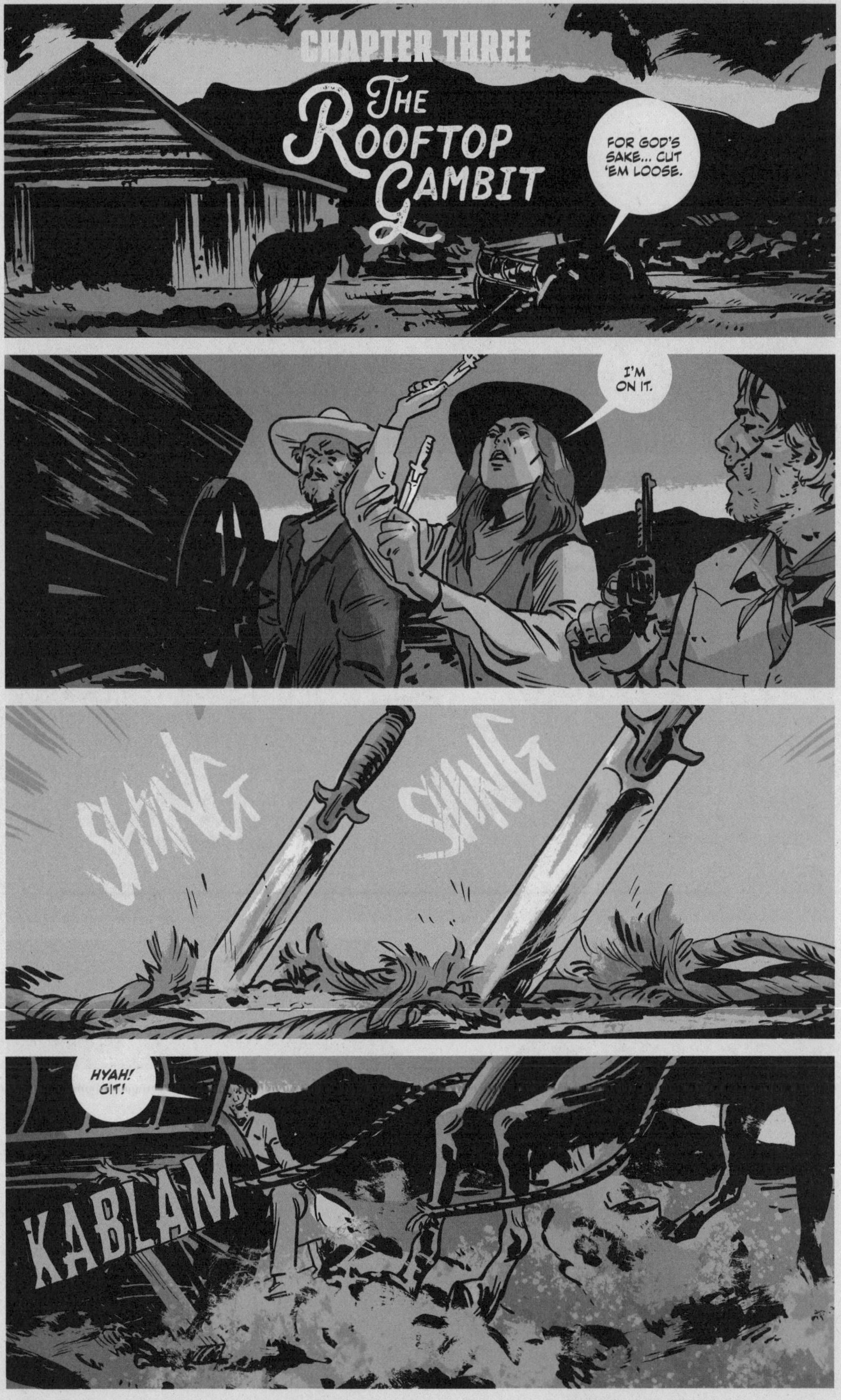

CHAPTER THREE
THE ROOFTOP GAMBIT
FOR GOD'S SAKE... CUT 'EM LOOSE.
I'M ON IT.
SHING
SHING
HYAH! GIT!
KABLAM

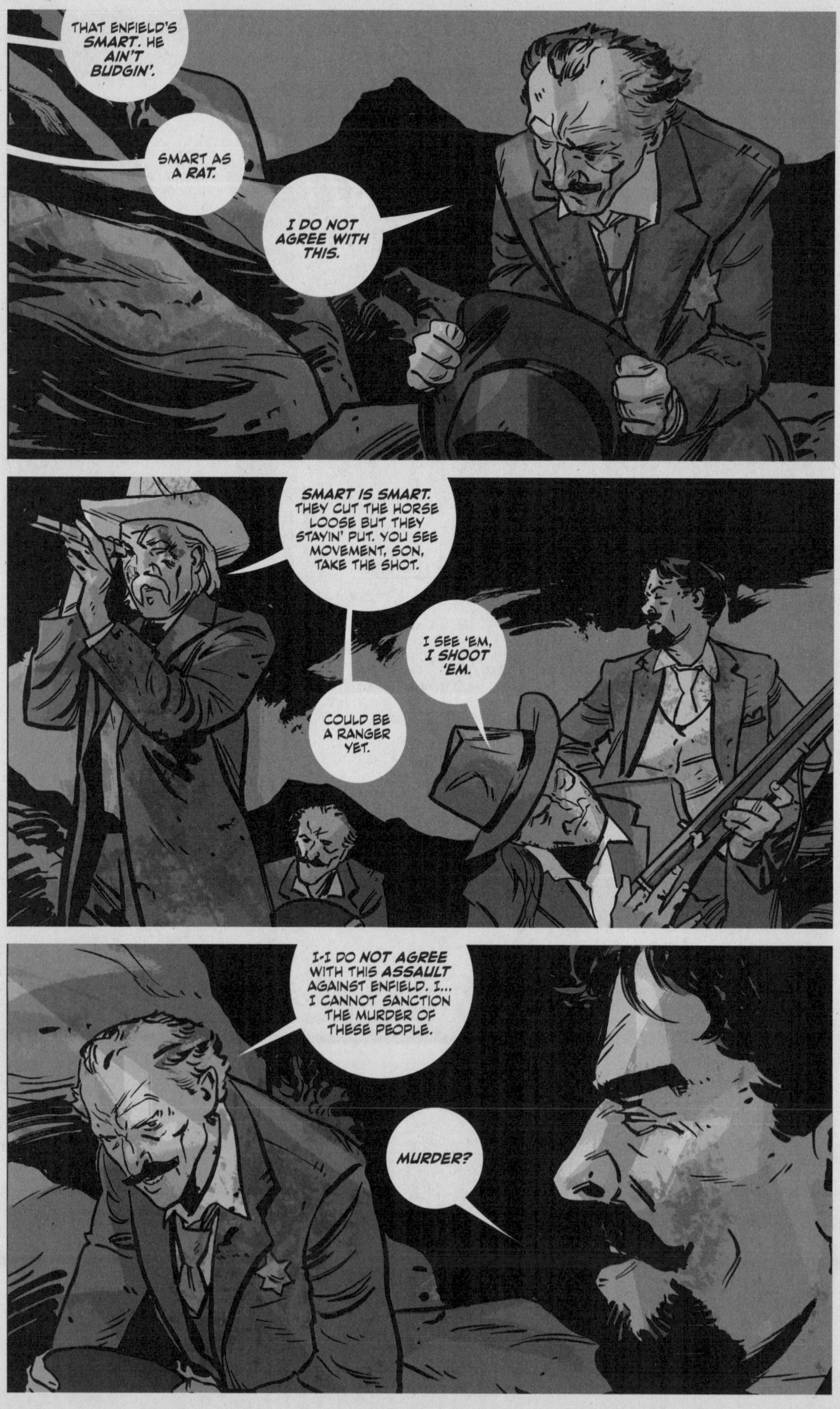
THAT ENFIELD'S SMART. HE AIN'T BUDGIN'.
SMART AS A RAT.
I DO NOT AGREE WITH THIS.
SMART IS SMART. THEY CUT THE HORSE LOOSE BUT THEY STAYIN' PUT. YOU SEE MOVEMENT, SON, TAKE THE SHOT.
COULD BE A RANGER YET.
I SEE 'EM, I SHOOT 'EM.
I-I DO NOT AGREE WITH THIS ASSAULT AGAINST ENFIELD. I... I CANNOT SANCTION THE MURDER OF THESE PEOPLE.
MURDER?

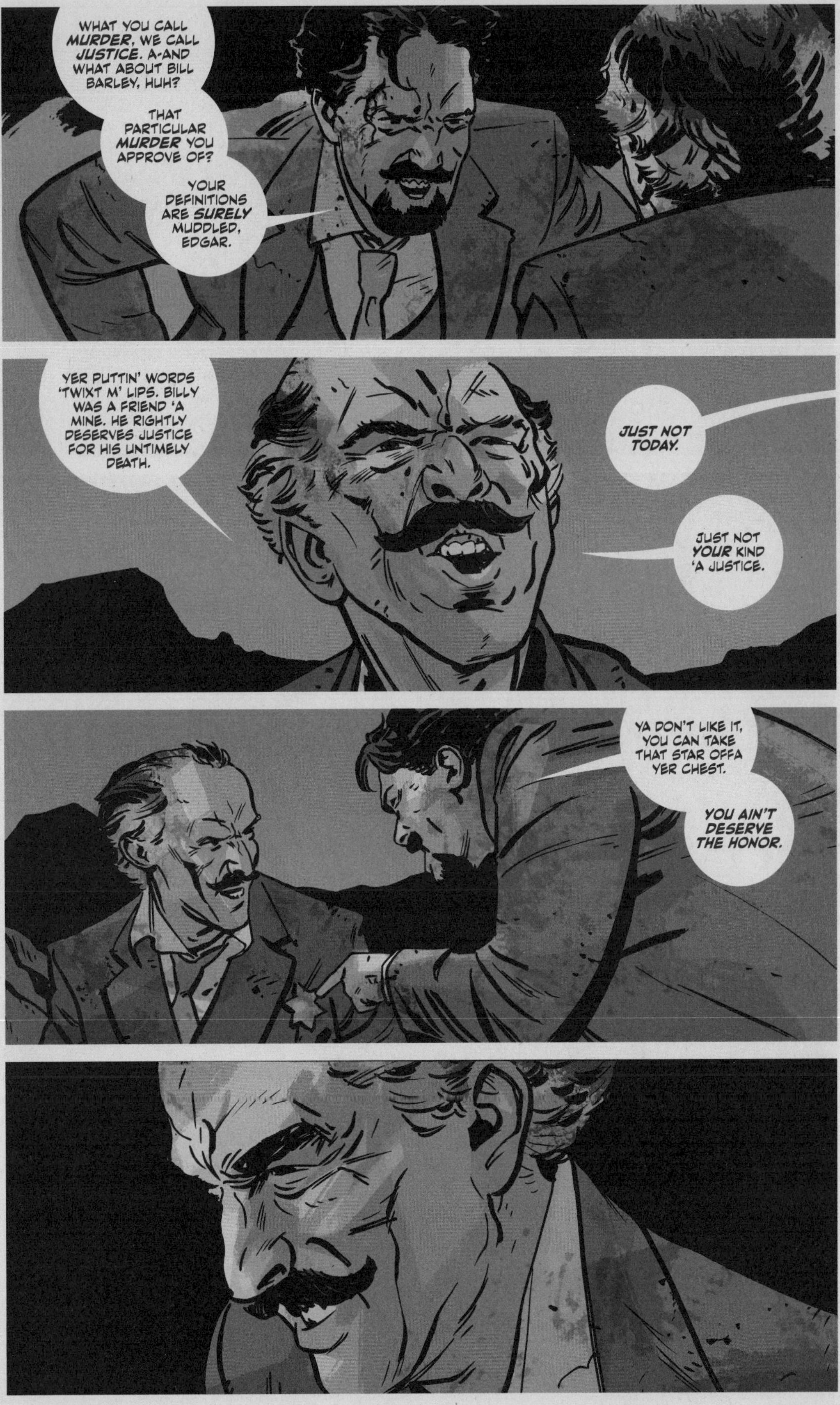
WHAT YOU CALL MURDER, WE CALL JUSTICE. A-AND WHAT ABOUT BILL BARLEY, HUH?
THAT PARTICULAR MURDER YOU APPROVE OF?
YOUR DEFINITIONS ARE SURELY MUDDLED, EDGAR.
YER PUTTIN' WORDS 'TWIXT M' LIPS. BILLY WAS A FRIEND 'A MINE. HE RIGHTLY DESERVES JUSTICE FOR HIS UNTIMELY DEATH.
JUST NOT TODAY.
JUST NOT YOUR KIND 'A JUSTICE.
YA DON'T LIKE IT, YOU CAN TAKE THAT STAR OFFA YER CHEST.
YOU AIN'T DESERVE THE HONOR.

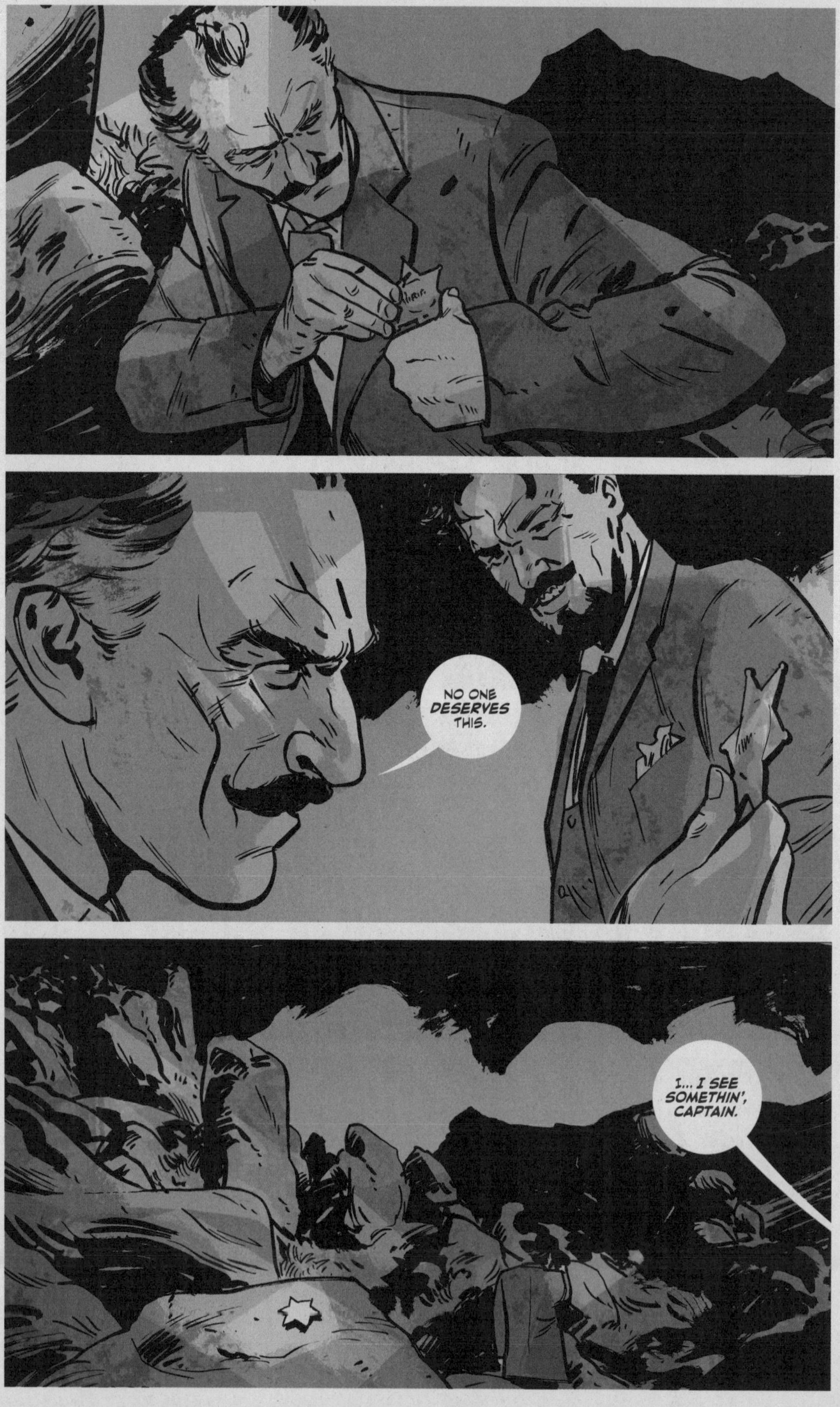
NO ONE DESERVES THIS.
I... I SEE SOMETHIN', CAPTAIN.

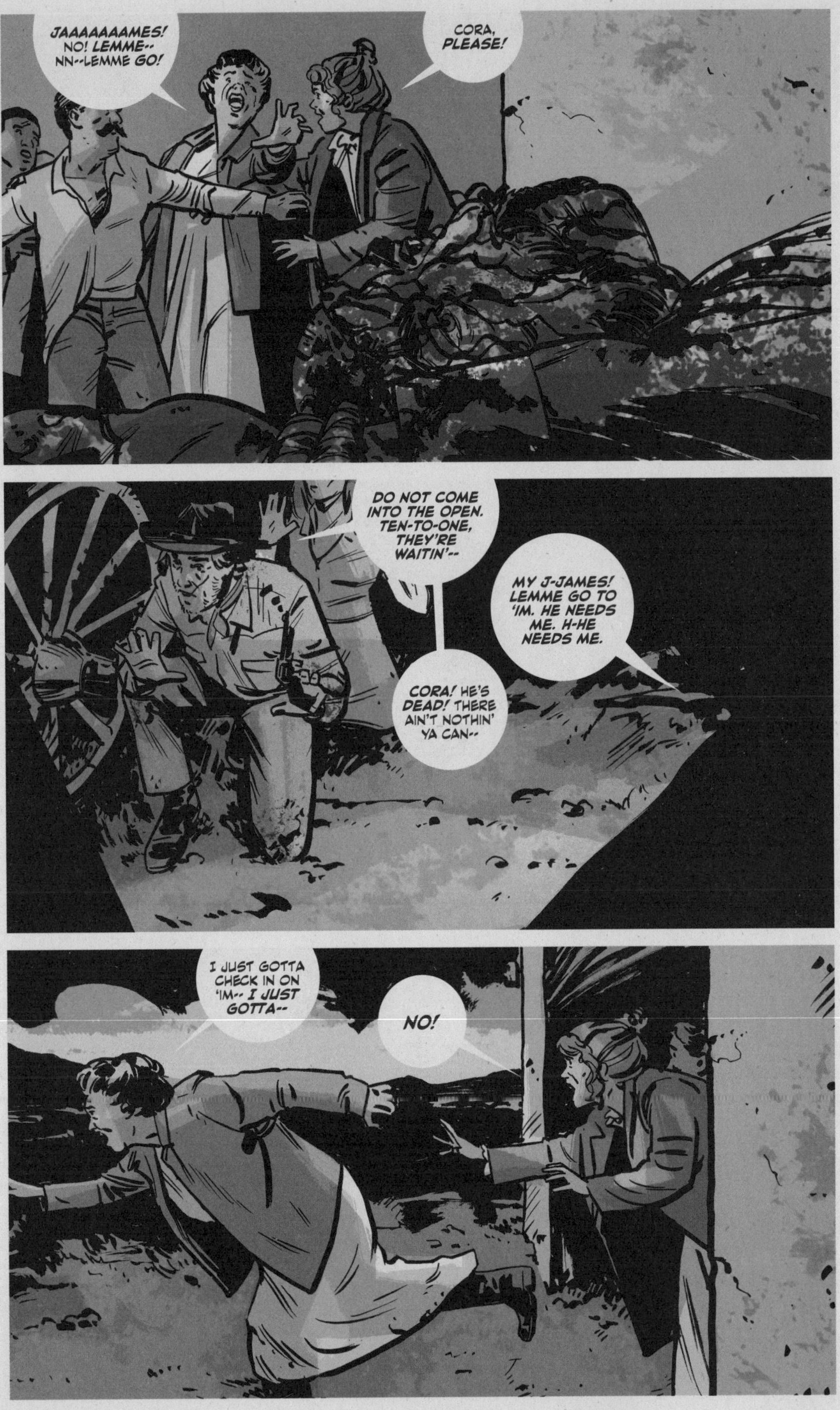
JAAAAAAAMES! NO! LEMME-- NN--LEMME GO!
CORA, PLEASE!
DO NOT COME INTO THE OPEN. TEN-TO-ONE, THEY'RE WAITIN'--
CORA! HE'S DEAD! THERE AIN'T NOTHIN' YA CAN--
MY J-JAMES! LEMME GO TO 'IM. HE NEEDS ME. H-HE NEEDS ME.
I JUST GOTTA CHECK IN ON 'IM-- I JUST GOTTA--
NO!

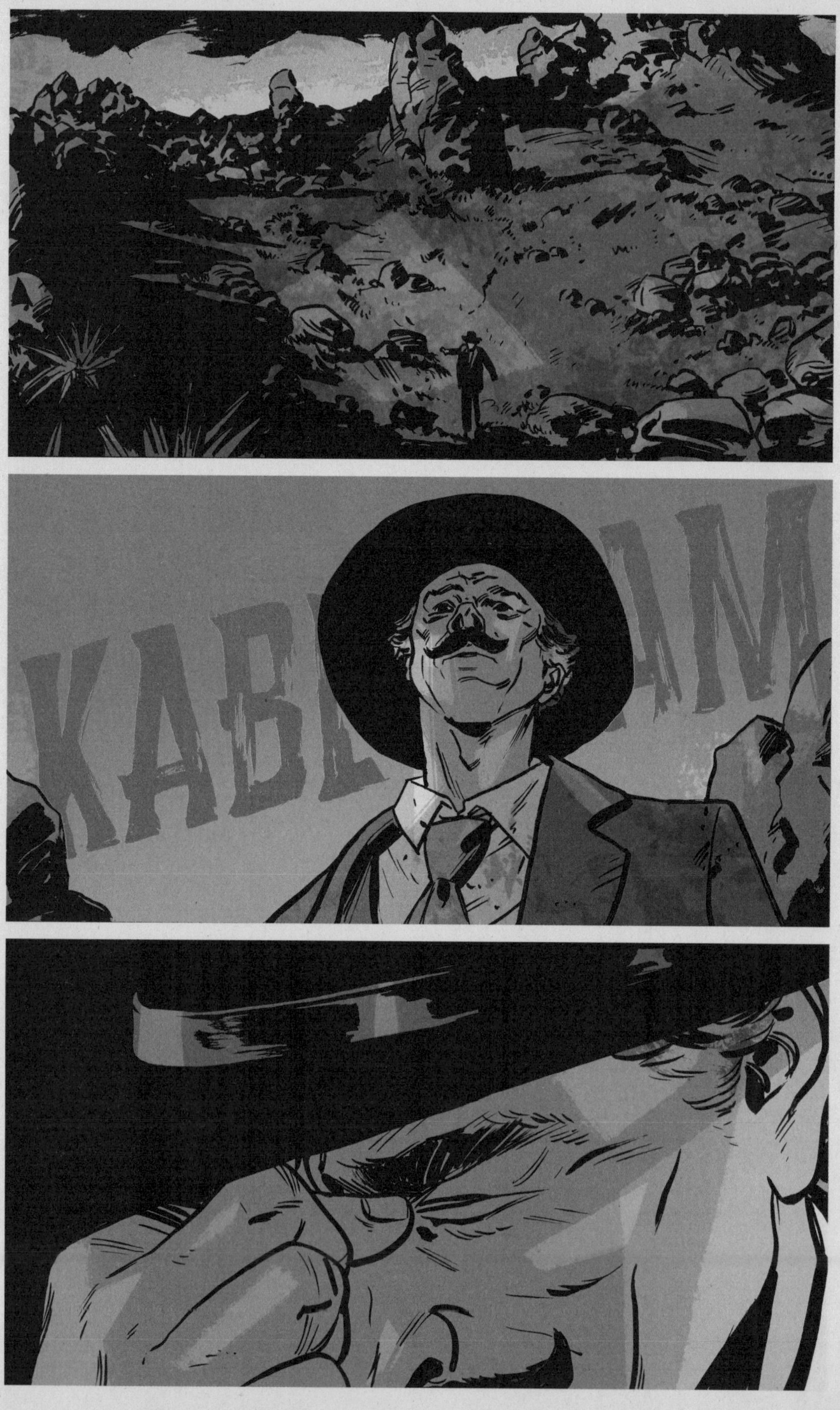
KABL AM

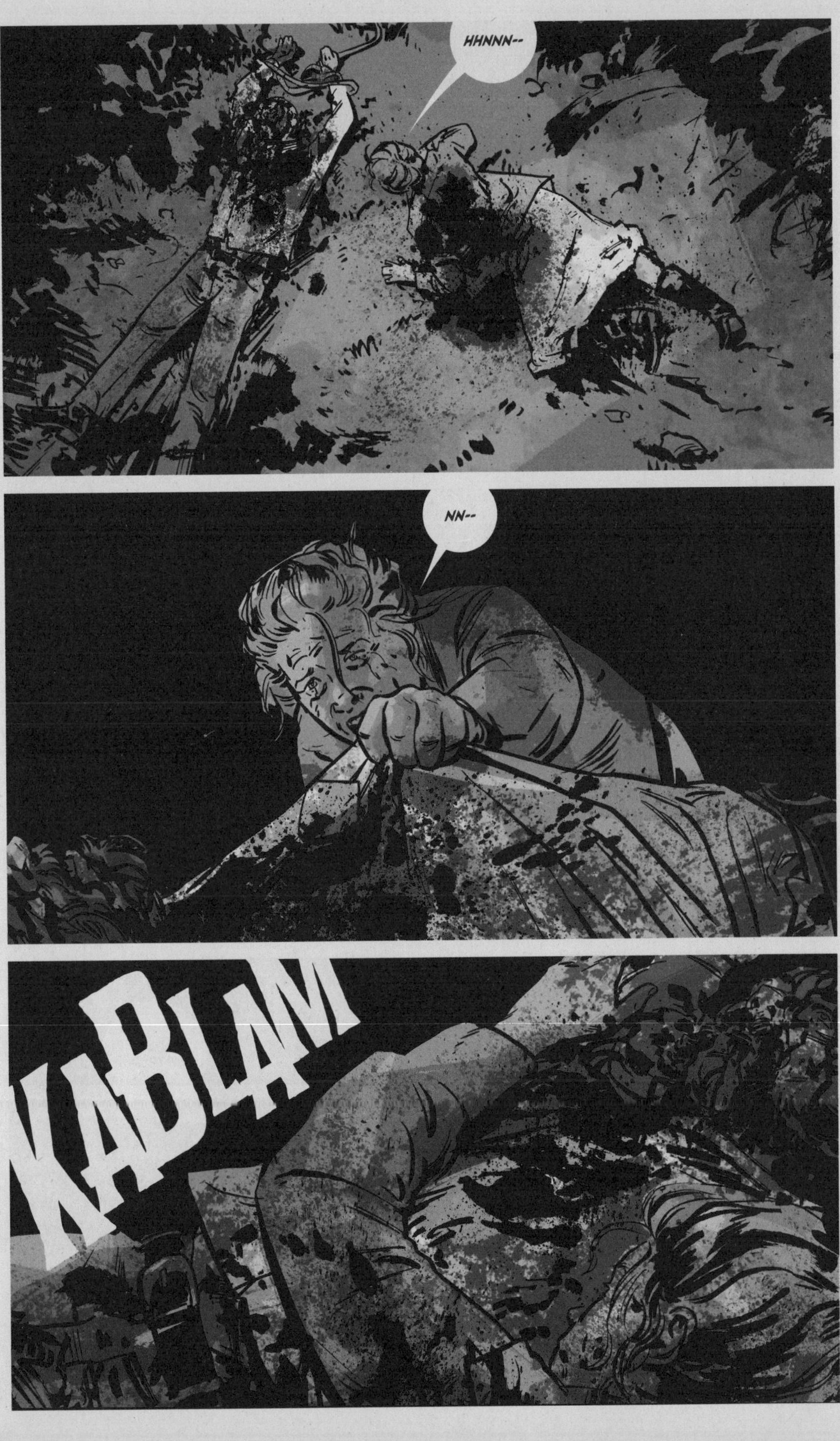
HHHNN--
NN--
KABLAM

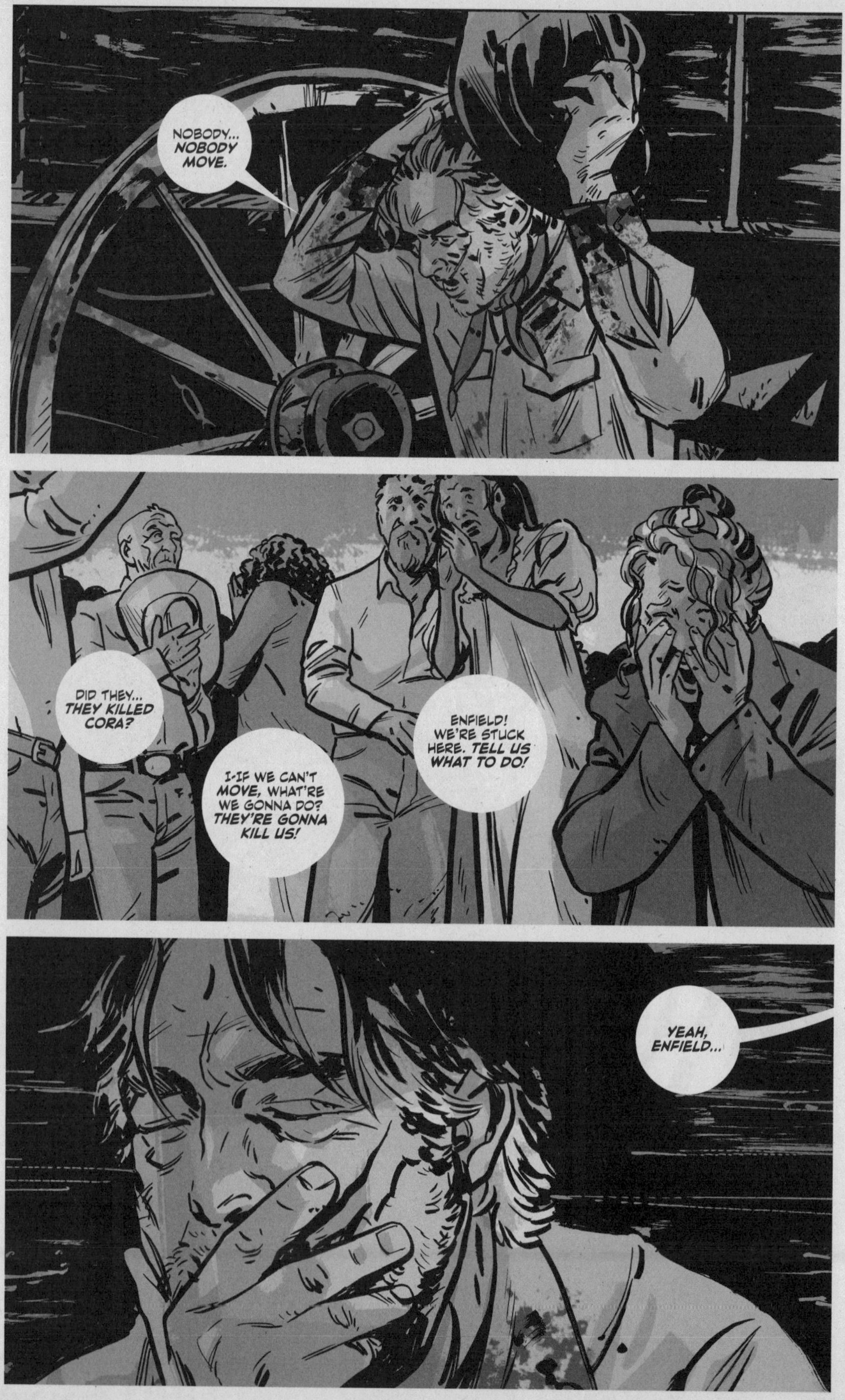
NOBODY... NOBODY MOVE.
DID THEY... THEY KILLED CORA?
I-IF WE CAN'T MOVE, WHAT'RE WE GONNA DO? THEY'RE GONNA KILL US!
ENFIELD! WE'RE STUCK HERE. TELL US WHAT TO DO!
YEAH, ENFIELD...

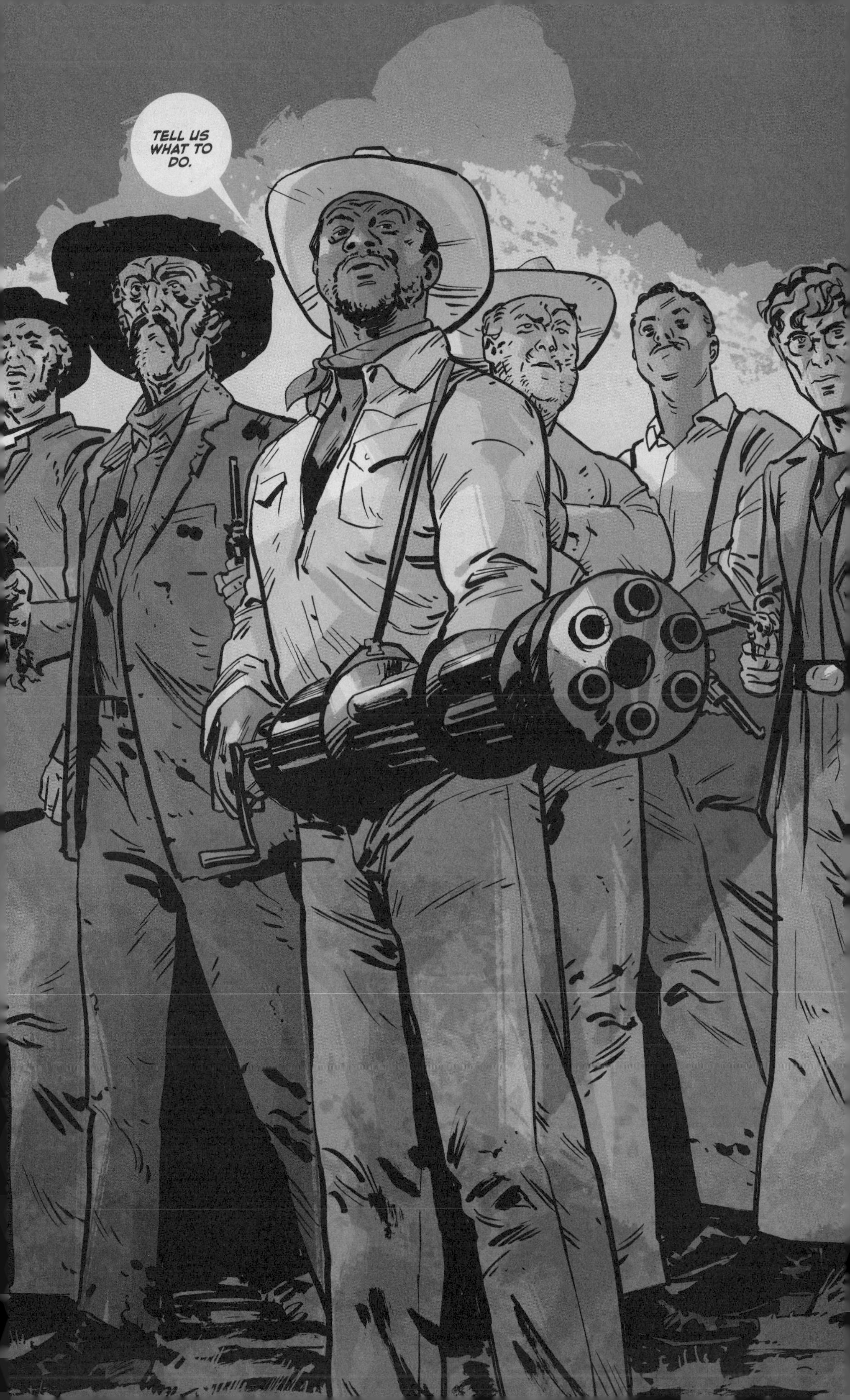
TELL US WHAT TO DO.

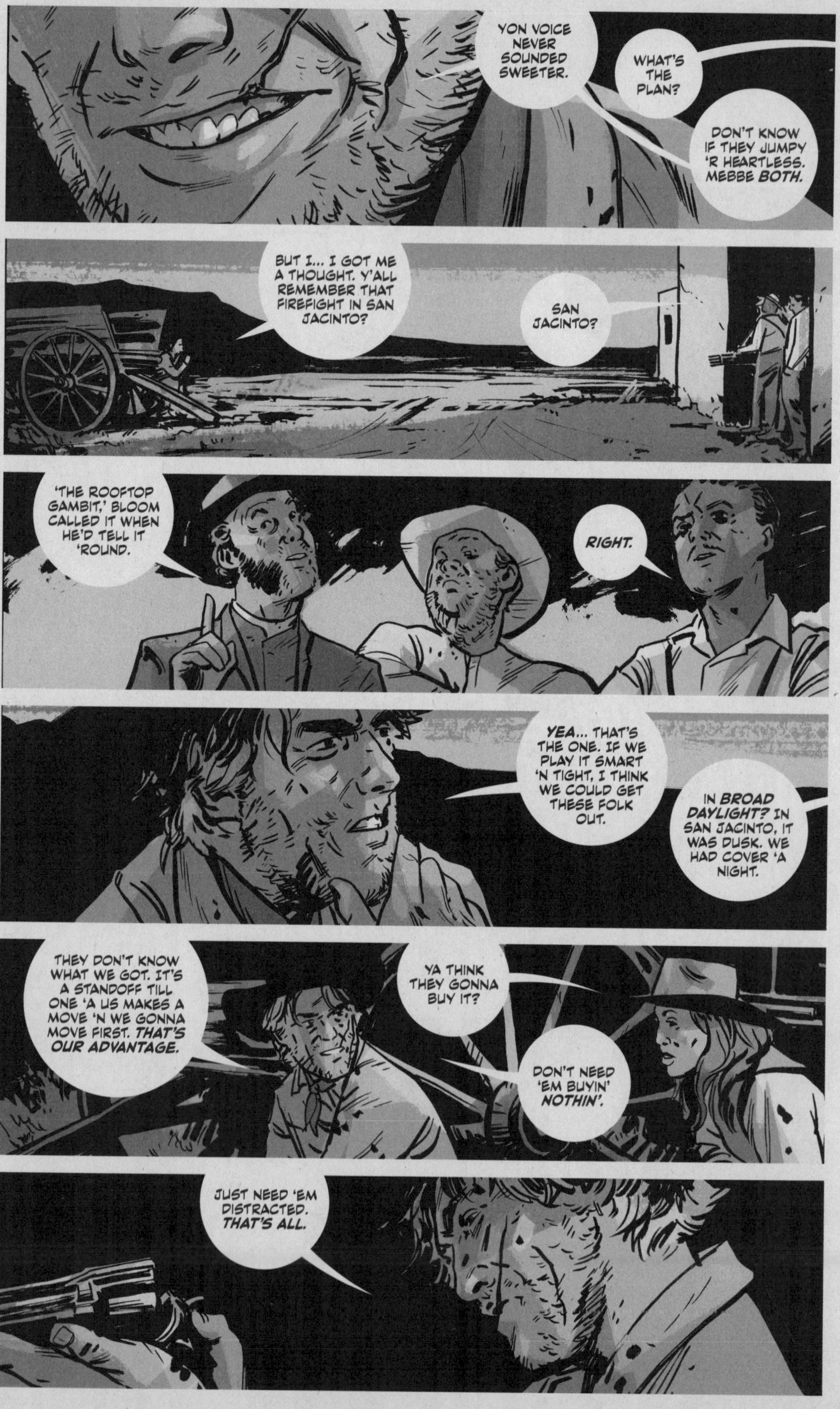
YON VOICE NEVER SOUNDED SWEETER.
WHAT'S THE PLAN?
DON'T KNOW IF THEY JUMPY 'R HEARTLESS. MEBBE *BOTH.*
BUT I... I GOT ME A THOUGHT. Y'ALL REMEMBER THAT FIREFIGHT IN SAN JACINTO?
SAN JACINTO?
'THE ROOFTOP GAMBIT,' BLOOM CALLED IT WHEN HE'D TELL IT 'ROUND.
RIGHT.
YEA... THAT'S THE ONE. IF WE PLAY IT SMART 'N TIGHT, I THINK WE COULD GET THESE FOLK OUT.
IN *BROAD DAYLIGHT?* IN SAN JACINTO, IT WAS DUSK. WE HAD COVER 'A NIGHT.
THEY DON'T KNOW WHAT WE GOT. IT'S A STANDOFF TILL ONE 'A US MAKES A MOVE 'N WE GONNA MOVE FIRST. *THAT'S OUR ADVANTAGE.*
YA THINK THEY GONNA BUY IT?
DON'T NEED 'EM BUYIN' *NOTHIN'.*
JUST NEED 'EM DISTRACTED. *THAT'S ALL.*

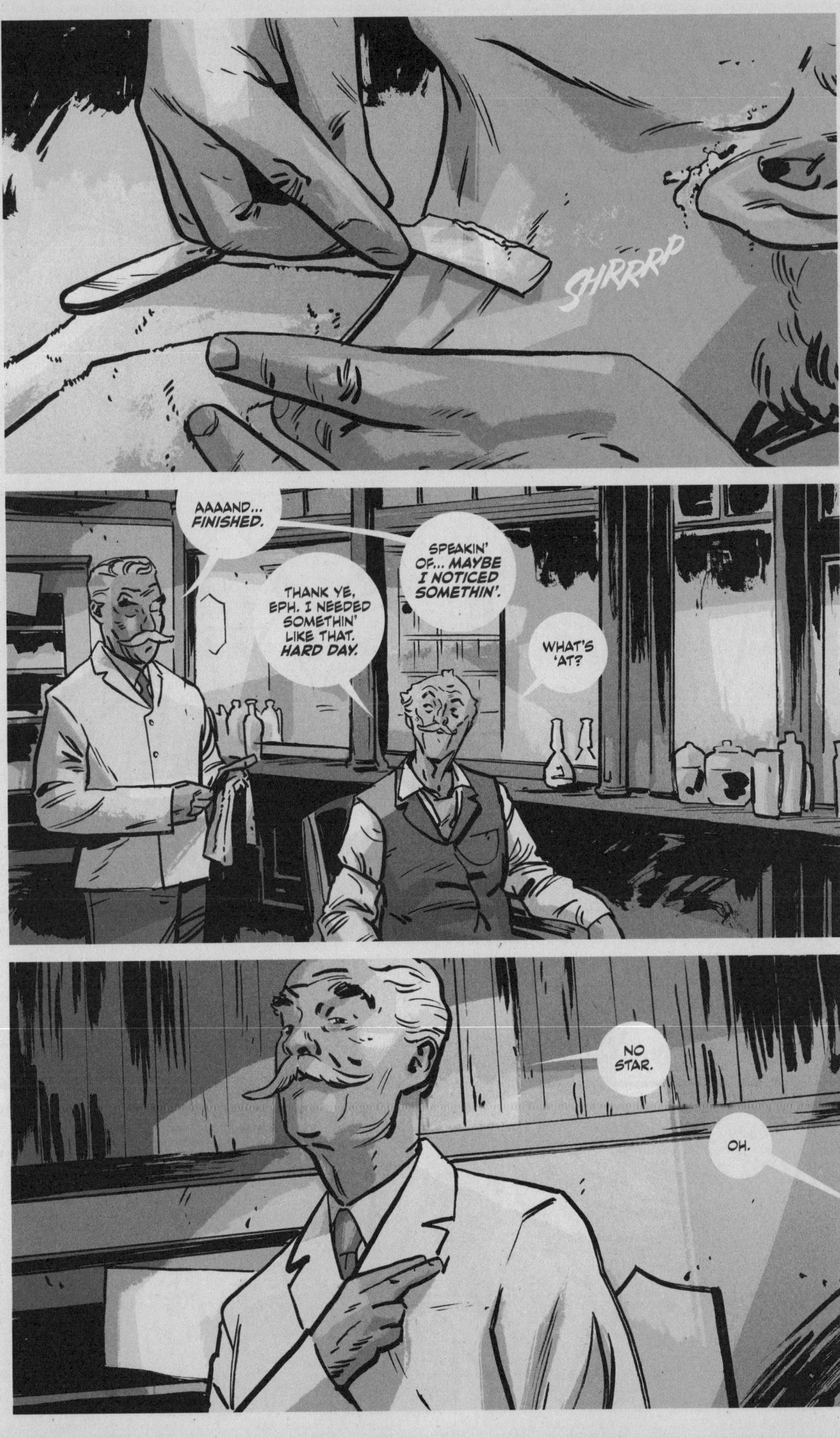
SHRRRP
AAAAND... FINISHED.
THANK YE, EPH. I NEEDED SOMETHIN' LIKE THAT. HARD DAY.
SPEAKIN' OF... MAYBE I NOTICED SOMETHIN'.
WHAT'S 'AT?
NO STAR.
OH.

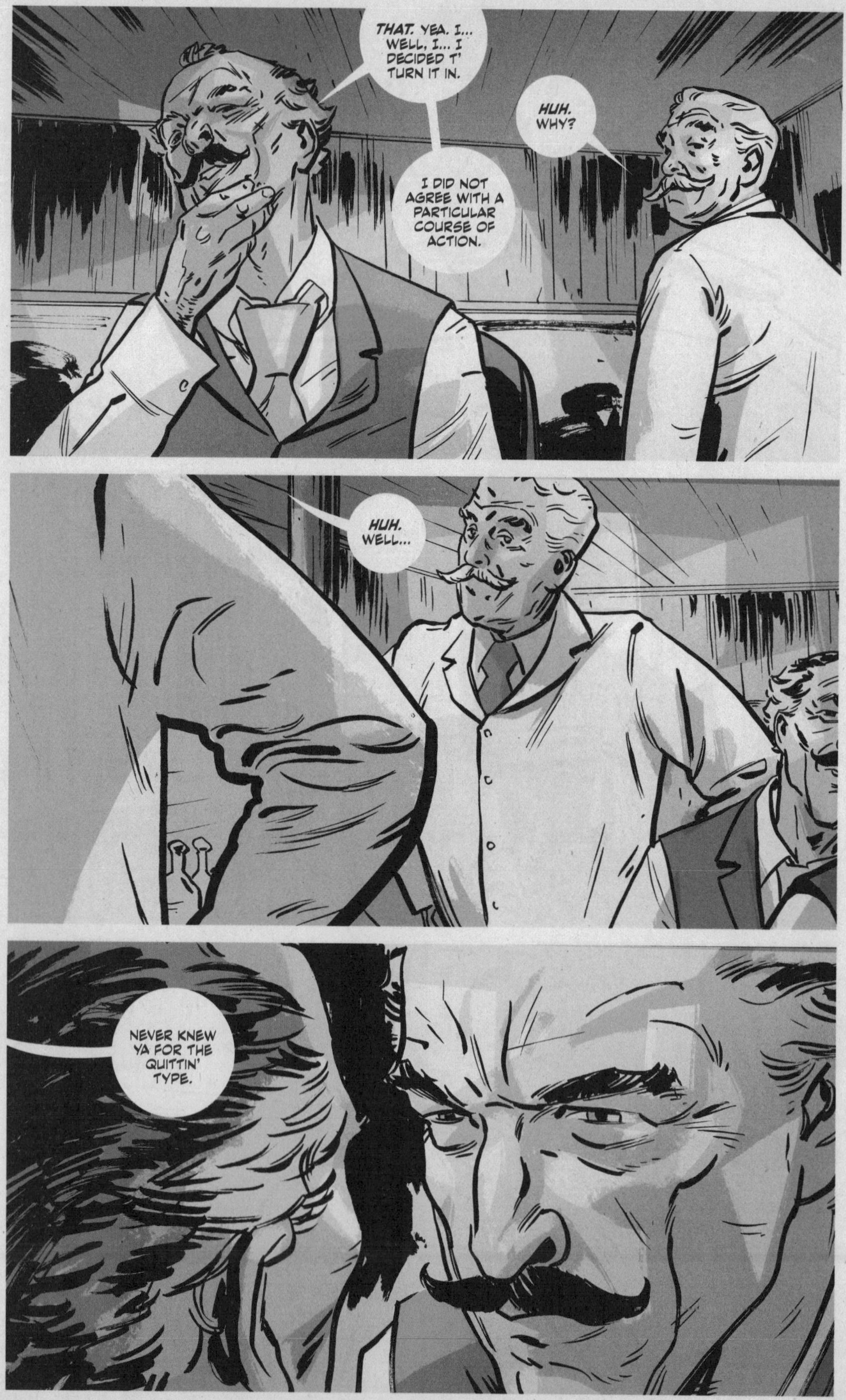
THAT. YEA. I... WELL, I... I DECIDED T' TURN IT IN.
HUH. WHY?
I DID NOT AGREE WITH A PARTICULAR COURSE OF ACTION.
HUH. WELL...
NEVER KNEW YA FOR THE QUITTIN' TYPE.

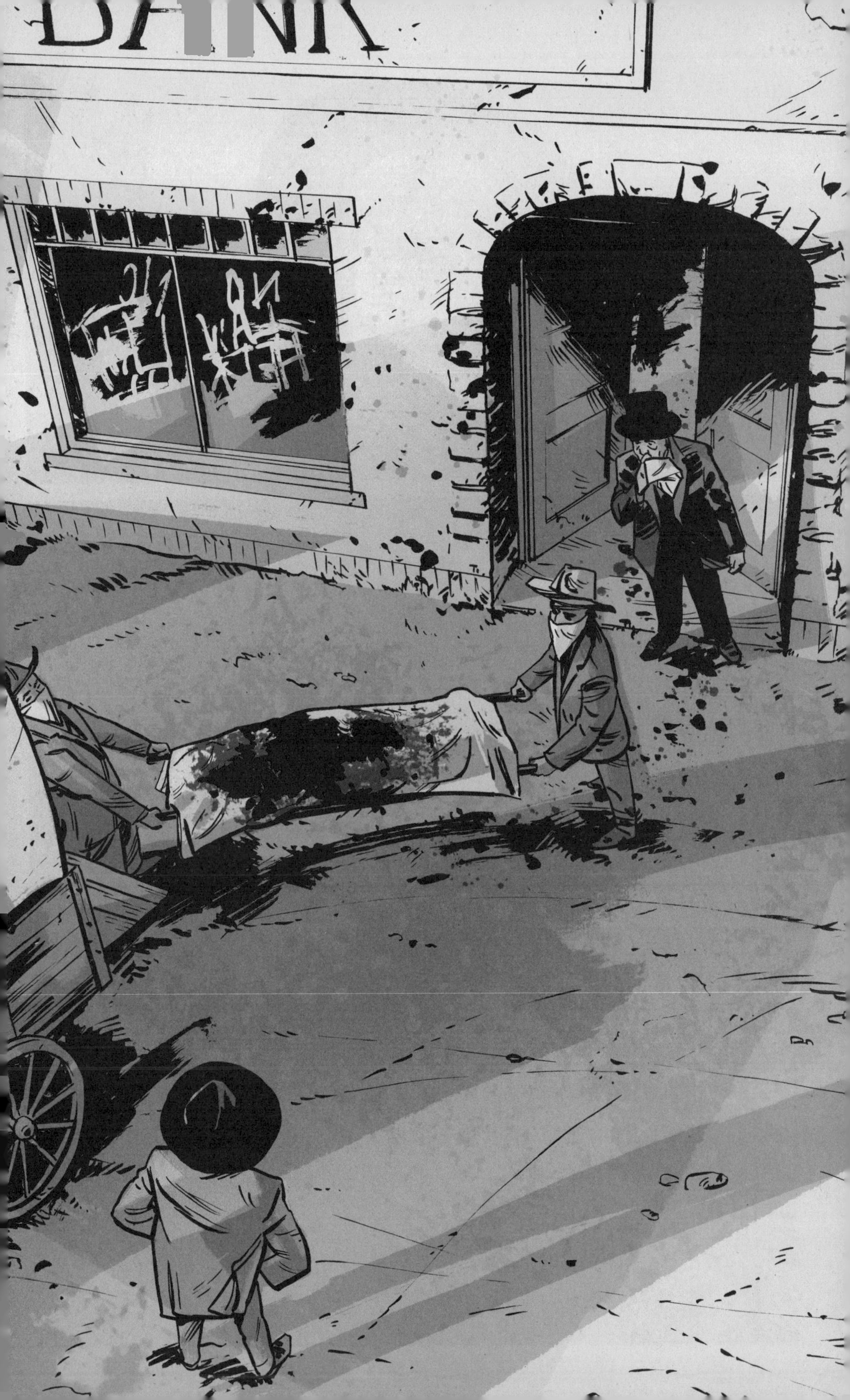
BANK

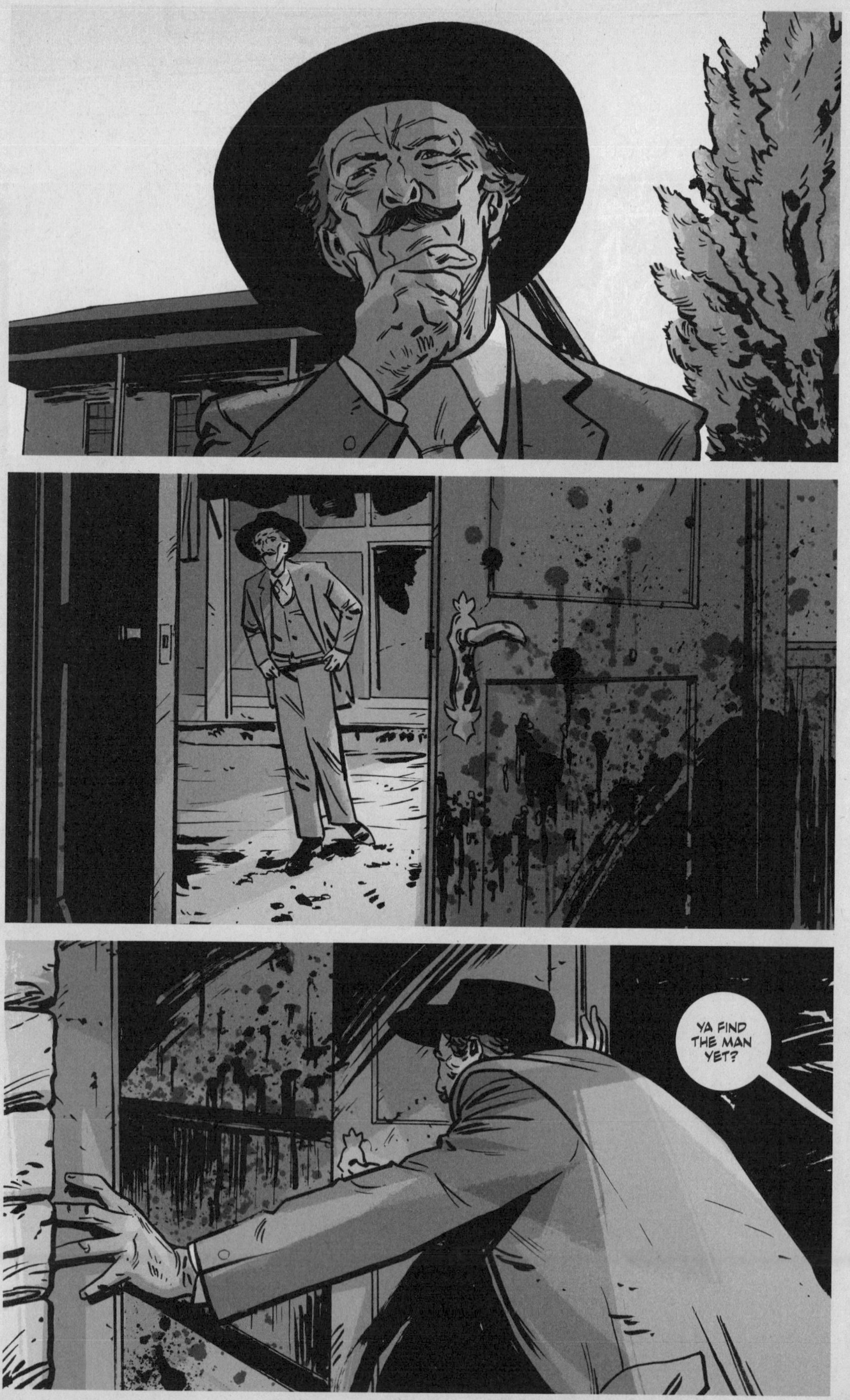
YA FIND THE MAN YET?

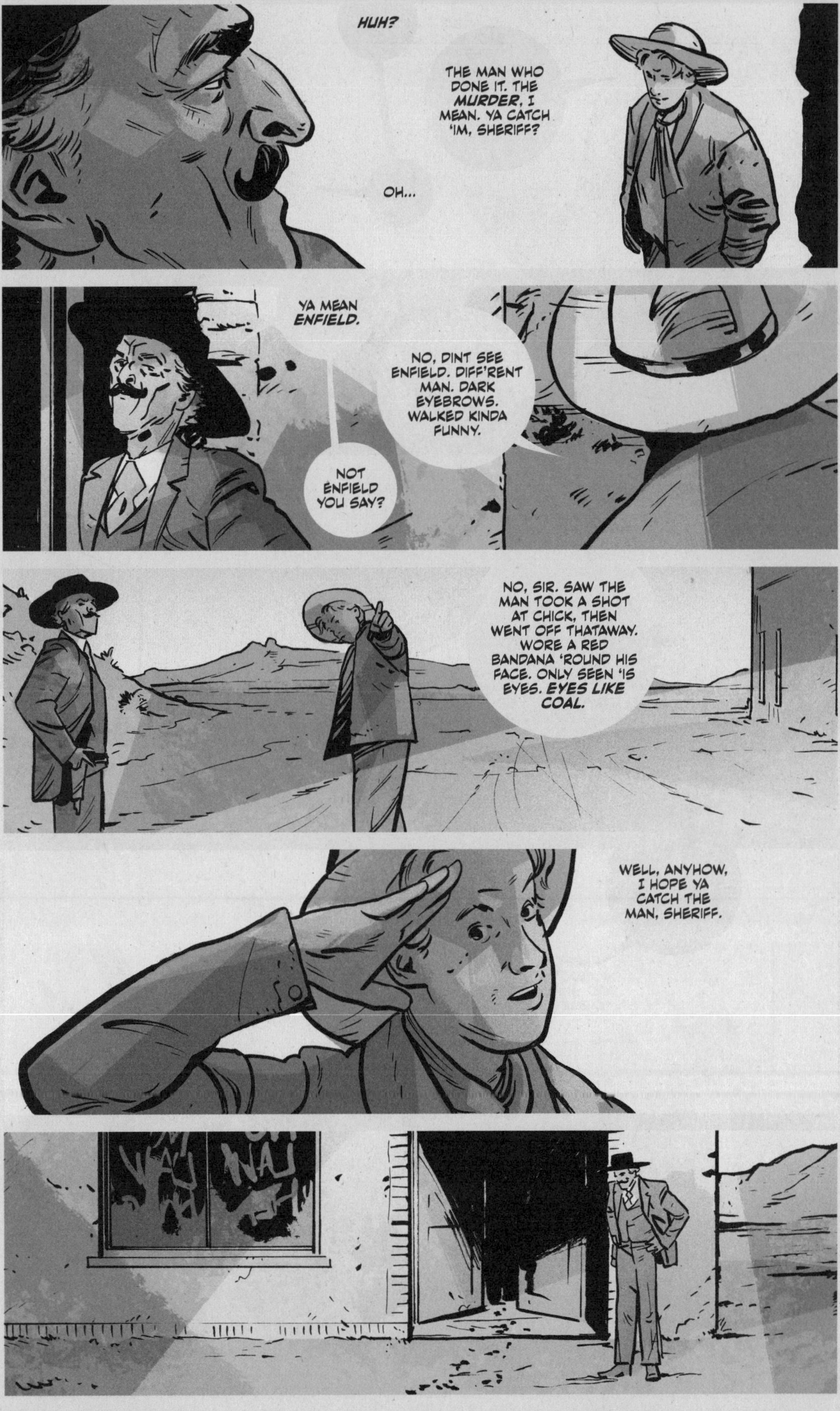
HUH?
THE MAN WHO DONE IT. THE MURDER, I MEAN. YA CATCH 'IM, SHERIFF?
OH...
YA MEAN ENFIELD.
NO, DINT SEE ENFIELD. DIFF'RENT MAN. DARK EYEBROWS. WALKED KINDA FUNNY.
NOT ENFIELD YOU SAY?
NO, SIR. SAW THE MAN TOOK A SHOT AT CHICK, THEN WENT OFF THATAWAY. WORE A RED BANDANA 'ROUND HIS FACE. ONLY SEEN 'IS EYES. EYES LIKE COAL.
WELL, ANYHOW, I HOPE YA CATCH THE MAN, SHERIFF.

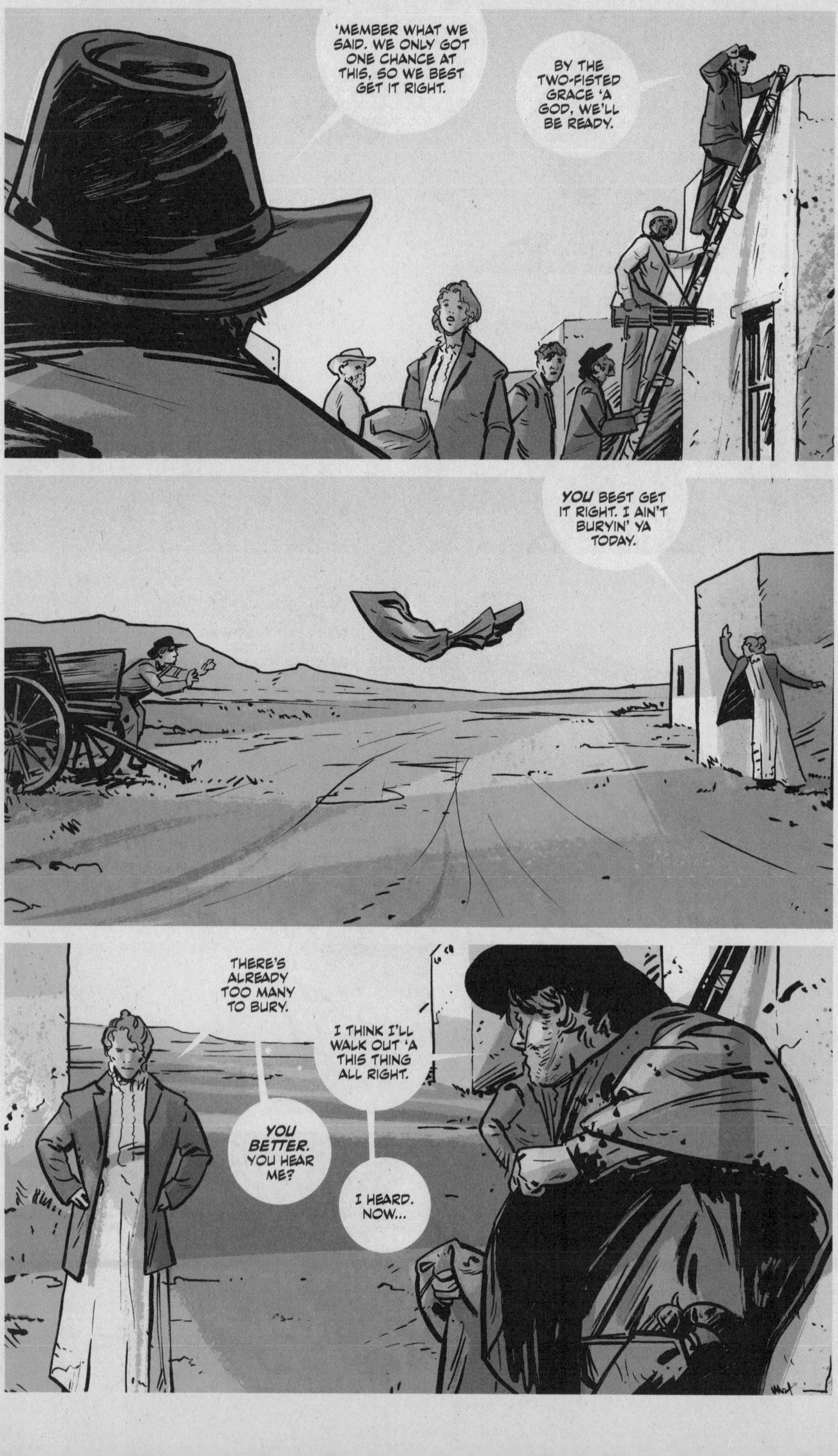

'MEMBER WHAT WE SAID. WE ONLY GOT ONE CHANCE AT THIS, SO WE BEST GET IT RIGHT.
BY THE TWO-FISTED GRACE 'A GOD, WE'LL BE READY.
YOU BEST GET IT RIGHT. I AIN'T BURYIN' YA TODAY.
THERE'S ALREADY TOO MANY TO BURY.
YOU BETTER. YOU HEAR ME?
I THINK I'LL WALK OUT 'A THIS THING ALL RIGHT.
I HEARD. NOW...

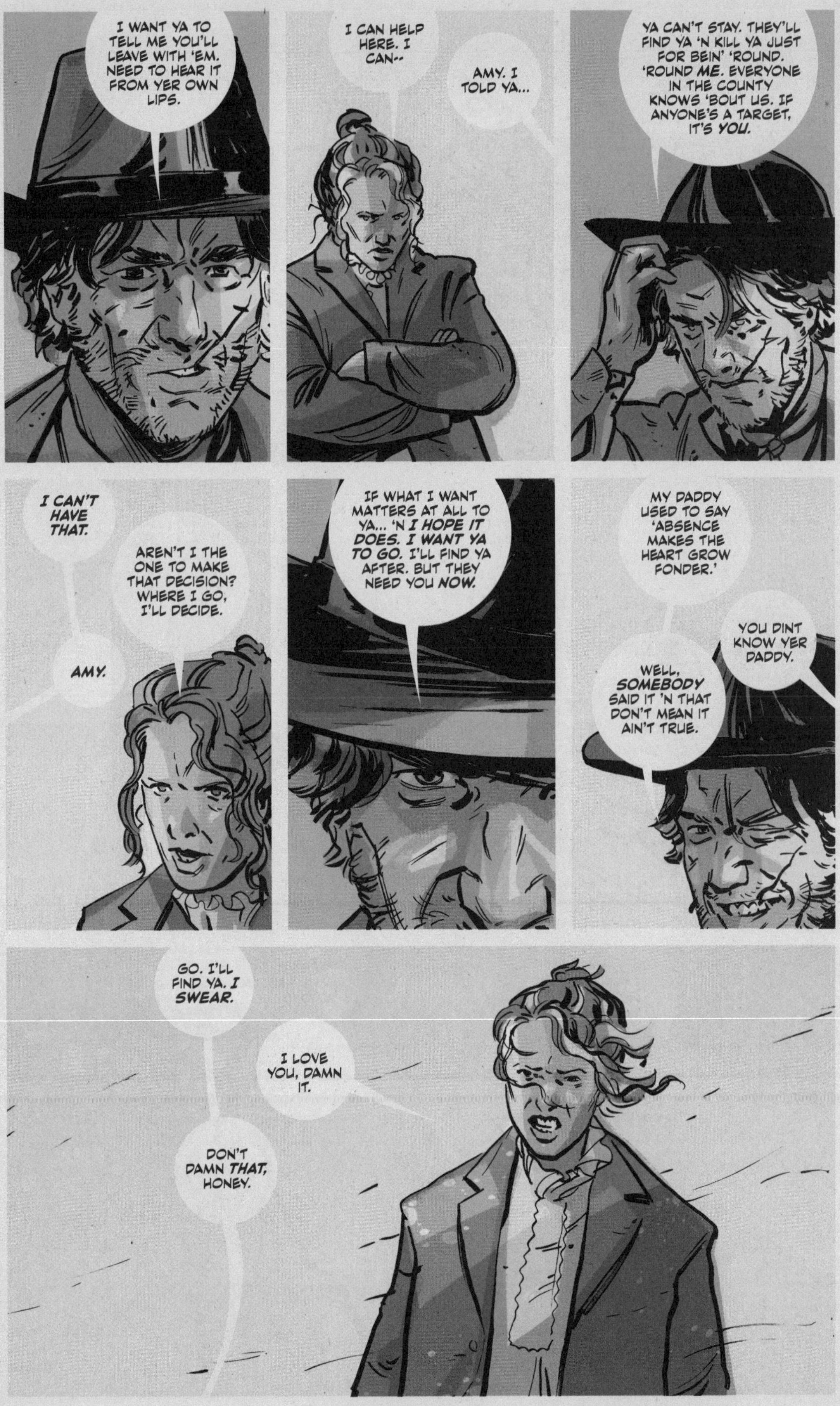

I WANT YA TO TELL ME YOU'LL LEAVE WITH 'EM. NEED TO HEAR IT FROM YER OWN LIPS.
I CAN HELP HERE. I CAN--
AMY. I TOLD YA...
YA CAN'T STAY. THEY'LL FIND YA 'N KILL YA JUST FOR BEIN' 'ROUND. 'ROUND *ME*. EVERYONE IN THE COUNTY KNOWS 'BOUT US. IF ANYONE'S A TARGET, IT'S *YOU*.
I CAN'T HAVE THAT.
ARE'NT I THE ONE TO MAKE THAT DECISION? WHERE I GO, I'LL DECIDE.
AMY.
IF WHAT I WANT MATTERS AT ALL TO YA... 'N *I HOPE IT DOES. I WANT YA TO GO.* I'LL FIND YA AFTER. BUT THEY NEED YOU *NOW.*
MY DADDY USED TO SAY 'ABSENCE MAKES THE HEART GROW FONDER.'
YOU DINT KNOW YER DADDY.
WELL, *SOMEBODY* SAID IT 'N THAT DON'T MEAN IT AIN'T TRUE.
GO. I'LL FIND YA. *I SWEAR.*
I LOVE YOU, DAMN IT.
DON'T DAMN *THAT,* HONEY.

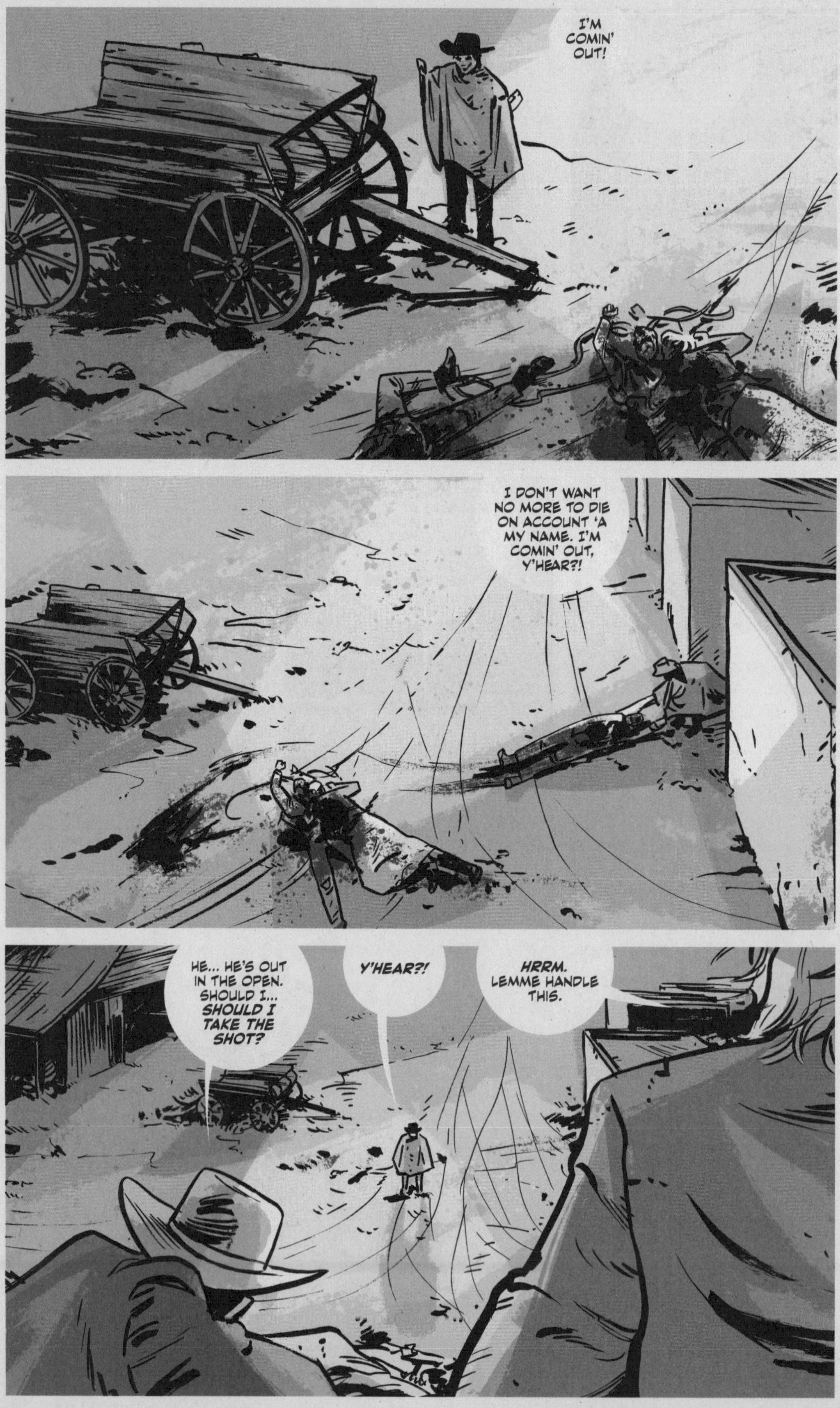
I'M COMIN' OUT!
I DON'T WANT NO MORE TO DIE ON ACCOUNT 'A MY NAME. I'M COMIN' OUT, Y'HEAR?!
HE... HE'S OUT IN THE OPEN. SHOULD I... SHOULD I TAKE THE SHOT?
Y'HEAR?!
HRRM. LEMME HANDLE THIS.

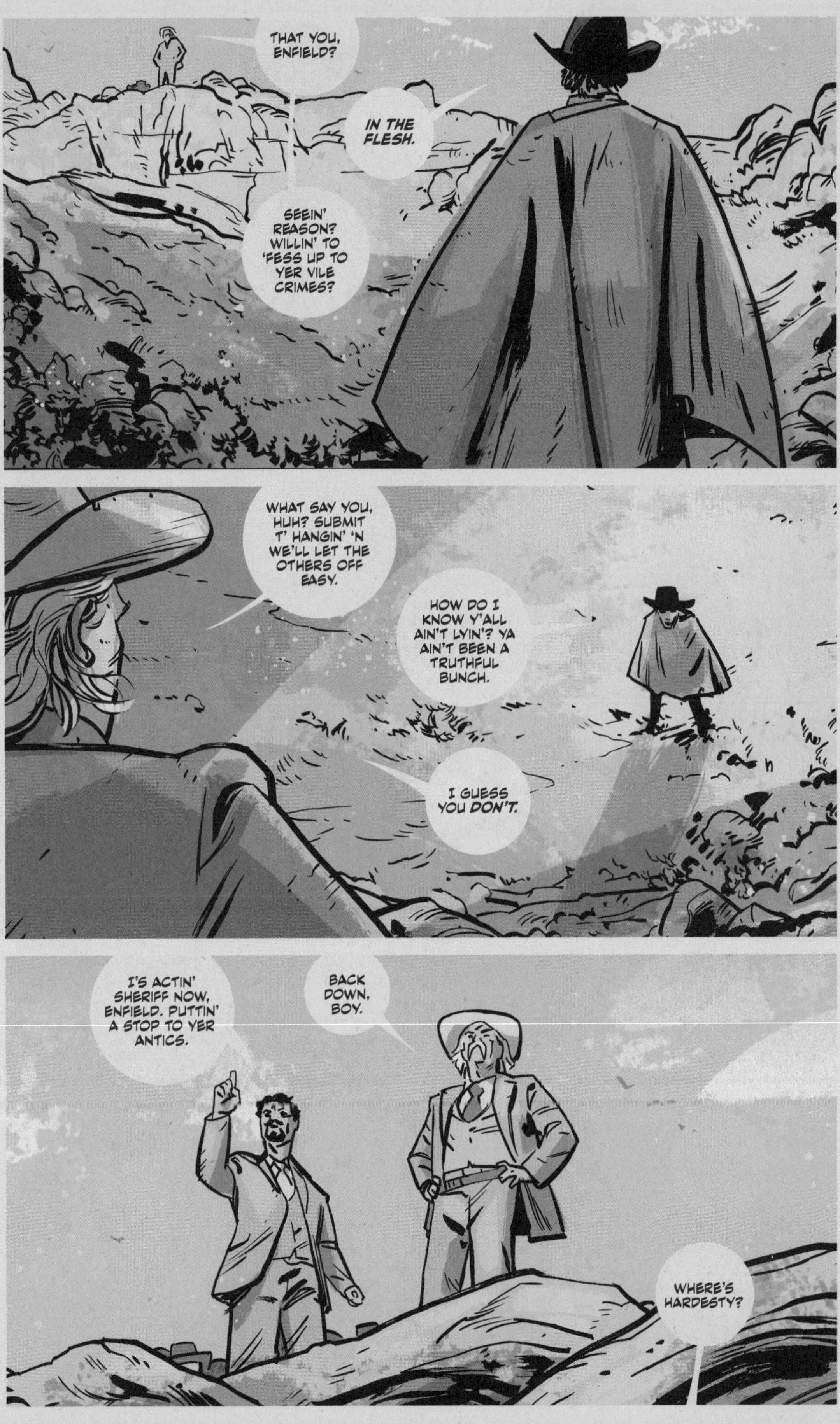
THAT YOU, ENFIELD?
IN THE FLESH.
SEEIN' REASON? WILLIN' TO 'FESS UP TO YER VILE CRIMES?
WHAT SAY YOU, HUH? SUBMIT T' HANGIN' 'N WE'LL LET THE OTHERS OFF EASY.
HOW DO I KNOW Y'ALL AIN'T LYIN'? YA AIN'T BEEN A TRUTHFUL BUNCH.
I GUESS YOU *DON'T.*
I'S ACTIN' SHERIFF NOW, ENFIELD. PUTTIN' A STOP TO YER ANTICS.
BACK DOWN, BOY.
WHERE'S HARDESTY?

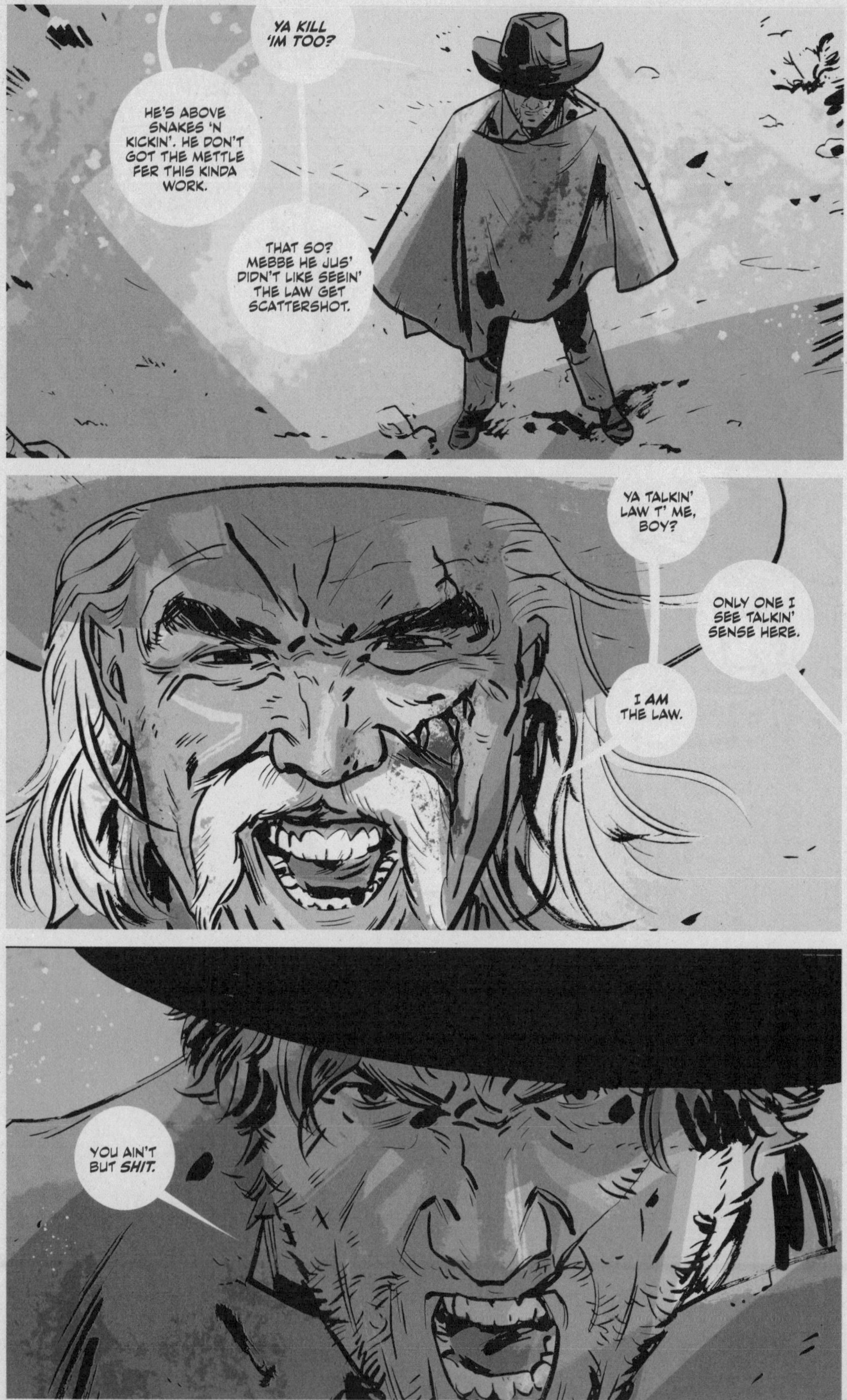
YA KILL 'IM TOO?
HE'S ABOVE SNAKES 'N KICKIN'. HE DON'T GOT THE METTLE FER THIS KINDA WORK.
THAT SO? MEBBE HE JUS' DIDN'T LIKE SEEIN' THE LAW GET SCATTERSHOT.
YA TALKIN' LAW T' ME, BOY?
I AM THE LAW.
ONLY ONE I SEE TALKIN' SENSE HERE.
YOU AIN'T BUT *SHIT.*

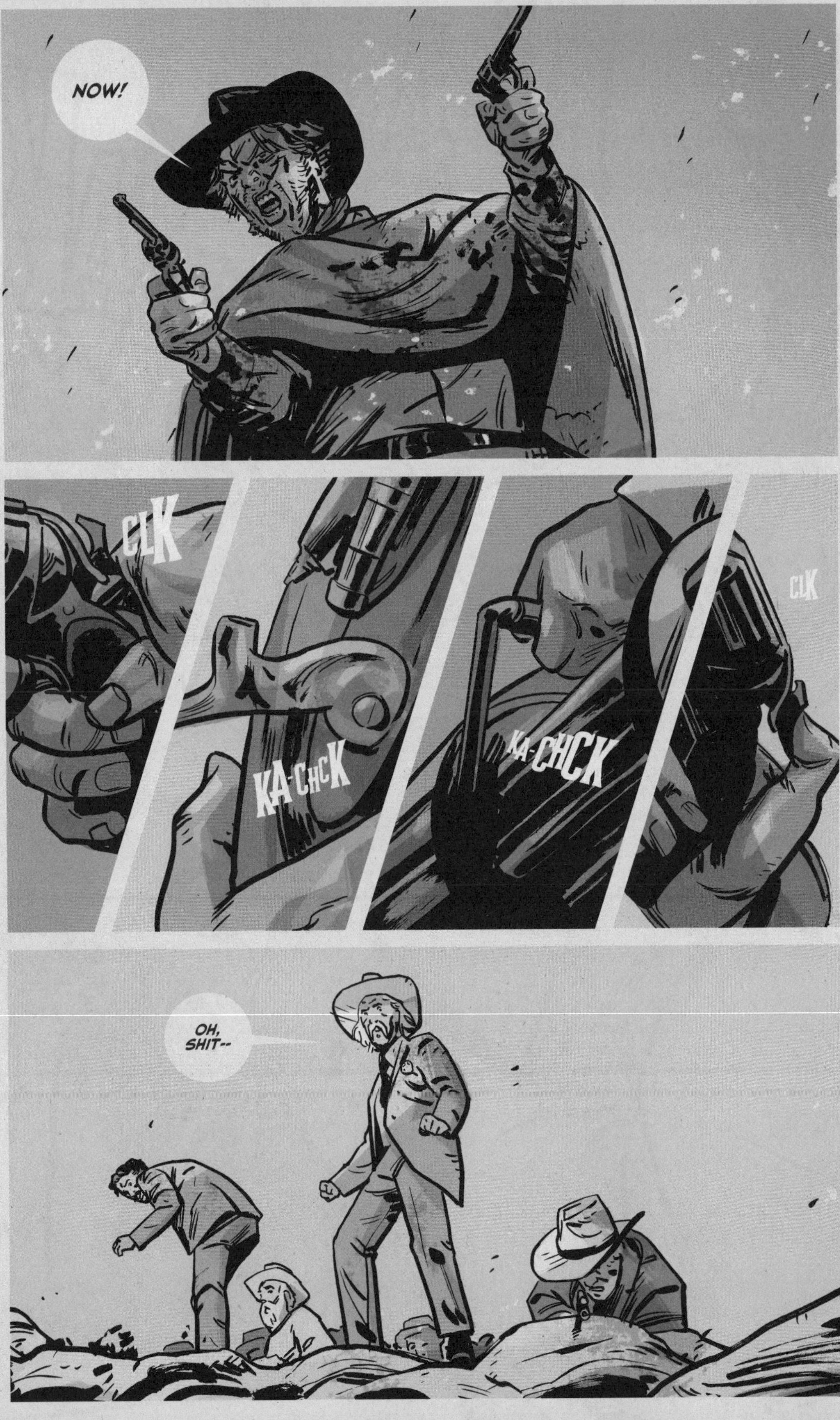
NOW!
CLK
KA-CHCK
KA-CHCK
CLK
OH, SHIT--

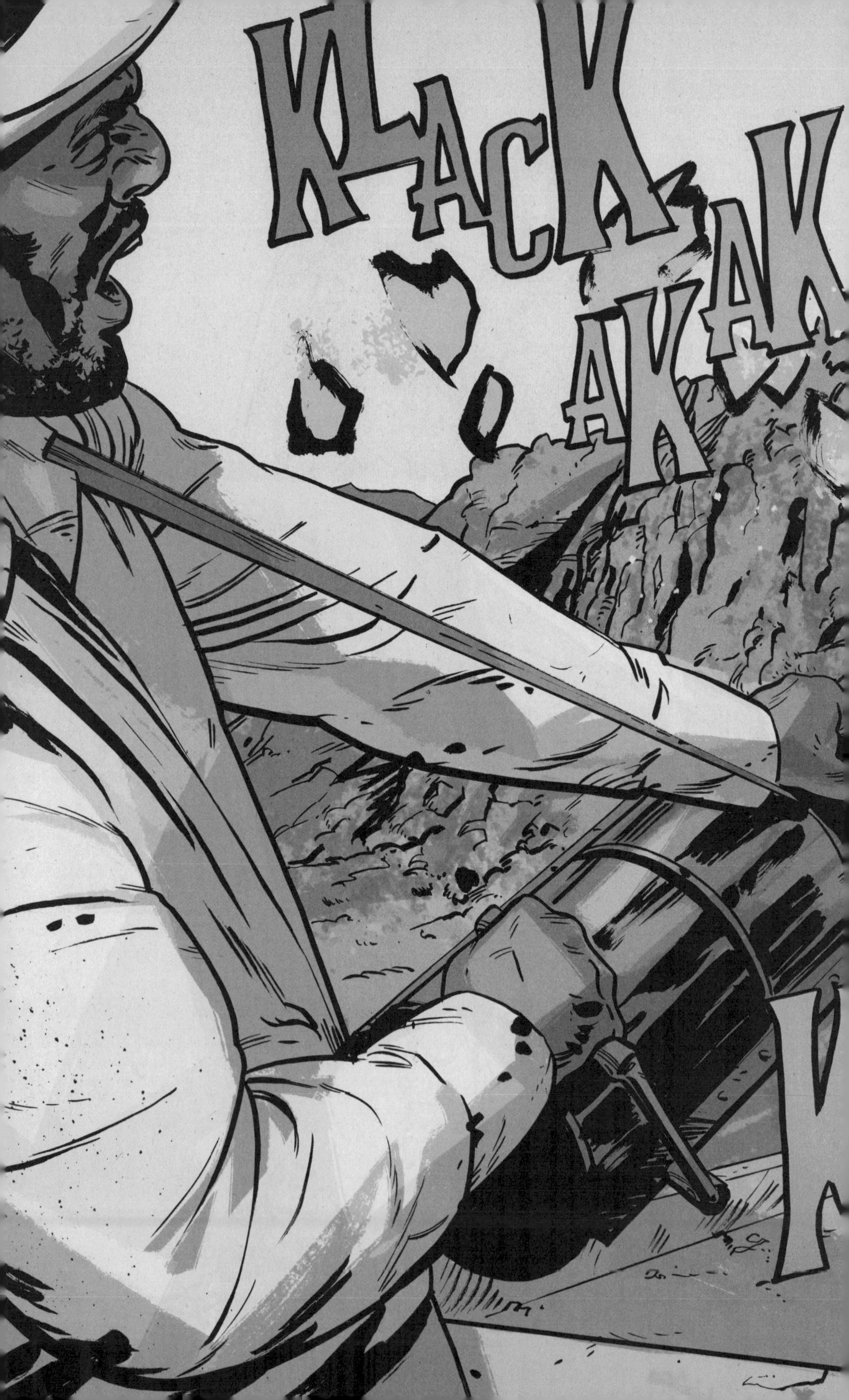
KLACKAKAK

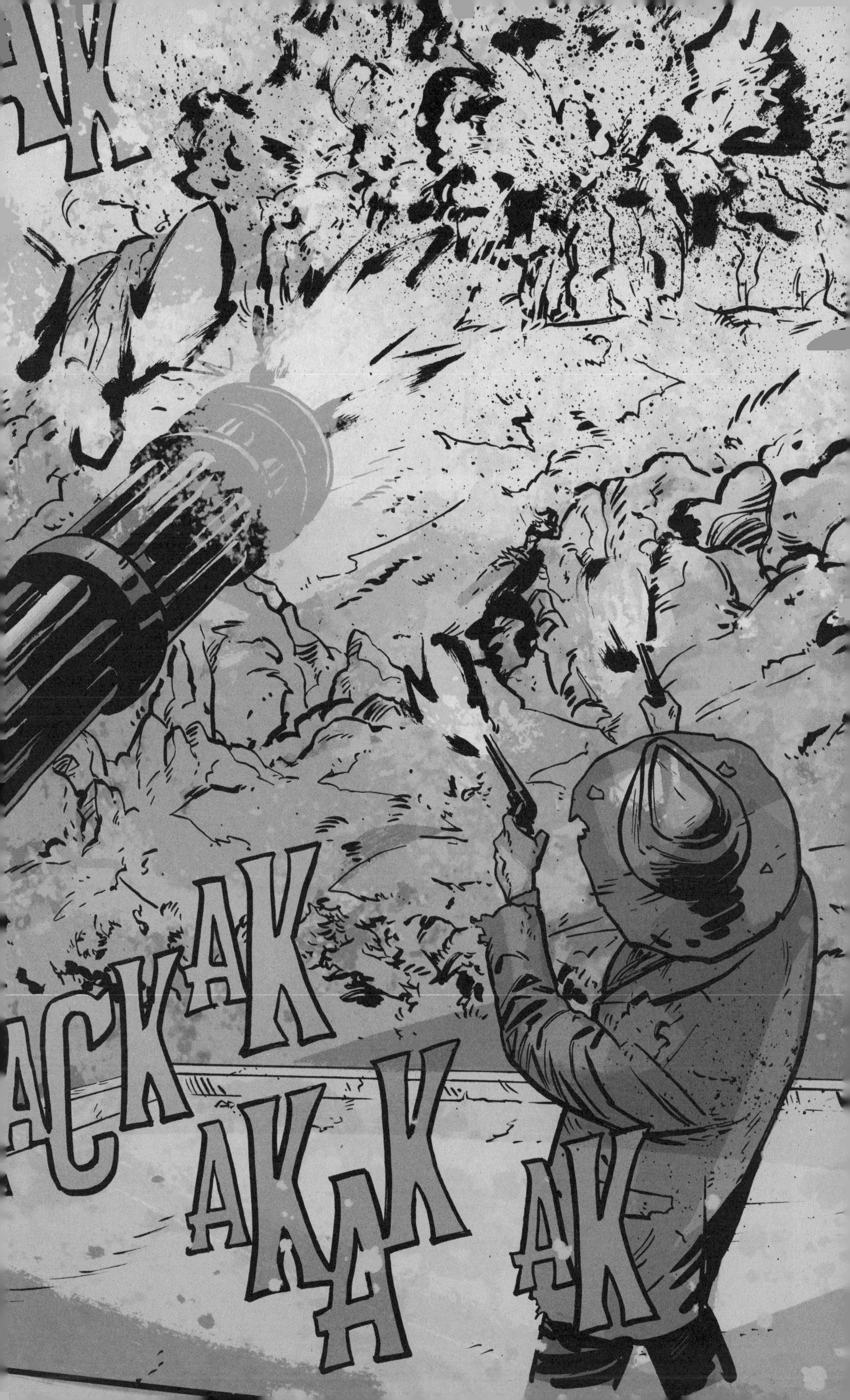
ACKAK
AKAK
AK

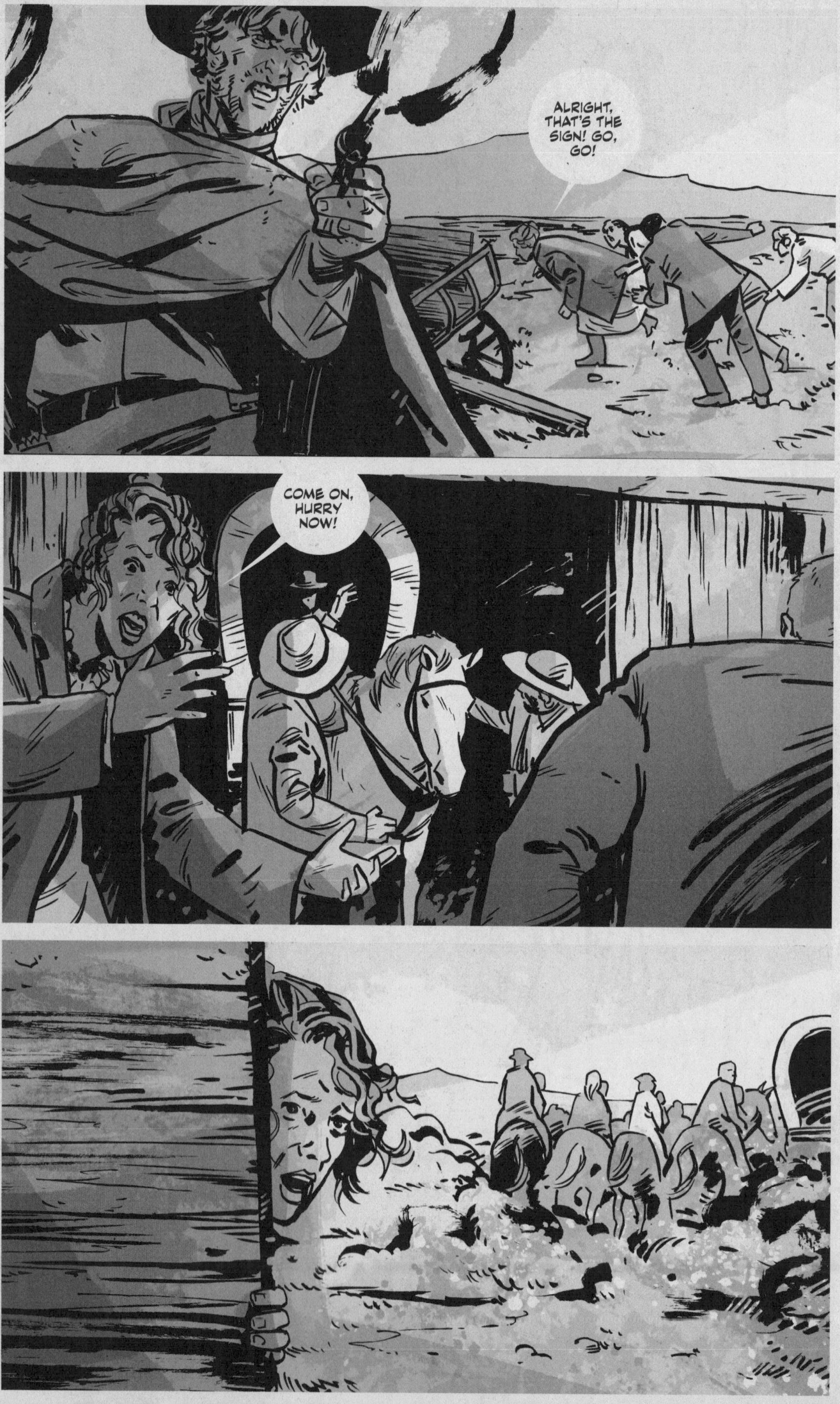
ALRIGHT, THAT'S THE SIGN! GO, GO!
COME ON, HURRY NOW!

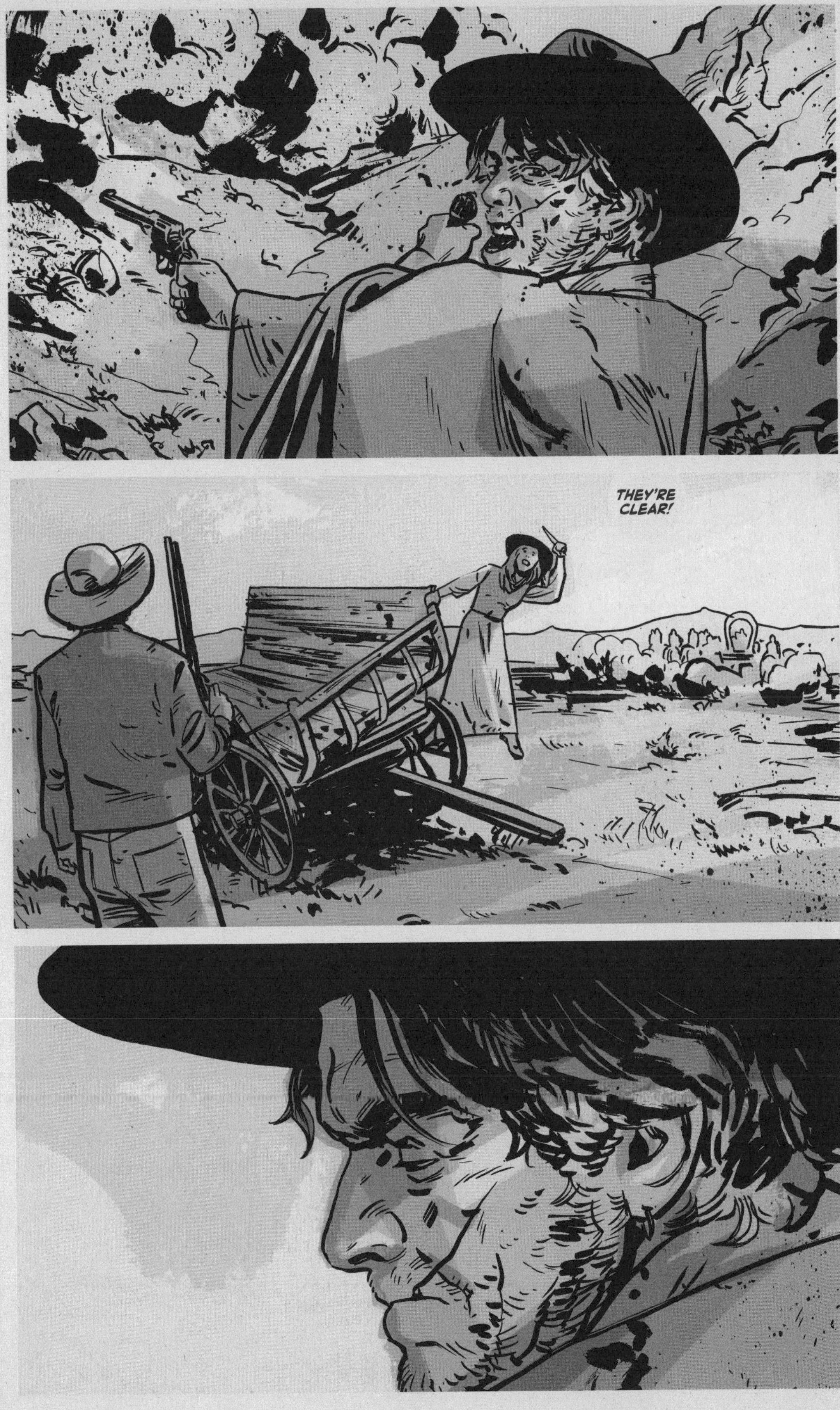
THEY'RE
CLEAR!

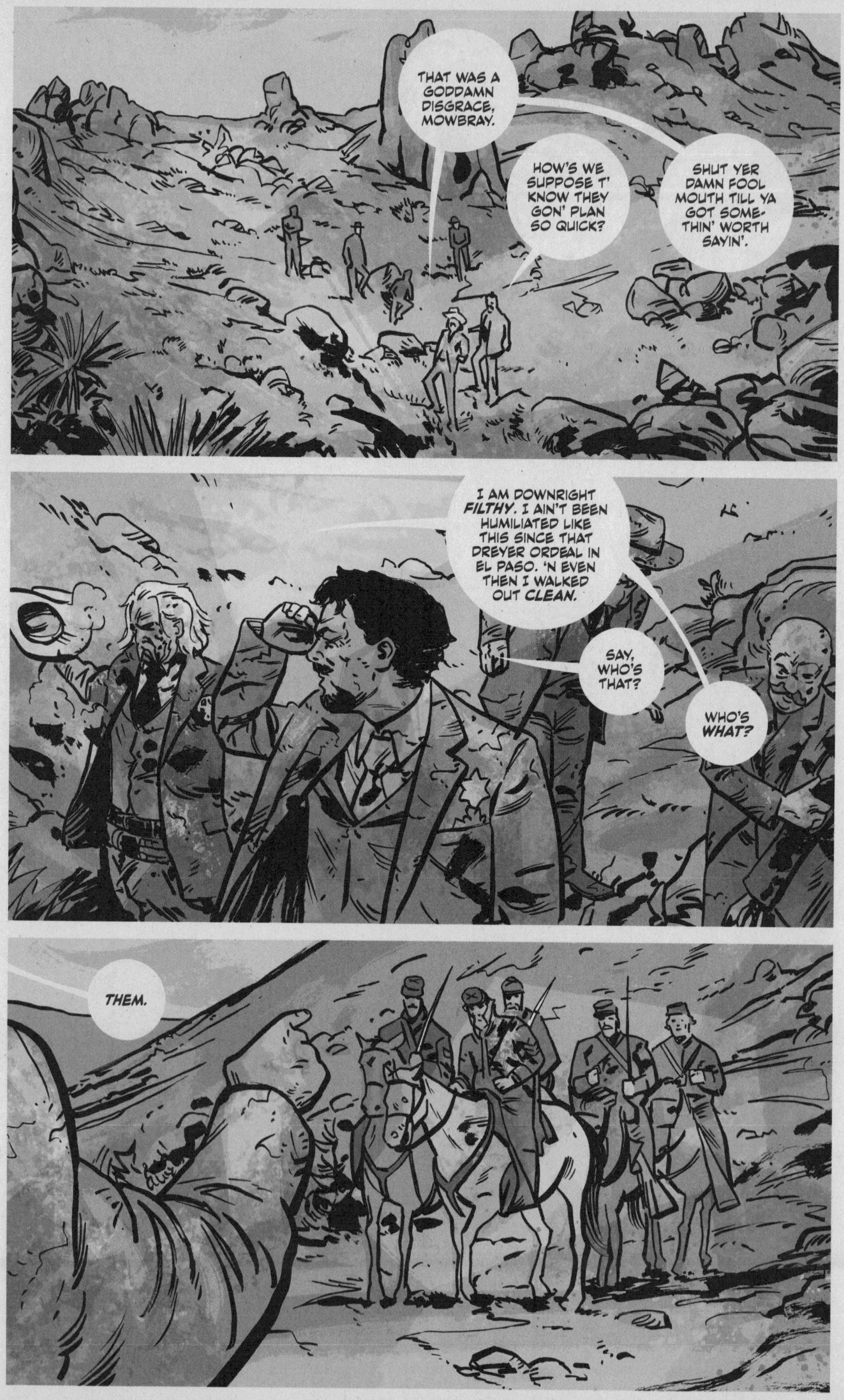
THAT WAS A GODDAMN DISGRACE, MOWBRAY.
HOW'S WE SUPPOSE T' KNOW THEY GON' PLAN SO QUICK?
SHUT YER DAMN FOOL MOUTH TILL YA GOT SOME-THIN' WORTH SAYIN'.
I AM DOWNRIGHT FILTHY. I AIN'T BEEN HUMILIATED LIKE THIS SINCE THAT DREYER ORDEAL IN EL PASO. 'N EVEN THEN I WALKED OUT CLEAN.
SAY, WHO'S THAT?
WHO'S WHAT?
THEM.

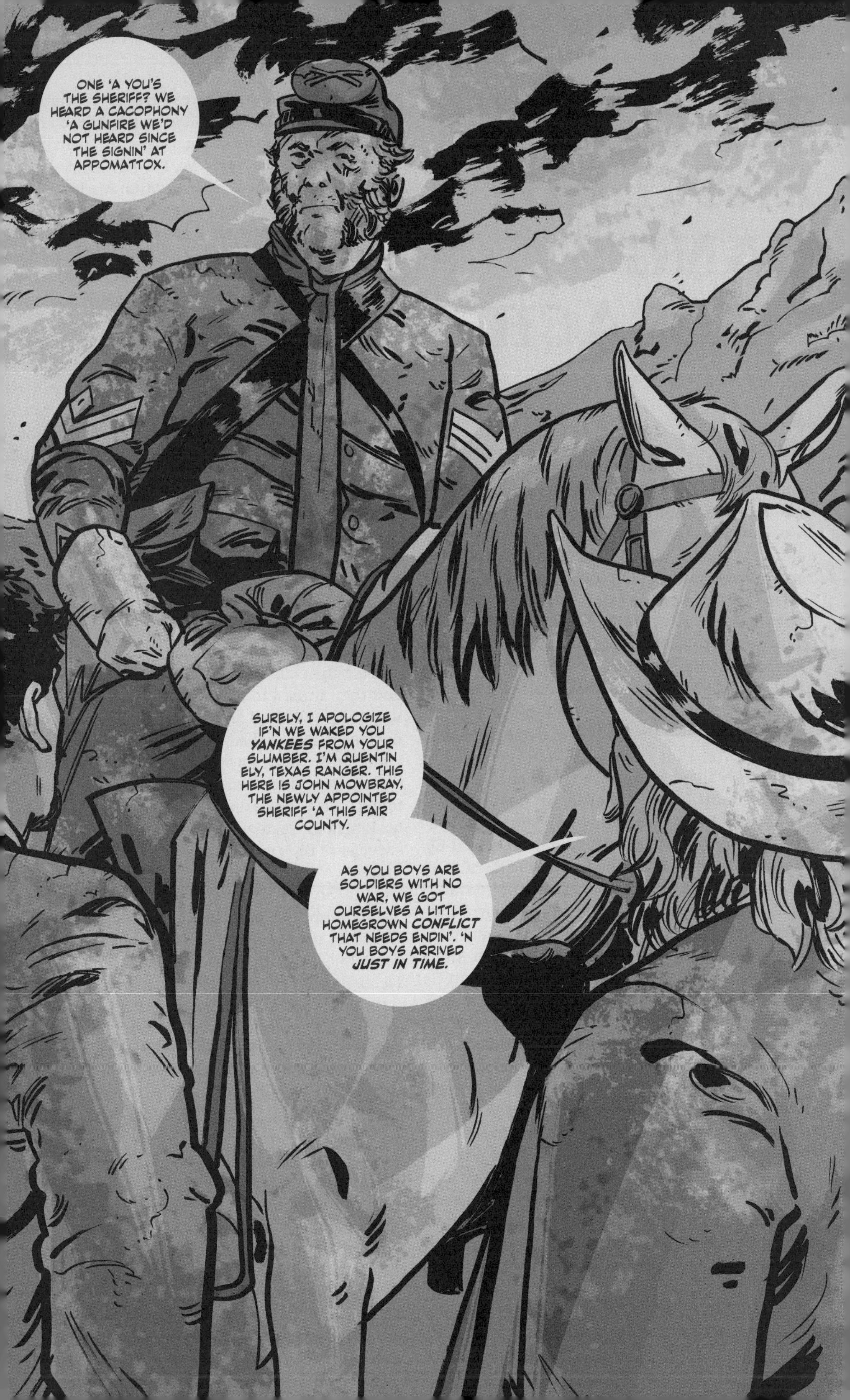
ONE 'A YOU'S THE SHERIFF? WE HEARD A CACOPHONY 'A GUNFIRE WE'D NOT HEARD SINCE THE SIGNIN' AT APPOMATTOX.
SURELY, I APOLOGIZE IF'N WE WAKED YOU *YANKEES* FROM YOUR SLUMBER. I'M QUENTIN ELY, TEXAS RANGER. THIS HERE IS JOHN MOWBRAY, THE NEWLY APPOINTED SHERIFF 'A THIS FAIR COUNTY.
AS YOU BOYS ARE SOLDIERS WITH NO WAR, WE GOT OURSELVES A LITTLE HOMEGROWN *CONFLICT* THAT NEEDS ENDIN'. 'N YOU BOYS ARRIVED *JUST IN TIME.*

THE ENFIELD GANG MASSACRE

cont'd.

But it wasn't for lack of trying; that much is abundantly clear.

Joining Mowbray on the opposite side of the battlefield was Captain Quentin Aloysius Ely of the Texas Rangers who led a fierce cadre of loyal Ambrose Countians with John Mowbray, and for a brief time, with Sheriff Edgar Clayton Hardesty. Each of these individuals was duly deputized for the conflict. In fact, my own grandfather was one of them. I never met the man, but from the brief few words I could scrounge from my father's beer-soaked lips, it sounds like he didn't care whether Enfield was guilty or not. What mattered was that he was hired for a job and he was going to see it through, no matter what. I suppose that was the temperament at the time, for good or ill. But it was not just the job itself, but Ely that helped push folks like my grandfather into battle. He was a respected man, one who brought with him a certain degree of authority. I believe that my grandfather would have followed Ely to the very gates of Hell, if he had asked. Ely was, in some ways, the ideal Texan to men like my grandfather. A stolid individual, fiercely independent, ready to meet any challenge with a well-placed bullet.

Captain Ely was born in 1812 in San Antonio, the specifics of which have been lost to time. He had displayed an aptitude for gunplay from an early age and, when he was able to, he joined up with the Texas Rangers. He spent much of his time riding with Stephen F. Austin himself, the de facto Father of Texas and founder of the Texas Rangers. He was known for his particularly cruel tendencies, though he himself noted that they were not cruel for pleasure. In what remains of his unpublished memoir, Ely wrote that, "what harsh effect my actions have on a man is unfortunate in the eyes of God but necessary to blind justice. I have traded kindness for bloodshed and would do so again one million times over if it were to keep [Texas] safe from the evils of the world."

In this writer's opinion, I certainly wouldn't call Ely a good man as we might think of it—you know, a morally sound, kind, considerate human being—but I also wouldn't call him evil either. From his perspective, he was following the rule of law—o● at least the law as he saw it. Does that mean he wa● right to do what he did? No, I would argue he wa● not. However, he was acting within his jurisdiction and the county had made it clear that they were interested in his services. It seems that this was the situation throughout his life and, if one is told something is right over and over without consequence they are no doubt going to believe that it is the way things ought to be.

Ely is perhaps most famous for his substantial role in the Enfield Gang Massacre, though there was one other skirmish in East Texas that really pu● his name on the map. The story goes that there wa● a young woman named Marguerite Townes who was horribly disfigured when her husband, Jerusalem Townes, thought that she had cheated on him with a wandering vagrant. It turns out that the attack was unprovoked and that Jerusalem had made the story up after he had drank too much cheap whisky and hit her too many times to recall. Ely wa● in the bar with several other Rangers when Marguerite stumbled in, her arm twisted unnaturally and her face a pulpy mess. When Ely inquired as to what happened she managed to utter her husband's name. When confronted, Jerusalem shot at the men and then turned to flee but was quickly caught. He was then castrated and paraded around town on a makeshift float pulled by two bulls. From that moment on, Ely was known for his harsh interpretation of frontier justice. It was said that when he rode into town, it was like an uncrowned king had returned to his kingdom. Take that with a grain of salt, but what survives of Ely's memoir makes that claim nearly six times.

So, it makes some sort of sense that when Ely took up residence in Ambrose County in 1875 when the county faced a tribulation, like the murder of Bill Barley and the subsequent killing of Chick Webb, they would seek out a man of his substantial standing. It is said, and Ely repeats this in his memoir, that he removed himself to West Texas not for action but for rest. He was looking to retire without saying the word but what he found instead was a powder keg primed and ready to explode with one man, John Mowbray, poised over the thing with a lit match.

Edgar Clayton Hardesty was the first sheriff in Ambrose County's history, though you'll be hard-pressed to find much information about him. What I've found, I've conjured from too many hours poring over Ely's self-aggrandizing memoir and from the earliest county documents that still exist. John Mowbray succeeded Hardesty as sheriff in the midst of the massacre and the history of Ambrose County has often been written to skirt around Hardesty's tenure and to prop up Mowbray's. I'd even argue that history has sought to wipe Hardesty's name from its pages entirely. Depending on what sources you refer to, you might come to believe that Mowbray was the first sheriff of the county. This is not the case, of course. Hardesty's 'disgrace', as Ely called it, took place because of his disagreement with how the Enfield Gang was being treated in what would become their final act. He was a man of the law and wanted to know the facts of the case but what Mowbray, Ely, and the rest of Ambrose County wanted was to see frontier justice done and to have it done with a swift and harsh hand.

By all accounts, Hardesty was a well-liked individual prior to his exit as sheriff. However, once he was deposed and Mowbray had taken the reins, he was a veritable pariah. He stayed on his ranch and rarely left. There is not much known about his final years, but he wouldn't survive long after the massacre. His tombstone states that he died in 1877, just two short years after the massacre, and doesn't offer an explanation as to its cause. He was predeceased by a wife and his children quickly sold the property and moved on to greener pastures. Quite literally, it seems. I've traced his descendants to the Pacific Northwest. When I reached out to his surviving family about any information they might have about their forebear, they explained that they did not know much. His great-granddaughter, Maggie Dreiberg, says that she was told that he was a good man and described to her as a Western cowboy like John Wayne in the movies. Her father, Robert, however, remembers a different picture. He says that his grandfather was a sad man, rattled with guilt. There is brief mention in Ely's memoir of Hardesty in seclusion at the end of his life and the drink becoming his companion, though I would take that description with a particularly large grain of salt. If I didn't know better, I'd say that Hardesty died of a broken heart. Not necessarily for the Enfield Gang themselves, but for what his county had become before his very eyes. Of course, I'm assuming a lot here, but I hope you will allow me some poetic license between the lines of hard evidence. Whatever the case, Hardesty was sheriff, then wasn't.

According to John Mowbray's account, he was chosen by the Lord God himself to lead Ambrose County in its time of need. However, if you peruse Ely's memoir, he quickly glosses over Mowbray's ascension to office. Ely writes, "Sheriff Hardesty did not have the stomach for the harsh work at hand, and thus stepped down from his position. I did not and do not agree with his conclusions, but I do respect his choice, disgraceful as it might be in the eyes of the law. A local man of some stripe named John Mowbray then took up the star and he stood beside me in the conflict till its end."
To Mowbray's mind, however, he was justice incarnate. In his published journal, which you can pur-

chase at several gift shops in Fort Lehane, he writes, "The sheriff's star had fallen to me like those from Heaven and, though it carried a considerable weight to its being, I felt no other recourse than to place it upon my chest and institute the justice that this young county had for so long been deprived of."

Okay, John Mowbray. We, of course, have the benefit of hindsight and over 120 years of history to examine while making our judgments, but Ely himself knew Mowbray to be the snake that he was right from the get-go. In the later sections of his memoir, Ely makes specific reference to Mowbray's sinister nature. He writes, "Mowbray fancies himself a warrior but has never faced war. He allows others to do the shooting while he signs his name to history and claims to have been the one with the hot pistol in his hand. A more sorry soul I cannot conjure, and I have met my fair share of despicable men."

Mowbray himself was from Kaskaskia, Illinois, originally. He was an unsuccessful businessman in his home state with failed venture after failed venture and quickly sought out the potential of this mysterious thing called the 'Wild West.' It seemed to have been the right move, fortunately for him, and he quickly and successfully established a saloon called 'The High Water' outside of the fort that offered drinks, gambling, and, well, let's say companionship. The High Water exists in Fort Lehane to this day, though the original building had burned to the ground in the early days of the twentieth century and was rebuilt by new ownership. Mowbray's success brought with it power which he used to control, as best he could, the state of things in Ambrose County. As we know well, the Enfield Gang's arrival threw Mowbray's grasp of the county into flux and he sought to maintain that control by any means necessary.

His published journals are available in gift shops, but these were not his only journals. The ones I have found in the county archives have cast an entirely new light on the man known as John Mowbray. To put it lightly, he was a troubled man who should have been confined to a cell. Instead, he was allowed to run a county.

To this day, I believe that Ambrose County suffers the curse of John Mowbray, a curse that runs deep down into the soil of this land and has poisoned it ever since. The purpose of this article, I suppose, is to provide an exorcism. I aim, in my small way, to save the soul of Ambrose County. To do this, we have to talk about a hard, simple truth: John Mowbray may not have pulled the trigger, but he certainly is the man responsible for the murder of Bill Barley and the countless deaths that followed over the next five days in 1875. And I intend to prove it.

TO BE CONTINUED.

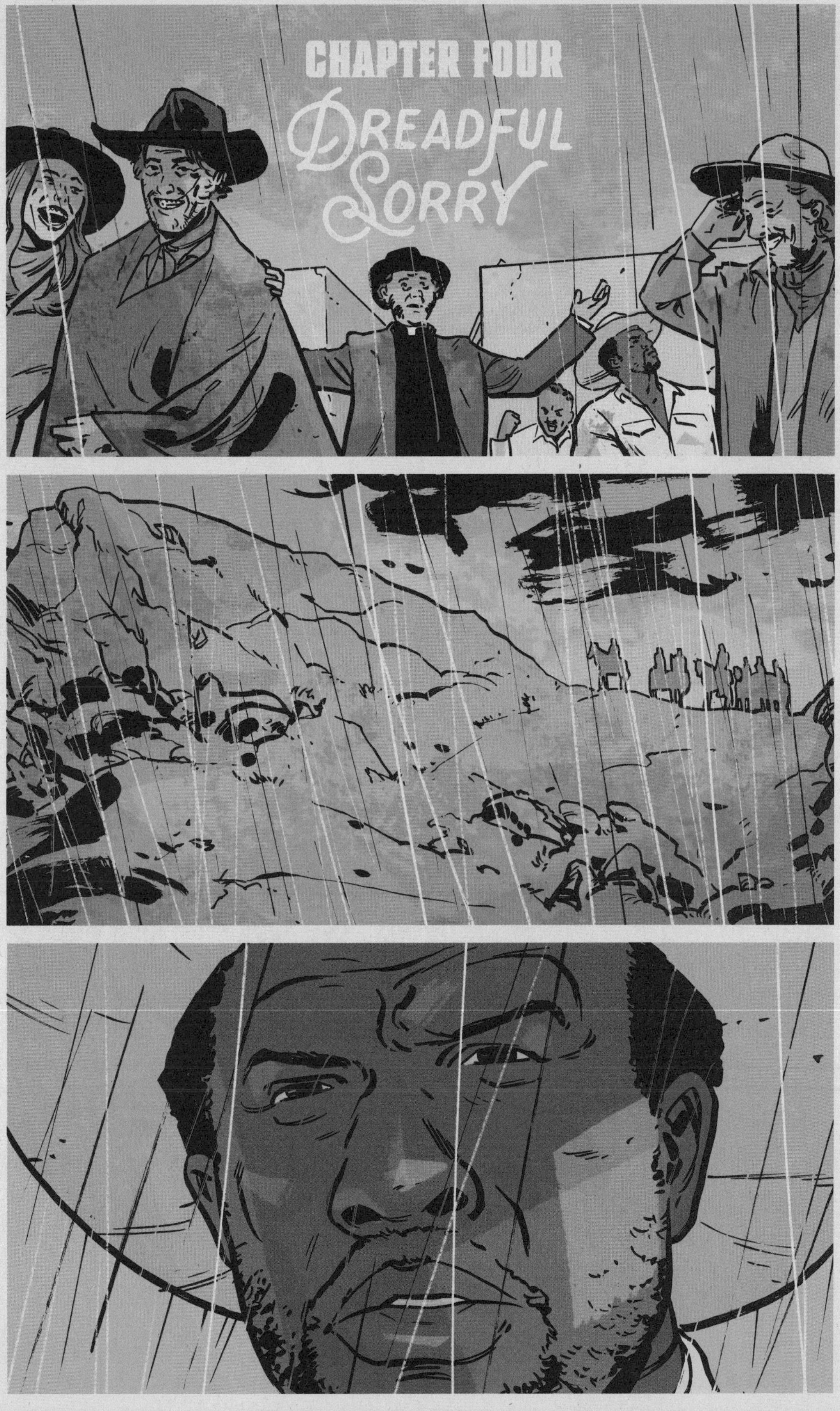
CHAPTER FOUR
DREADFUL SORRY

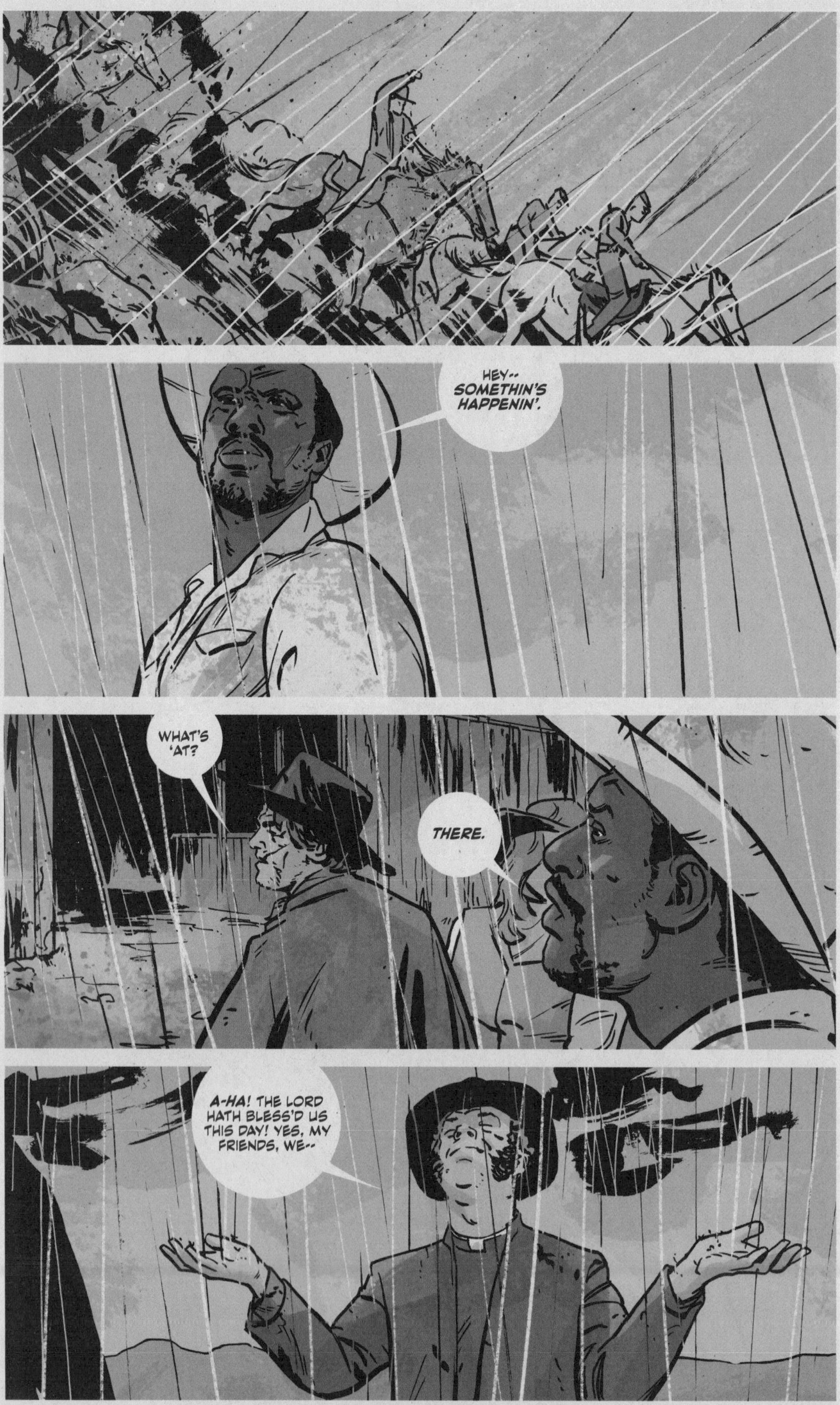
HEY--
SOMETHIN'S HAPPENIN'.
WHAT'S 'AT?
THERE.
A-HA! THE LORD HATH BLESS'D US THIS DAY! YES, MY FRIENDS, WE--

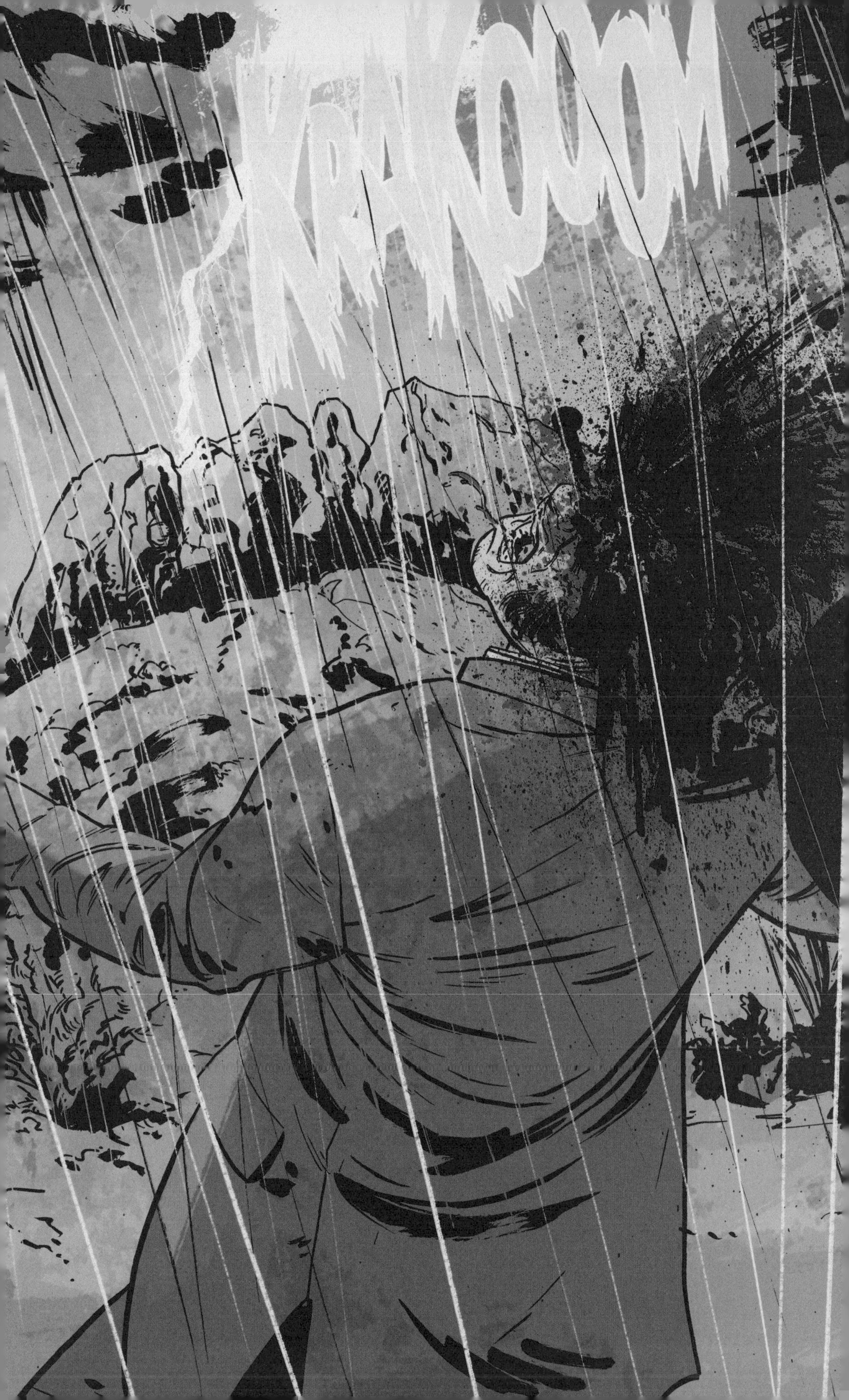
KRAKOOOM

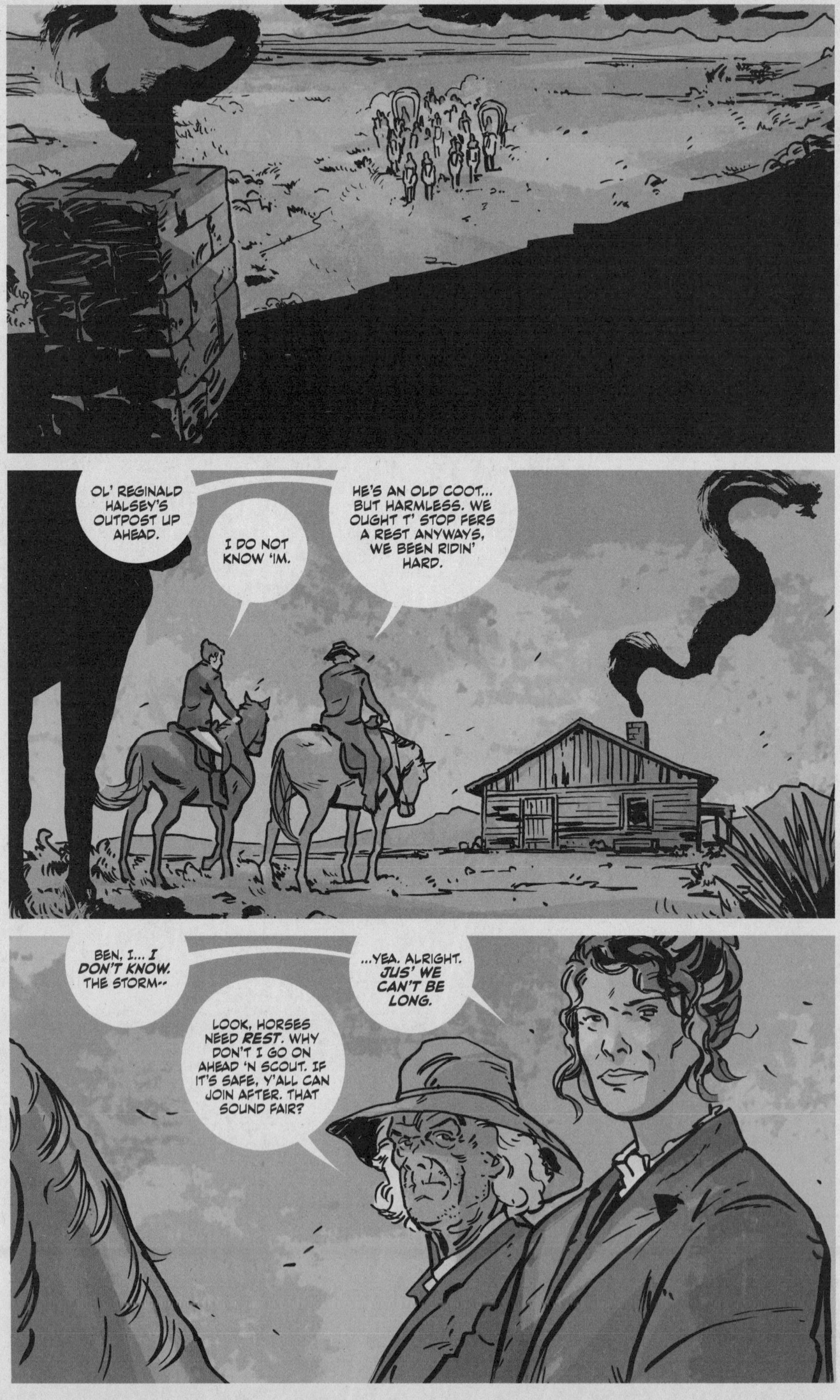
OL' REGINALD HALSEY'S OUTPOST UP AHEAD.
I DO NOT KNOW 'IM.
HE'S AN OLD COOT... BUT HARMLESS. WE OUGHT T' STOP FERS A REST ANYWAYS, WE BEEN RIDIN' HARD.
BEN, I... *I DON'T KNOW.* THE STORM--
LOOK, HORSES NEED *REST*. WHY DON'T I GO ON AHEAD 'N SCOUT. IF IT'S SAFE, Y'ALL CAN JOIN AFTER. THAT SOUND FAIR?
...YEA. ALRIGHT. *JUS' WE CAN'T BE LONG.*

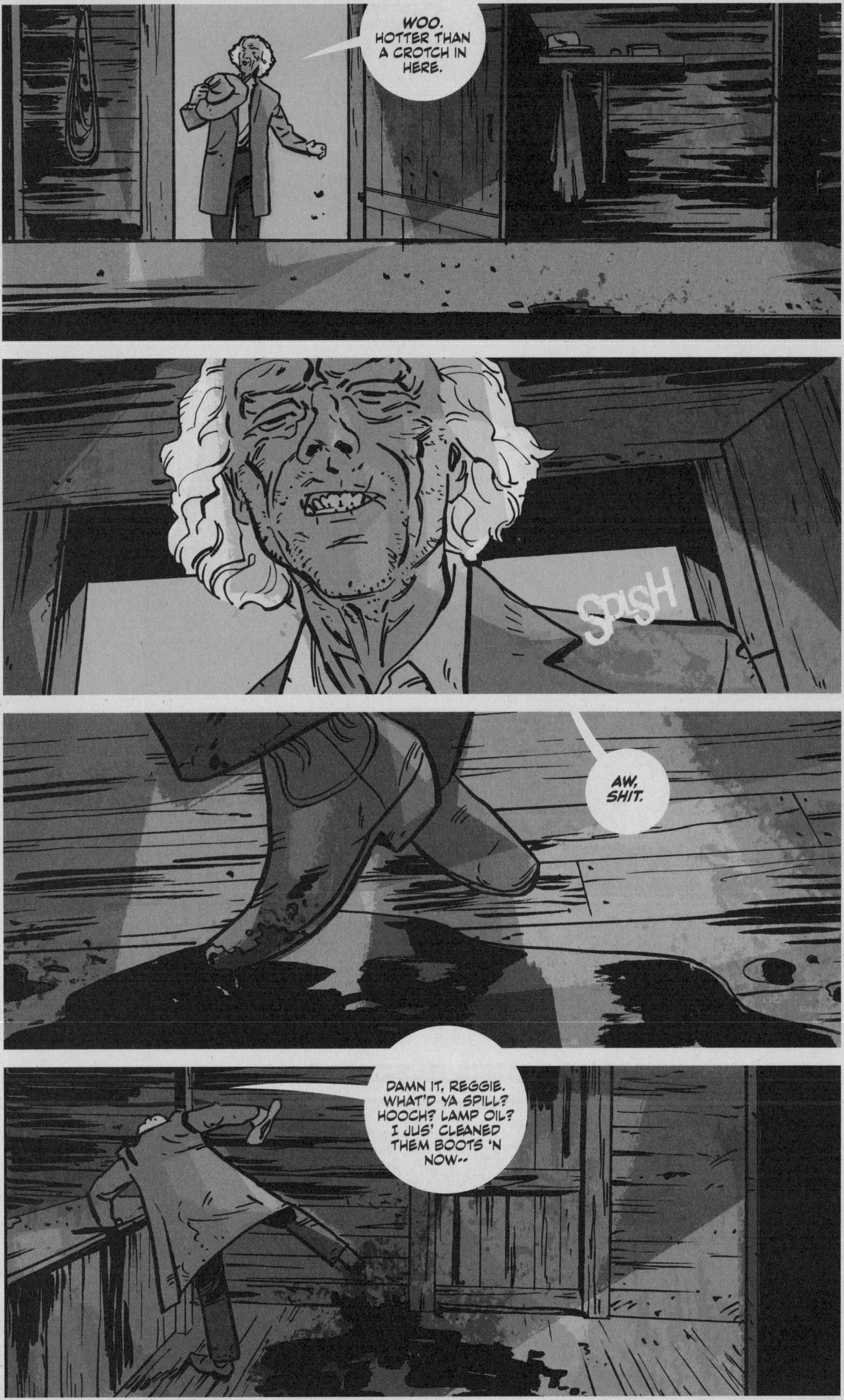
WOO. HOTTER THAN A CROTCH IN HERE.
SPLSH
AW, SHIT.
DAMN IT, REGGIE. WHAT'D YA SPILL? HOOCH? LAMP OIL? I JUS' CLEANED THEM BOOTS 'N NOW--

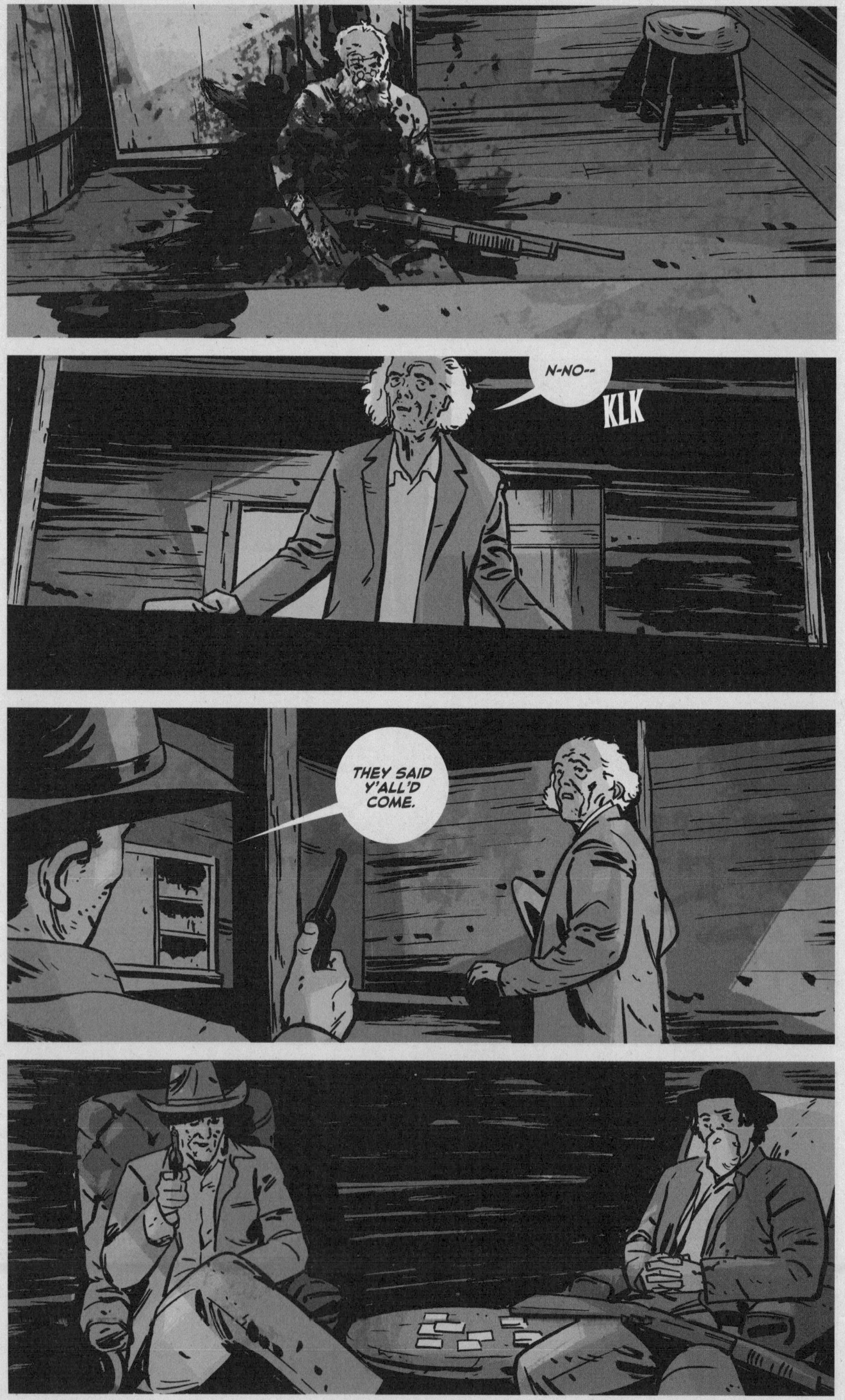
N-NO--
KLK
THEY SAID Y'ALL'D COME.

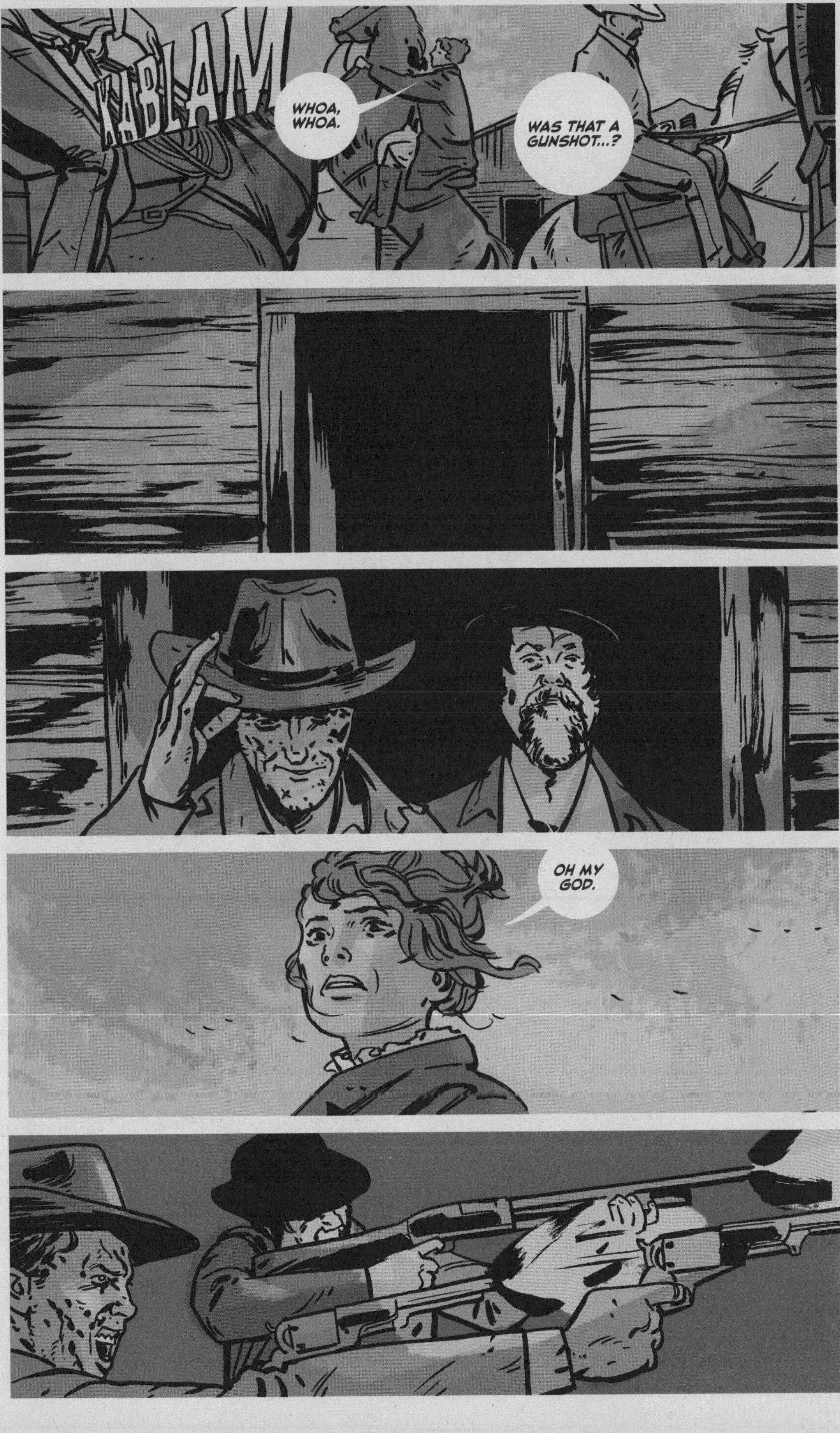
KABLAM
WHOA, WHOA.
WAS THAT A GUNSHOT...?
OH MY GOD.

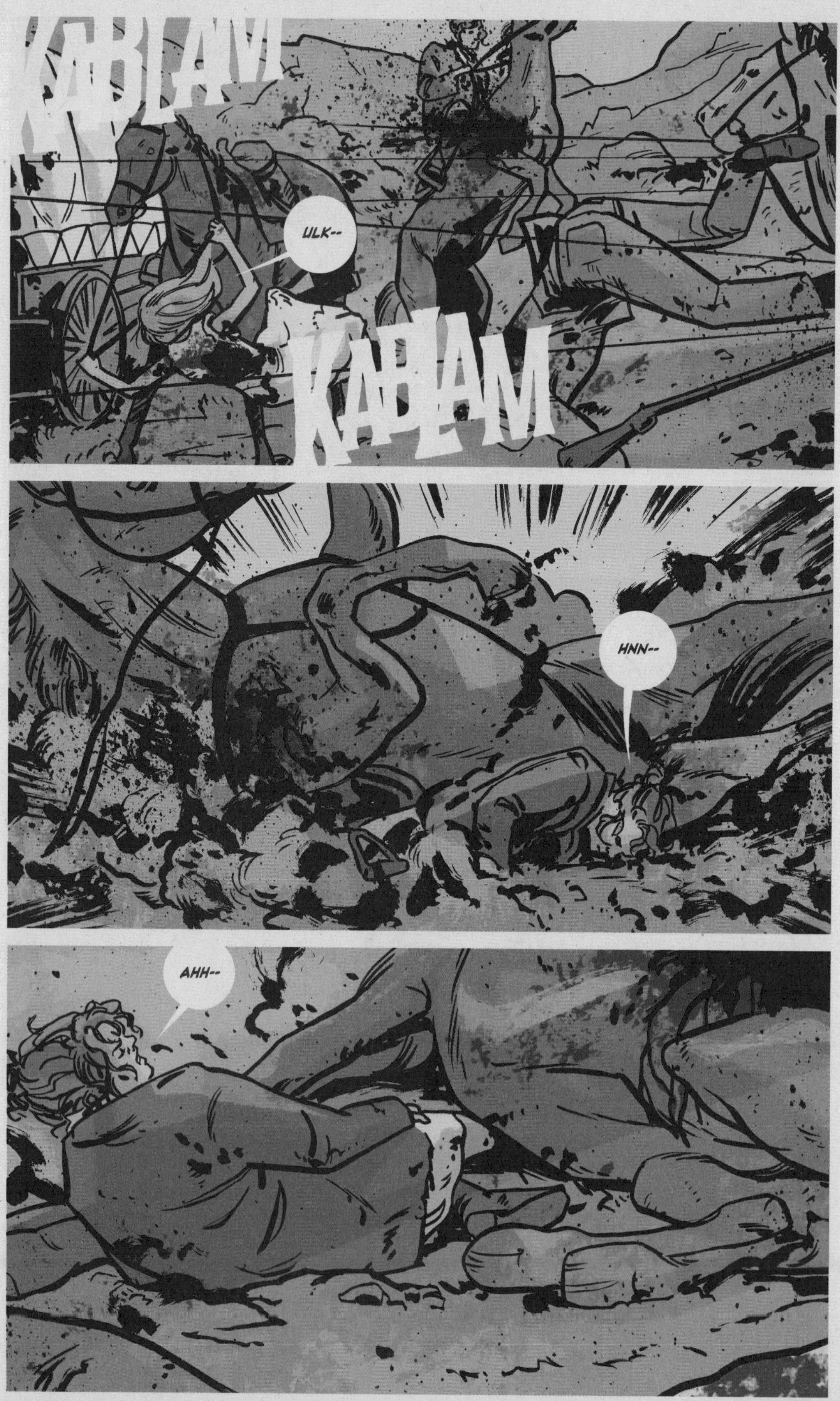
KABLAM
ULK--
KABLAM
HNN--
AHH--

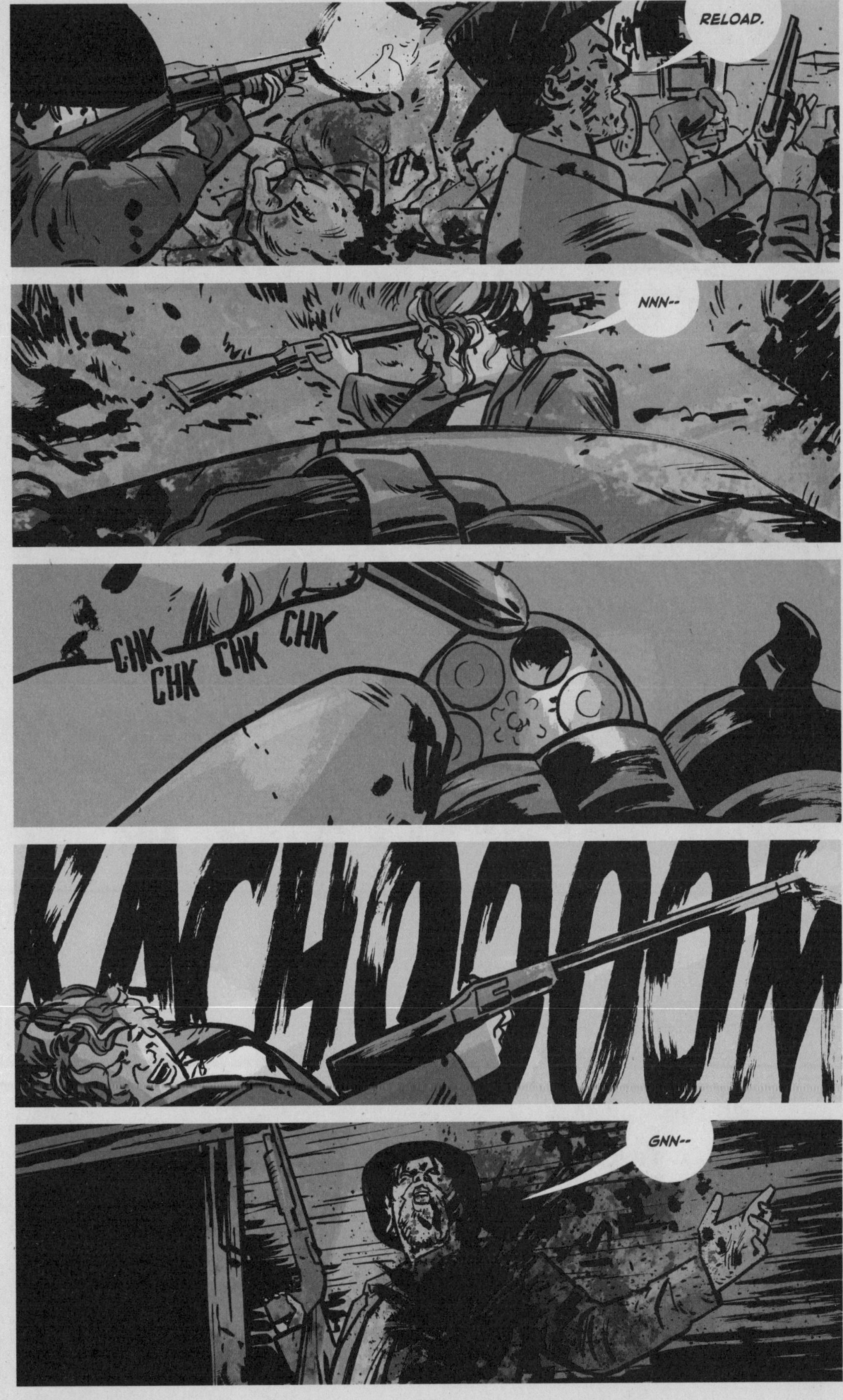
RELOAD.
NNN--
CHK
CHK
CHK
CHK
KACHOOOOM
GNN--

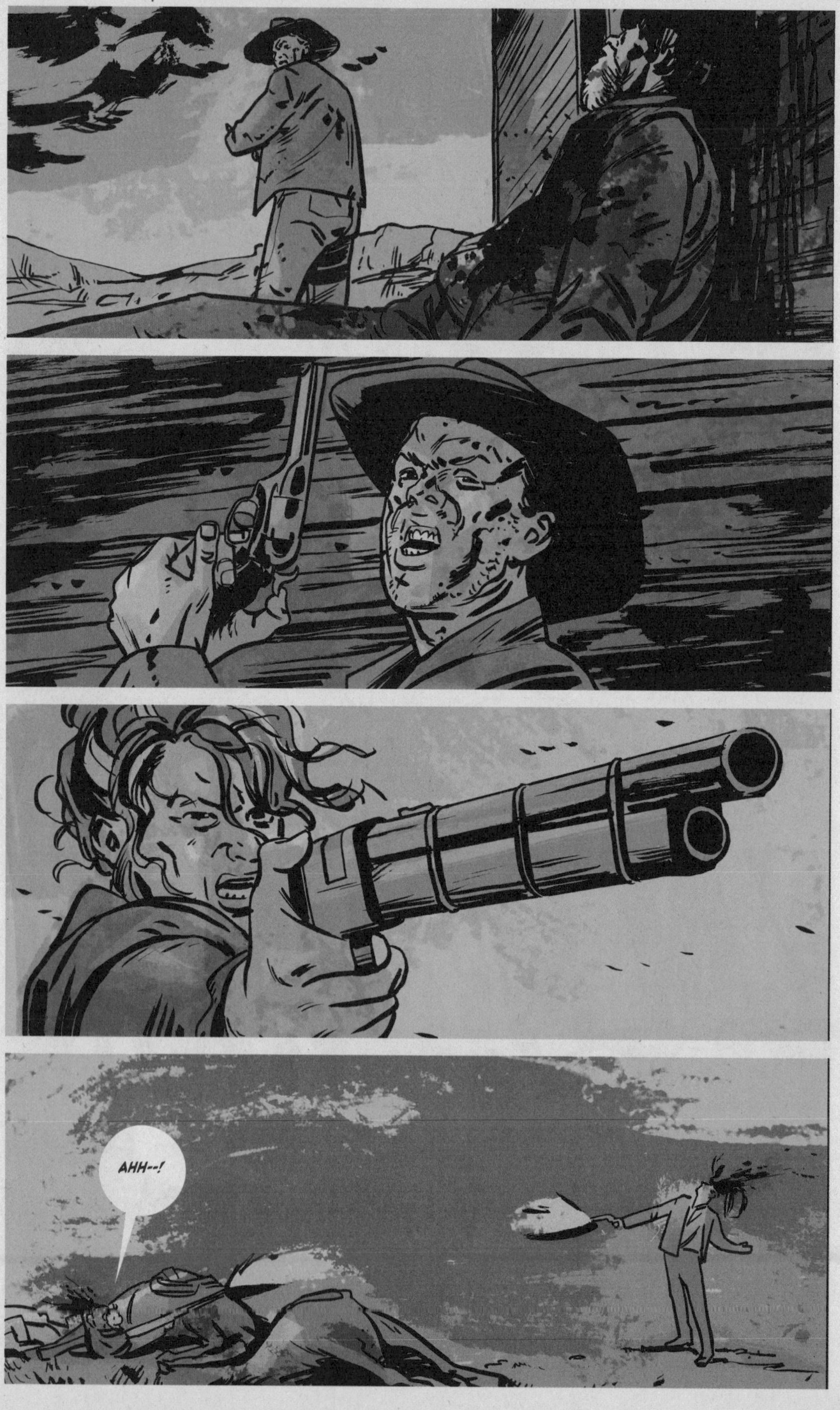
AHH--!

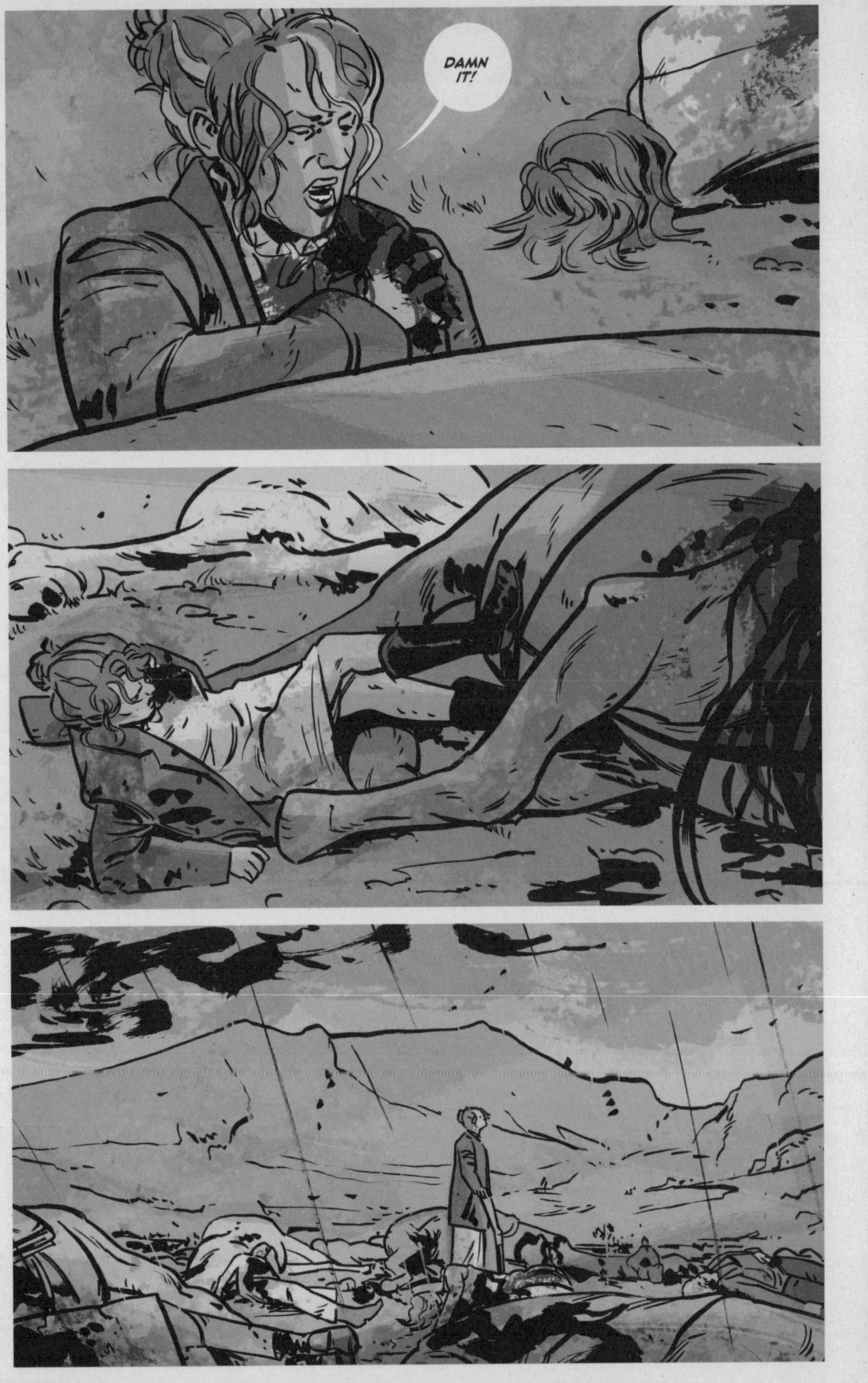
DAMN IT!

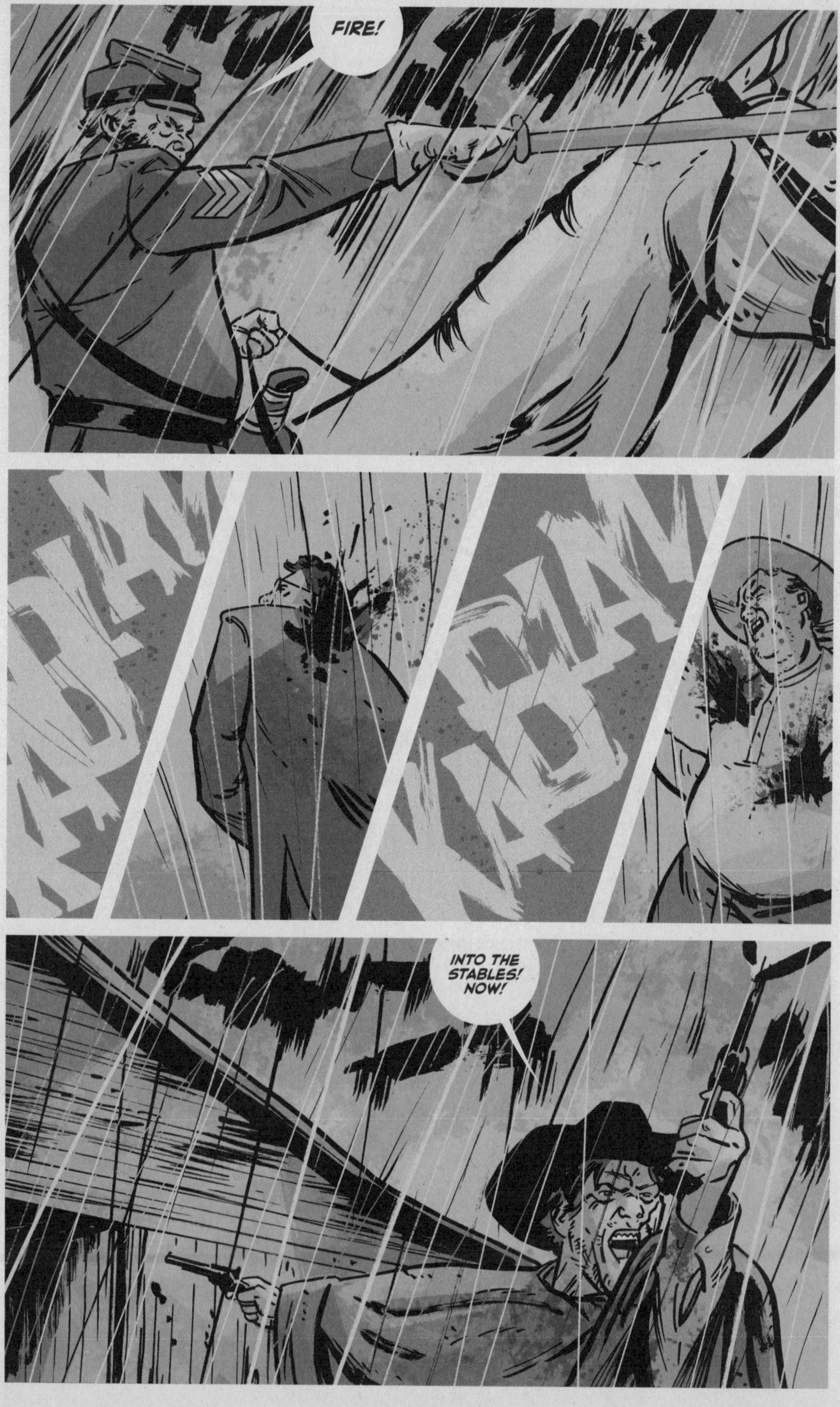
FIRE!
INTO THE STABLES! NOW!

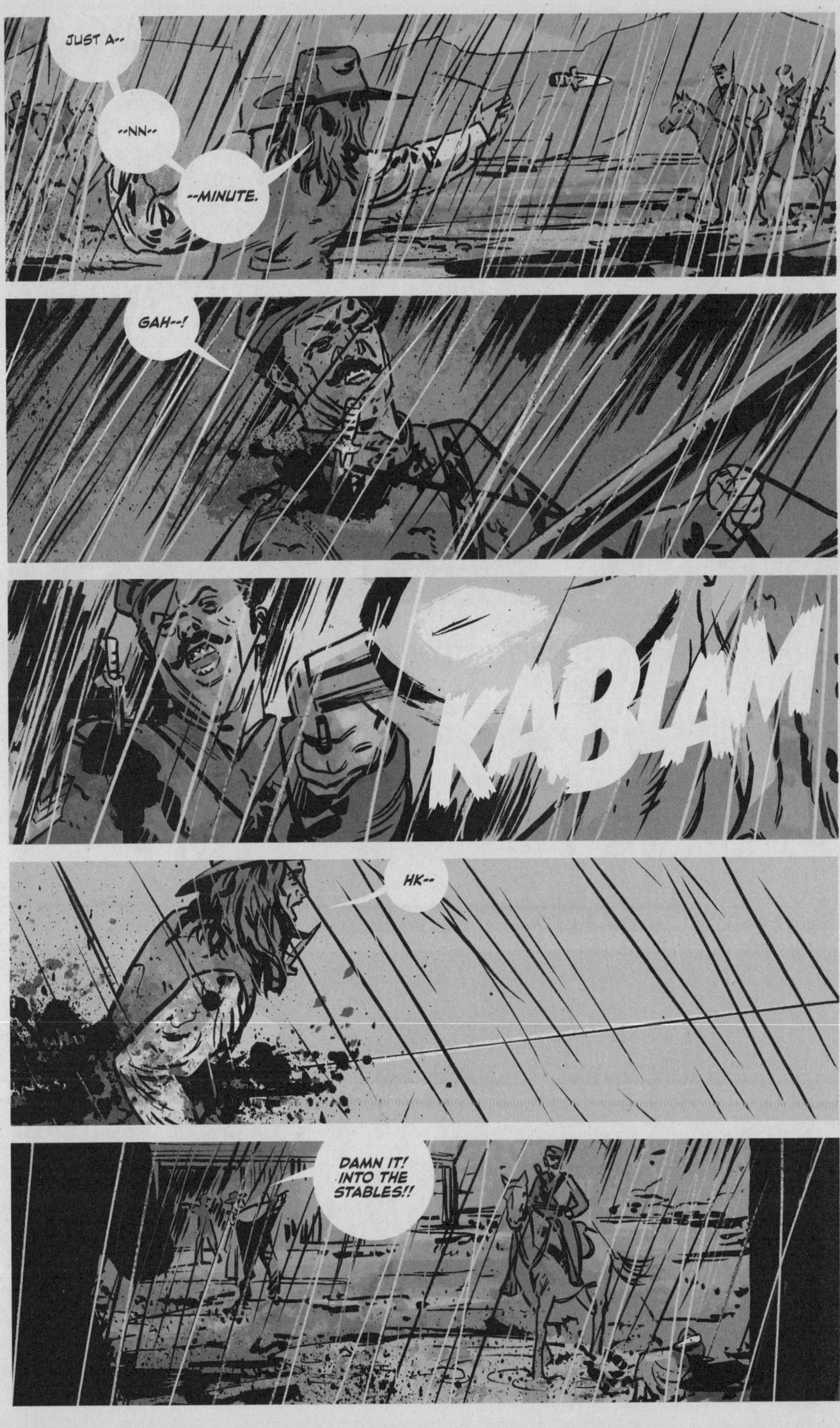
JUST A--
--NN--
--MINUTE.
GAH--!
KABLAM
HK--
DAMN IT! INTO THE STABLES!!

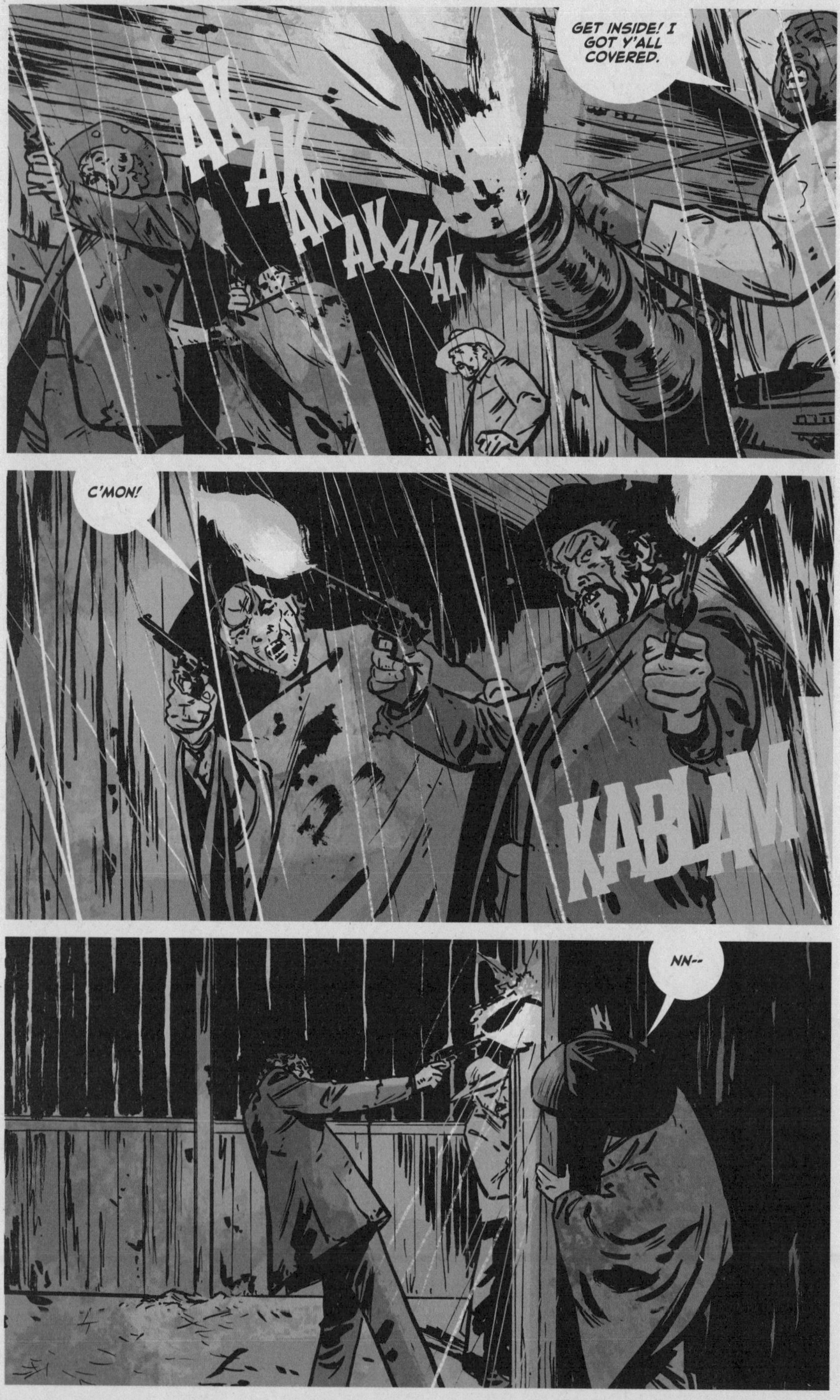
GET INSIDE! I GOT Y'ALL COVERED.
AK AK AK AK AK AK AK AK
C'MON!
KABLAM
NN--

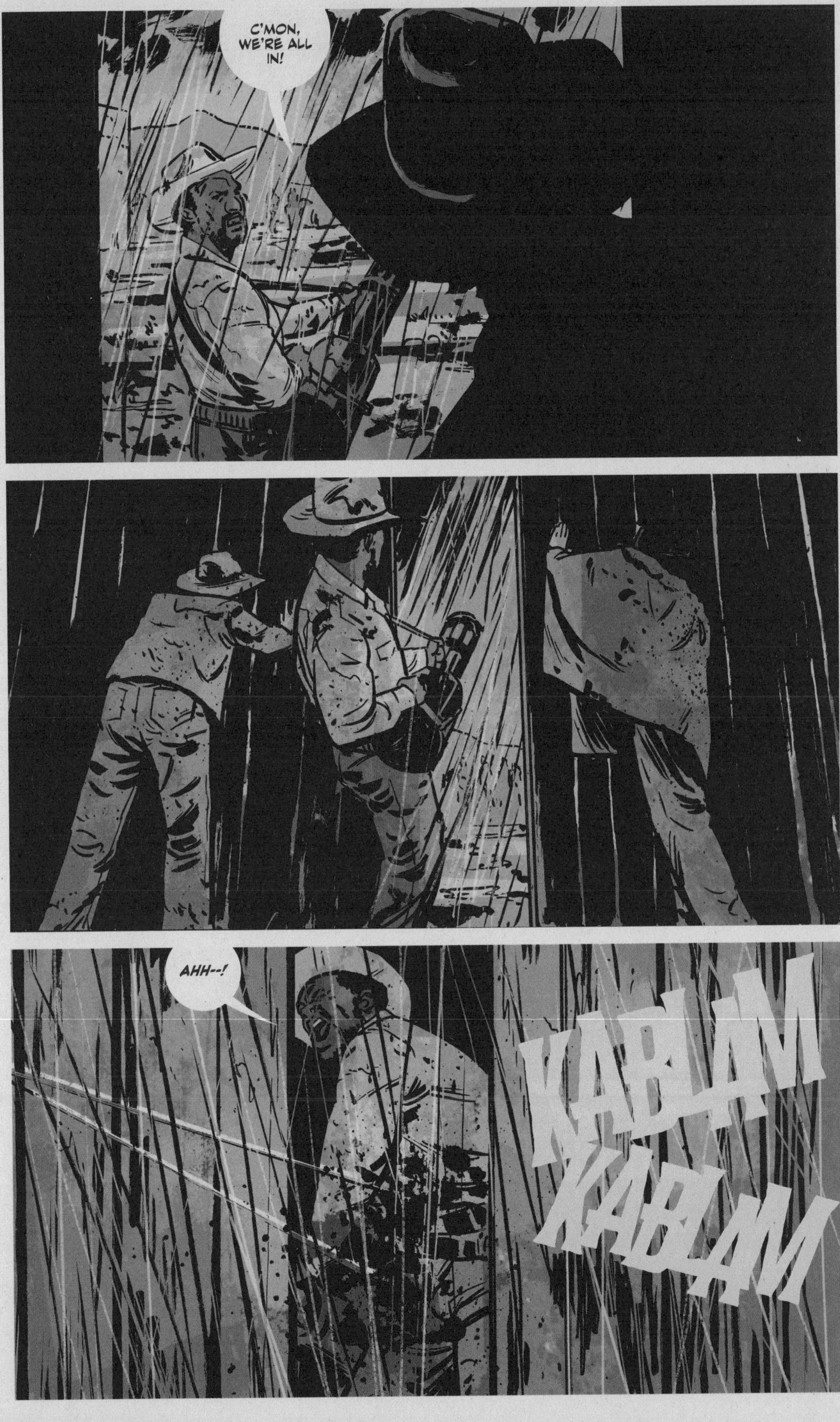
C'MON, WE'RE ALL IN!
AHH--!
KABLAM
KABLAM

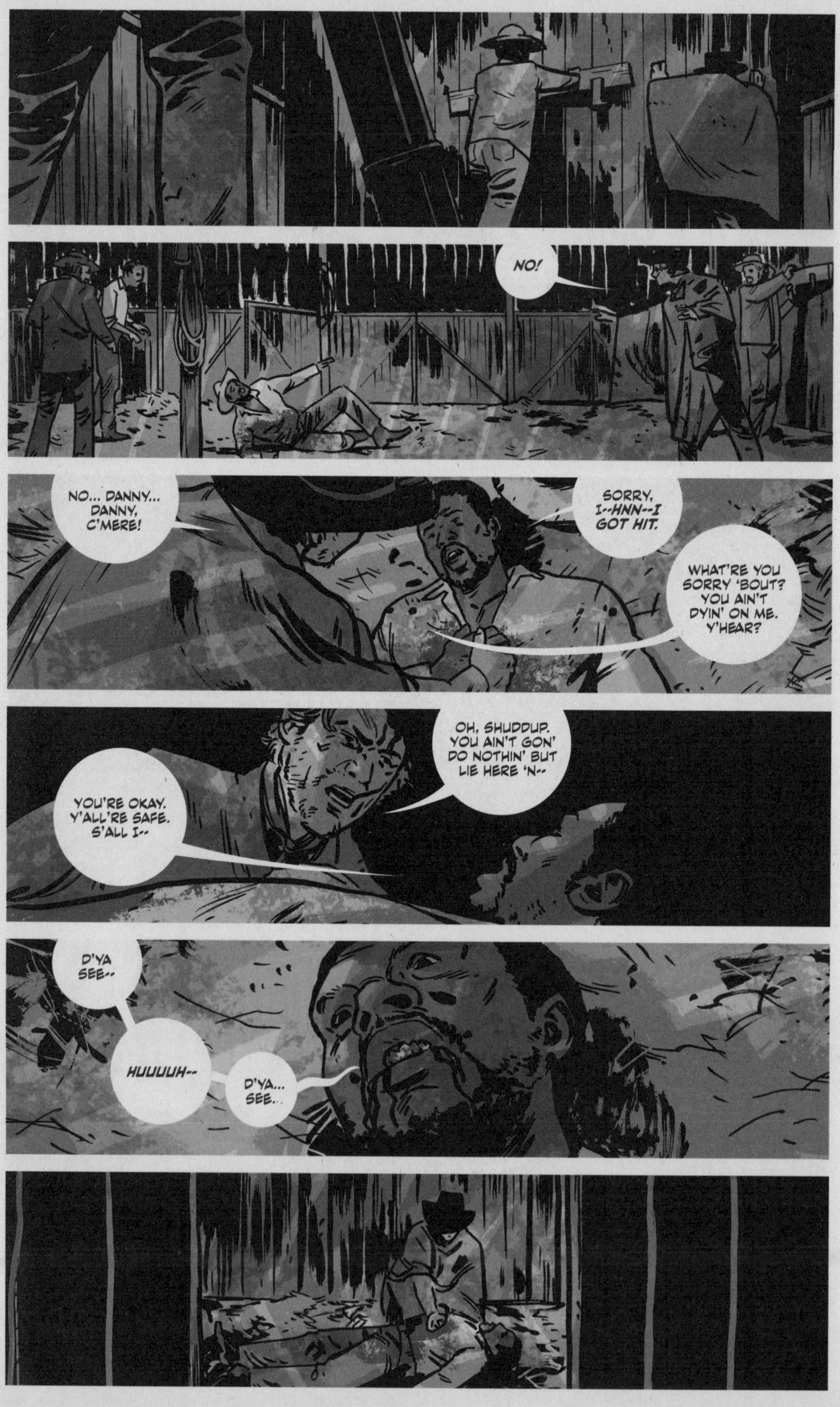
NO!
NO... DANNY... DANNY, C'MERE!
SORRY, I--HNN--I GOT HIT.
WHAT'RE YOU SORRY 'BOUT? YOU AIN'T DYIN' ON ME. Y'HEAR?
OH, SHUDDUP. YOU AIN'T GON' DO NOTHIN' BUT LIE HERE 'N--
YOU'RE OKAY. Y'ALL'RE SAFE. S'ALL I--
D'YA SEE--
HUUUUUH--
D'YA... SEE...

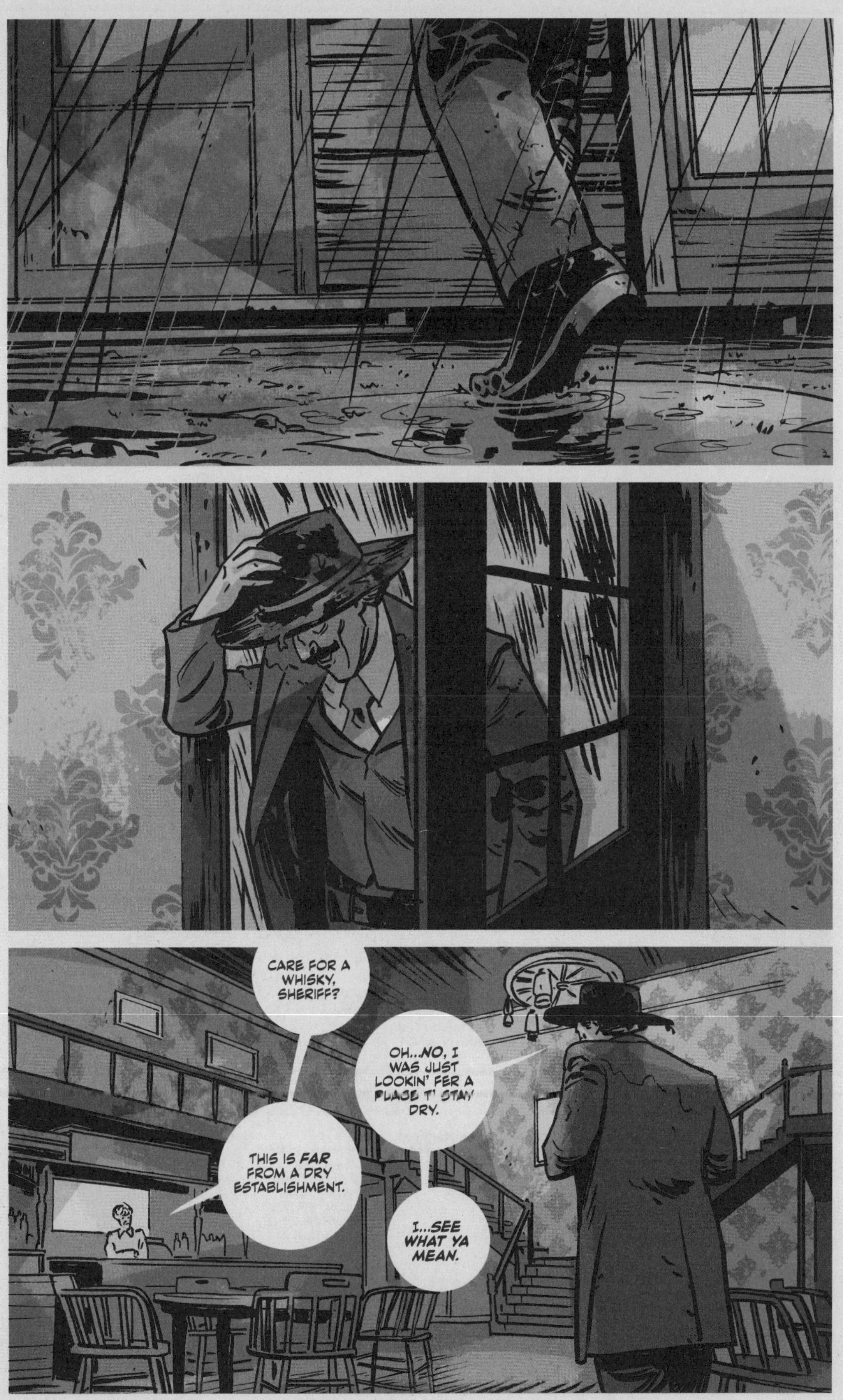
CARE FOR A WHISKY, SHERIFF?
OH...NO, I WAS JUST LOOKIN' FER A PLACE T' STAY DRY.
THIS IS FAR FROM A DRY ESTABLISHMENT.
I...SEE WHAT YA MEAN.

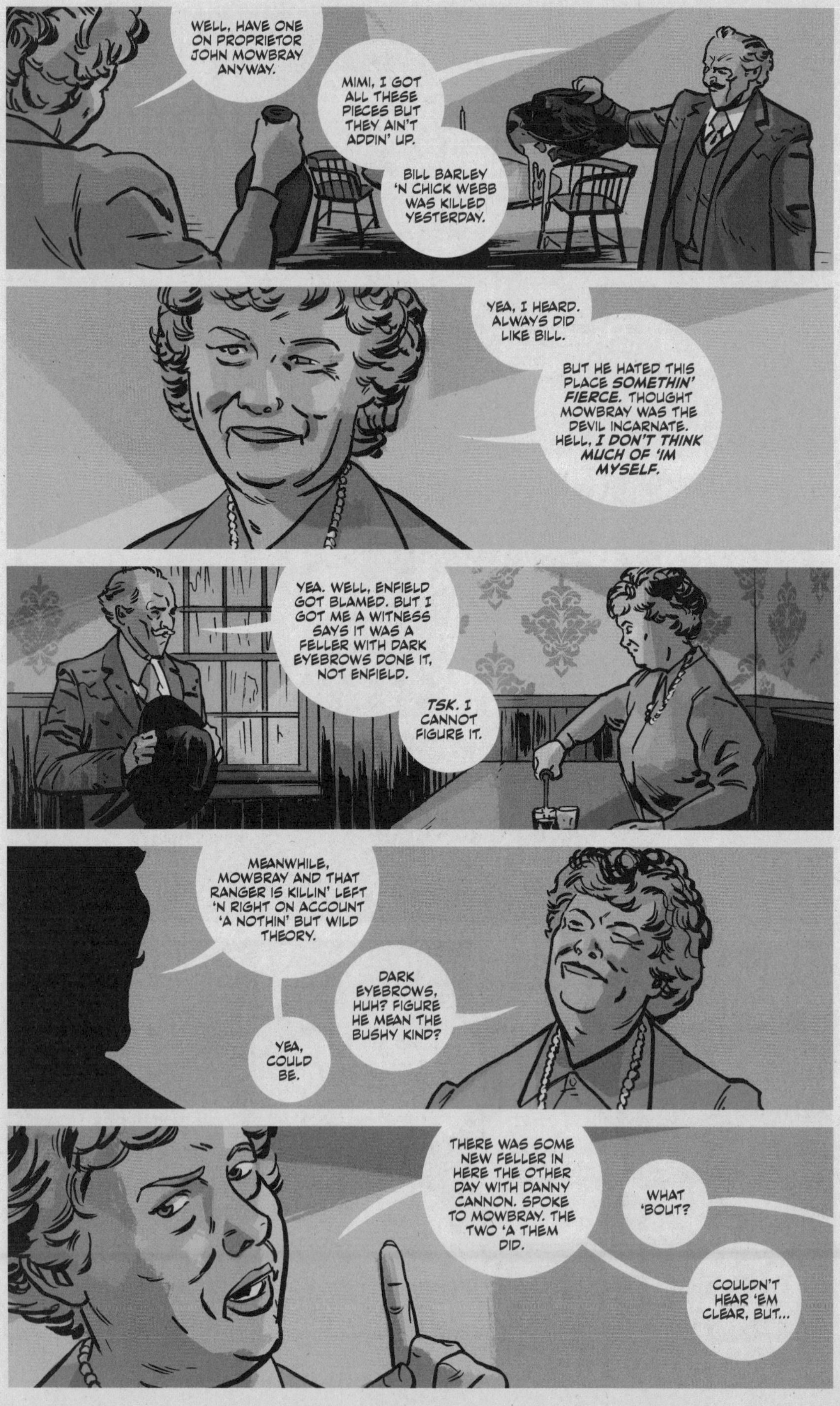
WELL, HAVE ONE ON PROPRIETOR JOHN MOWBRAY ANYWAY.
MIMI, I GOT ALL THESE PIECES BUT THEY AIN'T ADDIN' UP.
BILL BARLEY 'N CHICK WEBB WAS KILLED YESTERDAY.
YEA, I HEARD. ALWAYS DID LIKE BILL.
BUT HE HATED THIS PLACE *SOMETHIN' FIERCE*. THOUGHT MOWBRAY WAS THE DEVIL INCARNATE. HELL, *I DON'T THINK MUCH OF 'IM MYSELF*.
YEA. WELL, ENFIELD GOT BLAMED. BUT I GOT ME A WITNESS SAYS IT WAS A FELLER WITH DARK EYEBROWS DONE IT, NOT ENFIELD.
TSK. I CANNOT FIGURE IT.
MEANWHILE, MOWBRAY AND THAT RANGER IS KILLIN' LEFT 'N RIGHT ON ACCOUNT 'A NOTHIN' BUT WILD THEORY.
DARK EYEBROWS, HUH? FIGURE HE MEAN THE BUSHY KIND?
YEA, COULD BE.
THERE WAS SOME NEW FELLER IN HERE THE OTHER DAY WITH DANNY CANNON. SPOKE TO MOWBRAY. THE TWO 'A THEM DID.
WHAT 'BOUT?
COULDN'T HEAR 'EM CLEAR, BUT...

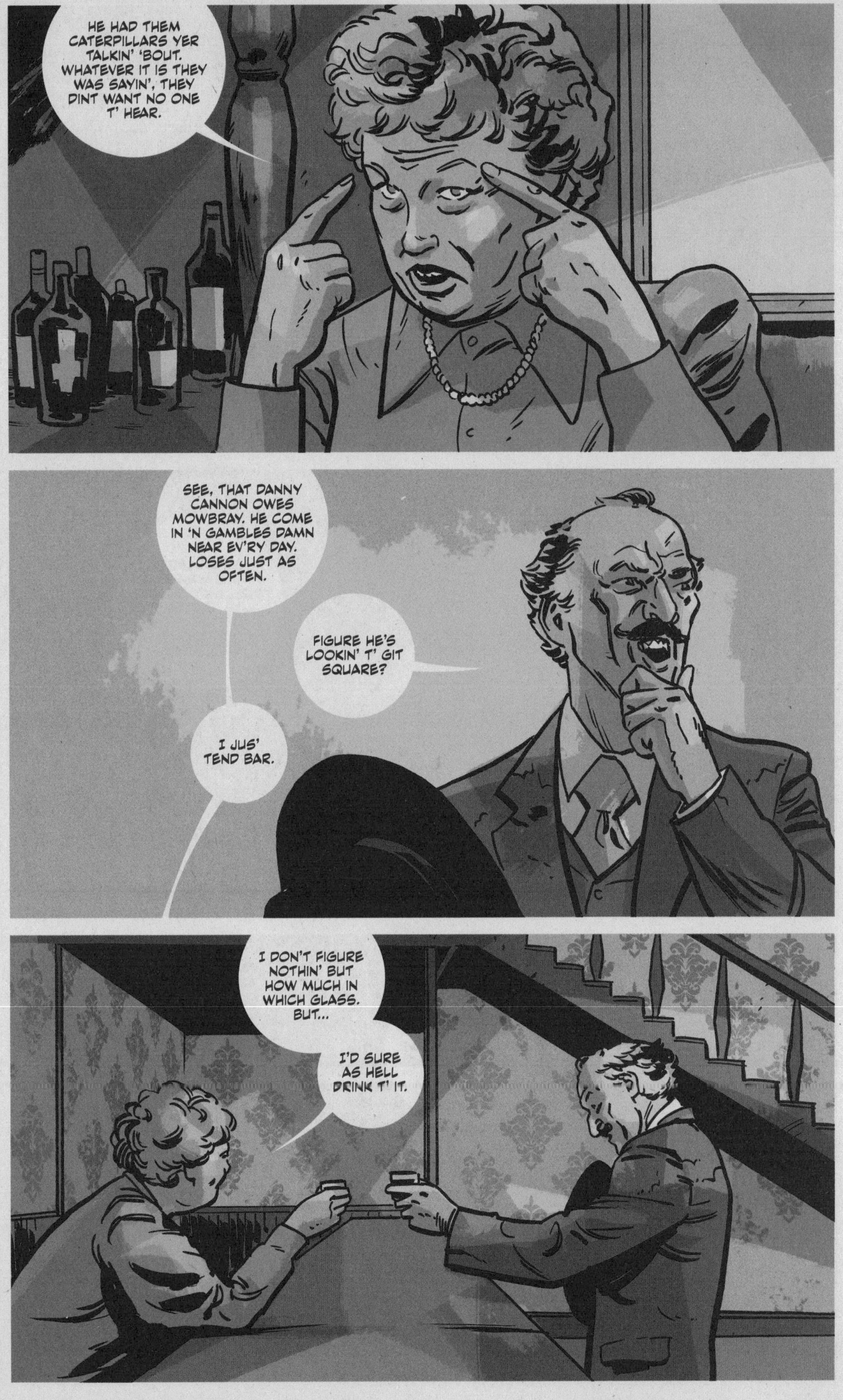
HE HAD THEM CATERPILLARS YER TALKIN' 'BOUT. WHATEVER IT IS THEY WAS SAYIN', THEY DINT WANT NO ONE T' HEAR.
SEE, THAT DANNY CANNON OWES MOWBRAY. HE COME IN 'N GAMBLES DAMN NEAR EV'RY DAY. LOSES JUST AS OFTEN.
FIGURE HE'S LOOKIN' T' GIT SQUARE?
I JUS' TEND BAR.
I DON'T FIGURE NOTHIN' BUT HOW MUCH IN WHICH GLASS. BUT...
I'D SURE AS HELL DRINK T' IT.

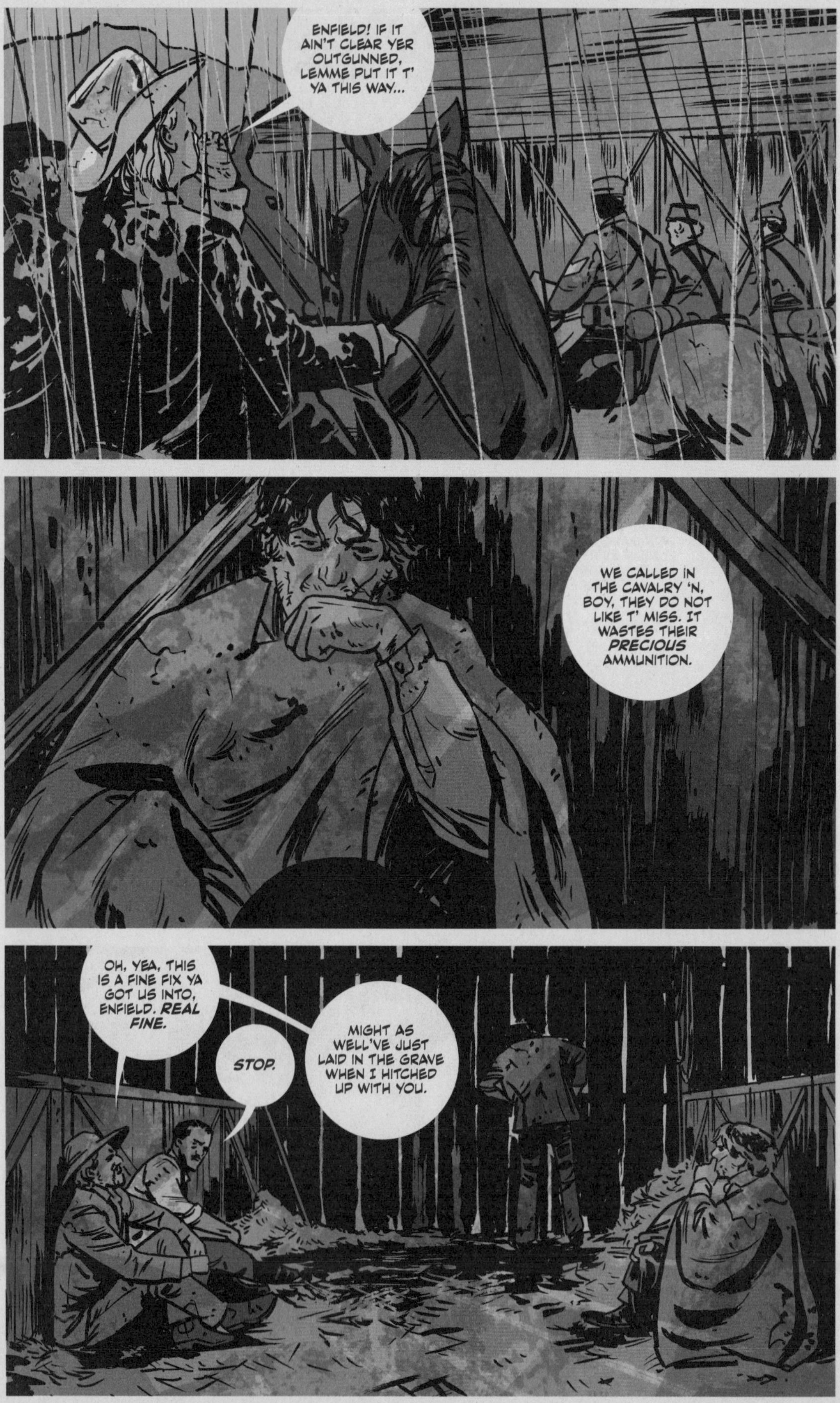
ENFIELD! IF IT AIN'T CLEAR YER OUTGUNNED, LEMME PUT IT T' YA THIS WAY...
WE CALLED IN THE CAVALRY 'N, BOY, THEY DO NOT LIKE T' MISS. IT WASTES THEIR *PRECIOUS* AMMUNITION.
OH, YEA, THIS IS A FINE FIX YA GOT US INTO, ENFIELD. *REAL FINE.*
MIGHT AS WELL'VE JUST LAID IN THE GRAVE WHEN I HITCHED UP WITH YOU.
STOP.

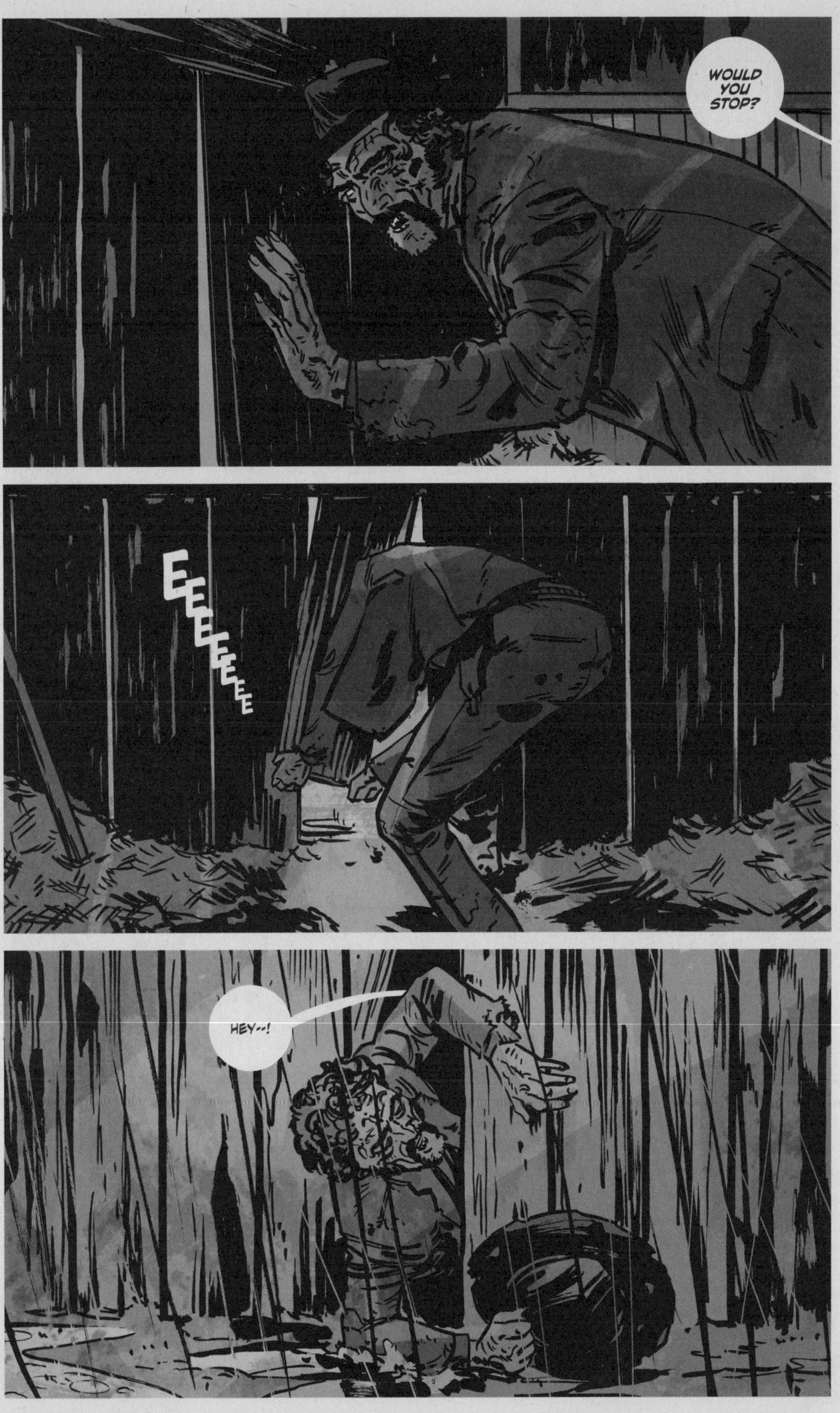
WOULD YOU STOP?
EEEEEEEE
HEY--!

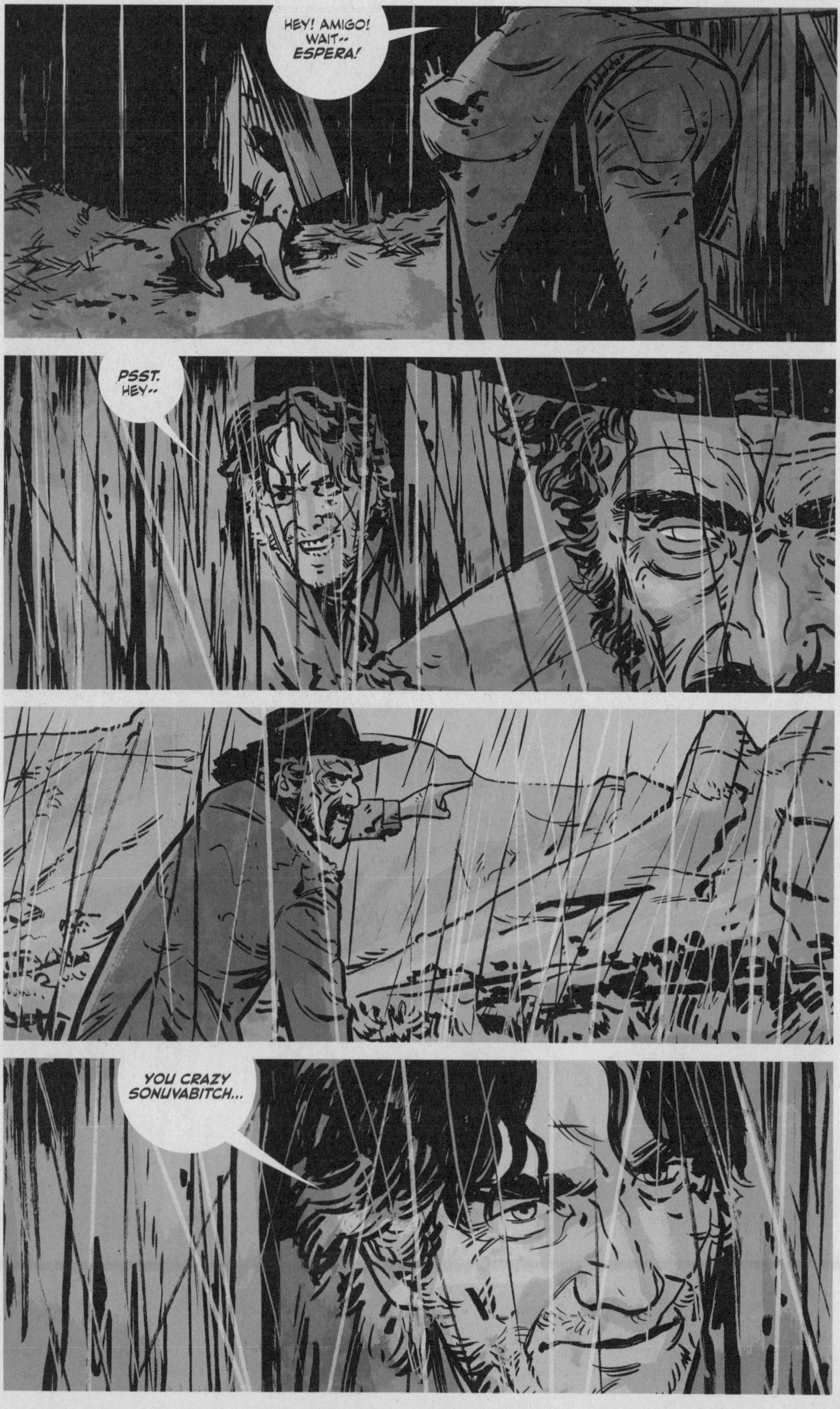
HEY! AMIGO! WAIT-- ESPERA!
PSST. HEY--
YOU CRAZY SONUVABITCH...

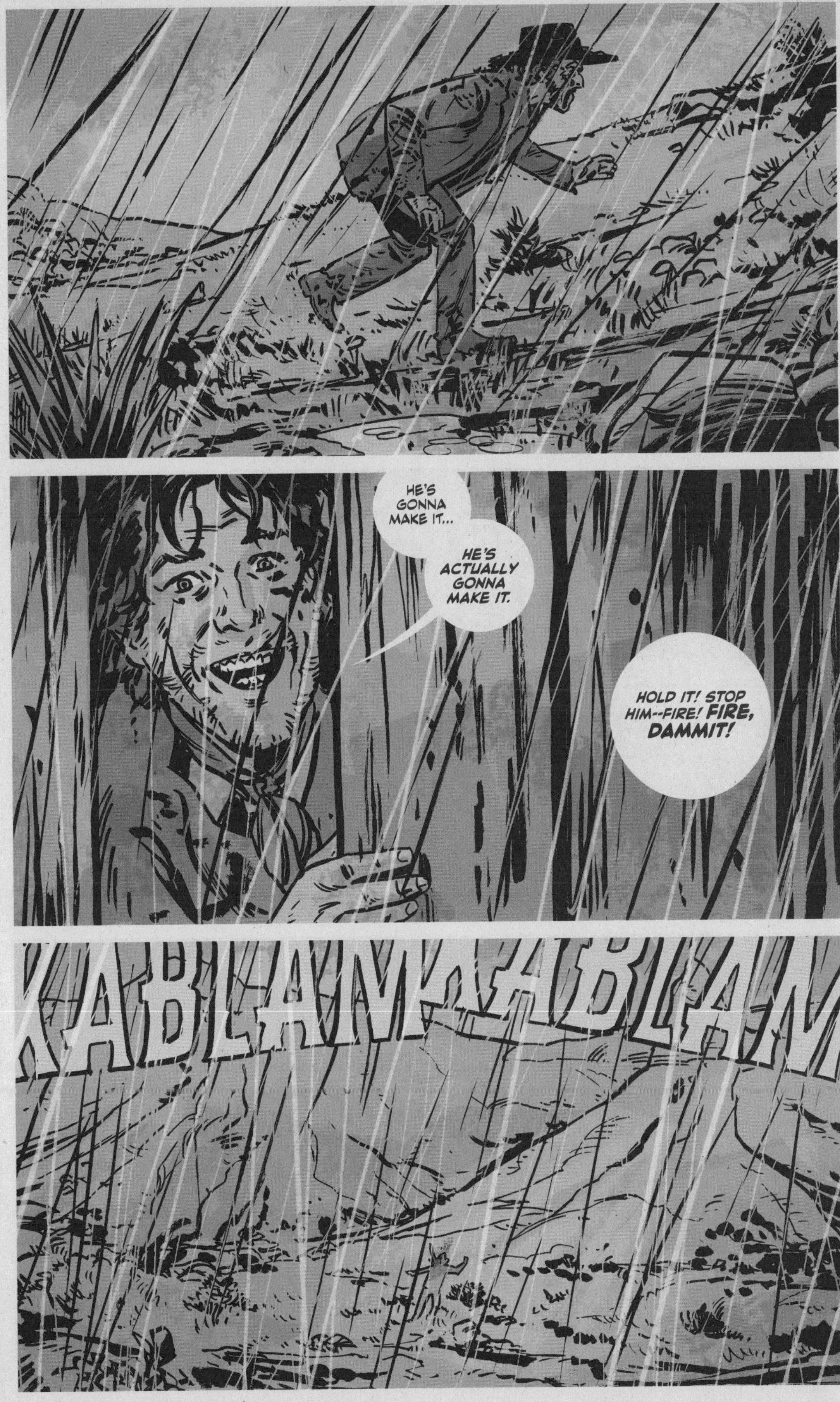
HE'S GONNA MAKE IT...
HE'S ACTUALLY GONNA MAKE IT.
HOLD IT! STOP HIM--FIRE! FIRE, DAMMIT!
KABLAM KABLAM

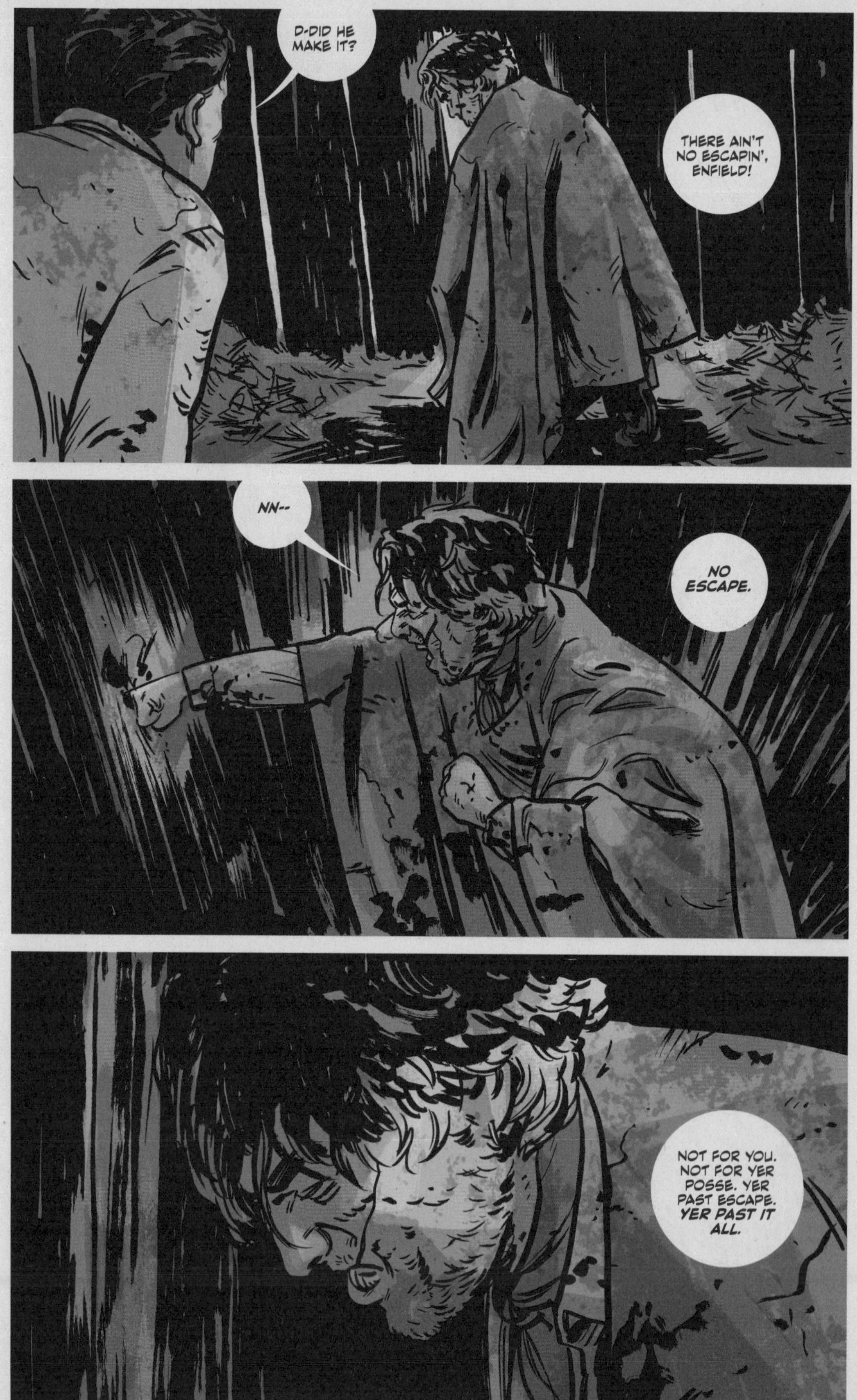
D-DID HE MAKE IT?
THERE AIN'T NO ESCAPIN', ENFIELD!
NN--
NO ESCAPE.
NOT FOR YOU. NOT FOR YER POSSE. YER PAST ESCAPE. YER PAST IT ALL.

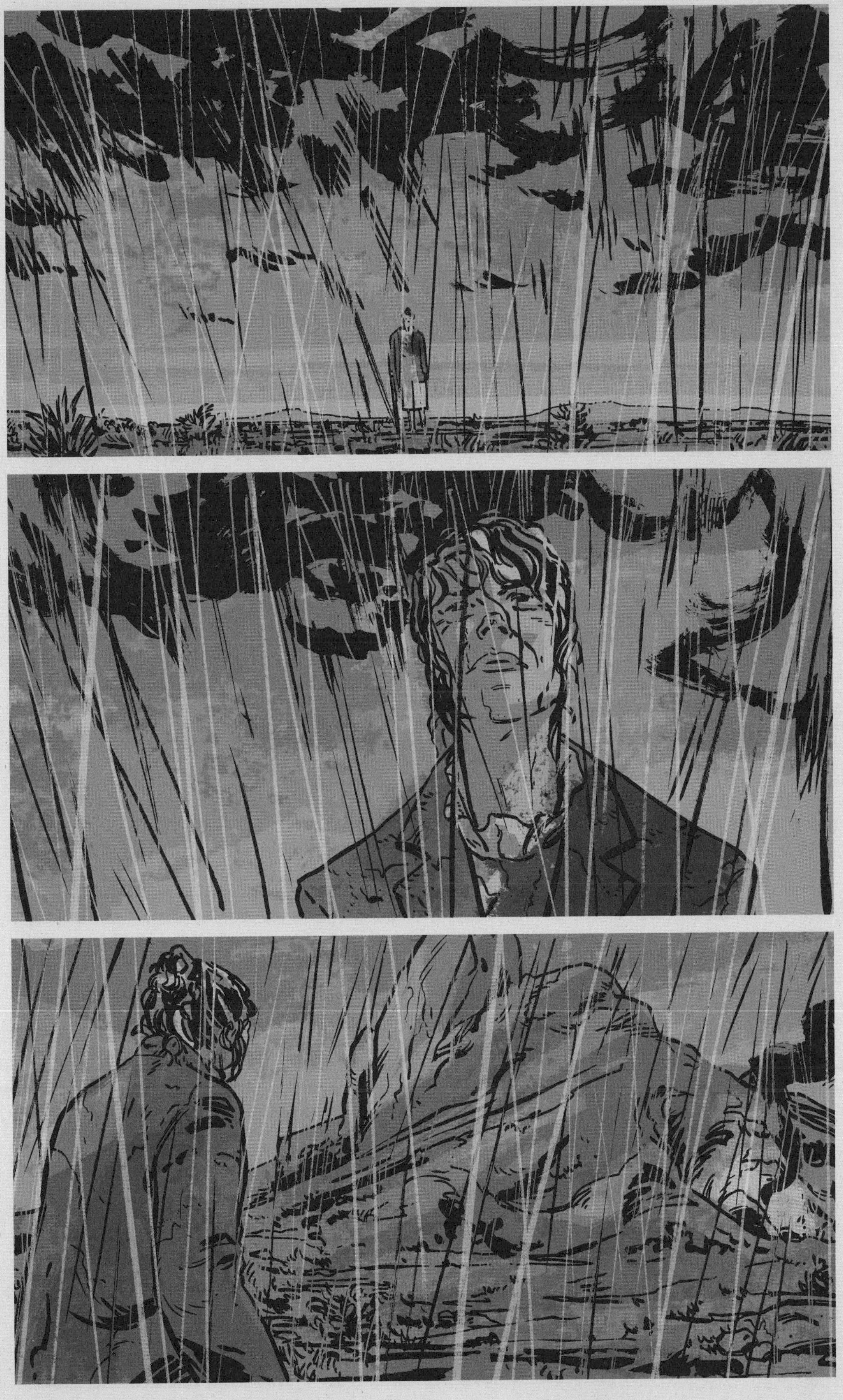

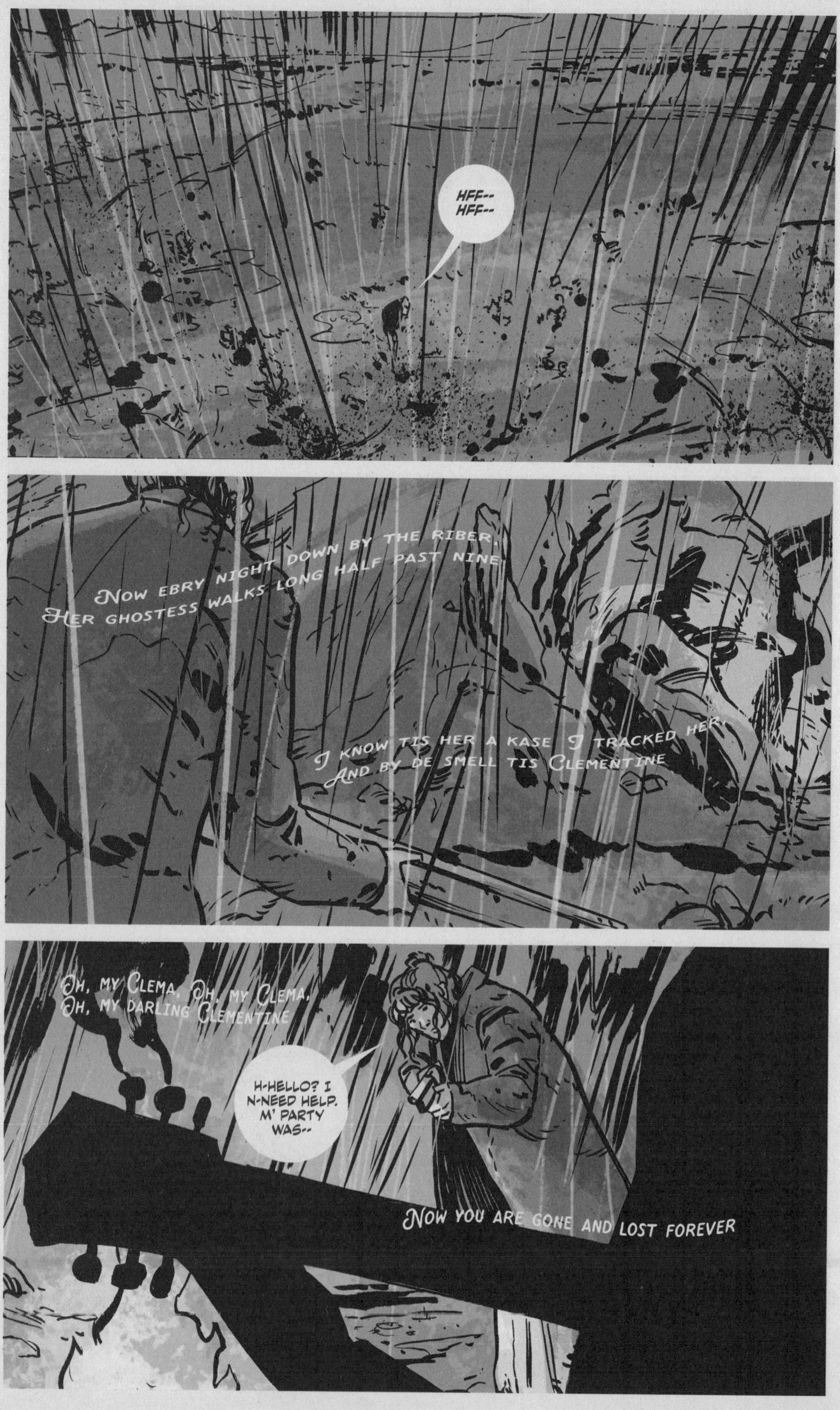

HFF-- HFF--
Now ebry night down by the riber, Her ghostess walks long half past nine.
I know tis her a kase I tracked her, And by de smell tis Clementine
Oh, my Clema, Oh, my Clema, Oh, my darling Clementine
H-HELLO? I N-NEED HELP. M' PARTY WAS--
Now you are gone and lost forever

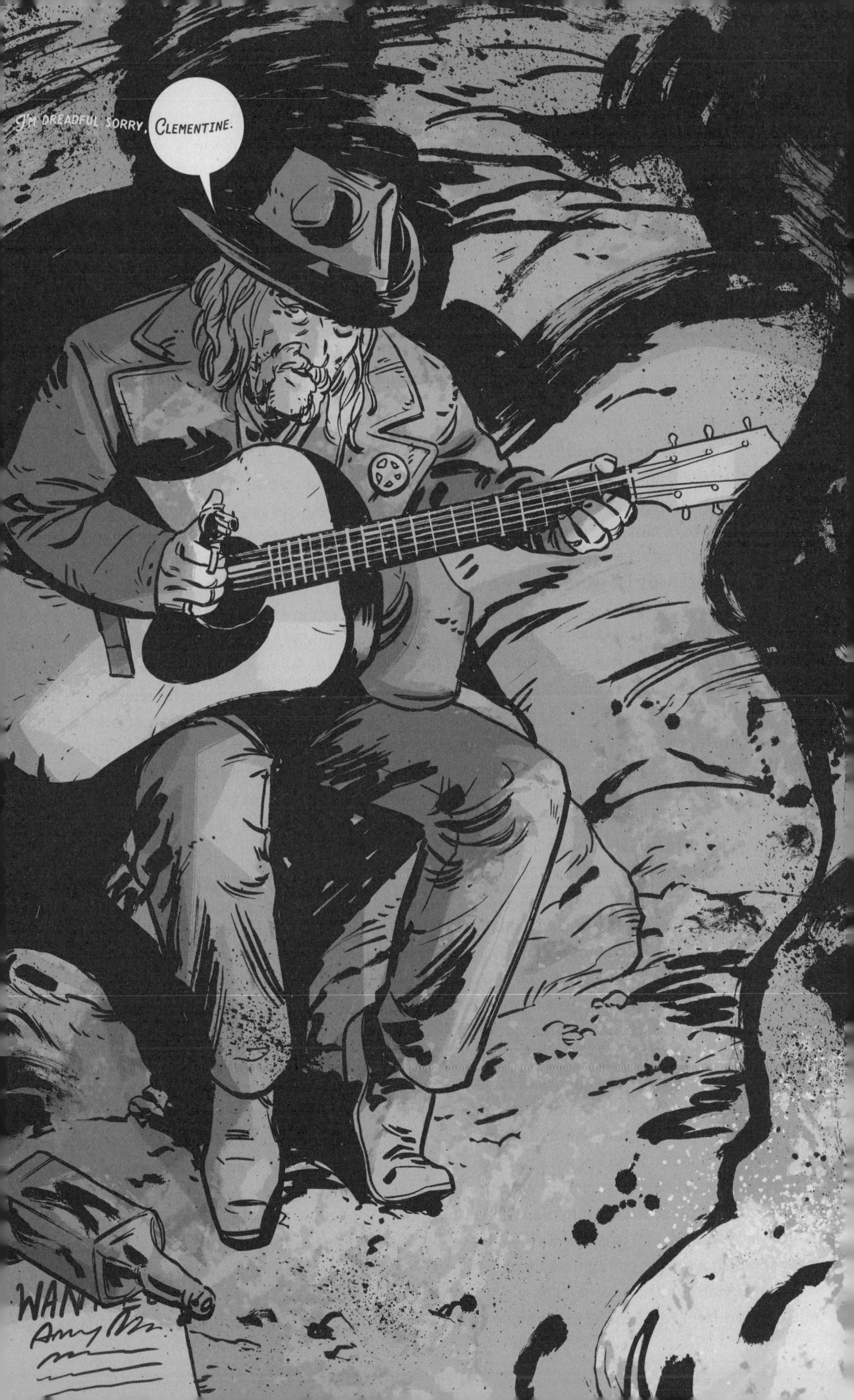
I'M DREADFUL SORRY, CLEMENTINE.

THE ENFIELD GANG MASSACRE

cont'd.

"I saw it as my duty to rid this county of these filthy souls. Men, women, or children; I saw no difference, nor will I. I believe, in fact, that it has been my purpose in this life to protect this county from the poison I believe these individuals bring with them in their very blood. By the grace of God, I shall persevere."

These are the words of John Mowbray, written in his private journal some time after The Enfield Gang Massacre took place. He does not specifically mention the massacre in this line, though it is implied. However, in the next paragraph, he goes into more detail on something only touched upon, in my research, in the journal of L.Q. West. "Despite the devious nature of such action," Mowbray writes, "I had colluded with individuals to ensure that the stain of Enfield and his evergrowing party of savages should be wiped clean from the county as if by the Hand of God Himself. I did not, nor could not, reveal my intentions to Captain Ely, the stalwart Texas Ranger who led the charge against Enfield, though I suspect he may have known more than his stolid demeanor let on.

"I had set the pieces in motion, and in so doing, I had begun the work that was for so long needed in this newborn county. But I could take no chance that the Enfield stain should evade the exacting Hand of Justice. I had known three gunfighters from my proprietary association with the High Water Saloon, an establishment that I have long thought a necessary evil to continue my true work at my shop. These three gunfighters I had sent east to Reginald Halsey's Outpost, a trading post some miles distant from Fort Lehane in Ambrose County.

They were instructed to wait four days for the appearance of any members of the Enfield Gang that might seek to escape and to summarily cut them down. I was informed later that they had completed their task quickly and well, though two had lost their lives in the ensuing chaos. One had departed earlier over some petty squabble with his partners and returned later with a gift, alone."

When I brought these journals to the attention of Nancy Gibbons, she was astonished. How these journals had been forgotten and buried in the county's archives remains a mystery, but there they were, waiting to be discovered. It is almost as if the ghost of John Mowbray were daring me or some other intrepid historian to find him out. Reading through his published journals, you are introduced to a clean-cut individual; a God-fearing man who fought for Truth, Justice, and the Ambrose Countian Way. But revealed in these private secondary journals is a man with a devious and sick mind. A man who saw his fellow citizens as pawns to be played rather than as individuals, who saw the county as his. He claimed to believe he was doing God's will, but I truly believe that he thought he was God in some strange, deluded way.

"This is a bombshell," Nancy Gibbons told me. "My hope is that we take this information and move toward a more inclusive future, one where we embrace the hard truths about our county."

We talked about the history of Ambrose County as having "sharp teeth." While this might seem to be a colorful metaphor, I do not think it is far off. We had both grown up in this county. We had both been brought up with its history. We had both loved its history, hell, it drove us both to our respective occupations. While we might still love the place we call home, and its history, we must acknowledge that there is a dark side to these things. Knowing and acknowledging it, I think that we can absolve the sins of this county and move toward the future that Ms. Gibbons imagines. But it will take time. I am sure that, once this article is released (or unleashed, depending on your perspective), there will be pushback. In fact, I am sure that there will be claims that the journal I have discovered was a fraud and that our founding father, John Mowbray, is innocent of these charges and I have been trying to sully his good name for a boost in sales.

To that, I bring forward corroborating evidence, written in the journal of L.Q. West. If you look through all readily available accounting of The Enfield Gang Massacre, you will find no mention of Reginald Halsey or his outpost. You will find no mention of gunfighters hired and sent around to take care of escaping members of the Enfield Gang. In fact, it is as if this whole section of Mowbray's journal never took place, as if he had concocted a singular work of fiction within his private journals. While L.Q. West was not present at the outpost for the incident, he was privy to its aftermath.

West writes that a single rider, a rancher on his way elsewhere, rode into town, with news that there were bodies scattered around the trading post. Men, women, children, even horses; all dead. The rancher looked rattled, sickened. He posited that it was Indians. His news was met with a figurative shrug and a party was reluctantly sent to bury the bodies where they lay, at Ely's orders. Mowbray insisted that the bodies be left to be picked clean by buzzards. He was ignored, thankfully. But no ceremony was given to these individuals. No markers were raised. It was as if these people had never even existed. The rancher left the town and did not return. West writes that the man looked as if he had just been taken ill by a disease unknown to man. Imaginative writing for a man of West's intelligence, but he couldn't be further from the truth. The disease was not contracted by the man himself. It was witnessed by him. And the disease is what we call apathy.

We do not know precisely where Reginald Halsey's Outpost was situated but we can make an educated guess based on its proximity to the outskirts of Fort Lehane. Contemporary writings place it about ten to twelve miles east (and slightly north) of Chihuahua, the easternmost locale in Fort Lehane. Today this ten to twelve mile area is a part of Ambrose County proper, though it was not at the time, as it was unincorporated land that belonged to Halsey. Together with Nancy Gibbons and the Ambrose County Historical Society, we have asked the State of Texas to mark this location for historical preservation and excavation, so that the truth might finally come to light. I have spoken to archaeologists at the University of Texas and they have expressed their interest in just such a dig. It's only a matter of time until it comes to fruition.

I am excited by this prospect. I am nonetheless unsettled, though, to think that ten-to-twelve miles away from where I played as a child with a tin six-shooter kablamming and kapowing, mimicking the grand stories I had been told about Enfield, his cronies, and the good guys that sent them to Hell, lay the bodies of the innocent slain. It sends a cold shiver down my spine.

I had been fooled. We had all been fooled.

TO BE CONTINUED.

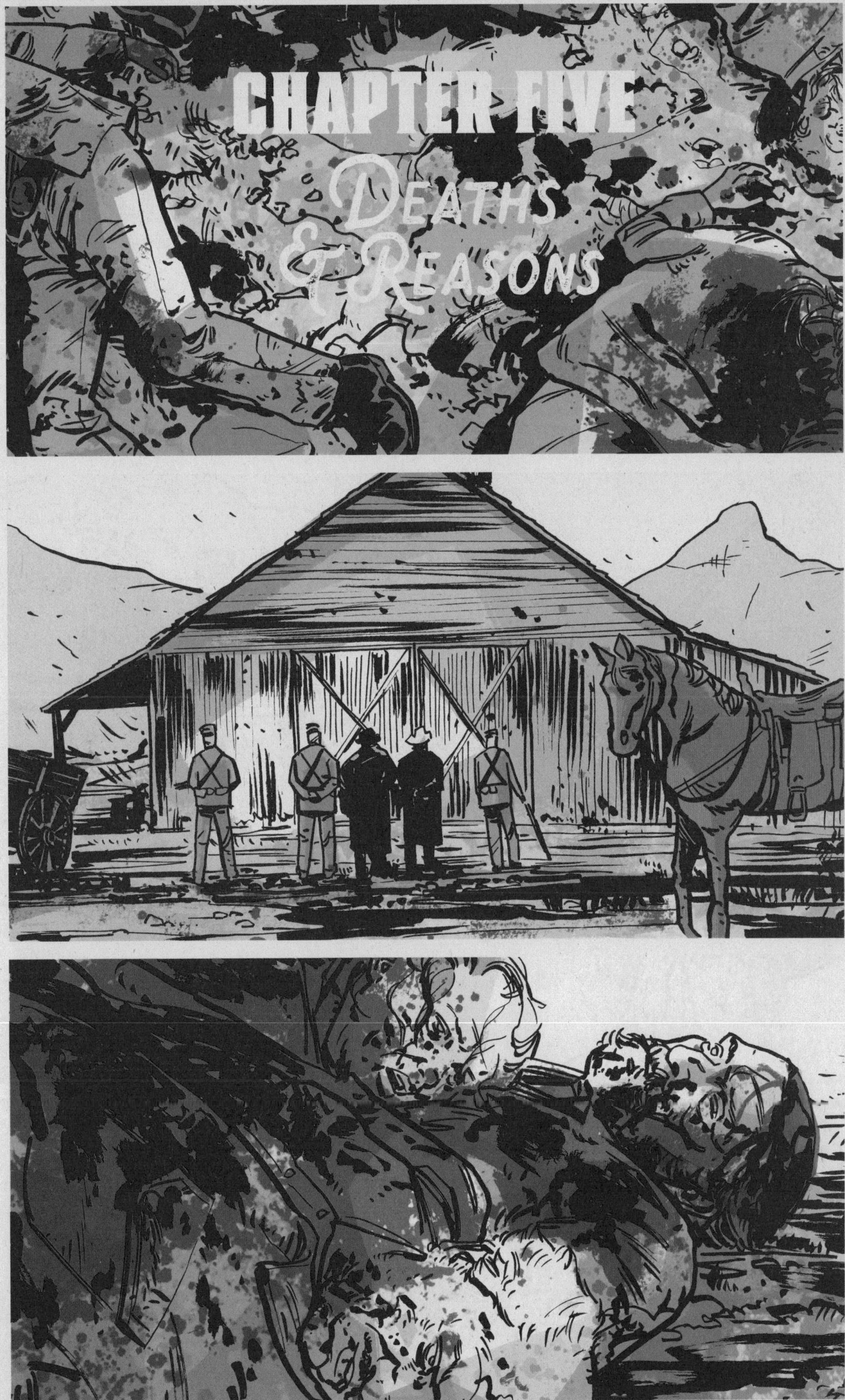
CHAPTER FIVE
DEATHS & REASONS

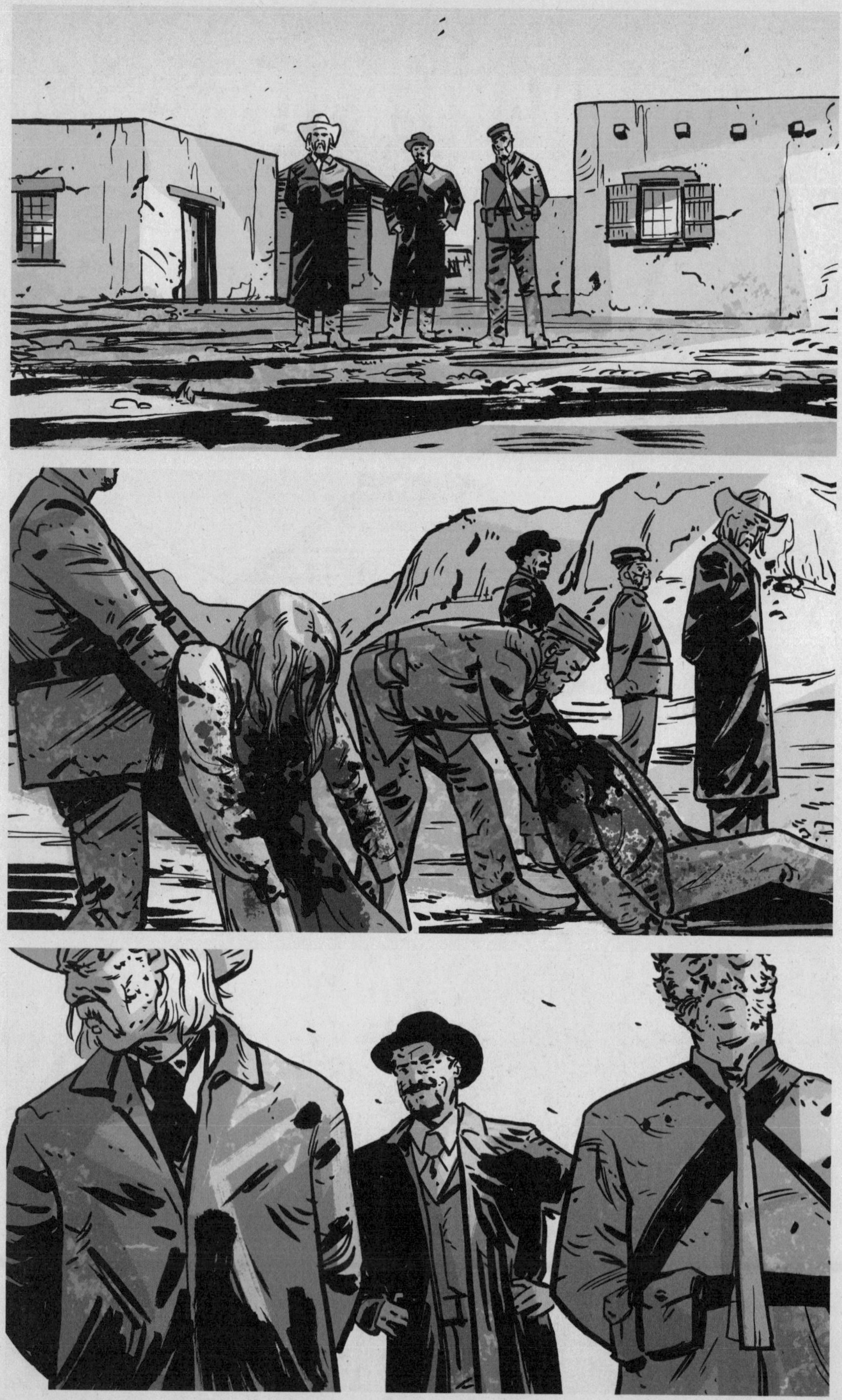

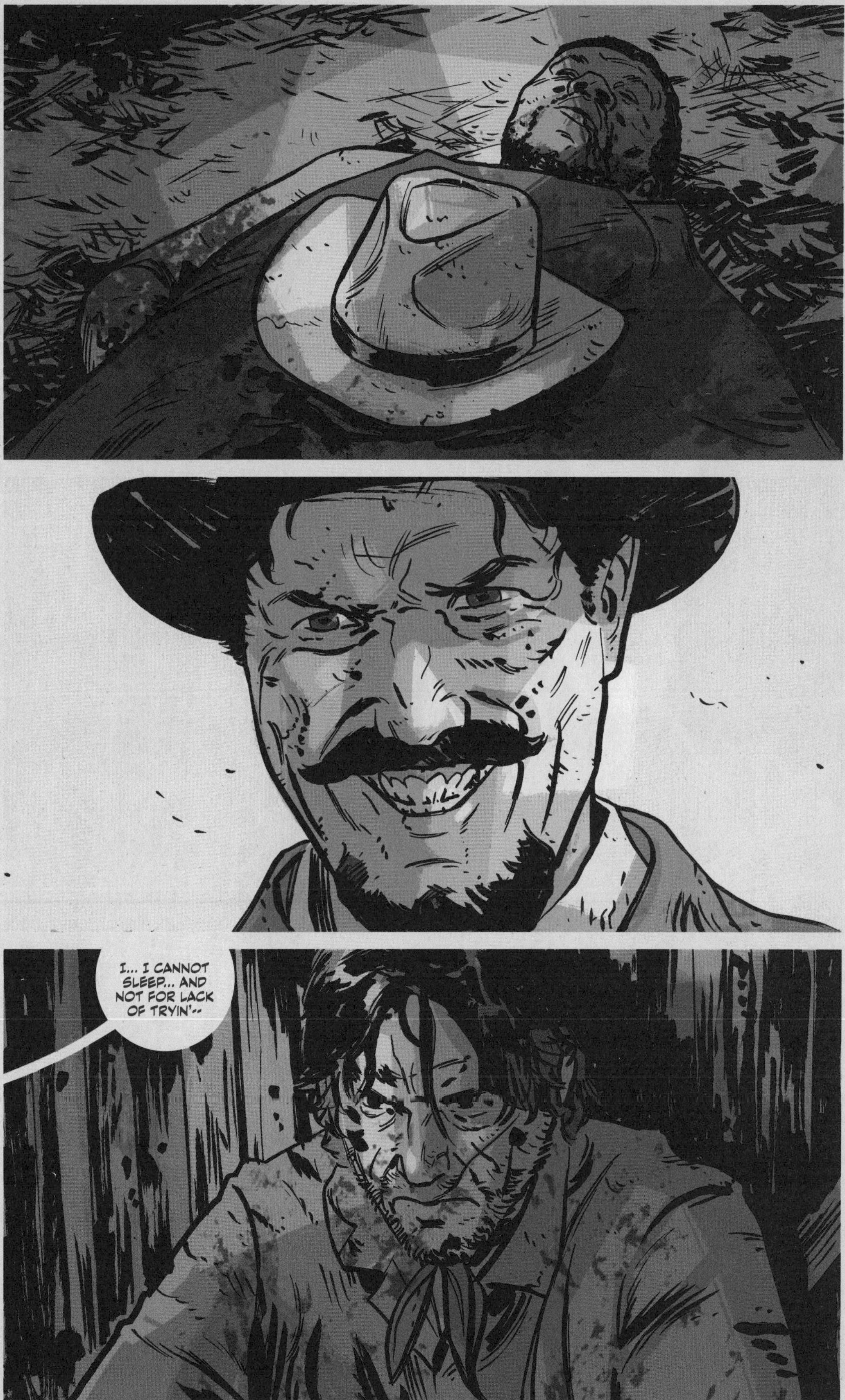
I... I CANNOT SLEEP... AND NOT FOR LACK OF TRYIN'--

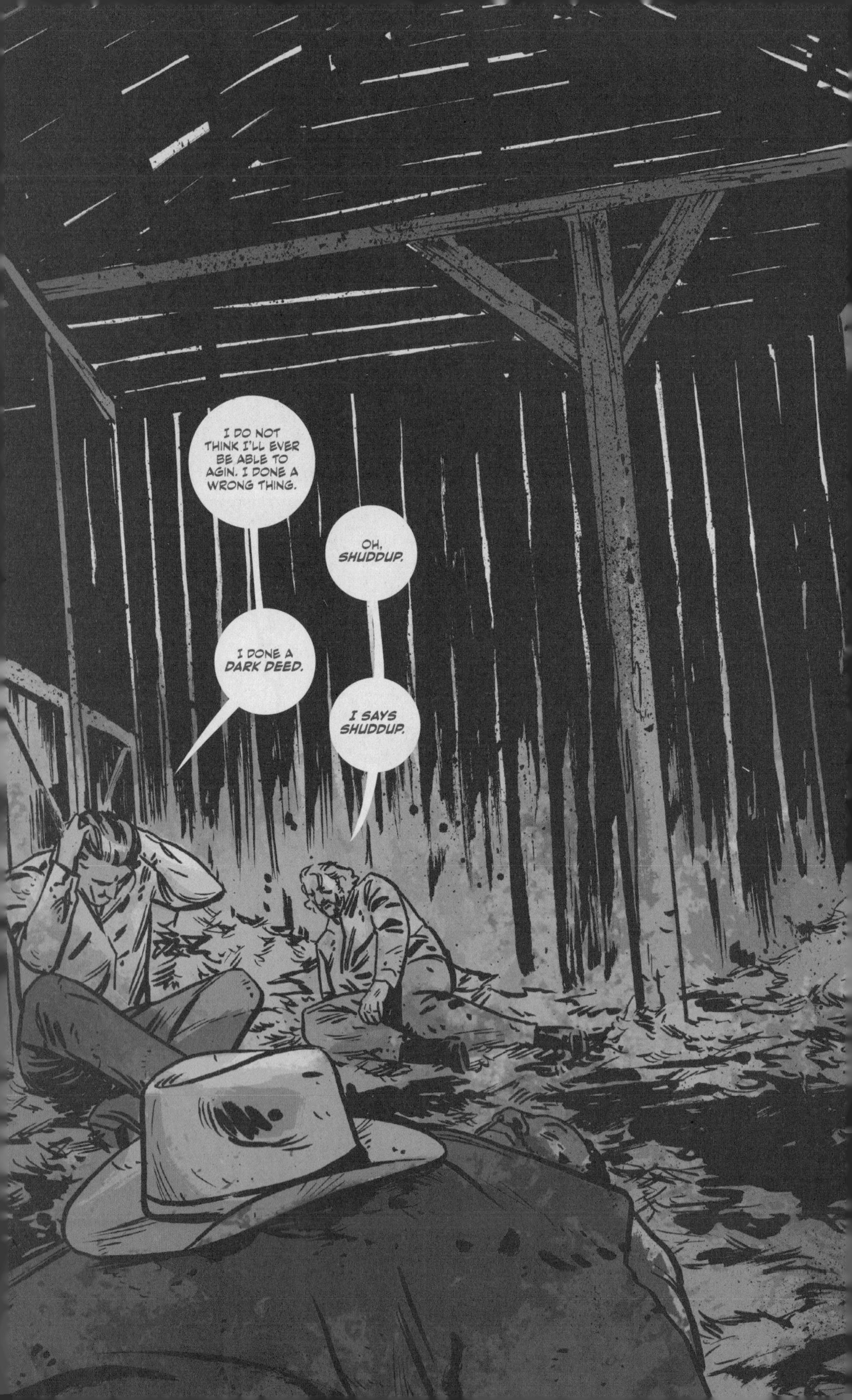
I DO NOT THINK I'LL EVER BE ABLE TO AGIN. I DONE A WRONG THING.
OH, SHUDDUP.
I DONE A DARK DEED.
I SAYS SHUDDUP.

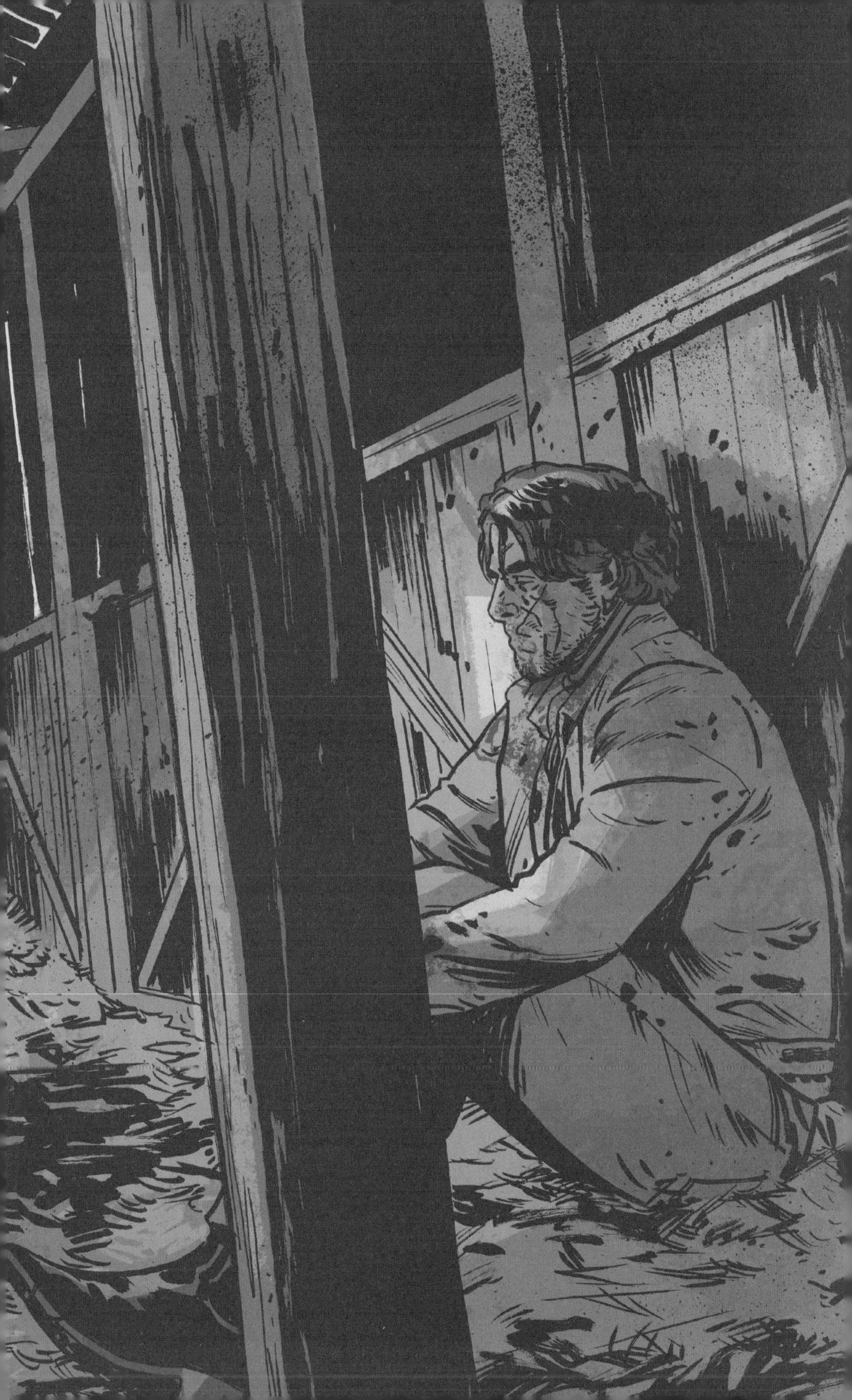

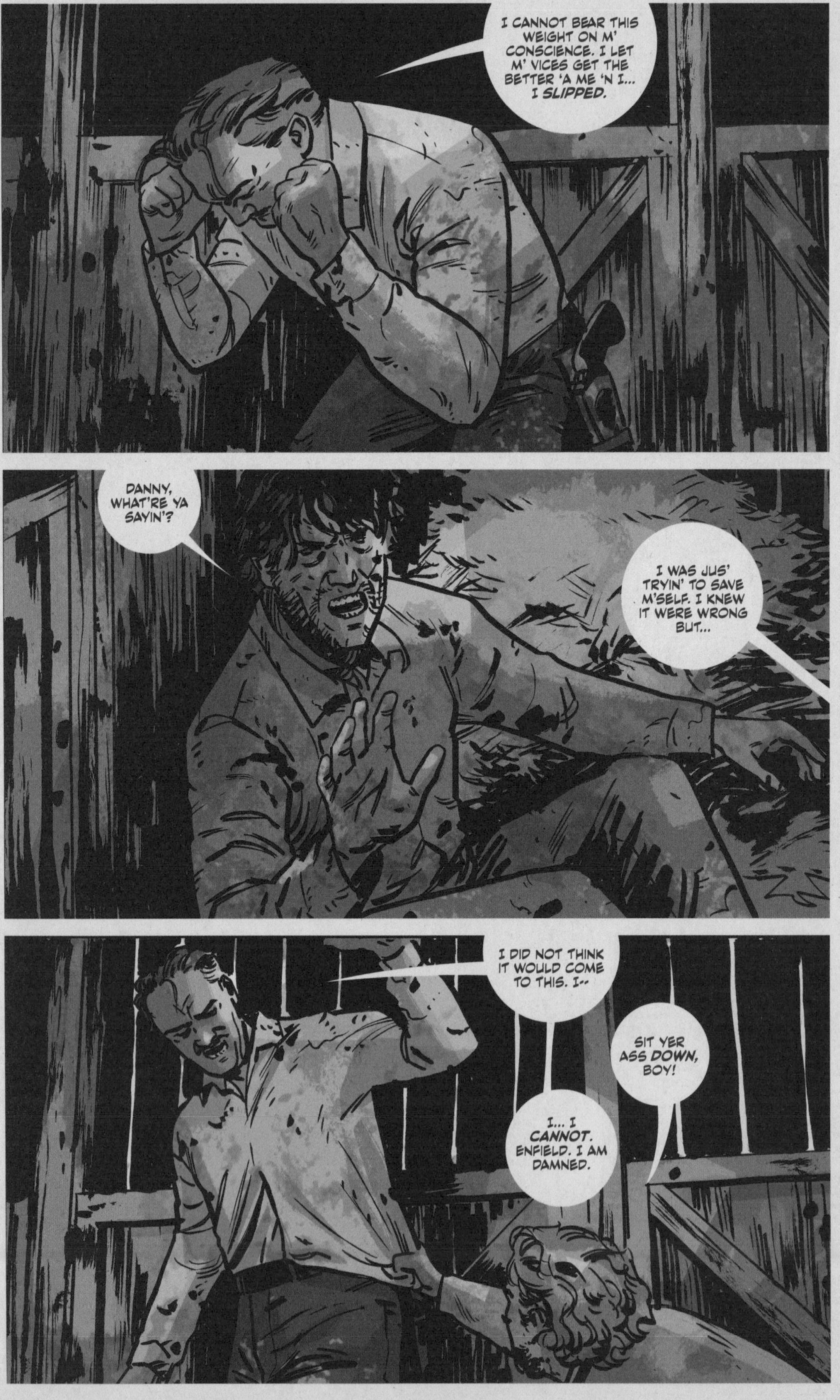
I CANNOT BEAR THIS WEIGHT ON M' CONSCIENCE. I LET M' VICES GET THE BETTER 'A ME 'N I... I SLIPPED.
DANNY, WHAT'RE YA SAYIN'?
I WAS JUS' TRYIN' TO SAVE M'SELF. I KNEW IT WERE WRONG BUT...
I DID NOT THINK IT WOULD COME TO THIS. I--
SIT YER ASS DOWN, BOY!
I... I CANNOT. ENFIELD. I AM DAMNED.

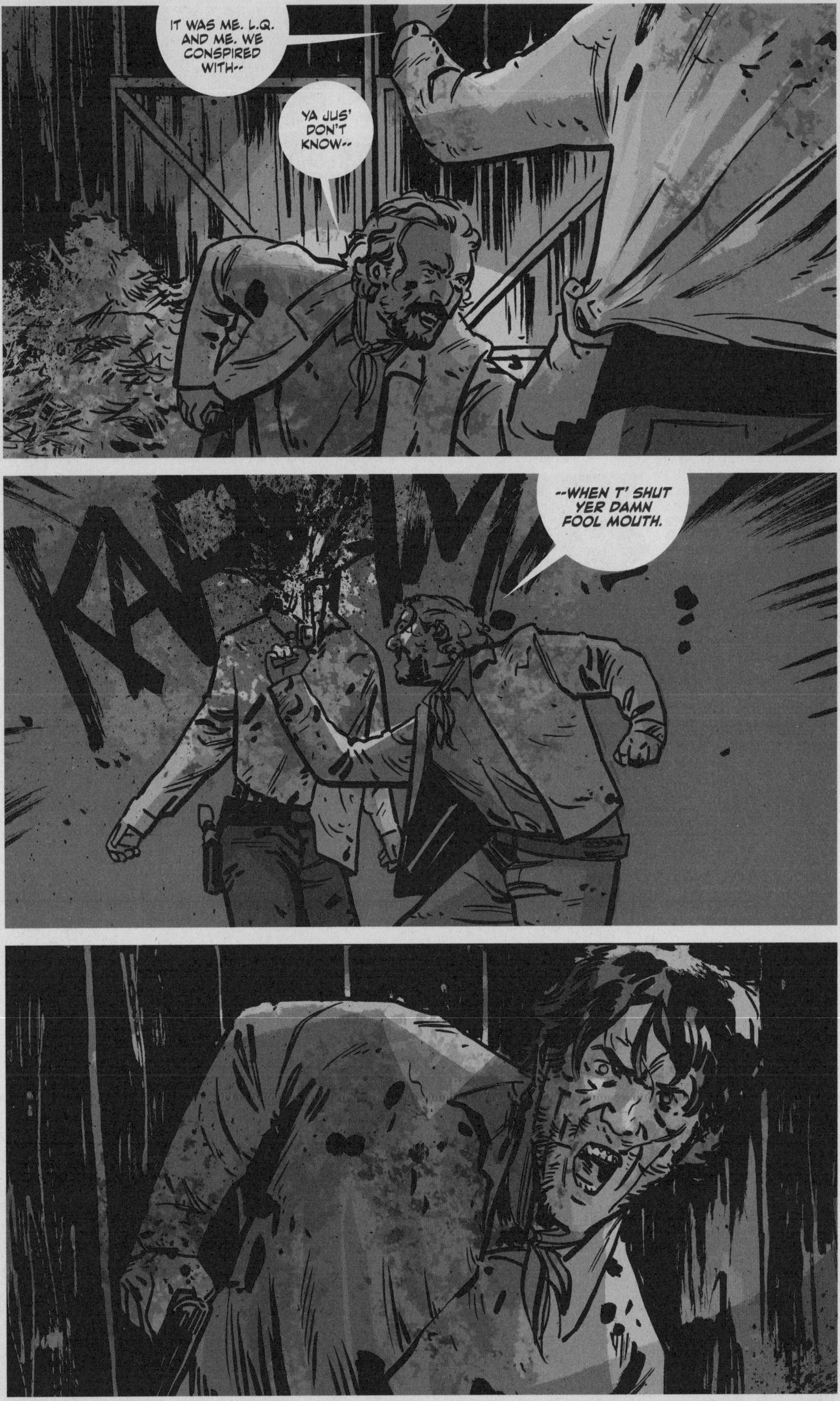
IT WAS ME. L.Q. AND ME. WE CONSPIRED WITH--
YA JUS' DON'T KNOW--
--WHEN T' SHUT YER DAMN FOOL MOUTH.

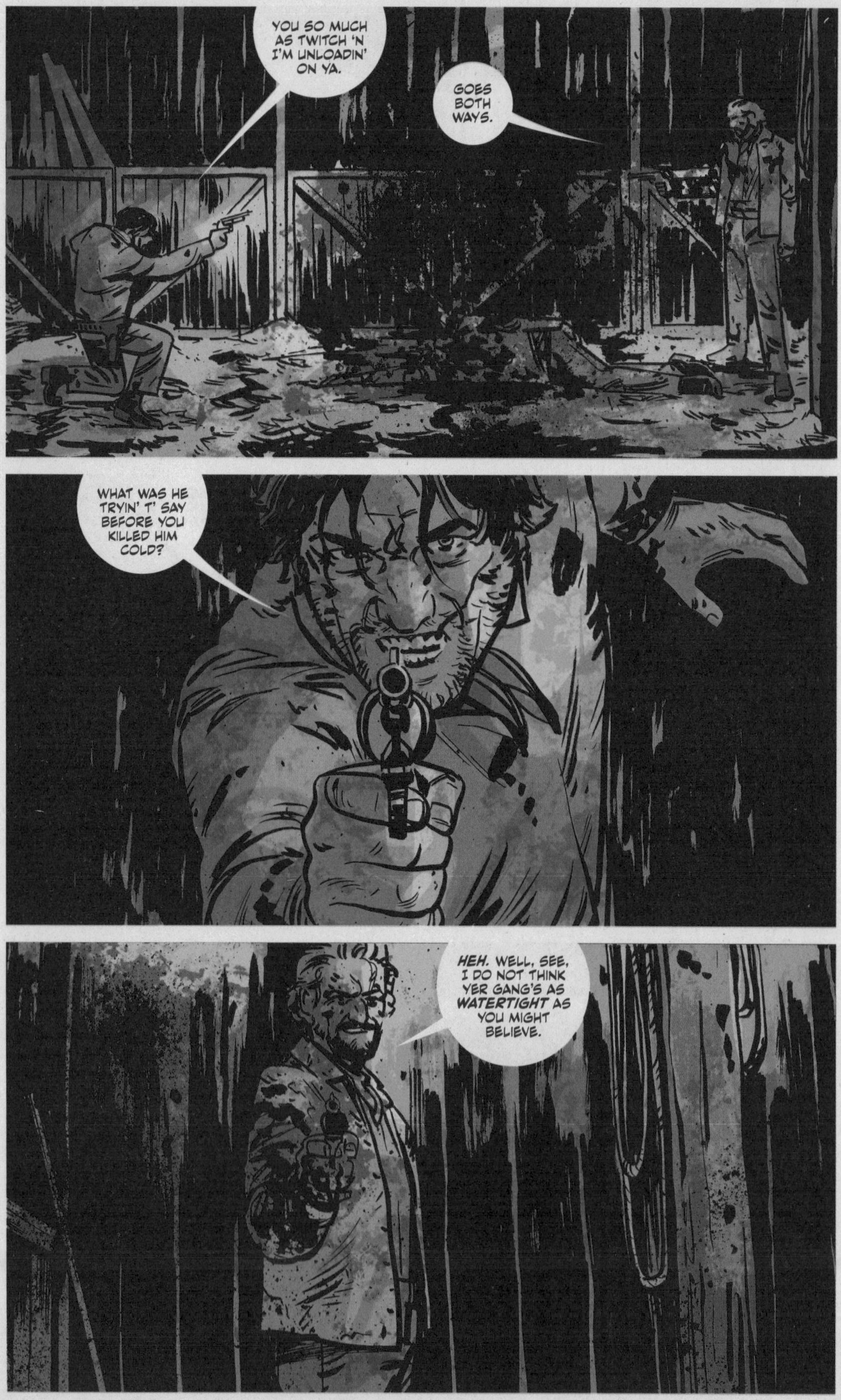
YOU SO MUCH AS TWITCH 'N I'M UNLOADIN' ON YA.
GOES BOTH WAYS.
WHAT WAS HE TRYIN' T' SAY BEFORE YOU KILLED HIM COLD?
HEH. WELL, SEE, I DO NOT THINK YER GANG'S AS WATERTIGHT AS YOU MIGHT BELIEVE.

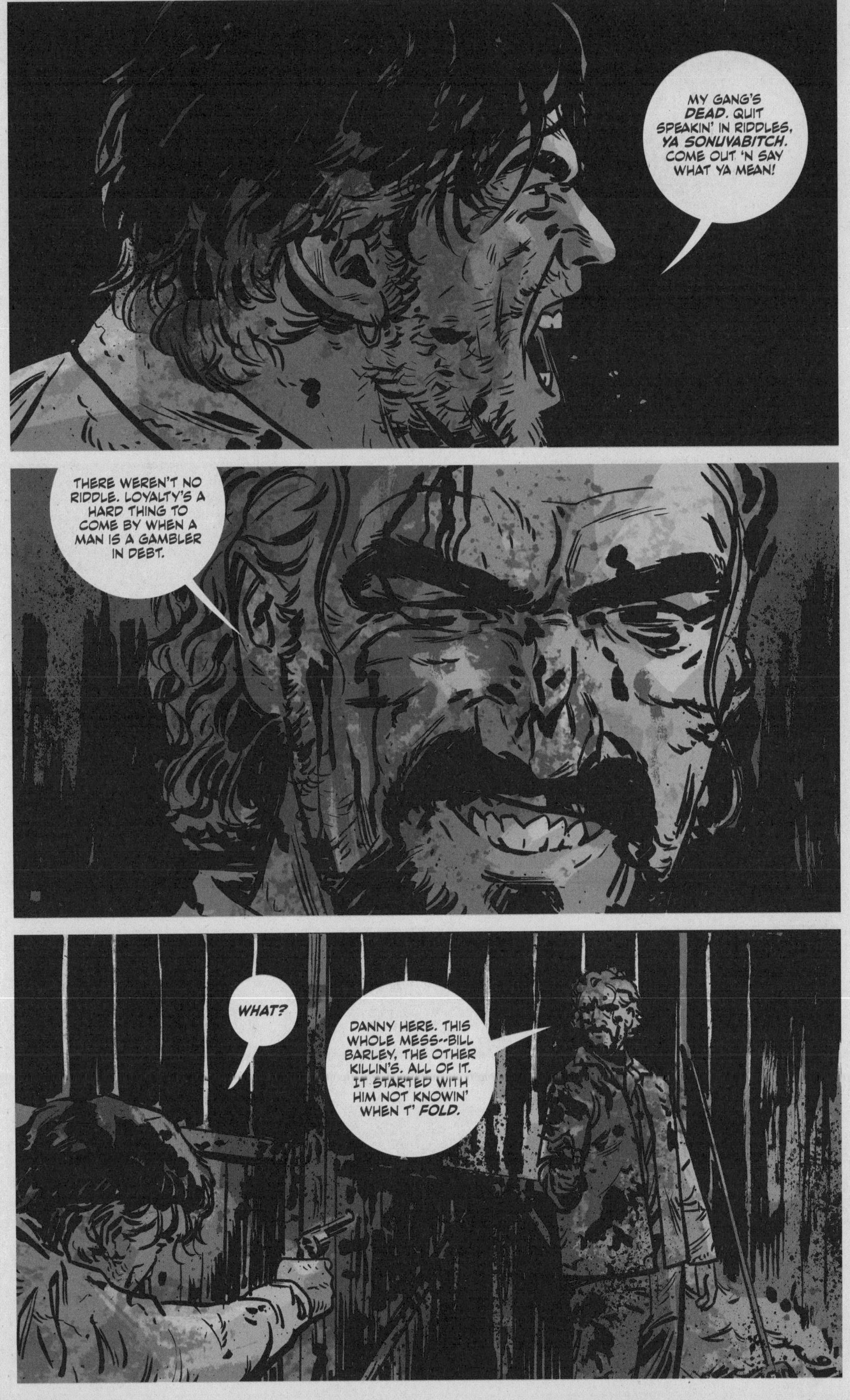
MY GANG'S DEAD. QUIT SPEAKIN' IN RIDDLES, YA SONUVABITCH. COME OUT 'N SAY WHAT YA MEAN!
THERE WEREN'T NO RIDDLE. LOYALTY'S A HARD THING TO COME BY WHEN A MAN IS A GAMBLER IN DEBT.
WHAT?
DANNY HERE. THIS WHOLE MESS--BILL BARLEY, THE OTHER KILLIN'S. ALL OF IT. IT STARTED WITH HIM NOT KNOWIN' WHEN T' FOLD.

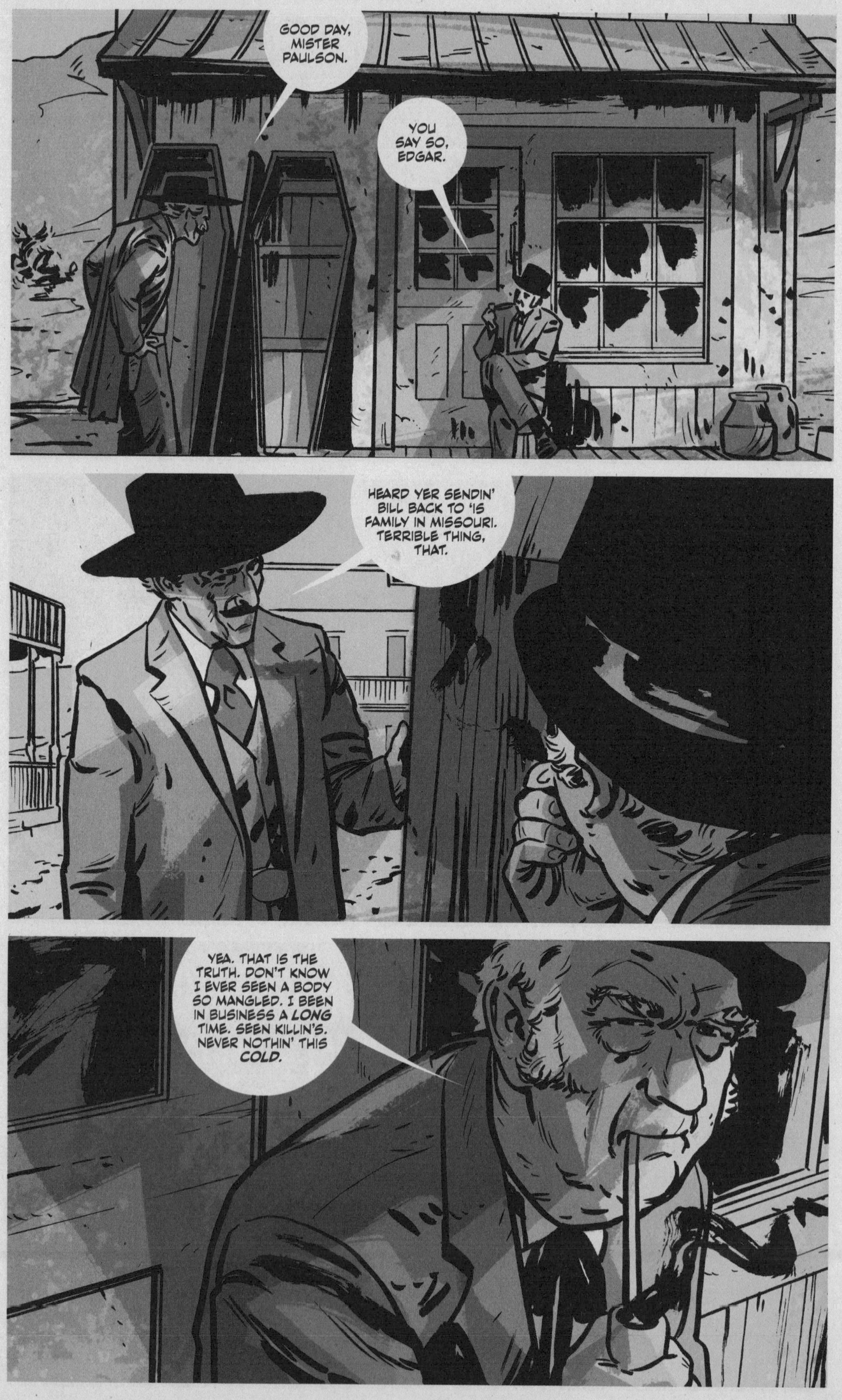
GOOD DAY, MISTER PAULSON.
YOU SAY SO, EDGAR.
HEARD YER SENDIN' BILL BACK TO 'IS FAMILY IN MISSOURI. TERRIBLE THING, THAT.
YEA. THAT IS THE TRUTH. DON'T KNOW I EVER SEEN A BODY SO MANGLED. I BEEN IN BUSINESS A *LONG* TIME. SEEN KILLIN'S. NEVER NOTHIN' THIS *COLD*.

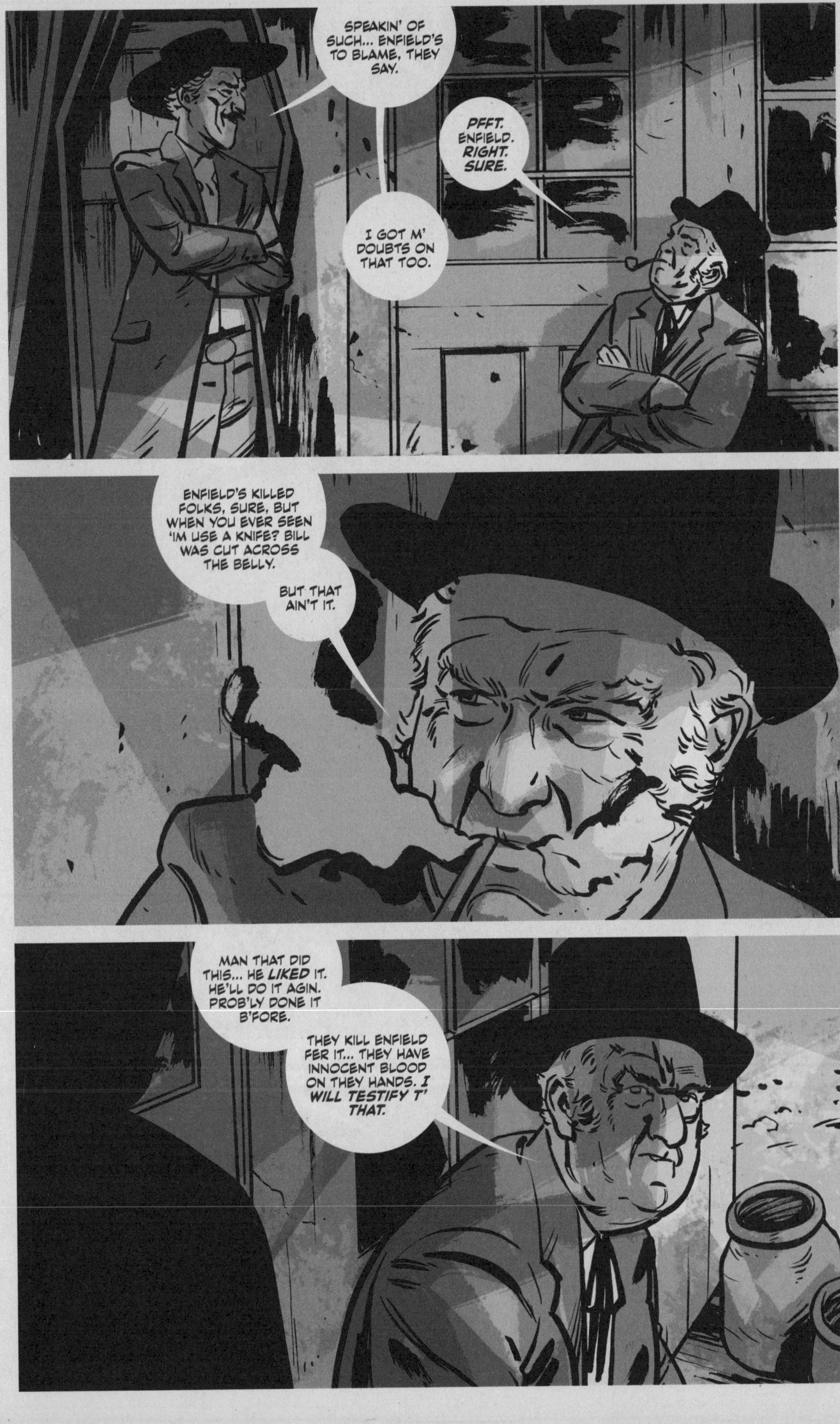
SPEAKIN' OF SUCH... ENFIELD'S TO BLAME, THEY SAY.
PFFT. ENFIELD. RIGHT. SURE.
I GOT M' DOUBTS ON THAT TOO.
ENFIELD'S KILLED FOLKS, SURE, BUT WHEN YOU EVER SEEN 'IM USE A KNIFE? BILL WAS CUT ACROSS THE BELLY.
BUT THAT AIN'T IT.
MAN THAT DID THIS... HE LIKED IT. HE'LL DO IT AGIN. PROB'LY DONE IT B'FORE.
THEY KILL ENFIELD FER IT... THEY HAVE INNOCENT BLOOD ON THEY HANDS. I WILL TESTIFY T' THAT.

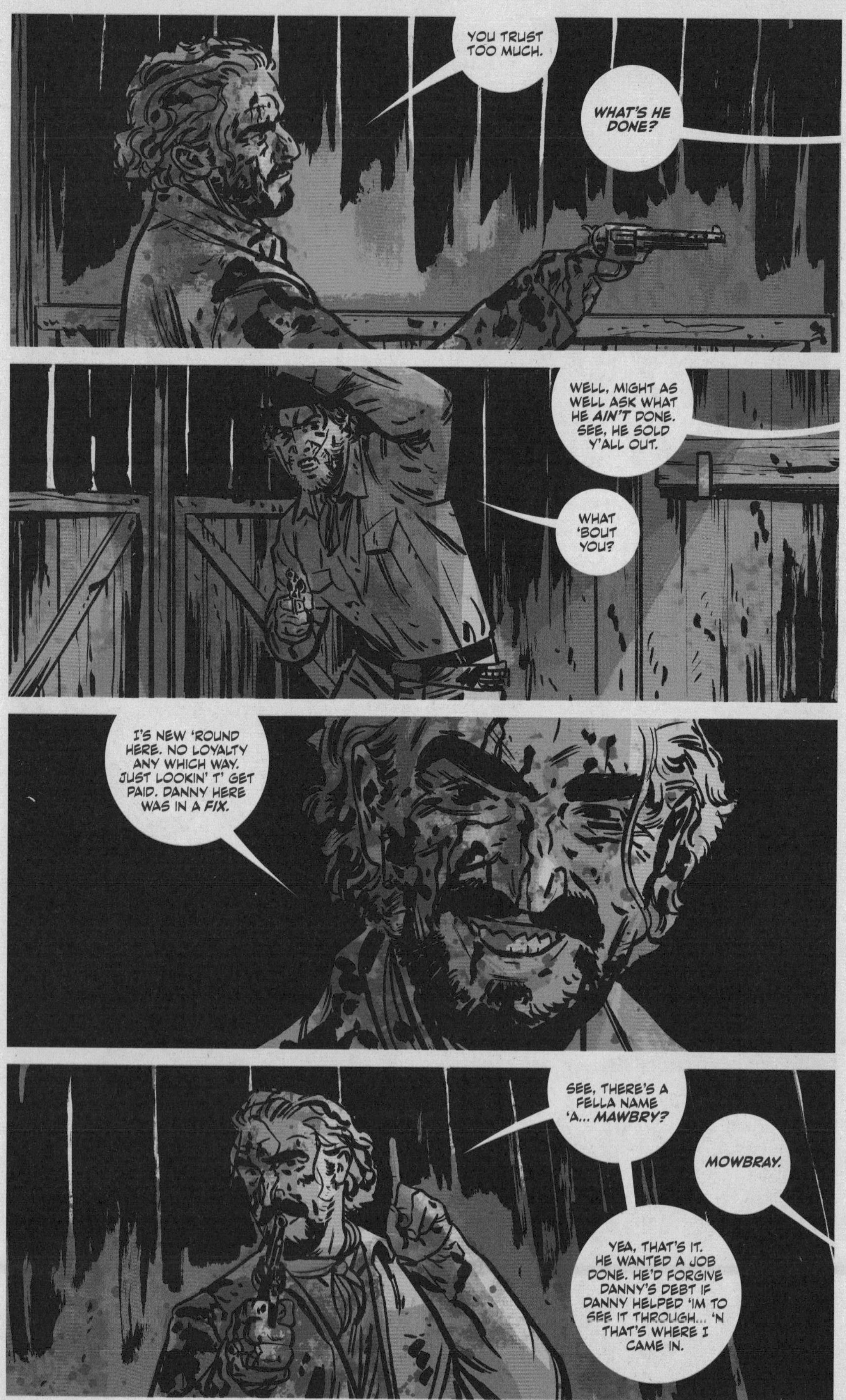
YOU TRUST TOO MUCH.
WHAT'S HE DONE?
WELL, MIGHT AS WELL ASK WHAT HE AIN'T DONE. SEE, HE SOLD Y'ALL OUT.
WHAT 'BOUT YOU?
I'S NEW 'ROUND HERE. NO LOYALTY ANY WHICH WAY. JUST LOOKIN' T' GET PAID. DANNY HERE WAS IN A FIX.
SEE, THERE'S A FELLA NAME 'A... MAWBRY?
MOWBRAY.
YEA, THAT'S IT. HE WANTED A JOB DONE. HE'D FORGIVE DANNY'S DEBT IF DANNY HELPED 'IM TO SEE IT THROUGH... 'N THAT'S WHERE I CAME IN.

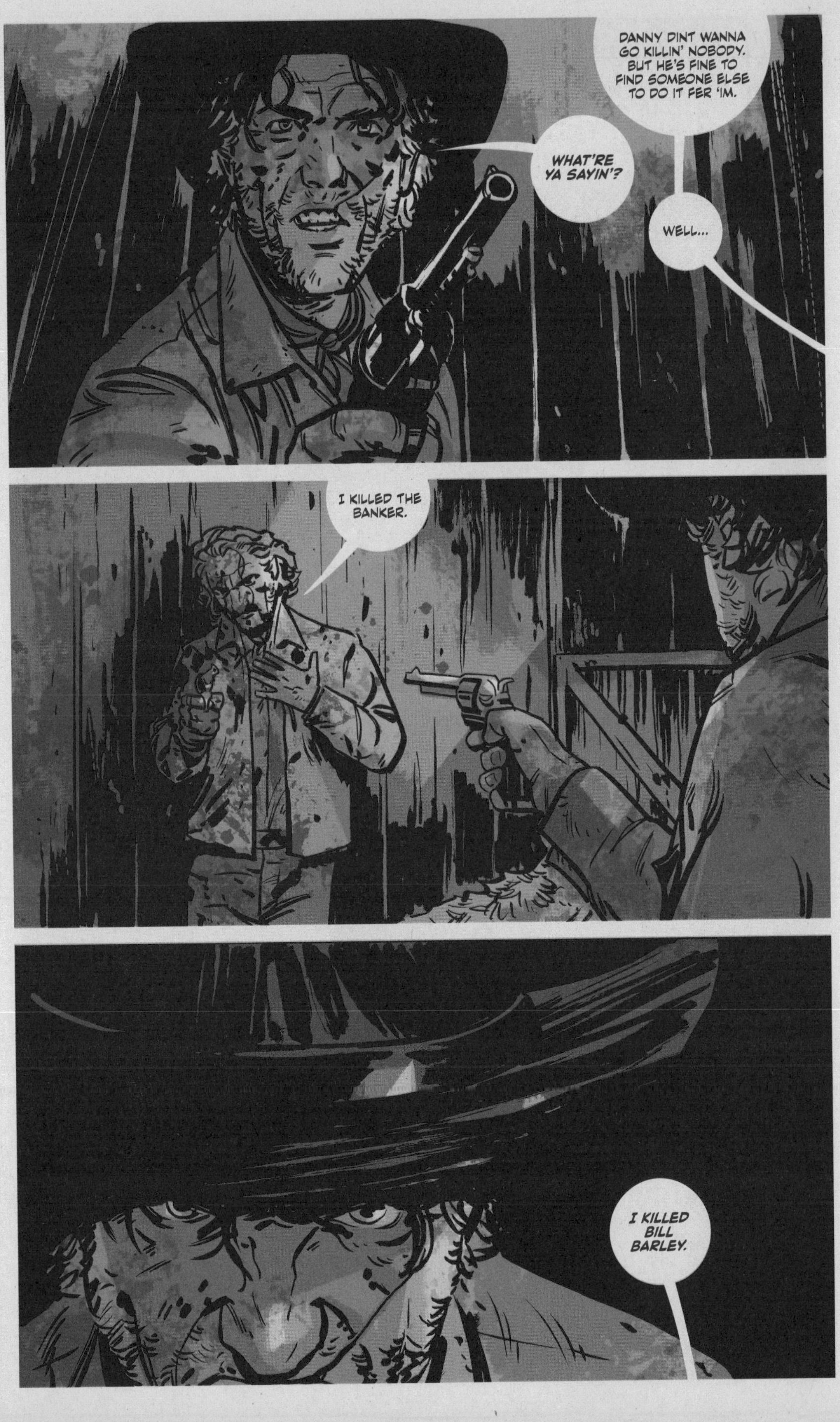
DANNY DINT WANNA GO KILLIN' NOBODY. BUT HE'S FINE TO FIND SOMEONE ELSE TO DO IT FER 'IM.
WHAT'RE YA SAYIN'?
WELL...
I KILLED THE BANKER.
I KILLED BILL BARLEY.

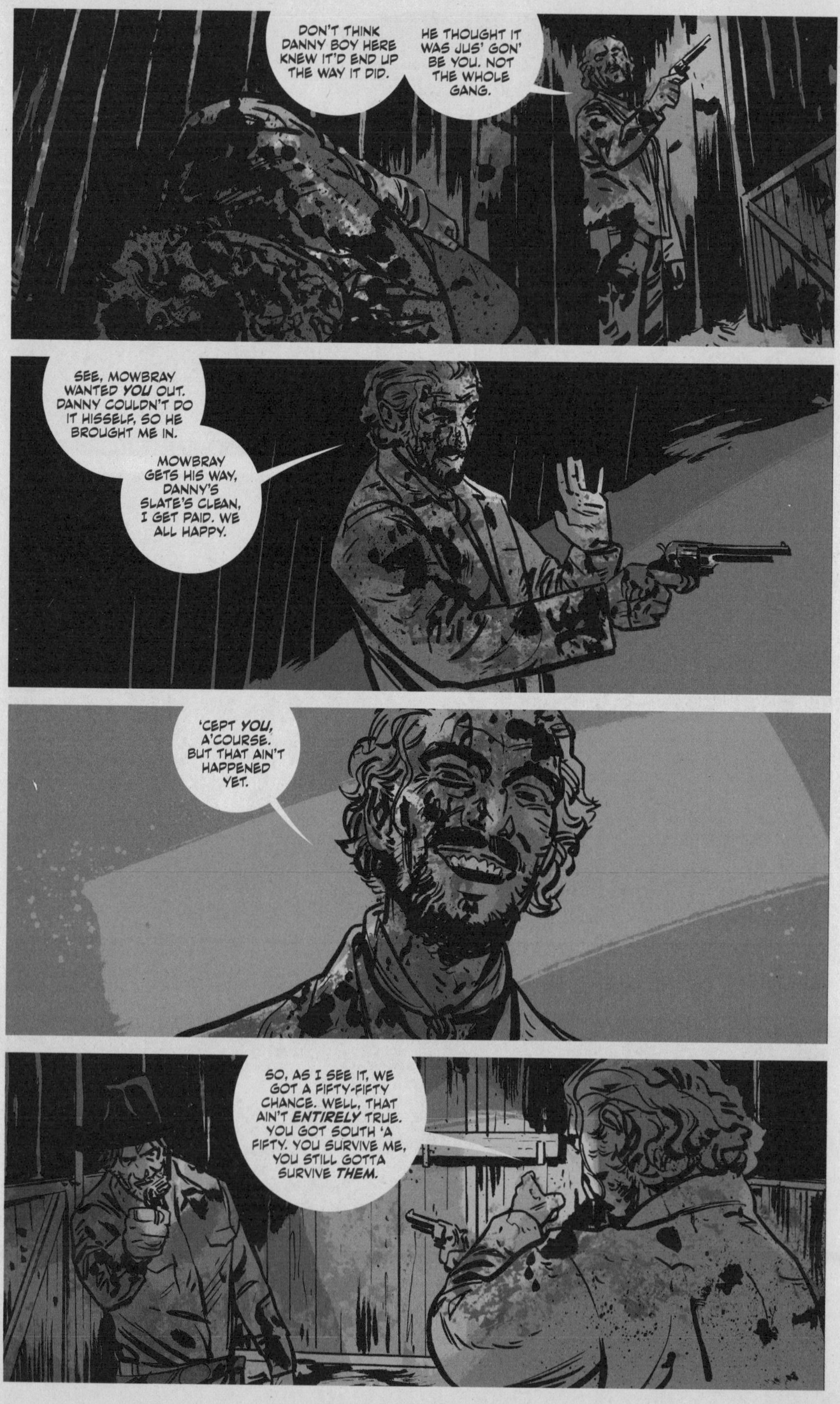
DON'T THINK DANNY BOY HERE KNEW IT'D END UP THE WAY IT DID.
HE THOUGHT IT WAS JUS' GON' BE YOU. NOT THE WHOLE GANG.
SEE, MOWBRAY WANTED *YOU* OUT. DANNY COULDN'T DO IT HISSELF, SO HE BROUGHT ME IN.
MOWBRAY GETS HIS WAY, DANNY'S SLATE'S CLEAN, I GET PAID. WE ALL HAPPY.
'CEPT *YOU*, A'COURSE. BUT THAT AIN'T HAPPENED YET.
SO, AS I SEE IT, WE GOT A FIFTY-FIFTY CHANCE. WELL, THAT AIN'T *ENTIRELY* TRUE. YOU GOT SOUTH 'A FIFTY. YOU SURVIVE ME, YOU STILL GOTTA SURVIVE *THEM*.

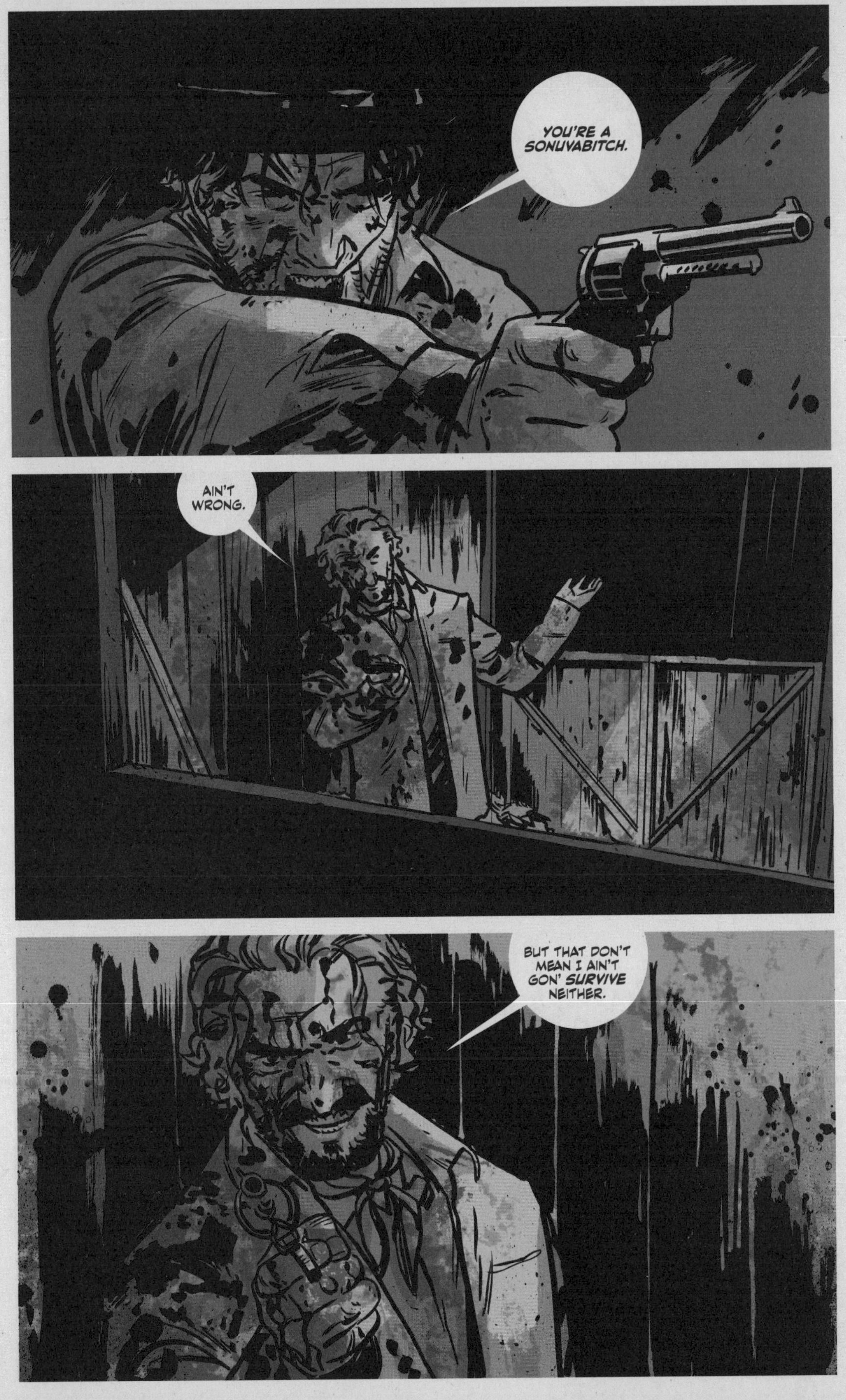
YOU'RE A SONUVABITCH.
AIN'T WRONG.
BUT THAT DON'T MEAN I AIN'T GON' *SURVIVE* NEITHER.

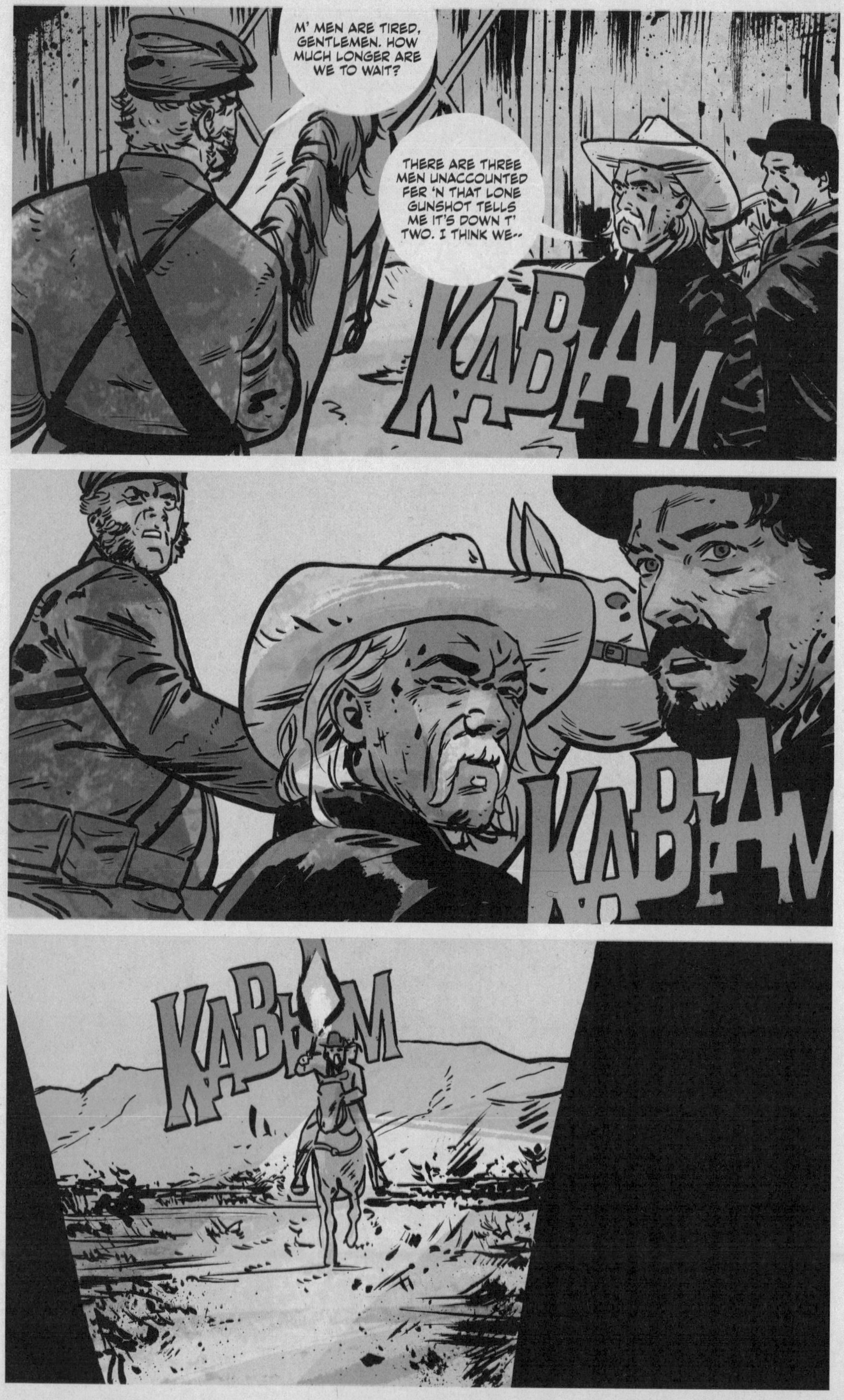

M' MEN ARE TIRED, GENTLEMEN. HOW MUCH LONGER ARE WE TO WAIT?
THERE ARE THREE MEN UNACCOUNTED FER 'N THAT LONE GUNSHOT TELLS ME IT'S DOWN T' TWO. I THINK WE--
KABLAM
KABLAM
KABLAM

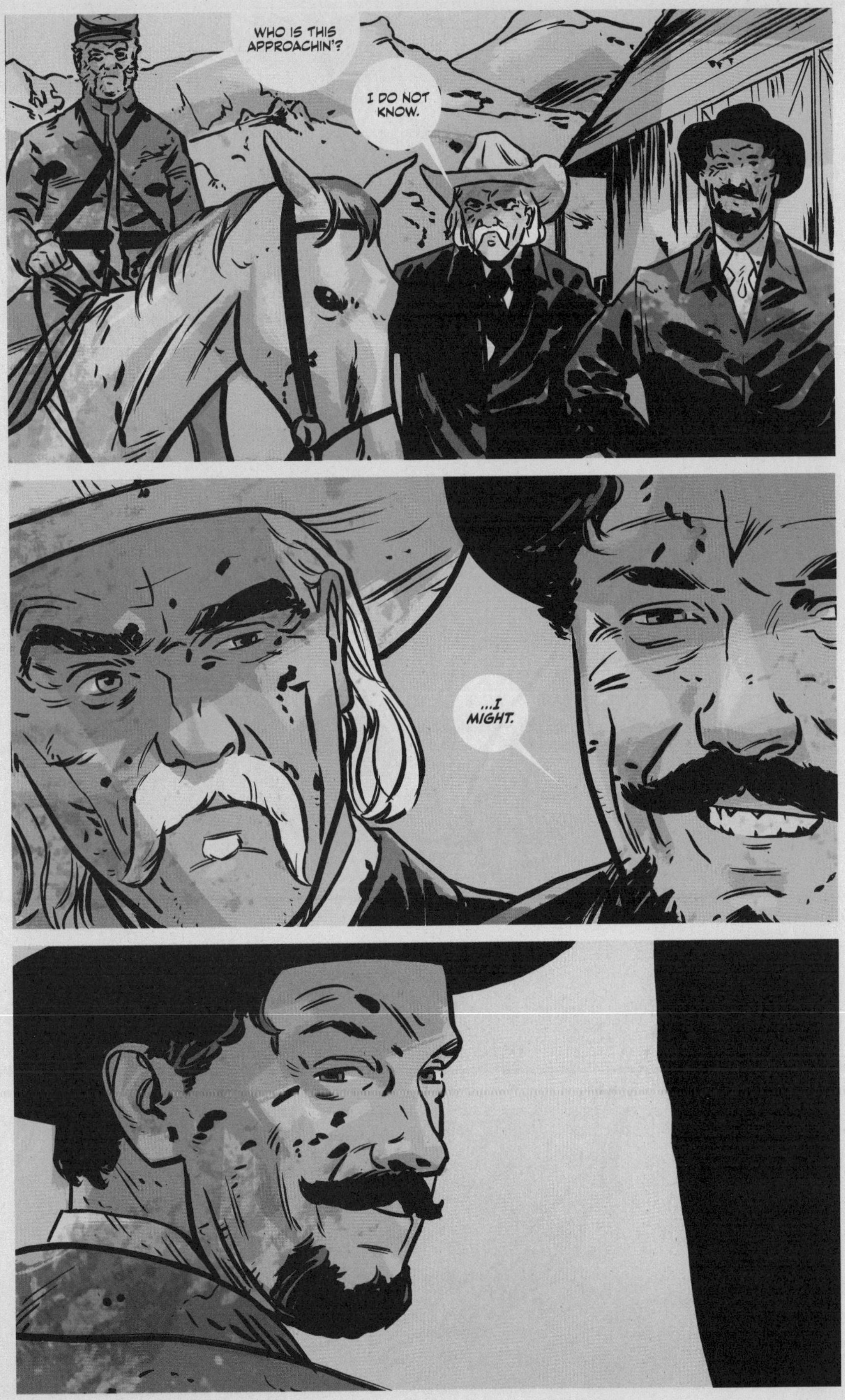
WHO IS THIS APPROACHIN'?
I DO NOT KNOW.
...I MIGHT.

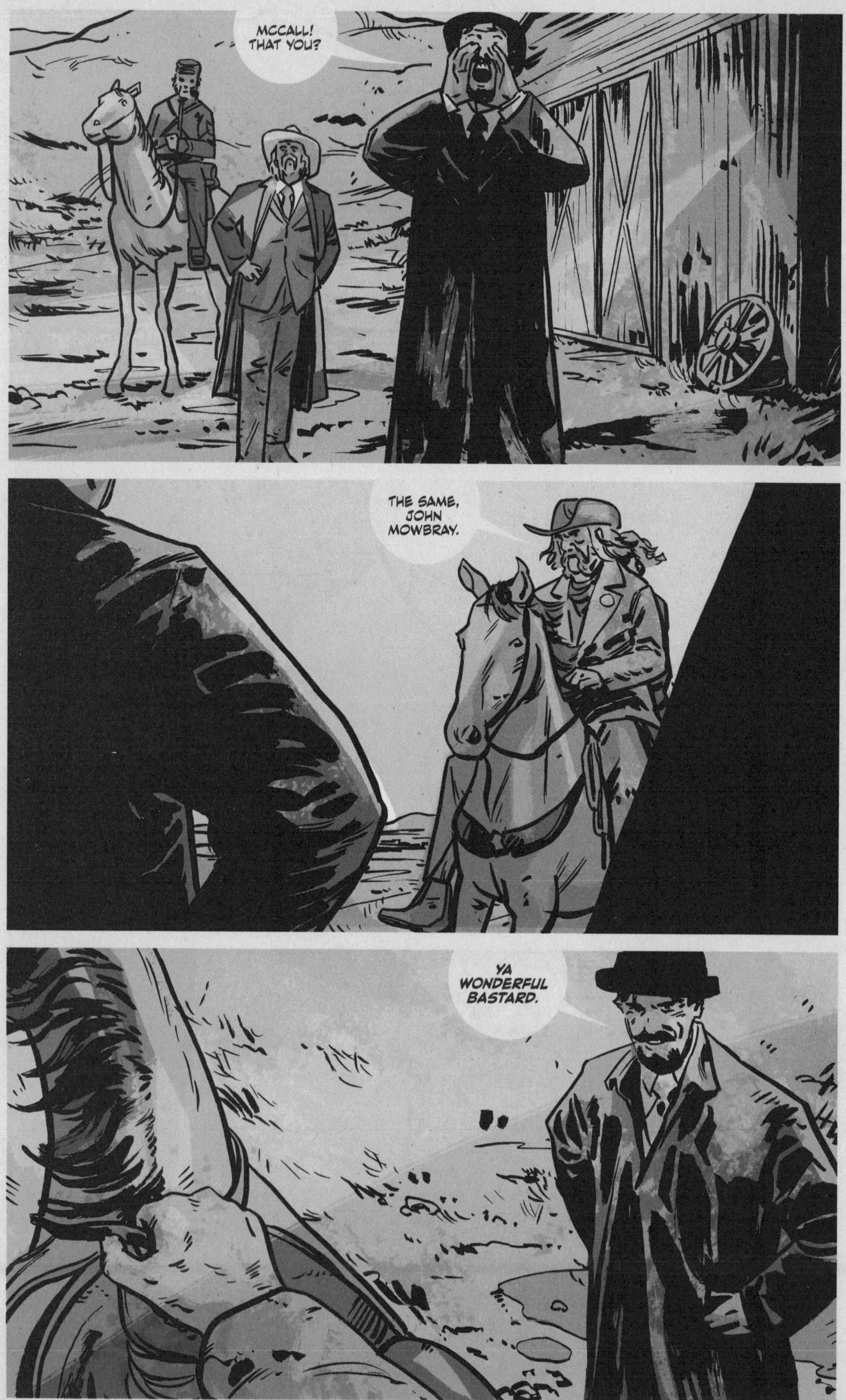
MCCALL! THAT YOU?
THE SAME, JOHN MOWBRAY.
YA WONDERFUL BASTARD.

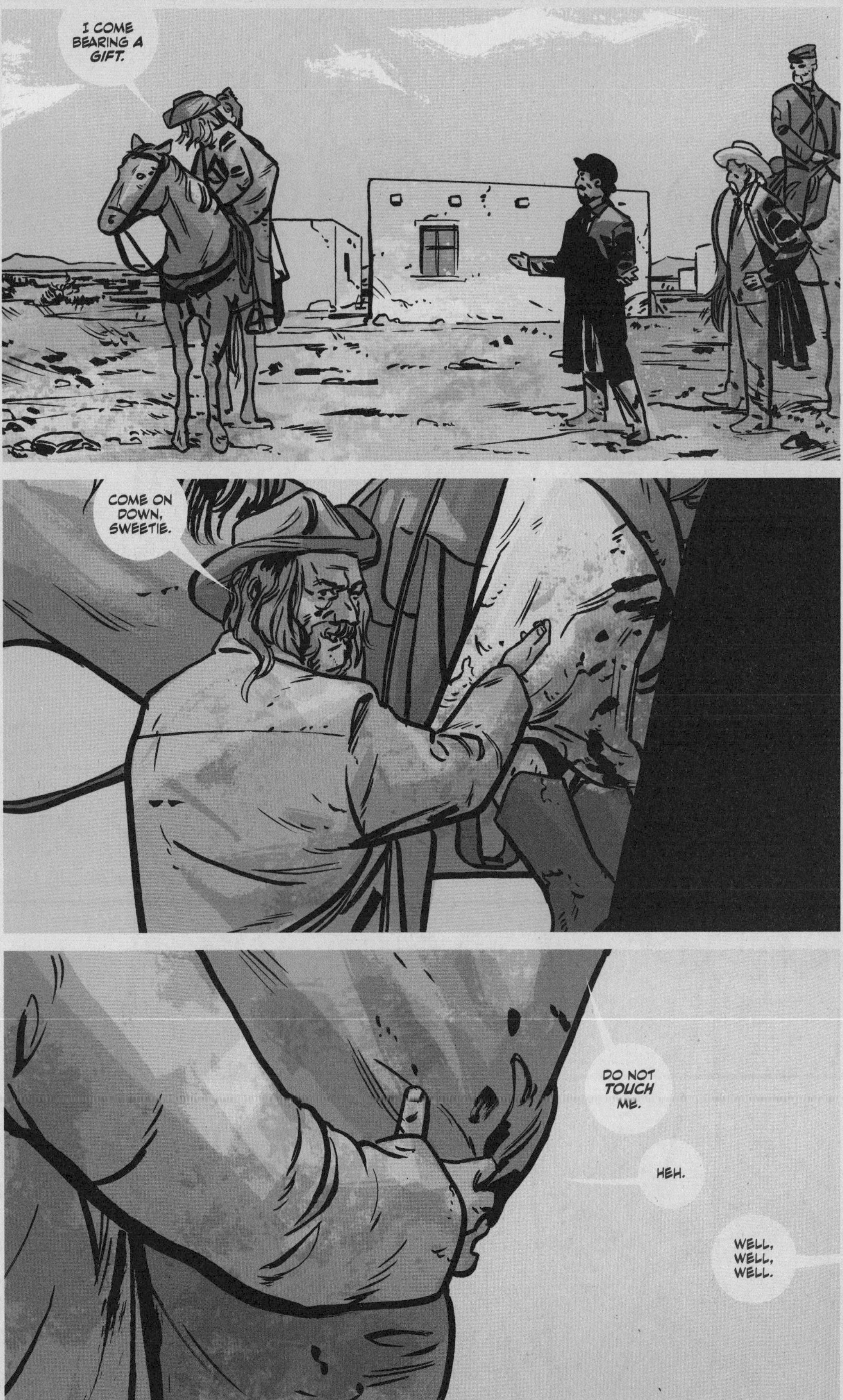
I COME BEARING A GIFT.
COME ON DOWN, SWEETIE.
DO NOT TOUCH ME.
HEH.
WELL, WELL, WELL.

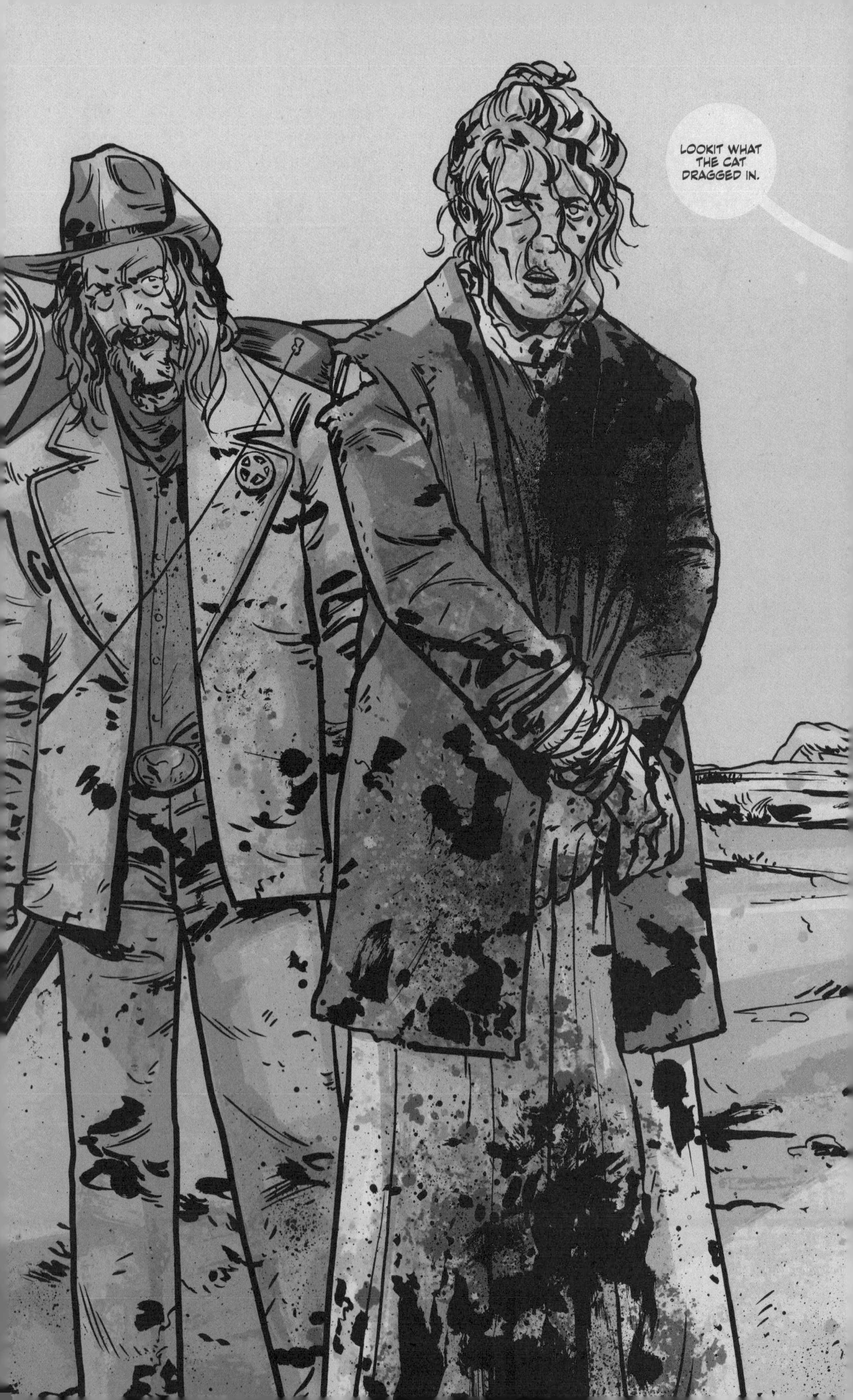
LOOKIT WHAT THE CAT DRAGGED IN.

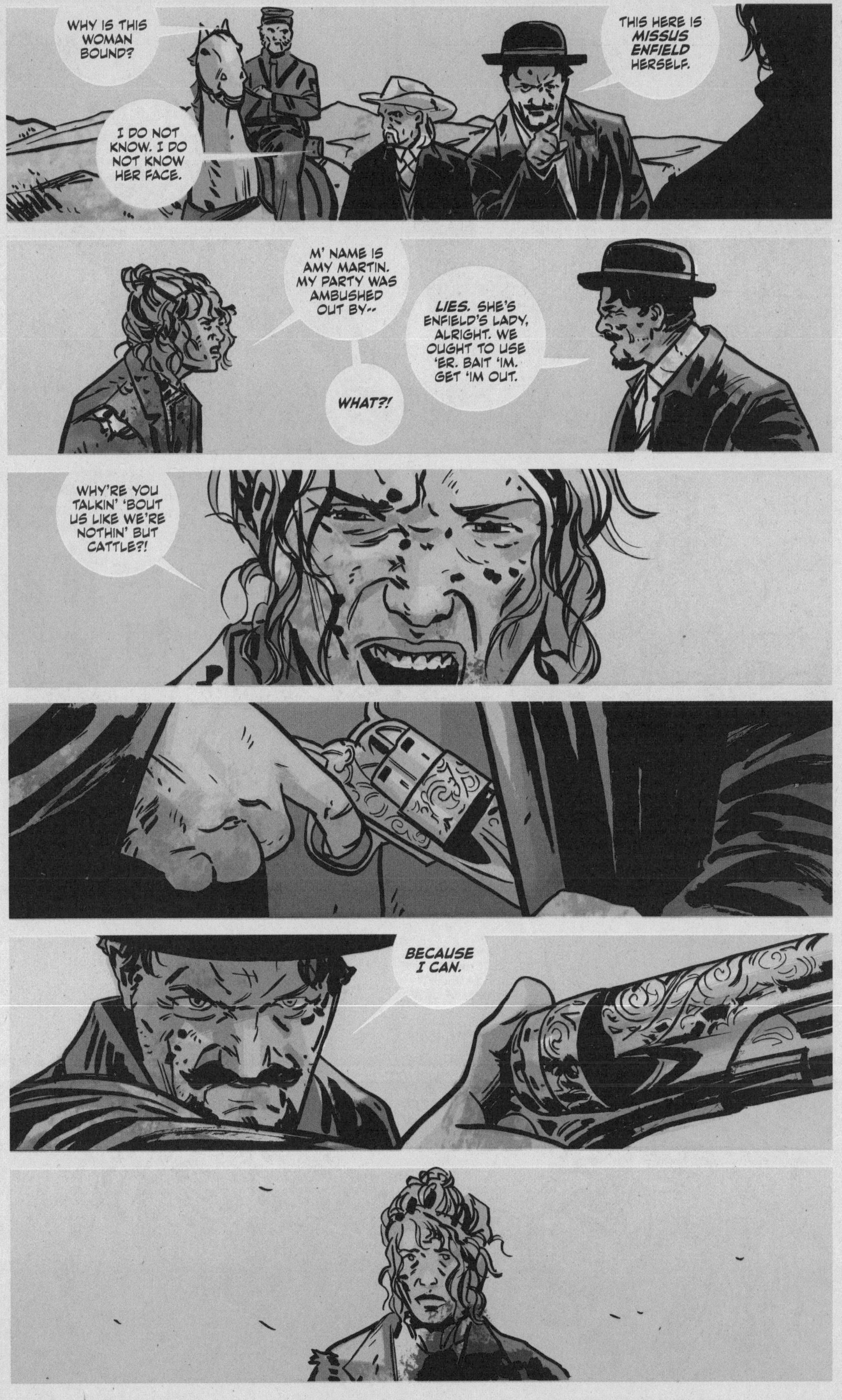
WHY IS THIS WOMAN BOUND?
THIS HERE IS *MISSUS ENFIELD* HERSELF.
I DO NOT KNOW. I DO NOT KNOW HER FACE.
M' NAME IS AMY MARTIN. MY PARTY WAS AMBUSHED OUT BY--
WHAT?!
LIES. SHE'S ENFIELD'S LADY, ALRIGHT. WE OUGHT TO USE 'ER. BAIT 'IM. GET 'IM OUT.
WHY'RE YOU TALKIN' 'BOUT US LIKE WE'RE NOTHIN' BUT CATTLE?!
BECAUSE I CAN.

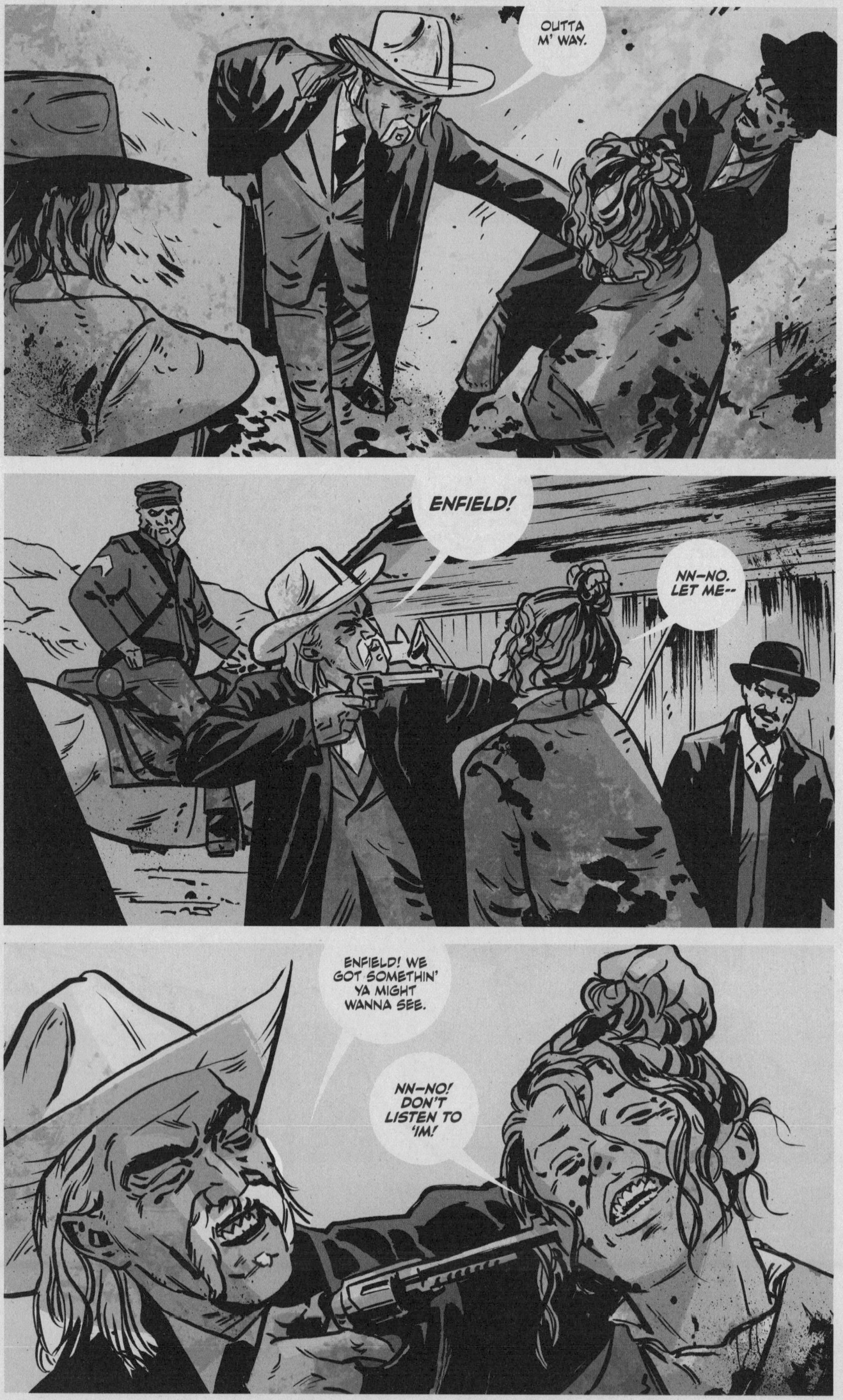
OUTTA M' WAY.
ENFIELD!
NN-NO. LET ME--
ENFIELD! WE GOT SOMETHIN' YA MIGHT WANNA SEE.
NN-NO! DON'T LISTEN TO 'IM!

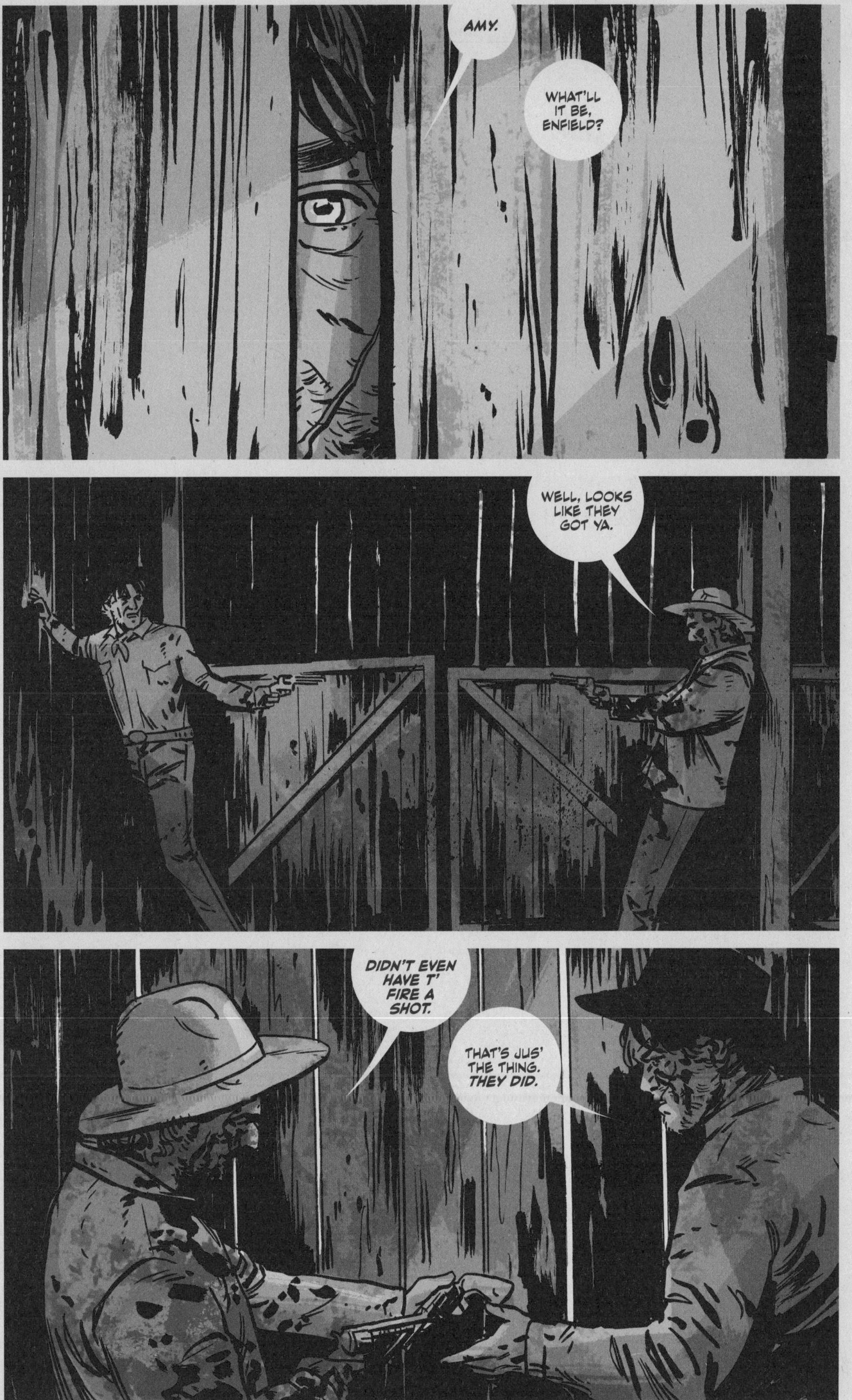

AMY.
WHAT'LL IT BE, ENFIELD?
WELL, LOOKS LIKE THEY GOT YA.
DIDN'T EVEN HAVE T' FIRE A SHOT.
THAT'S JUS' THE THING. THEY DID.

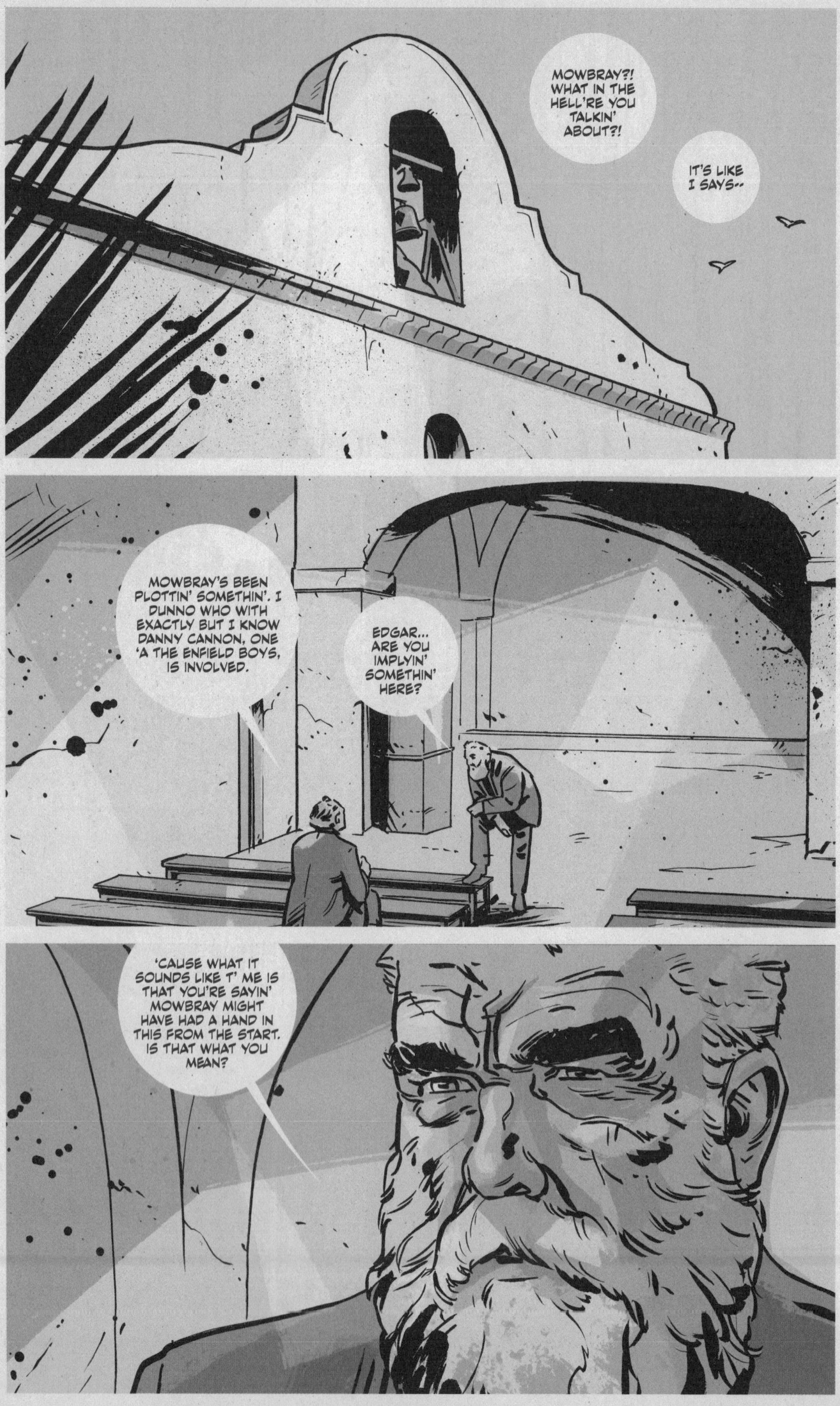
MOWBRAY?! WHAT IN THE HELL'RE YOU TALKIN' ABOUT?!
IT'S LIKE I SAYS--
MOWBRAY'S BEEN PLOTTIN' SOMETHIN'. I DUNNO WHO WITH EXACTLY BUT I KNOW DANNY CANNON, ONE 'A THE ENFIELD BOYS, IS INVOLVED.
EDGAR... ARE YOU IMPLYIN' SOMETHIN' HERE?
'CAUSE WHAT IT SOUNDS LIKE T' ME IS THAT YOU'RE SAYIN' MOWBRAY MIGHT HAVE HAD A HAND IN THIS FROM THE START. IS THAT WHAT YOU MEAN?

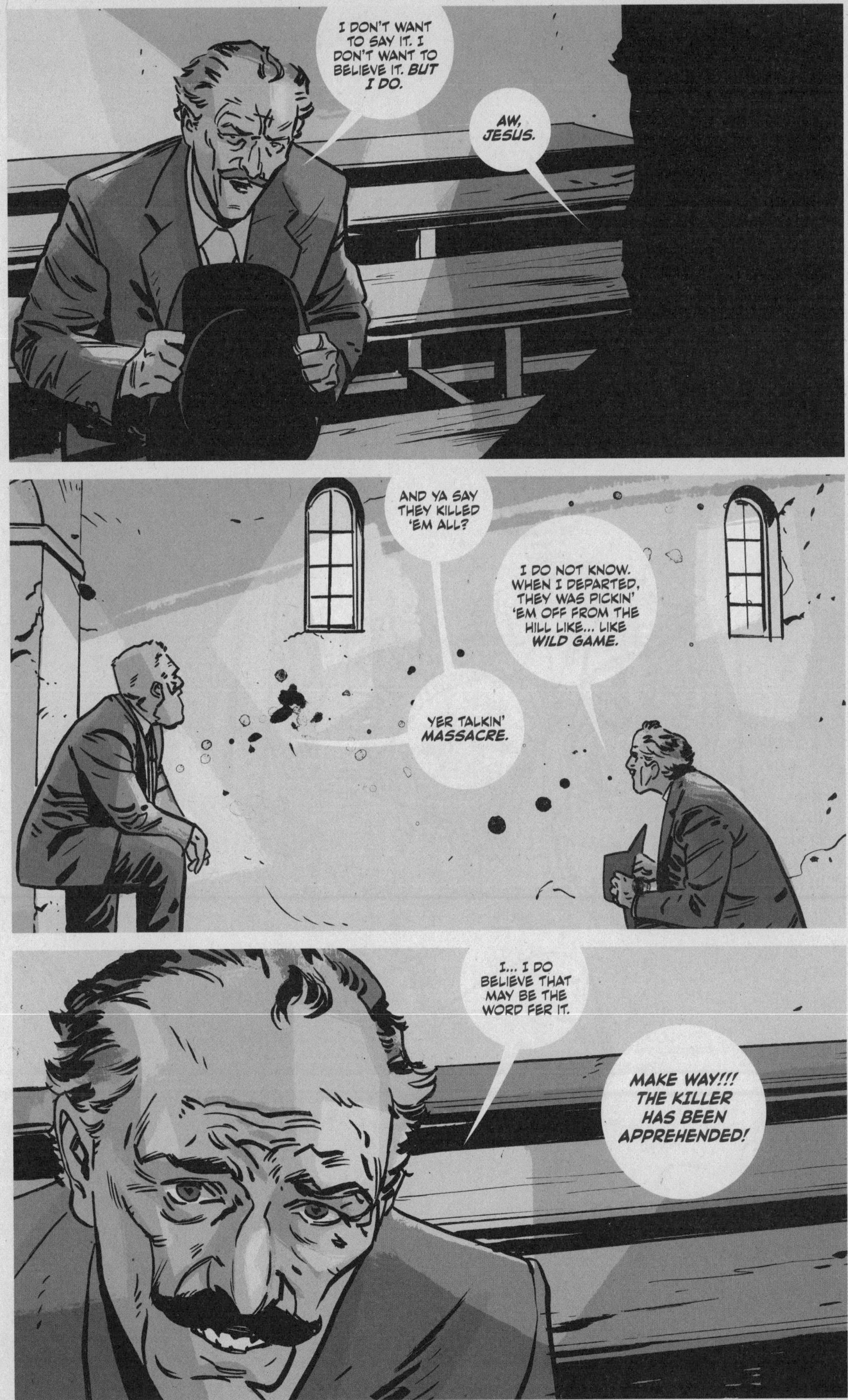
I DON'T WANT TO SAY IT. I DON'T WANT TO BELIEVE IT. BUT I DO.
AW, JESUS.
AND YA SAY THEY KILLED 'EM ALL?
I DO NOT KNOW. WHEN I DEPARTED, THEY WAS PICKIN' 'EM OFF FROM THE HILL LIKE... LIKE WILD GAME.
YER TALKIN' MASSACRE.
I... I DO BELIEVE THAT MAY BE THE WORD FER IT.
MAKE WAY!!! THE KILLER HAS BEEN APPREHENDED!

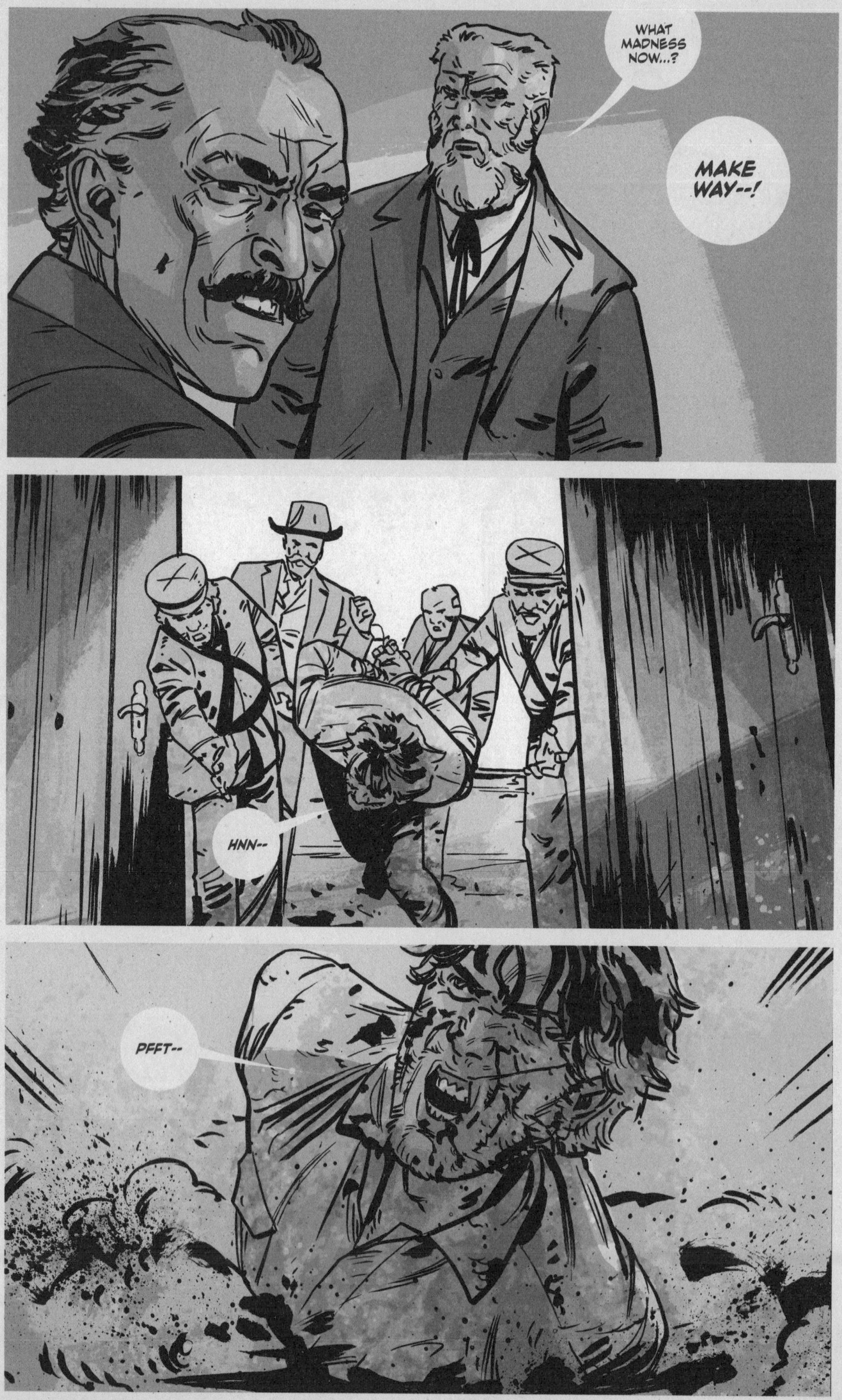
WHAT MADNESS NOW...?
MAKE WAY--!
HNN--
PFFT--

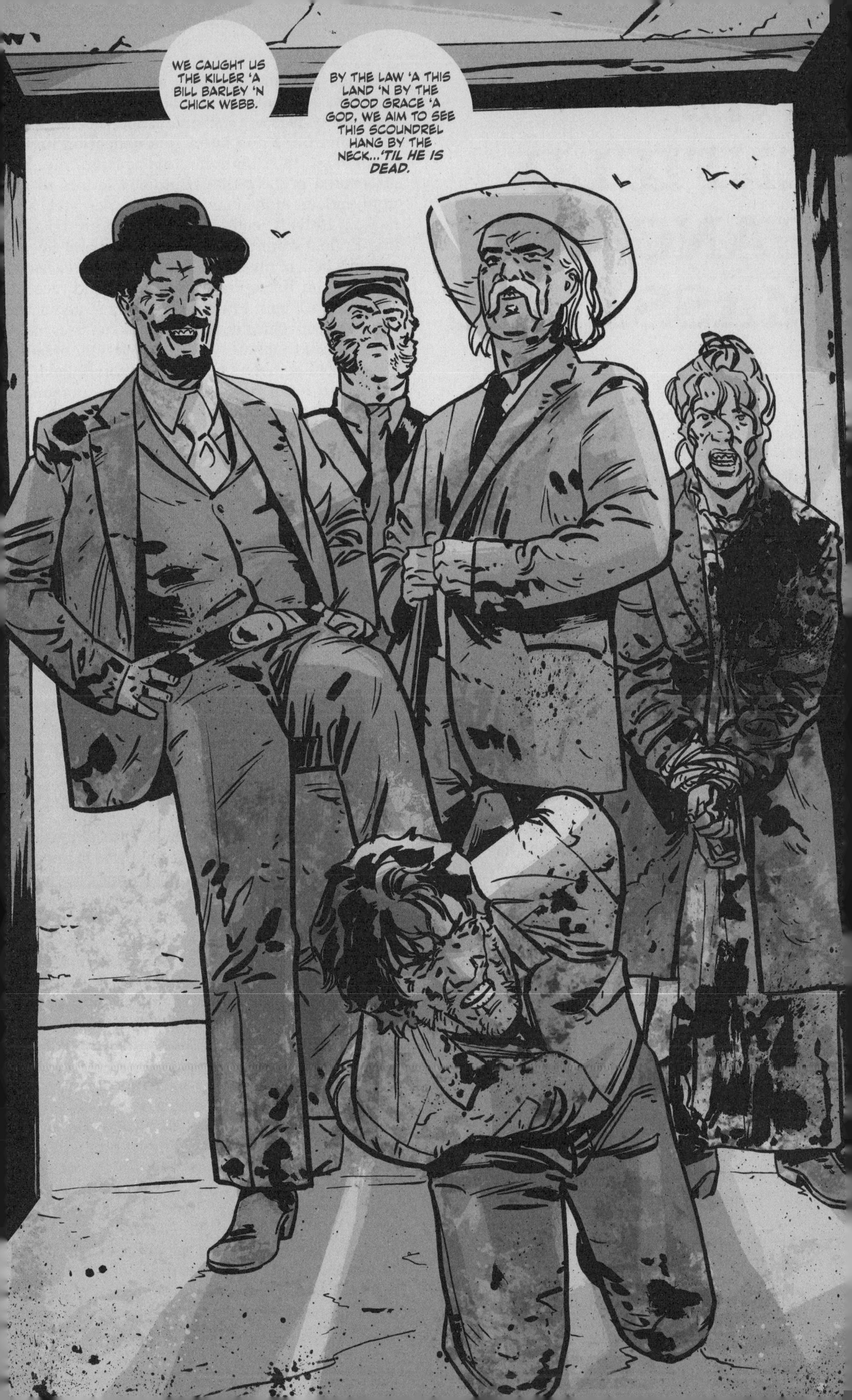
WE CAUGHT US THE KILLER 'A BILL BARLEY 'N CHICK WEBB.
BY THE LAW 'A THIS LAND 'N BY THE GOOD GRACE 'A GOD, WE AIM TO SEE THIS SCOUNDREL HANG BY THE NECK...'TIL HE IS DEAD.

THE ENFIELD GANG MASSACRE

cont'd.

Fooled or not, it is the truth, and we must make amends with it. We must admit our folly and move toward a future in which this shall never happen again. My family is, at least in some small part, entangled in the darkness that John Mowbray brought down upon this county. But reading more, learning more, you start to wonder if John Mowbray was the soul who brought Evil to Ambrose County or if the Evil had always been, as if it has been a festering boil, growing with each passing second, with every sunrise and sunset. Bad and evil things have been happening everywhere across the world since time immemorial, it's true.. But this place, the place I am writing these very words, in fact, has a penchant for the damned.

Why that is, I can't say. I don't dare take a guess, even an educated one. All that I can tell you is that, in my brief time on this earth, I have uncovered the systematic destruction of an entire group of people in The Enfield Gang Massacre, I have lived through the horrors of The Cult of Night kidnappings and murders in 1981, and I have seen a vile serial killer traipse through our land and take our brightest from us too soon. There has been more, of course. There has been much more. Worse things have happened elsewhere, of course. But these things happened here. Not only that, they happened to people that I have known. This is not a large county. Yet, these things happen, as if the bad things are drawn to us like a moth to flame. Or a predator to prey. I am curious if my mentioning this might exorcize that apparent attractiveness to Evil. Perhaps my own superstition will be soothed. I pray that is the case, though I feel in my bones that it will continue to bring darkness to the county, and that John Mowbray was not the first, nor the last.

Which brings me, somewhat reluctantly, to the true gold mine discovery of The Enfield Gang Massacre. I have glossed over a certain, vital person and this was on purpose. Her name was Amy Martin. As I had mentioned previously, Amy Martin was Enfield's lover.

In April of 1994, I had befriended a man by the name of Franklin Durango. He lives in Minneapolis, Minnesota, where he has a wife, two sons and, recently, a granddaughter. What brought us together was my research for this very article. Franklin, or Frankie, as he likes to be called, is a collector of Western ephemera. Boots, belts, spurs and other odds and ends. In a collection he had purchased in Oklahoma at auction, he had discovered a chest that contained letters to and from various individuals from approximately 1877 to 1914. He had read or heard about my research into Enfield from somebody or other and he had gotten a hold of my phone number through a friend. I was at the Texas Record offices when I received a phone call from Frankie. He told me about this chest and, specifically, told me about a letter inside of it that he thought I would find very interesting. It was from someone named "Clayton Enfield." He had asked me if I'd ever heard of this person, on account of my research, and I had told him no, I had no knowledge of a Clayton Enfield. Frankie told me that he'd send this letter down to me via express mail and said no more.

"YOU START TO WONDER IF JOHN MOWBRAY WAS THE SOUL WHO BROUGHT EVIL TO AMBROSE COUNTY OR IF THE EVIL HAD ALWAYS BEEN"

I was, of course, curious, but there was no indication that this Clayton Enfield was in any way connected to Montgomery Enfield, nor The Enfield Gang Massacre. For one thing, Enfield's relatives lived in Arkansas and bore a different last name. It's also a last name that belongs to many individuals not necessarily related to the gang or the massacre. The fact that this letter was housed in Oklahoma also called into question its connection to Enfield. Enfield had spent some time in Oklahoma but there was no reason to believe that he had established roots there in any form.

So, to say that I was skeptical is to put it lightly. My initial thought was that I would receive this letter, peruse it briefly, thank Frankie for the thought but explain that simply mentioning a particular name was not enough to establish connection between two people—especially when those two people were divided by thirty-some years.

I was not waiting patiently. In fact, I was not waiting at all. Once I set the phone down with Frankie, I had nearly forgotten about the subject altogether until I received a knock on the door where stood a tall mailman asking me to sign for a large envelope. I did, accepted the envelope, then went

nside. I walked to my kitchen, slid a knife under
ne taped-shut flap, then opened the envelope and
emoved its contents. Held between two cardboard
lats and sheathed in plastic was the letter. I care-
ully removed it, inspected it briefly, then opened it.

To be sure, this was an interesting piece
egardless of its contents. But once I began
eading, I realized the significance of this letter in
ne saga of The Enfield Gang Massacre. Why? Well,
, was because the letter was seemingly written by
he son of Edward Montgomery Enfield. A son that
hould, by all accounts, not exist.

Nowhere, in all of my research, had I read
nything about a son. Nor was there even an
nkling of such a being existing. Yet, here he was.
Clayton Enfield.

The contents themselves were nothing
erribly illuminating. It revolved around troubles
vith a particular ranch owner named Talford,
omewhere east of Tulsa. But where things got
particularly interesting was in its last paragraph.
Clayton writes that he is awaiting the arrival of
his mother by train who is traveling west from
Arkansas. Her name, he writes, is Amy.

Of course, this could have been mere
coincidence. These are not particularly unique
names, Enfield and Amy, but the chance that those
wo names should arrive in the same letter, dated
after the turn of the century, is where I believe this
etter moves squarely into the realm of possibility,
or, more accurately, high probability.

I immediately phoned my editor, Dorothy
Harman, and told her that I believed I had discovered something interesting pertaining to the
Enfield Gang Massacre. Dorothy has always been
a champion of mine but has been fairly critical of
my work revolving around the Enfield Gang and the
massacre. She's approving this piece of writing, so I
eel I must be honest here and say that I don't think
she was wrong to be. This is an incredibly heated
subject, one that has been a staple of West Texas
history and myth for more than a century. To
urn the tables on folks and tell them that their
mythology isn't worth a damn is like telling a
child Santa Claus doesn't exist. It will likely cause
outrage, fear, and even hostility. I had always pooh-
poohed that notion, claiming that the facts are
the facts and it is my job to report them. Dorothy,
however, in her infinite wisdom, refused to run
any article stabbing a hole in history unless I had
concrete evidence (I had not yet found L.Q.'s
ournal, nor Mowbray's personal journal. This letter
from Clayton Enfield was proverbial gas in the
engine that got the pistons of this story working).

Now, here I was with not so much evidence
but a clue. Perhaps, I surmised, if this singular
letter existed, maybe there were others as well.
Once I was off the phone with Dorothy, who en-
couraged me to pursue the lead, I called Frankie
back and asked him where he had purchased
the letter. He told me where, specifically, but told
me that there were no more letters in the chest
written by Clayton Enfield, nor was there any to or

from Amy Martin. It seems that, over the years,
collectors had gathered letters from various sources
and dropped them all into this chest, not knowing
that their collection contained a morsel of a clue
to what happened in July of 1875 in Ambrose
County, Texas. I thanked Frankie, asked him to let
me know if he discovered anything else, then got
off the phone.

I recall a sense of purpose about this
discovery, an almost buzzing anticipation. I had
stumbled upon something that could be the most
interesting and, frankly, monumental discoveries in
Texas history in years.

Up to this point, it was unknown what
had happened to Amy Martin during the Enfield
Gang Massacre. It was assumed that she was killed
along with the others, her body likely buried in an
unmarked grave somewhere in Fort Lehane along
with the rest.

But if she was getting on a train in Arkansas and heading to Oklahoma in 1906, she was very
much alive.

In my mind, this opened up a door of
possibilities. If Amy was alive, perhaps there were
others that had survived as well. This, of course,
would turn out to be untrue. As we've previously
discussed, most of Chihuahua was executed in
some form or other during the days of the massacre.
But Amy Martin, the lover of Enfield, lived. My mind
raced with questions. How? Why?

I traveled to Little Rock, Arkansas and
scoured their records, searching for any mention
of an Amy Martin in either a census or in land
ownership and sales. I was turning up nothing.
I then contacted a friend of mine, Bill Buck, in
Oklahoma and asked him to check his records for
me to see if there was either a Clayton Enfield or
an Amy Martin. He told me he'd call me back if he
found anything.

Months passed. I had moved on to other
stories. But then one day, the phone rang. It was
Bill. He told me that there was not mention of one
of the individuals I was searching for, but both, in
records belonging to Rogers County, Oklahoma. It
seems that this Amy, listed as Amy Westley, had
lived with Clayton on a ranch there, which he sold
in 1920. The family had apparently relocated to
Connecticut following that but had since moved
down to New Jersey where they currently reside.
Today in Montclair, New Jersey, there is a woman
named Lanna. She is married to a man named
Thomas Byrne. They have no children. If my
information was true, Lanna Byrne may be the last
living descendant of Edward Montgomery Enfield.

I called them cold on a Wednesday afternoon and introduced myself as a man shaking a
hornet's nest in West Texas. I told Lanna I wanted
to know more about her surname, Enfield, and
more than that, I wanted to know if I could meet
her. I had a lot that I wanted to discuss.

TO BE CONTINUED.

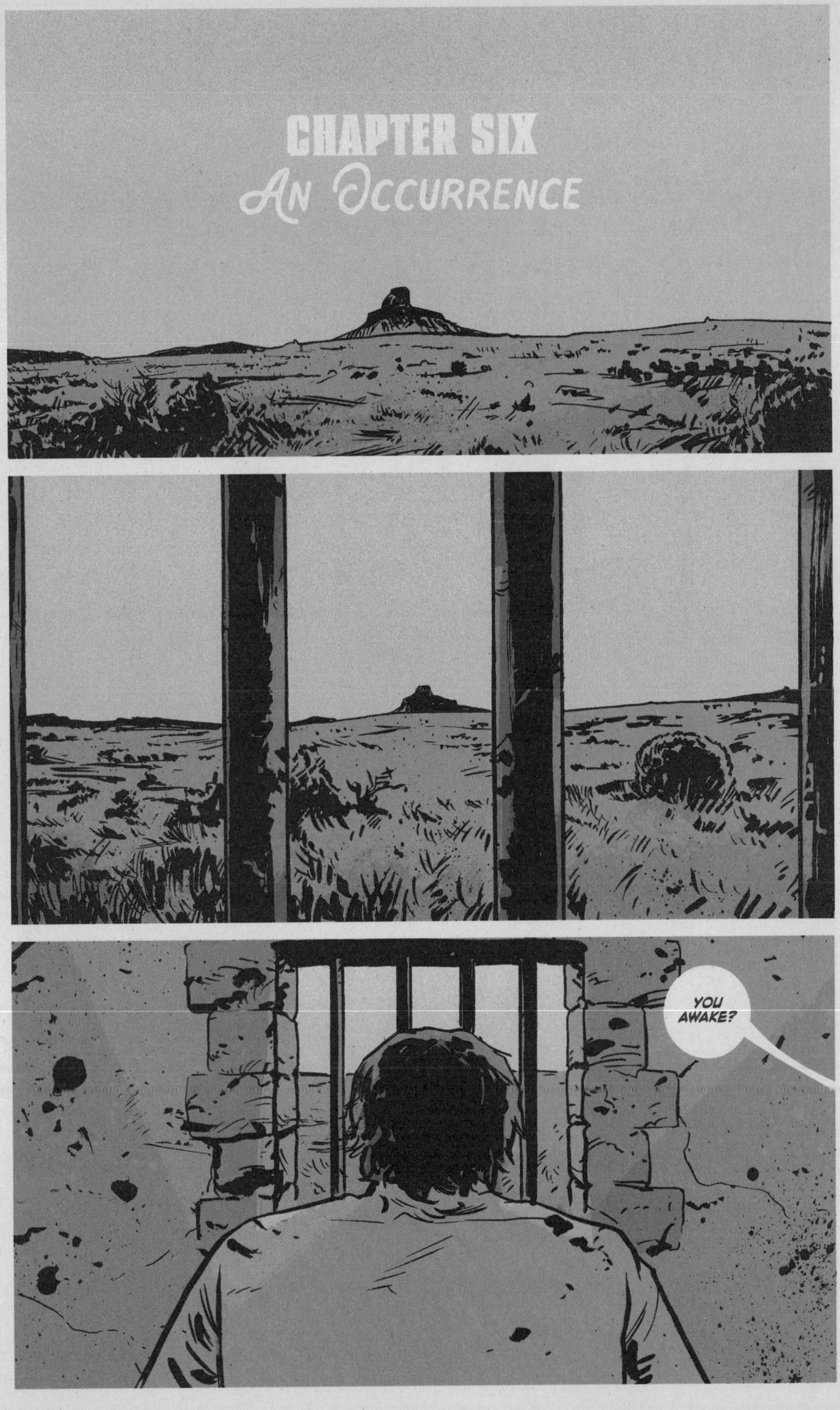
CHAPTER SIX
An Occurrence
YOU AWAKE?

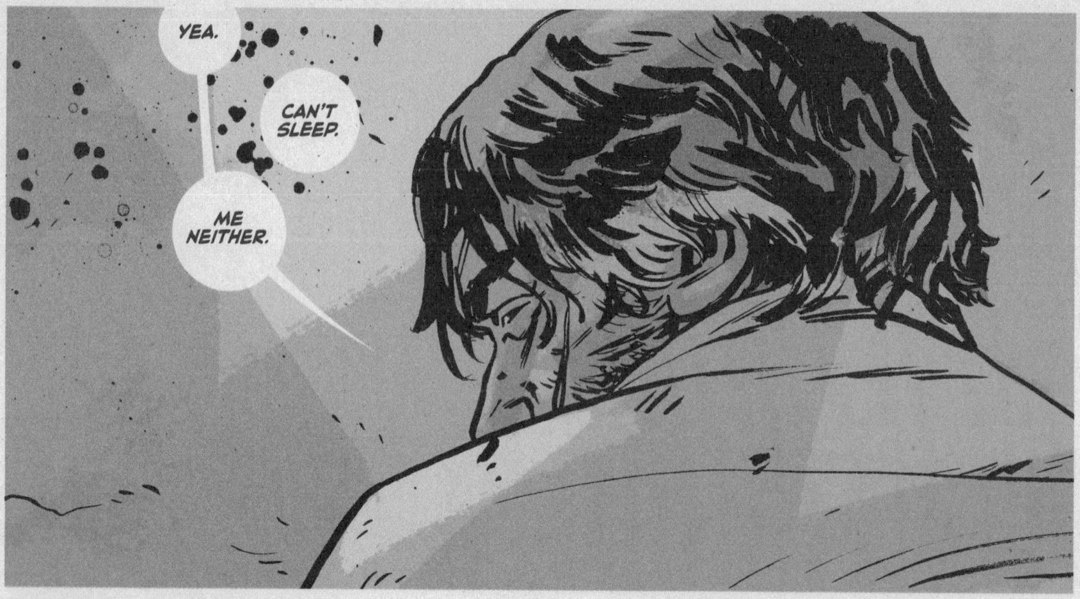
YEA.
CAN'T SLEEP.
ME NEITHER.

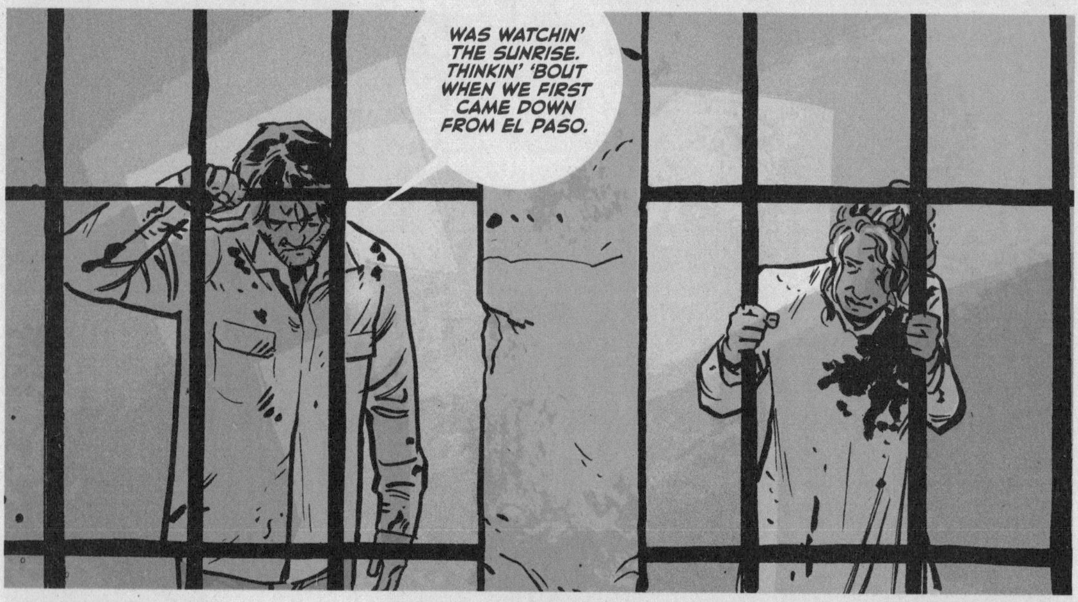
WAS WATCHIN' THE SUNRISE. THINKIN' 'BOUT WHEN WE FIRST CAME DOWN FROM EL PASO.

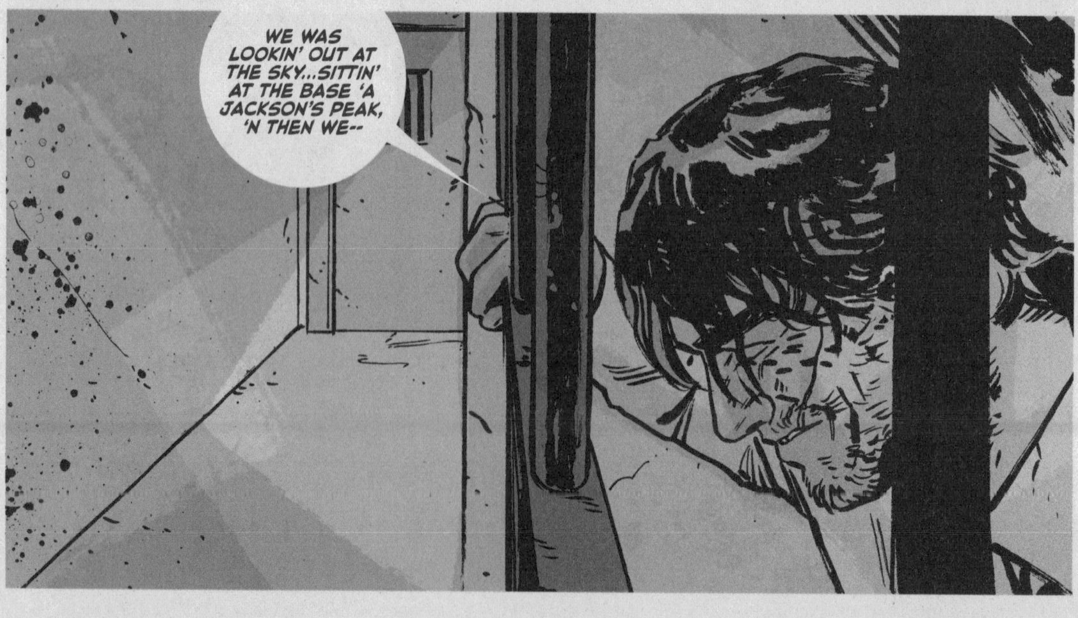
WE WAS LOOKIN' OUT AT THE SKY...SITTIN' AT THE BASE 'A JACKSON'S PEAK, 'N THEN WE--

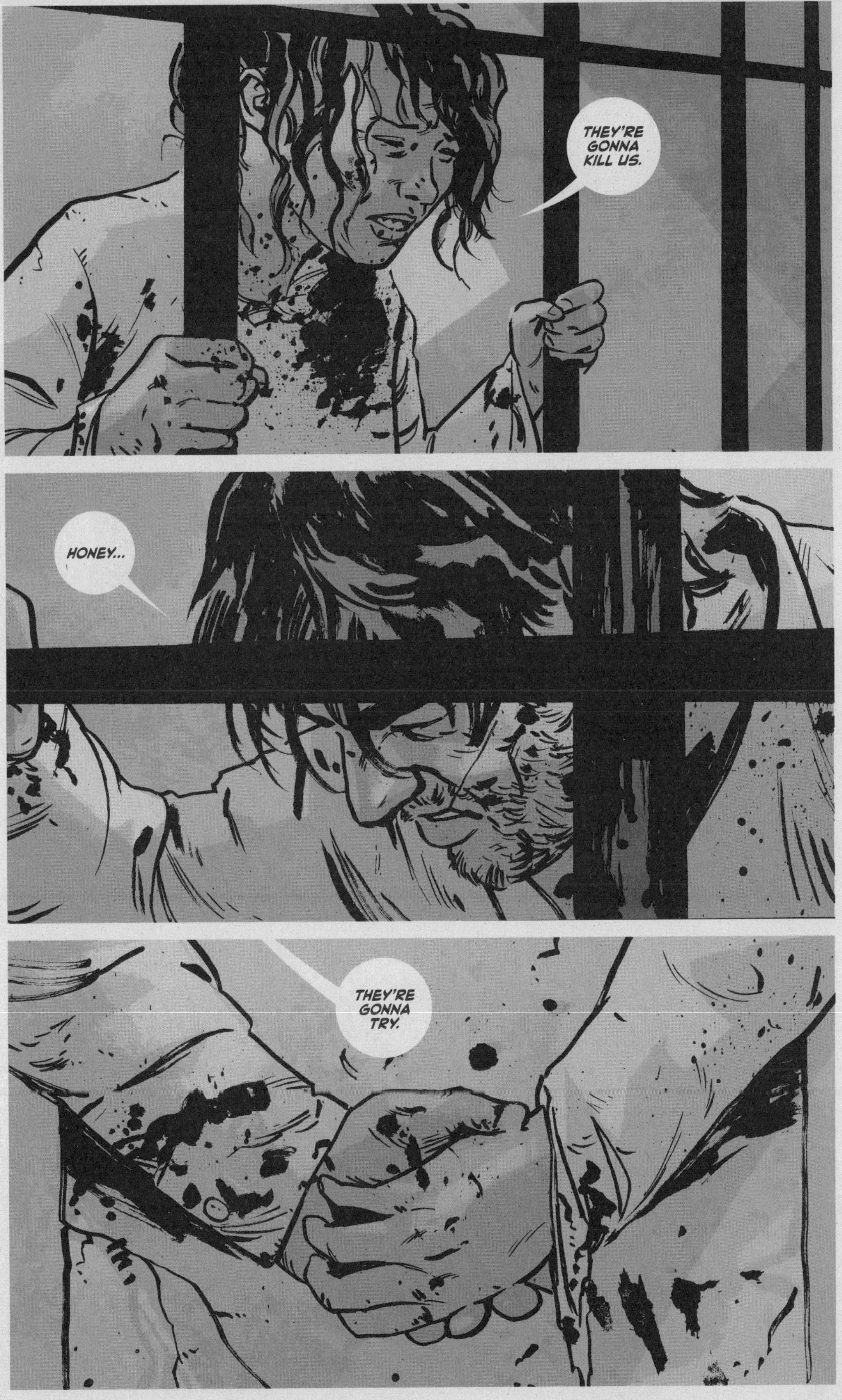
THEY'RE GONNA KILL US.
HONEY...
THEY'RE GONNA TRY.

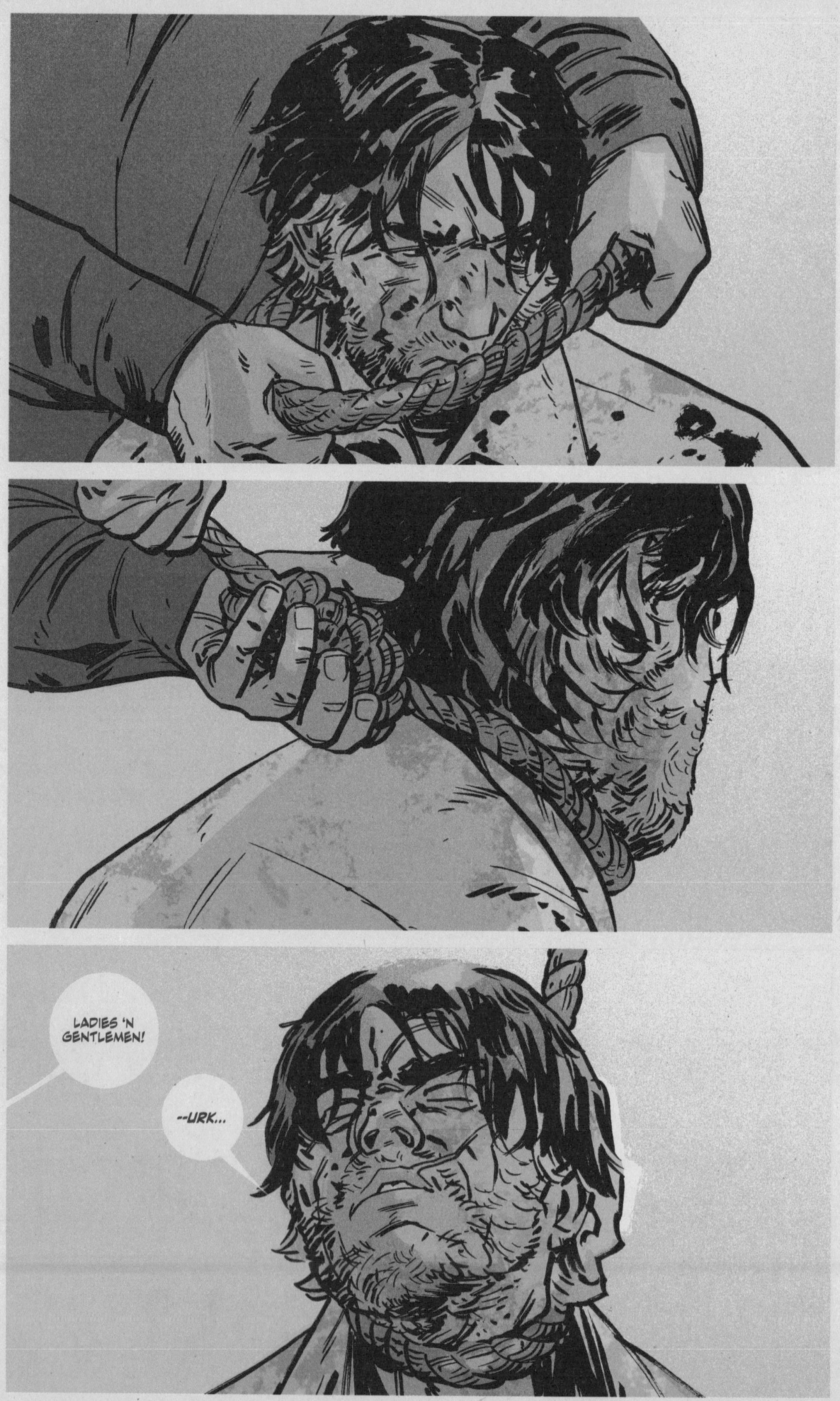
LADIES 'N GENTLEMEN!
--URK...

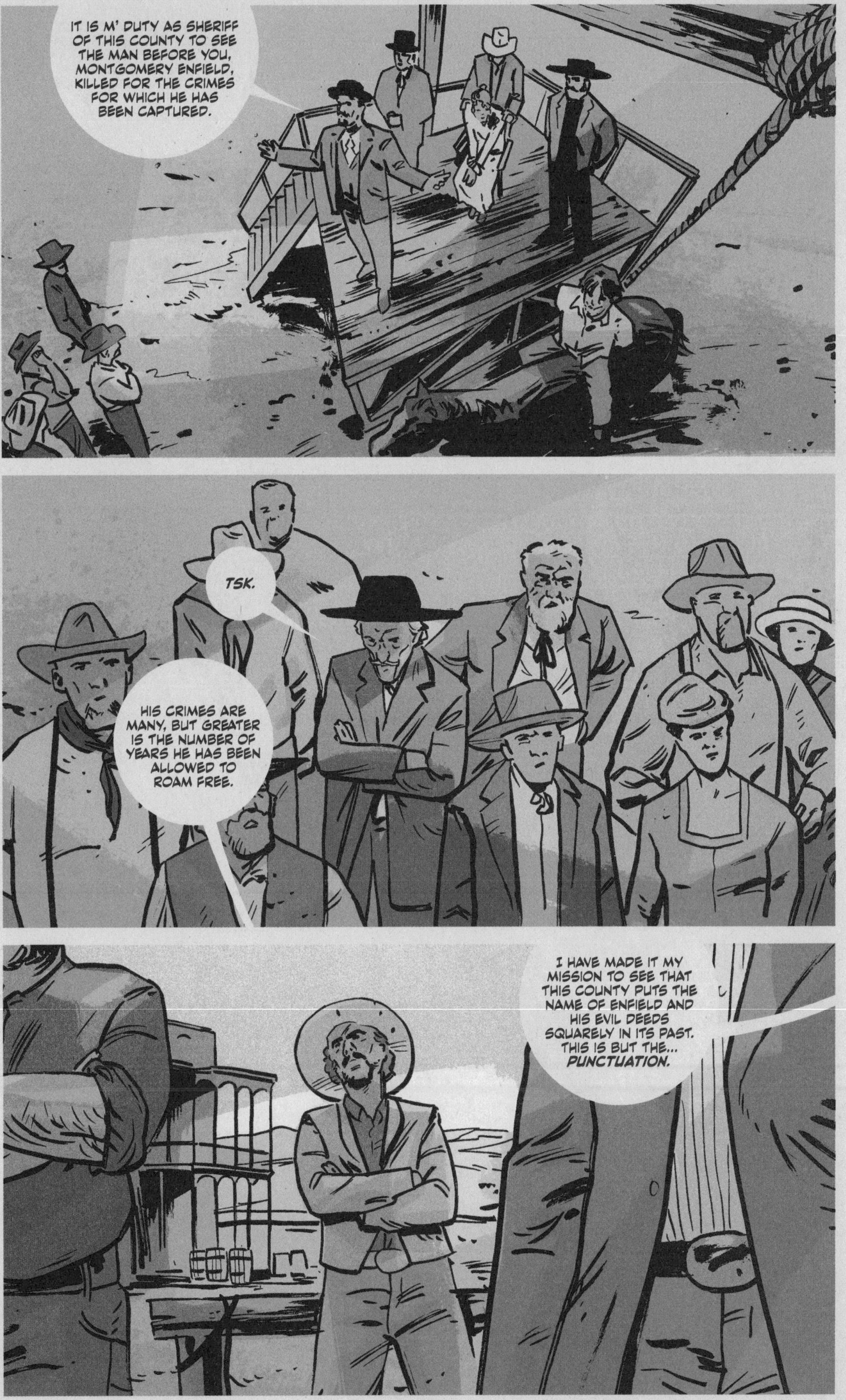
IT IS M' DUTY AS SHERIFF OF THIS COUNTY TO SEE THE MAN BEFORE YOU, MONTGOMERY ENFIELD, KILLED FOR THE CRIMES FOR WHICH HE HAS BEEN CAPTURED.
TSK.
HIS CRIMES ARE MANY, BUT GREATER IS THE NUMBER OF YEARS HE HAS BEEN ALLOWED TO ROAM FREE.
I HAVE MADE IT MY MISSION TO SEE THAT THIS COUNTY PUTS THE NAME OF ENFIELD AND HIS EVIL DEEDS SQUARELY IN ITS PAST. THIS IS BUT THE... *PUNCTUATION.*

HE HAS KILLED TWO OF OUR FRIENDS THIS PAST WEEK. *TWO!* CHICK WEBB 'N BILL BARLEY. THERE MAY BE OTHERS, BUT I AM, AS YET, UNAWARE. STILL...

TWO IS STILL *TWO TOO MANY.* I STAND PROUD BEFORE YOU, STEADFAST IN OUR DECISION. THIS MAN, FOR HIS RADICAL ACTIONS AND IDEALS, MUST *HANG.*

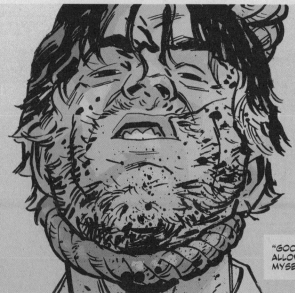

AND GOD, IN HIS INFINITE WISDOM, SHALL BE THE FINAL JUDGE OF HIS SOUL.

"GOOD MORNIN'. PLEASE ALLOW ME TO INTRODUCE MYSELF..."

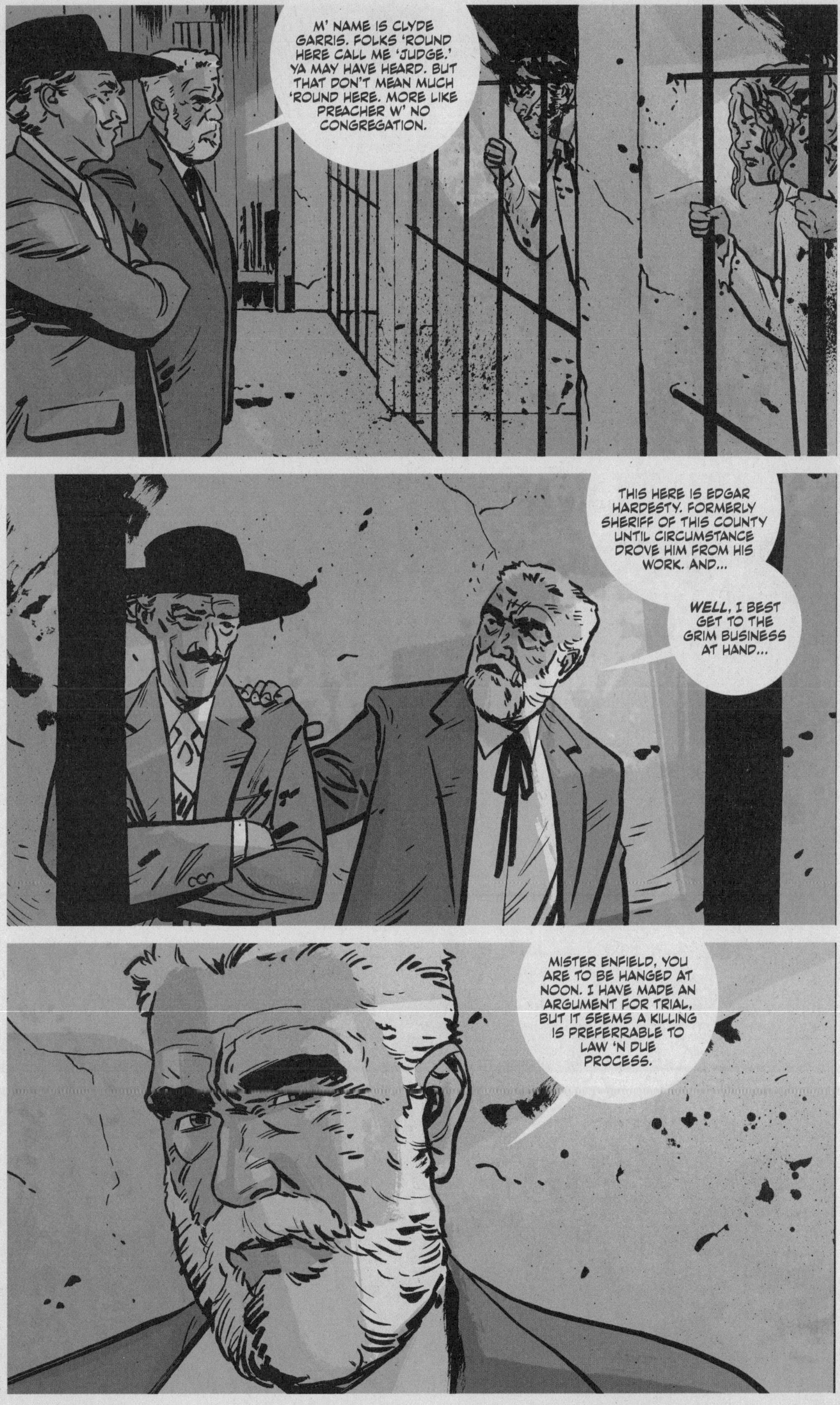
M' NAME IS CLYDE GARRIS. FOLKS 'ROUND HERE CALL ME 'JUDGE.' YA MAY HAVE HEARD. BUT THAT DON'T MEAN MUCH 'ROUND HERE. MORE LIKE PREACHER W' NO CONGREGATION.
THIS HERE IS EDGAR HARDESTY. FORMERLY SHERIFF OF THIS COUNTY UNTIL CIRCUMSTANCE DROVE HIM FROM HIS WORK. AND...
WELL, I BEST GET TO THE GRIM BUSINESS AT HAND...
MISTER ENFIELD, YOU ARE TO BE HANGED AT NOON. I HAVE MADE AN ARGUMENT FOR TRIAL, BUT IT SEEMS A KILLING IS PREFERRABLE TO LAW 'N DUE PROCESS.

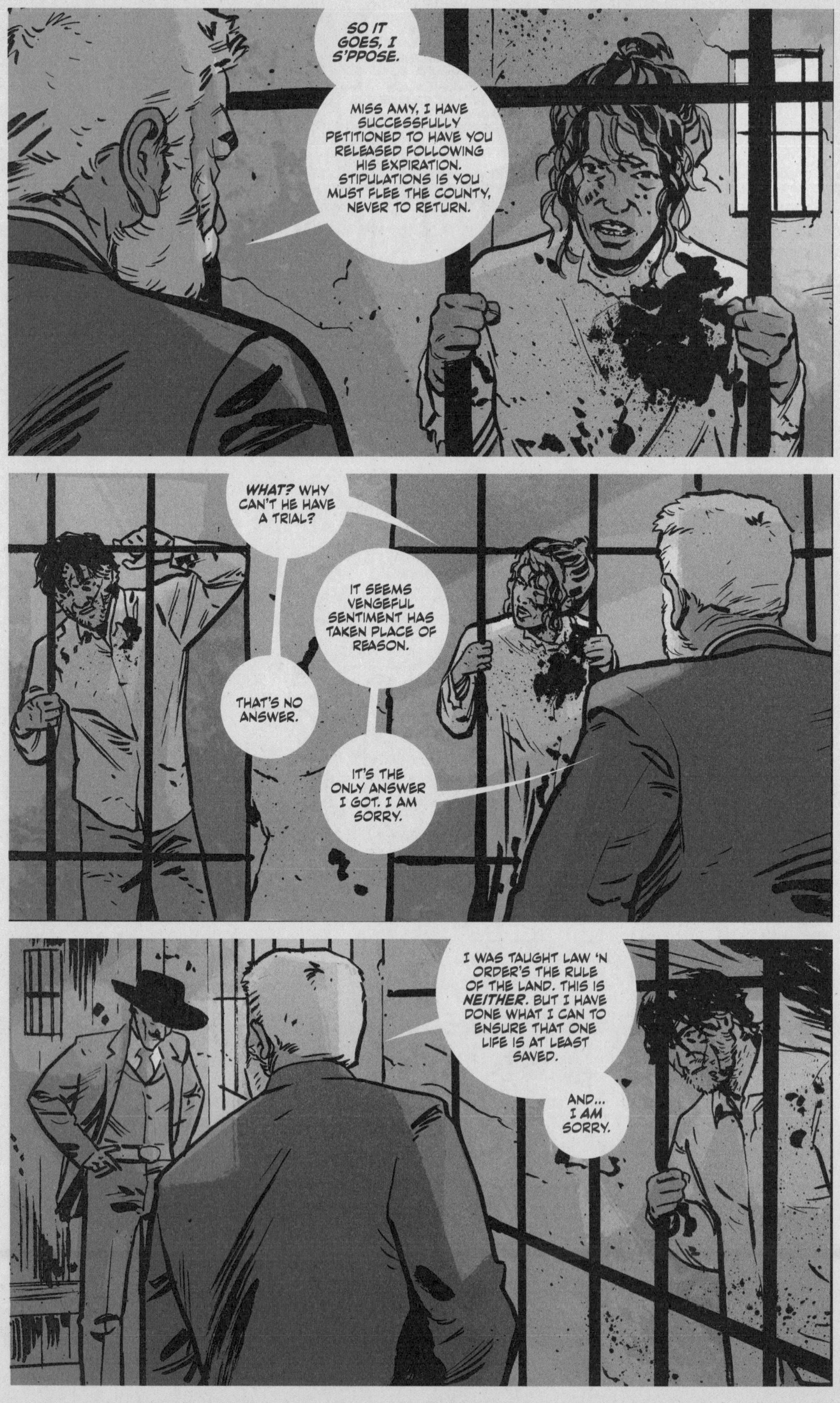
SO IT GOES, I S'PPOSE.
MISS AMY, I HAVE SUCCESSFULLY PETITIONED TO HAVE YOU RELEASED FOLLOWING HIS EXPIRATION. STIPULATIONS IS YOU MUST FLEE THE COUNTY, NEVER TO RETURN.
WHAT? WHY CAN'T HE HAVE A TRIAL?
IT SEEMS VENGEFUL SENTIMENT HAS TAKEN PLACE OF REASON.
THAT'S NO ANSWER.
IT'S THE ONLY ANSWER I GOT. I AM SORRY.
I WAS TAUGHT LAW 'N ORDER'S THE RULE OF THE LAND. THIS IS NEITHER. BUT I HAVE DONE WHAT I CAN TO ENSURE THAT ONE LIFE IS AT LEAST SAVED.
AND... I AM SORRY.

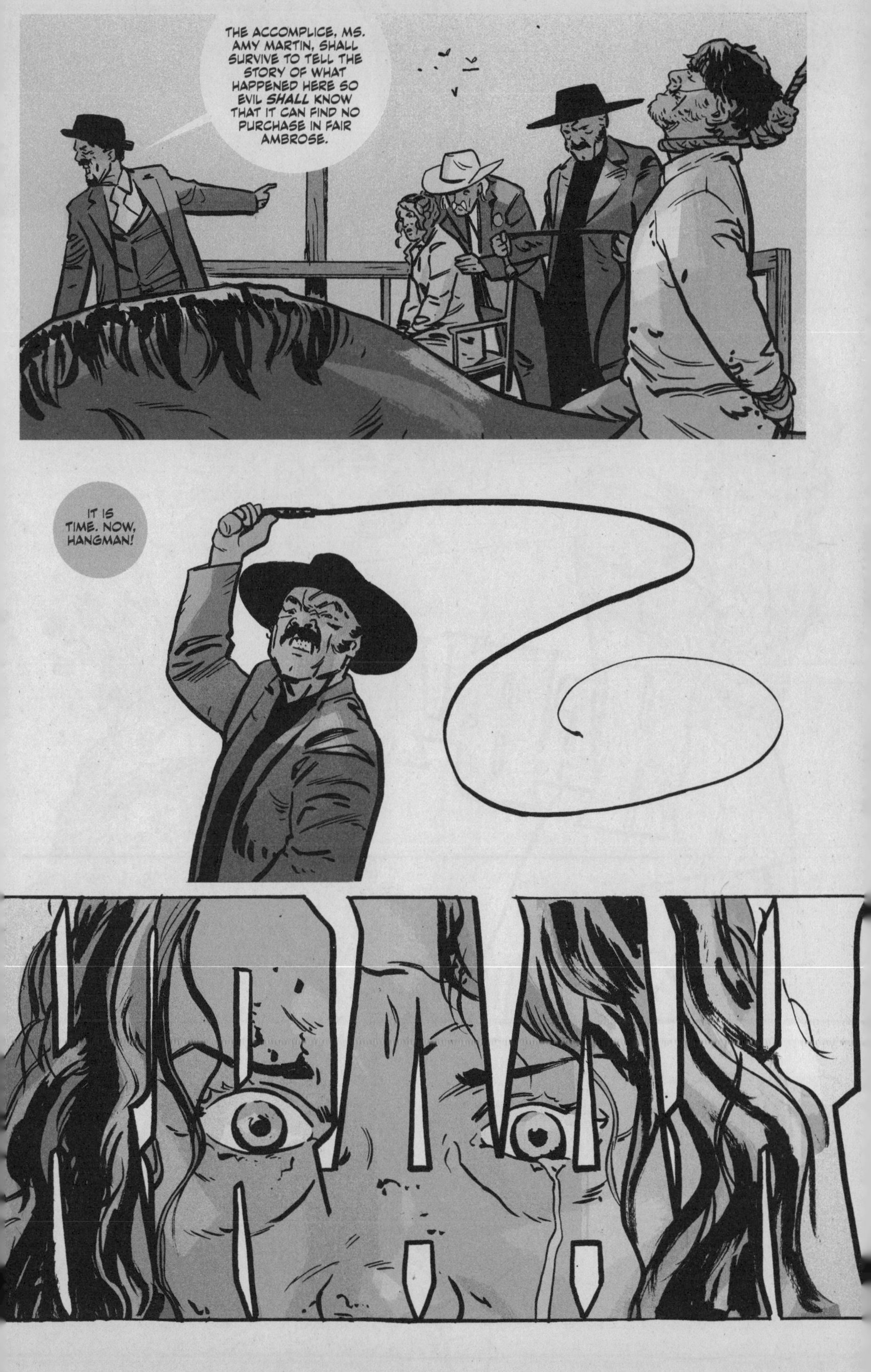
THE ACCOMPLICE, MS. AMY MARTIN, SHALL SURVIVE TO TELL THE STORY OF WHAT HAPPENED HERE SO EVIL *SHALL* KNOW THAT IT CAN FIND NO PURCHASE IN FAIR AMBROSE.
IT IS TIME. NOW, HANGMAN!

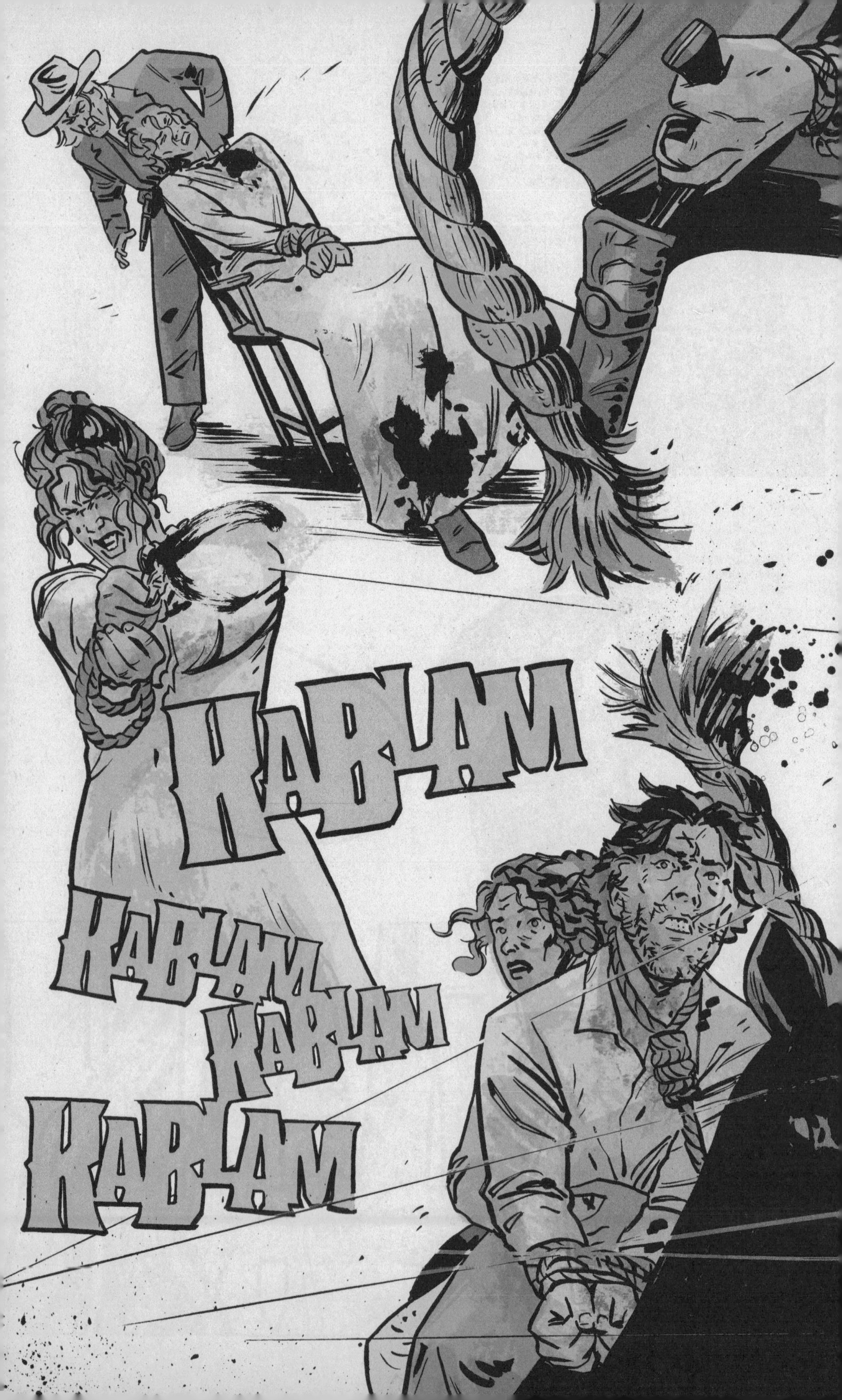
KABLAM
KABLAM
KABLAM
KABLAM

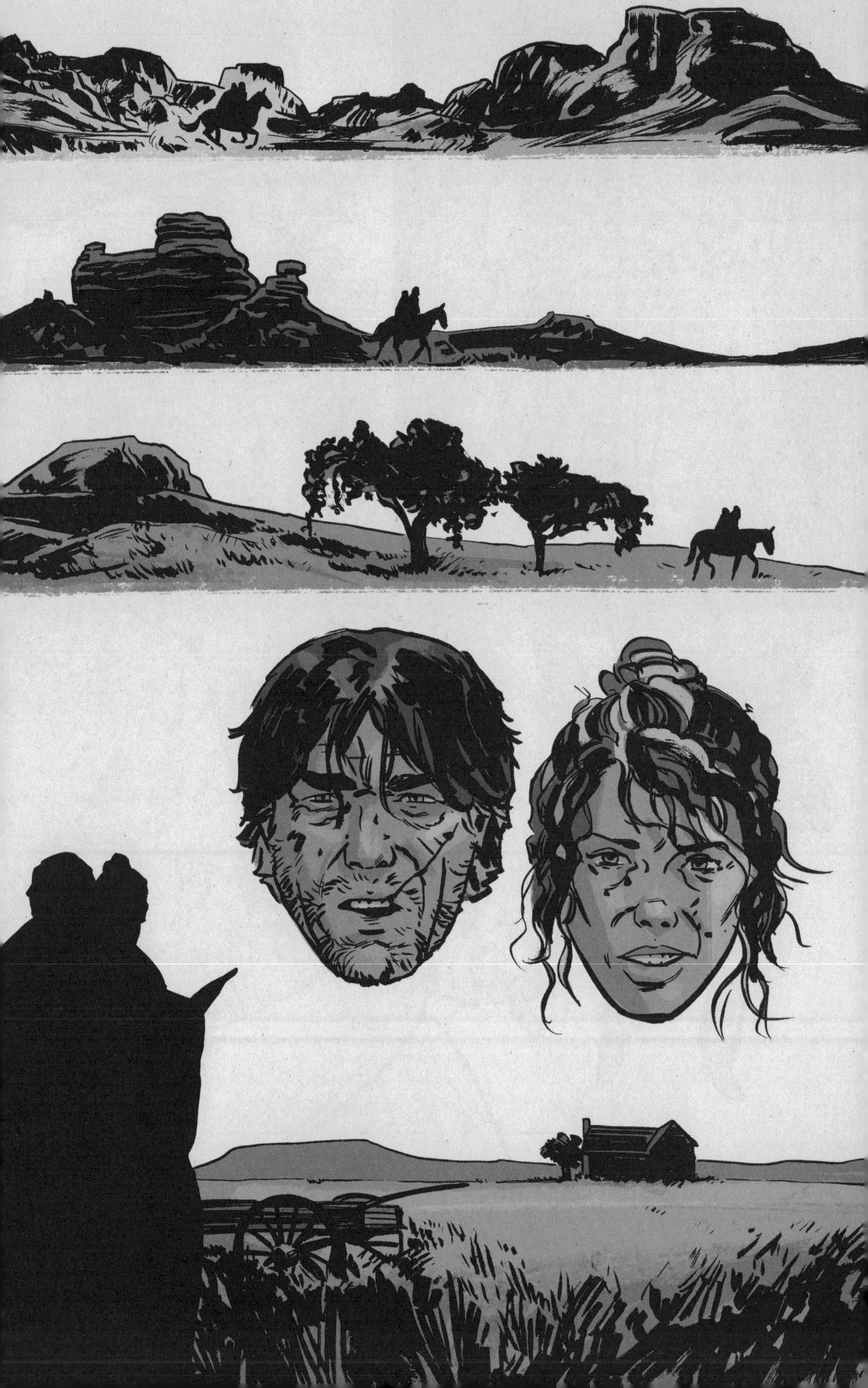

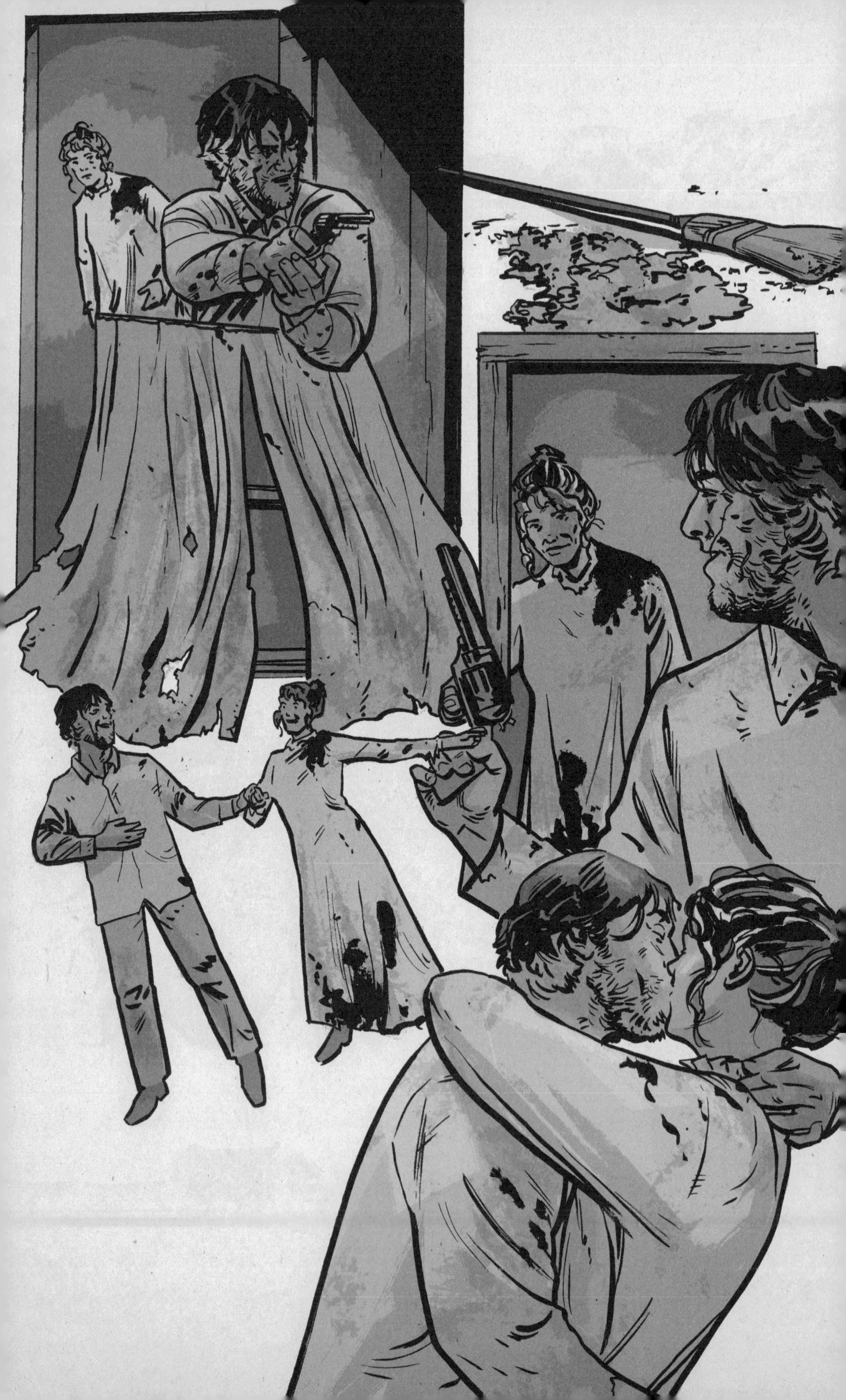

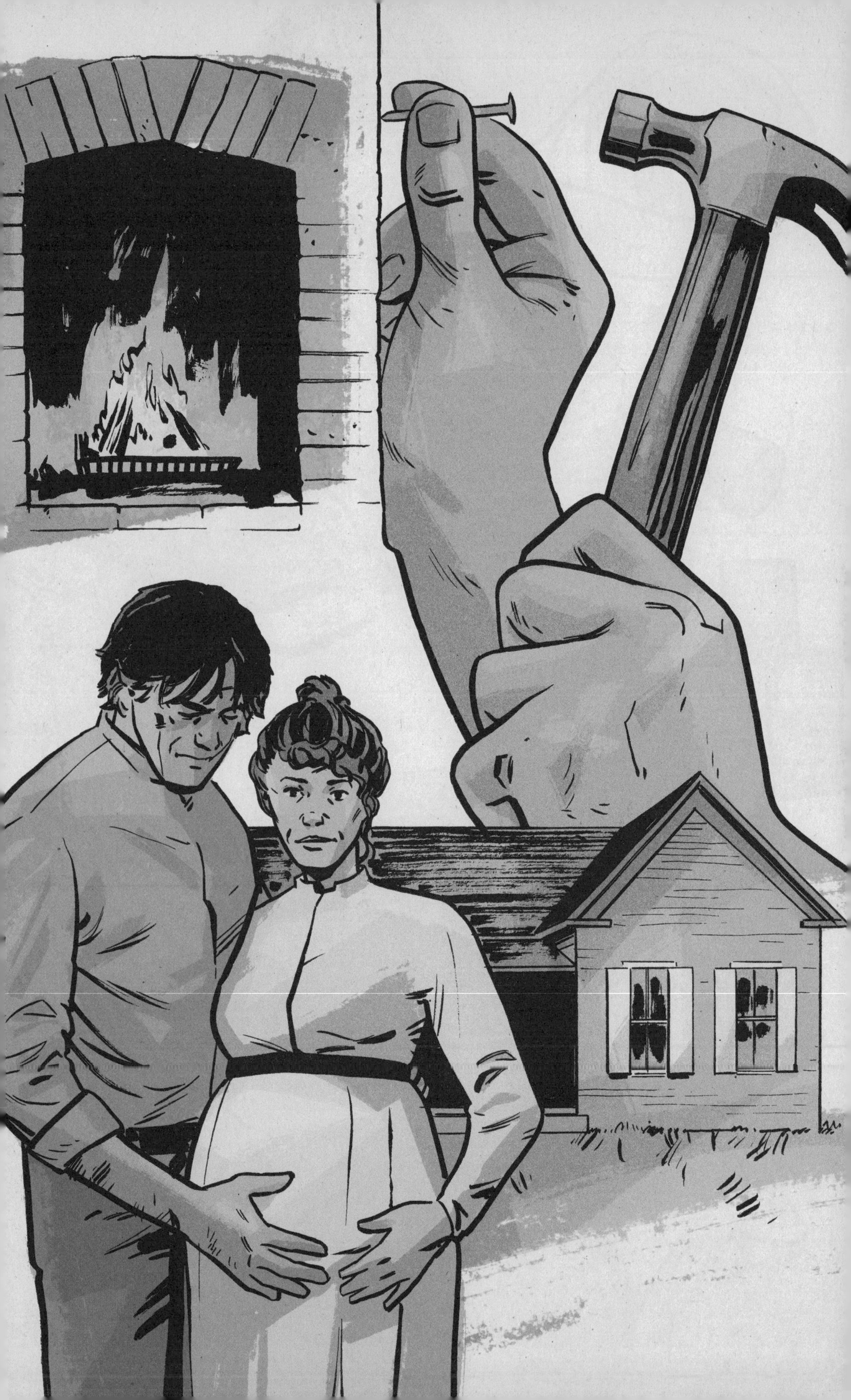

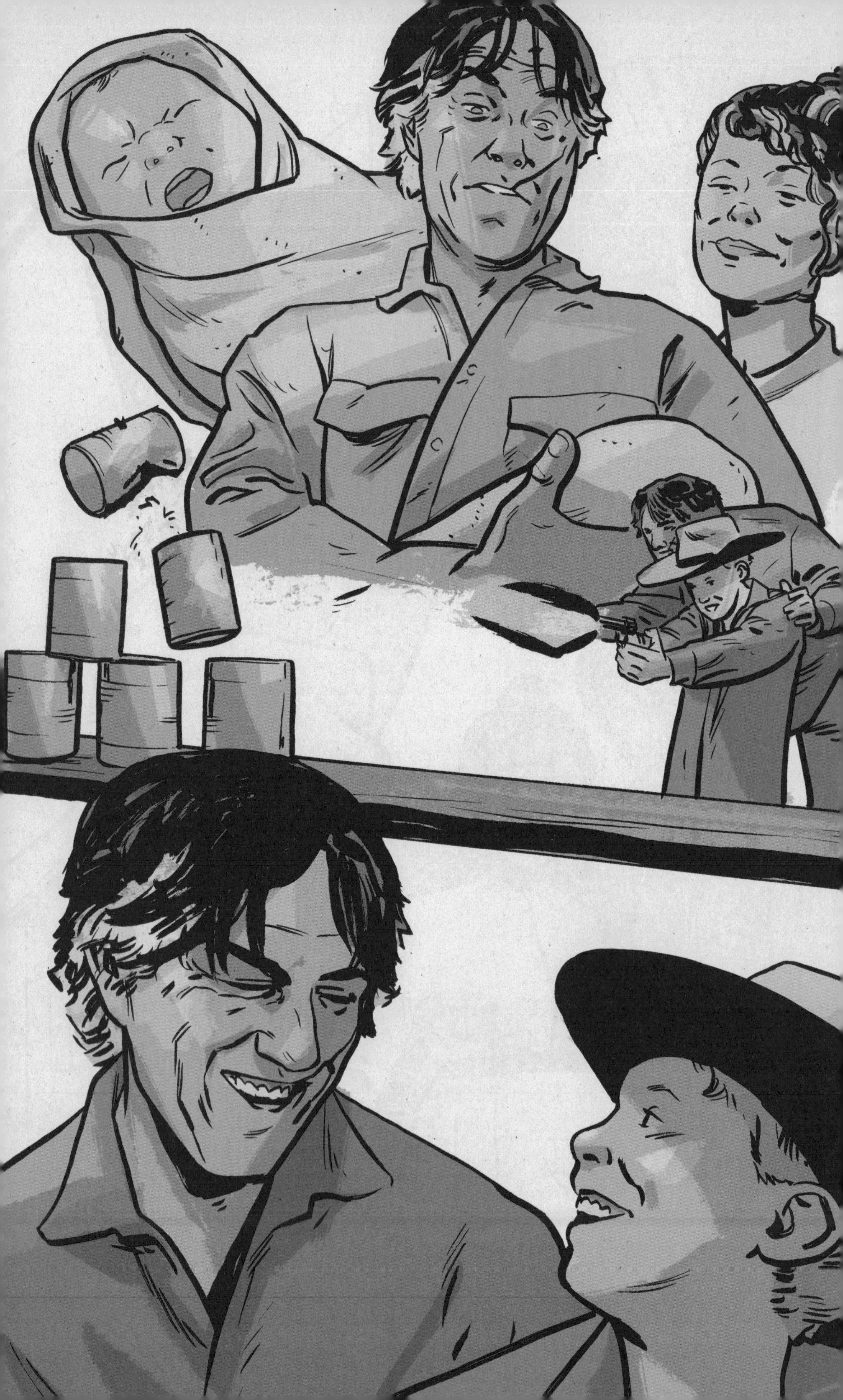

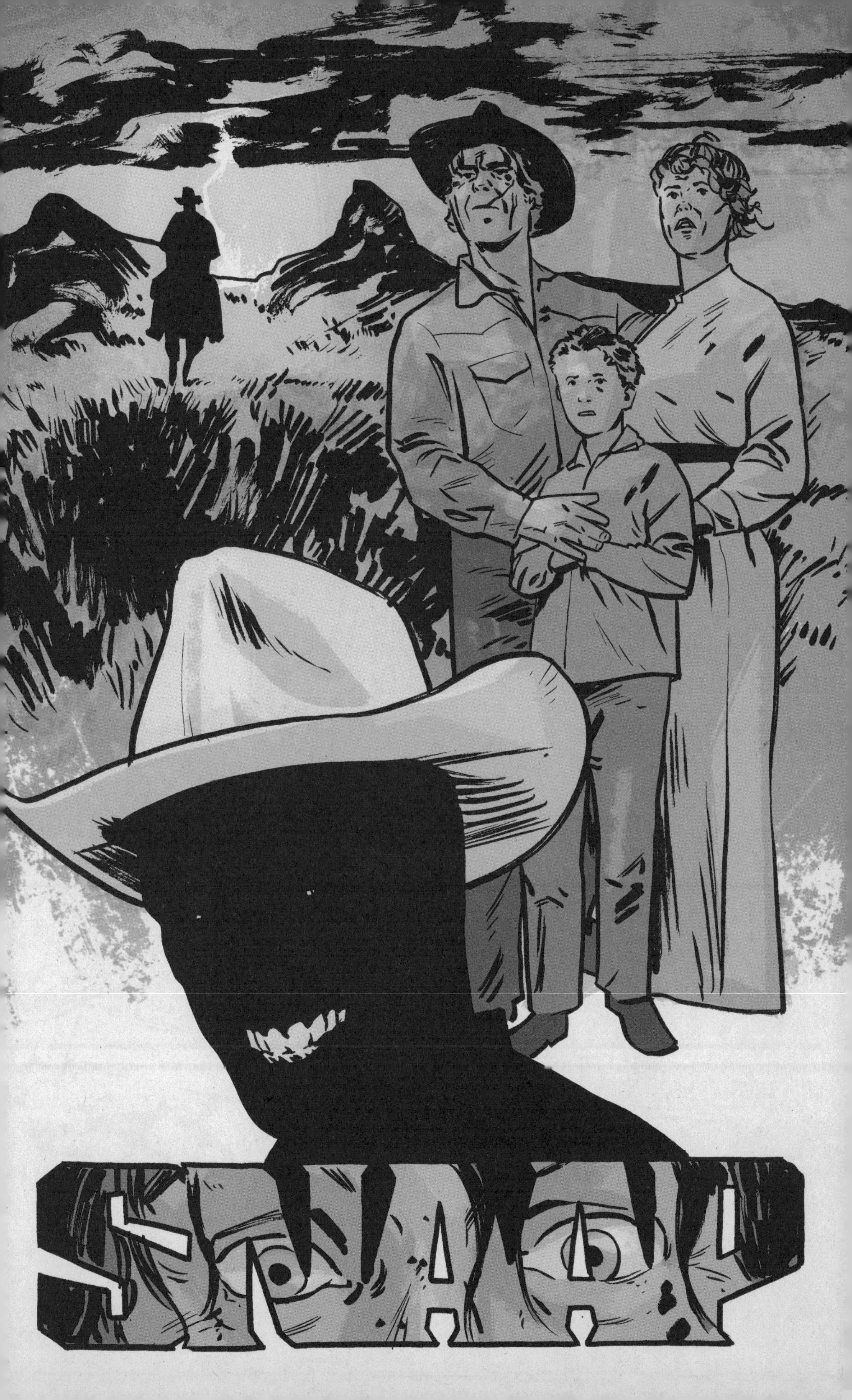

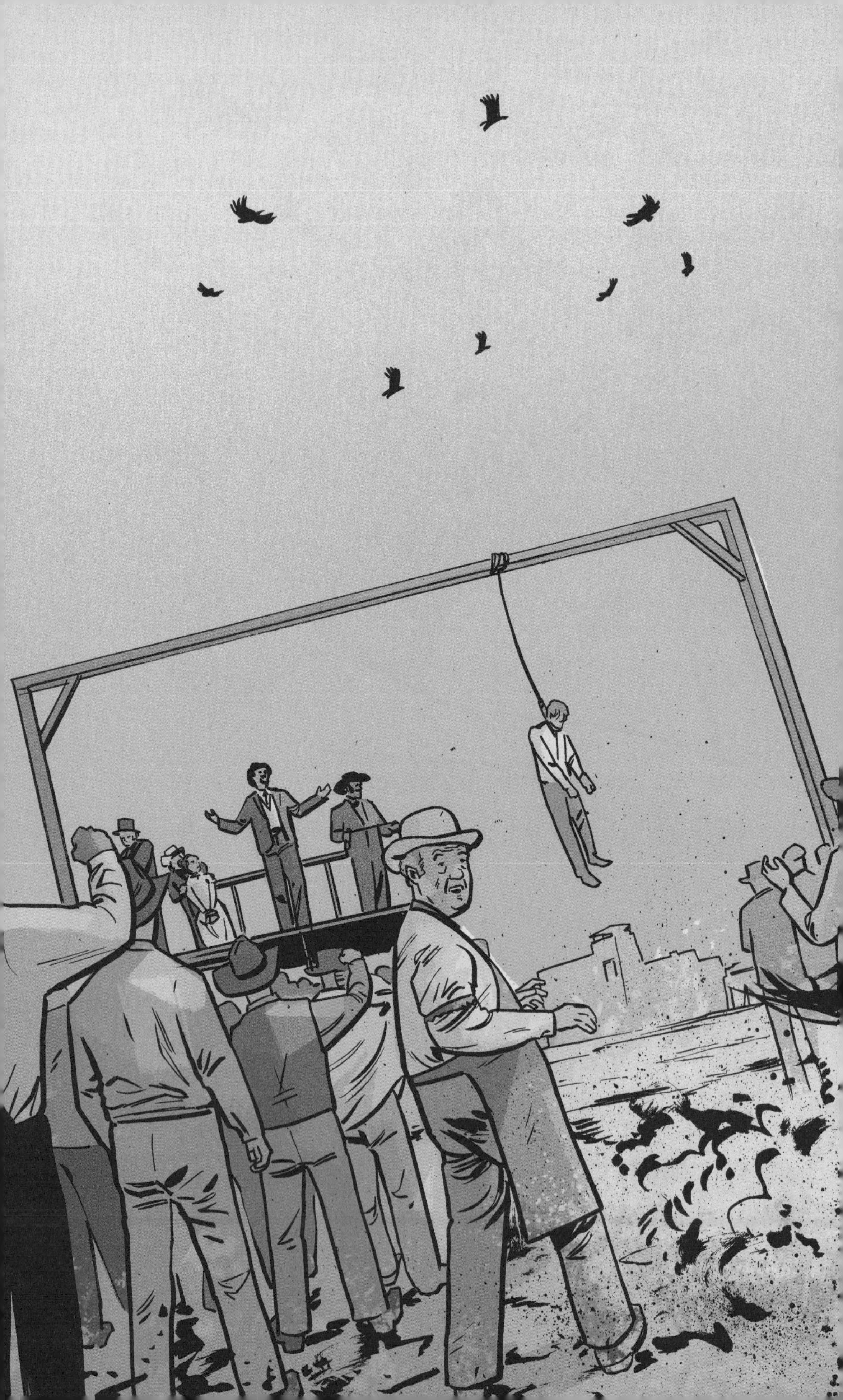

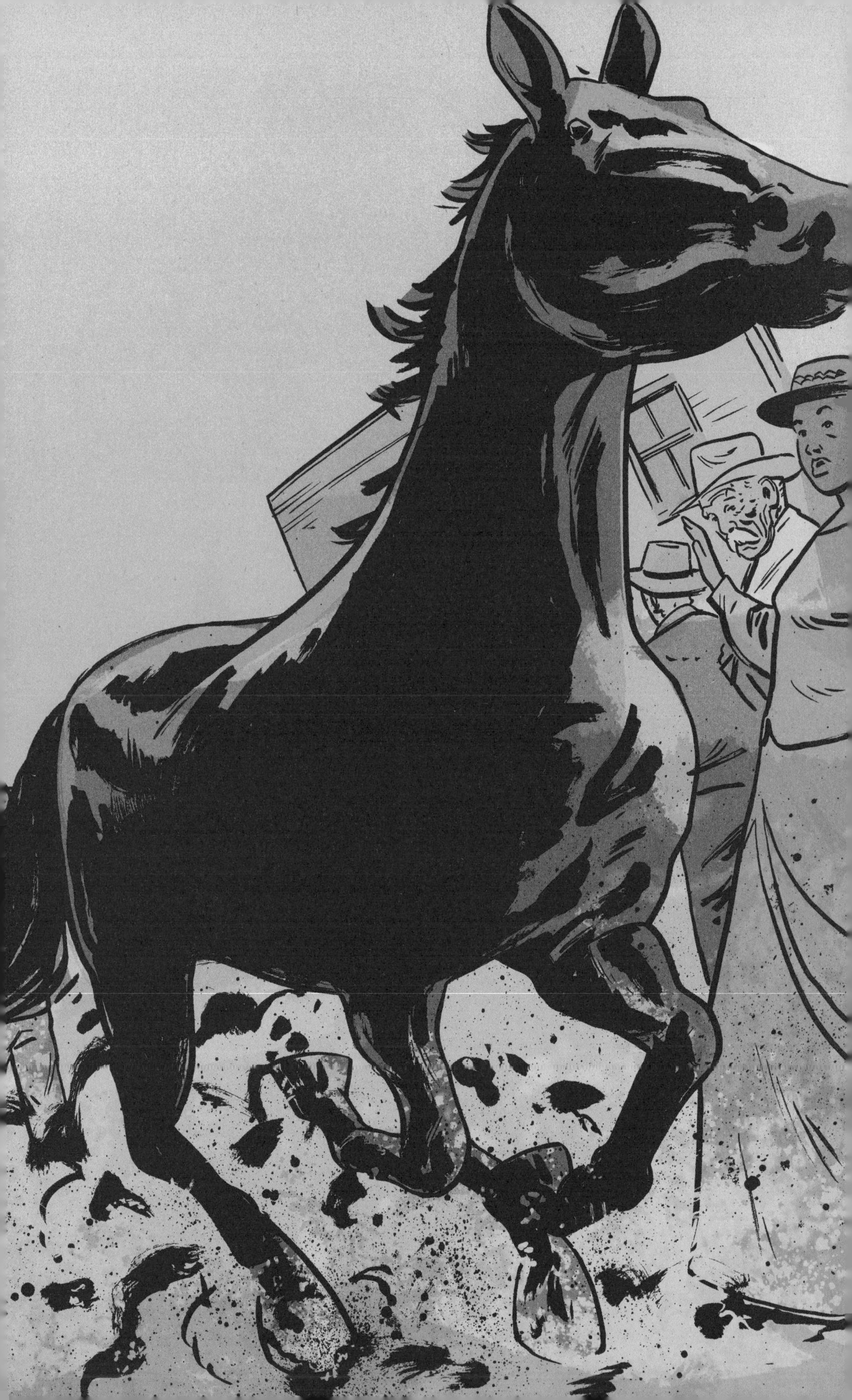

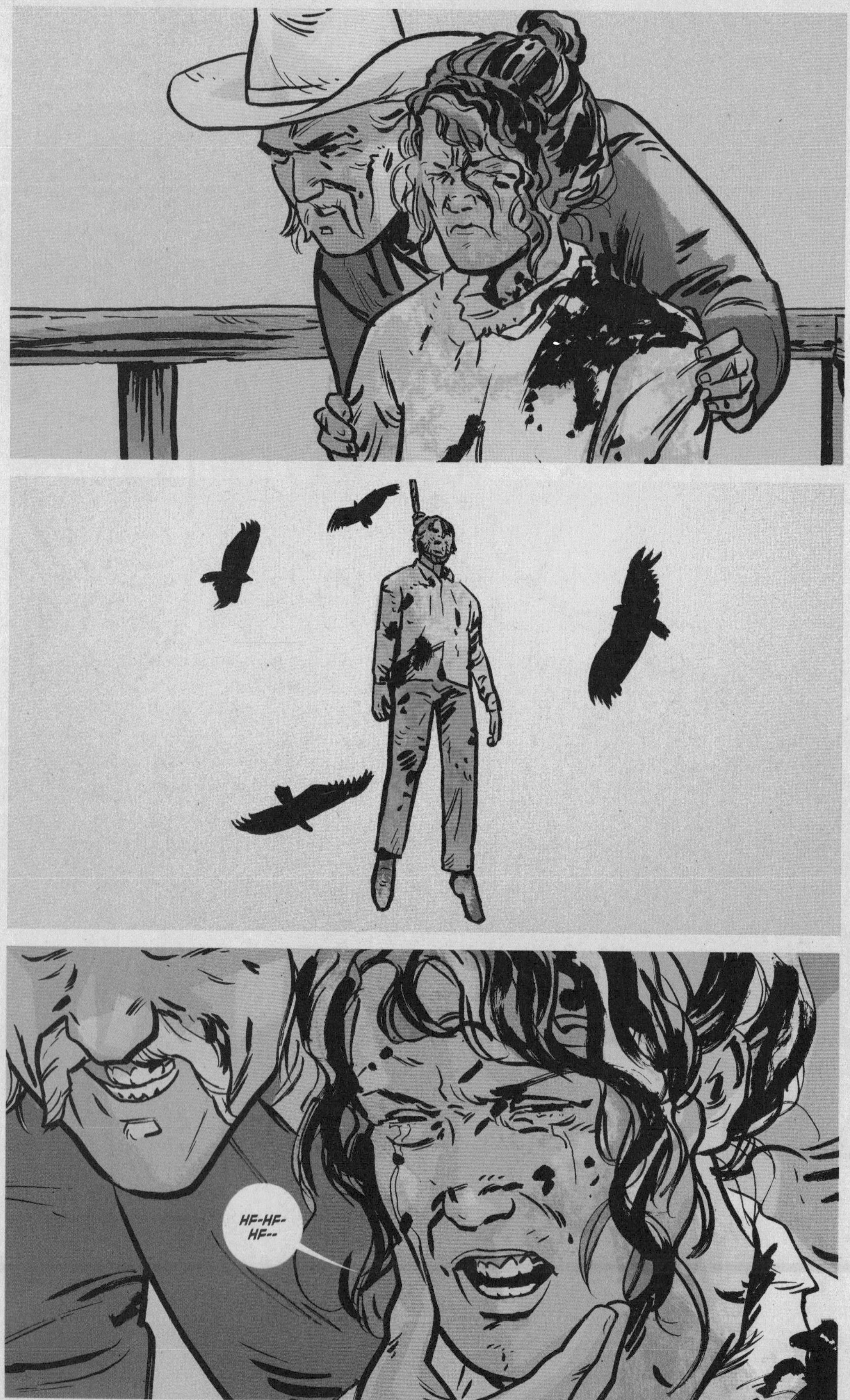
HF-HF-
HF--

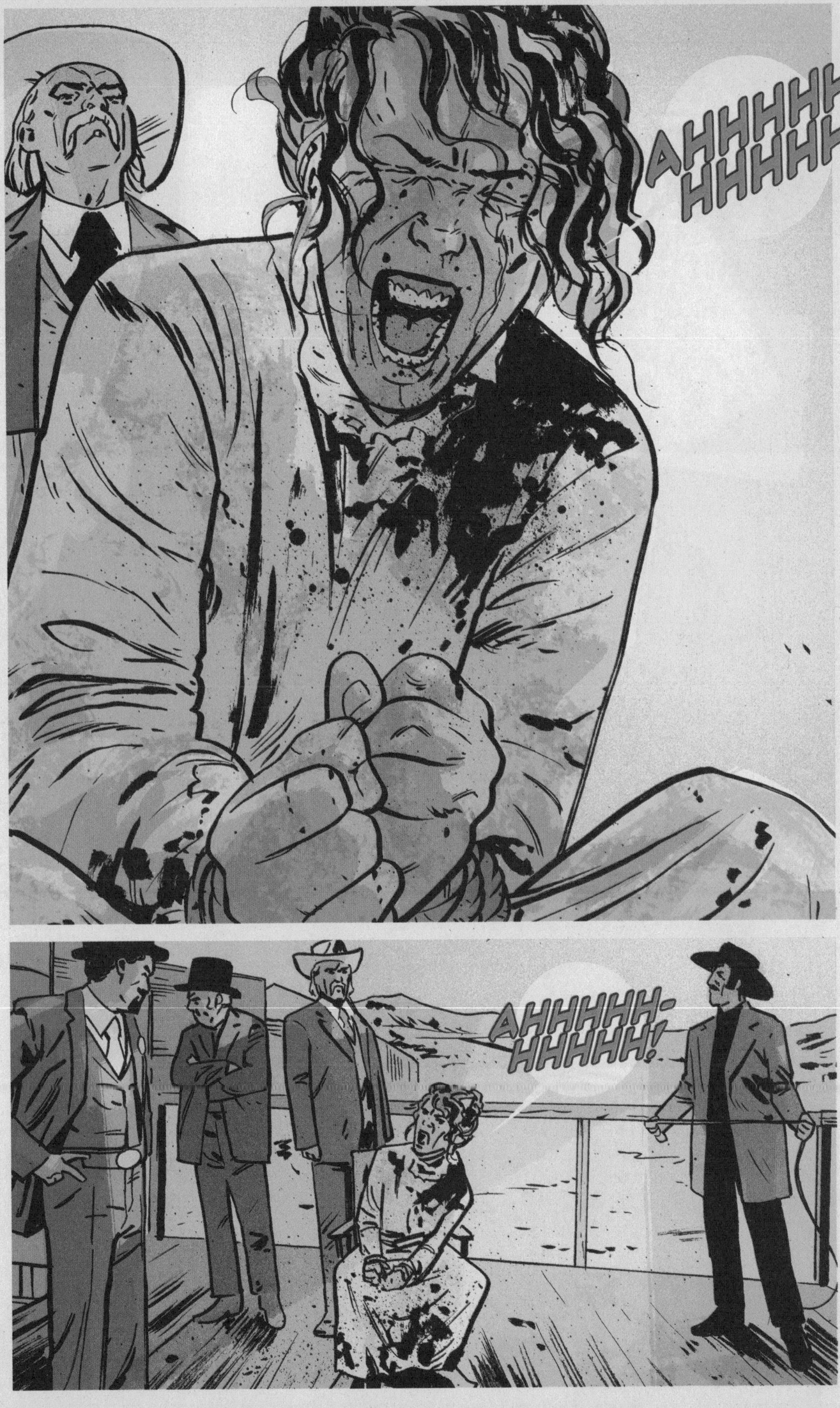
AHHHHH-HHHHH!
AHHHHH-HHHHH!

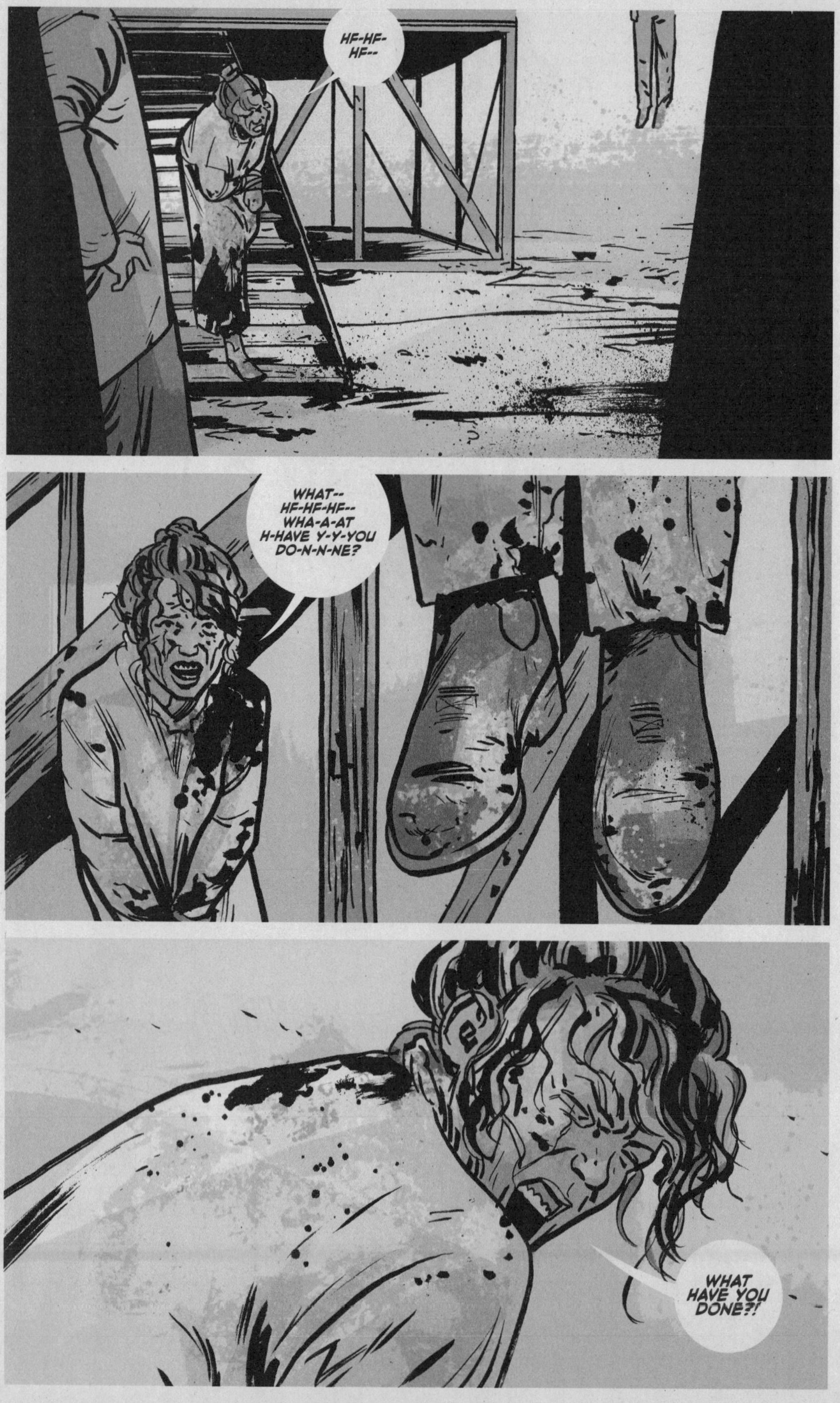
HF-HF-HF--
WHAT-- HF-HF-HF-- WHA-A-AT H-HAVE Y-Y-YOU DO-N-N-NE?
WHAT HAVE YOU DONE?!

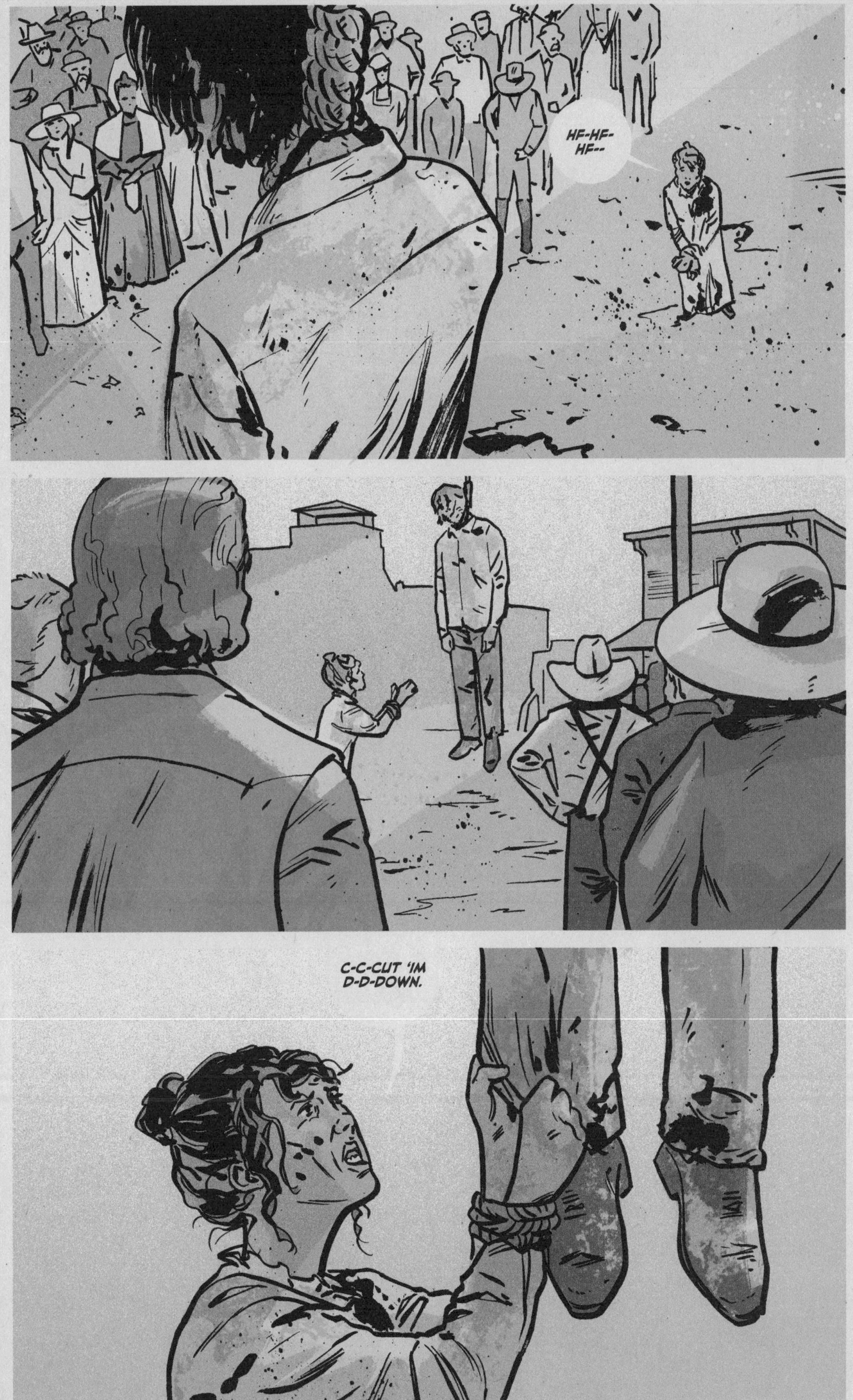
HF-HF-HF--
C-C-CUT 'IM D-D-DOWN.

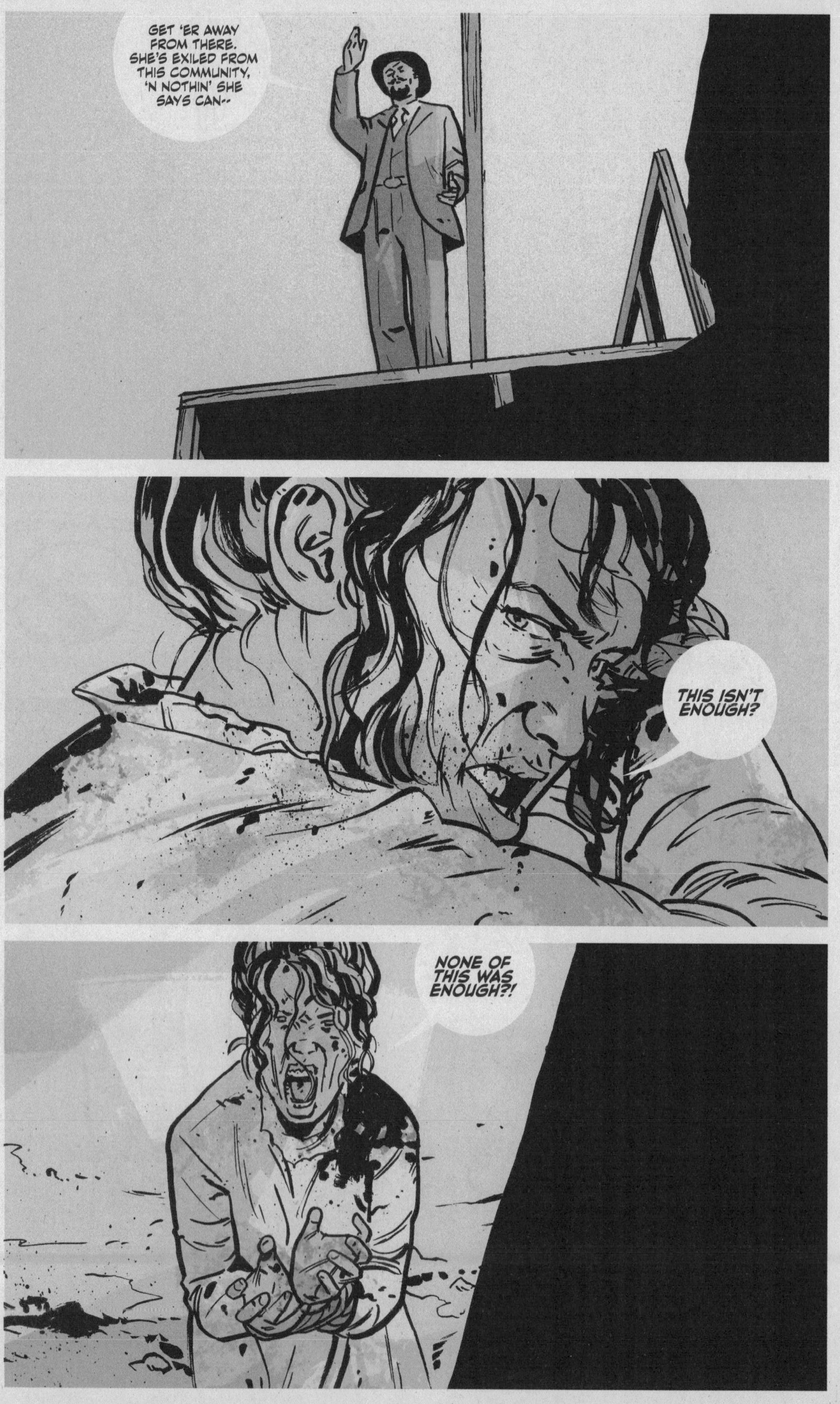
GET 'ER AWAY FROM THERE. SHE'S EXILED FROM THIS COMMUNITY, 'N NOTHIN' SHE SAYS CAN--
THIS ISN'T ENOUGH?
NONE OF THIS WAS ENOUGH?!

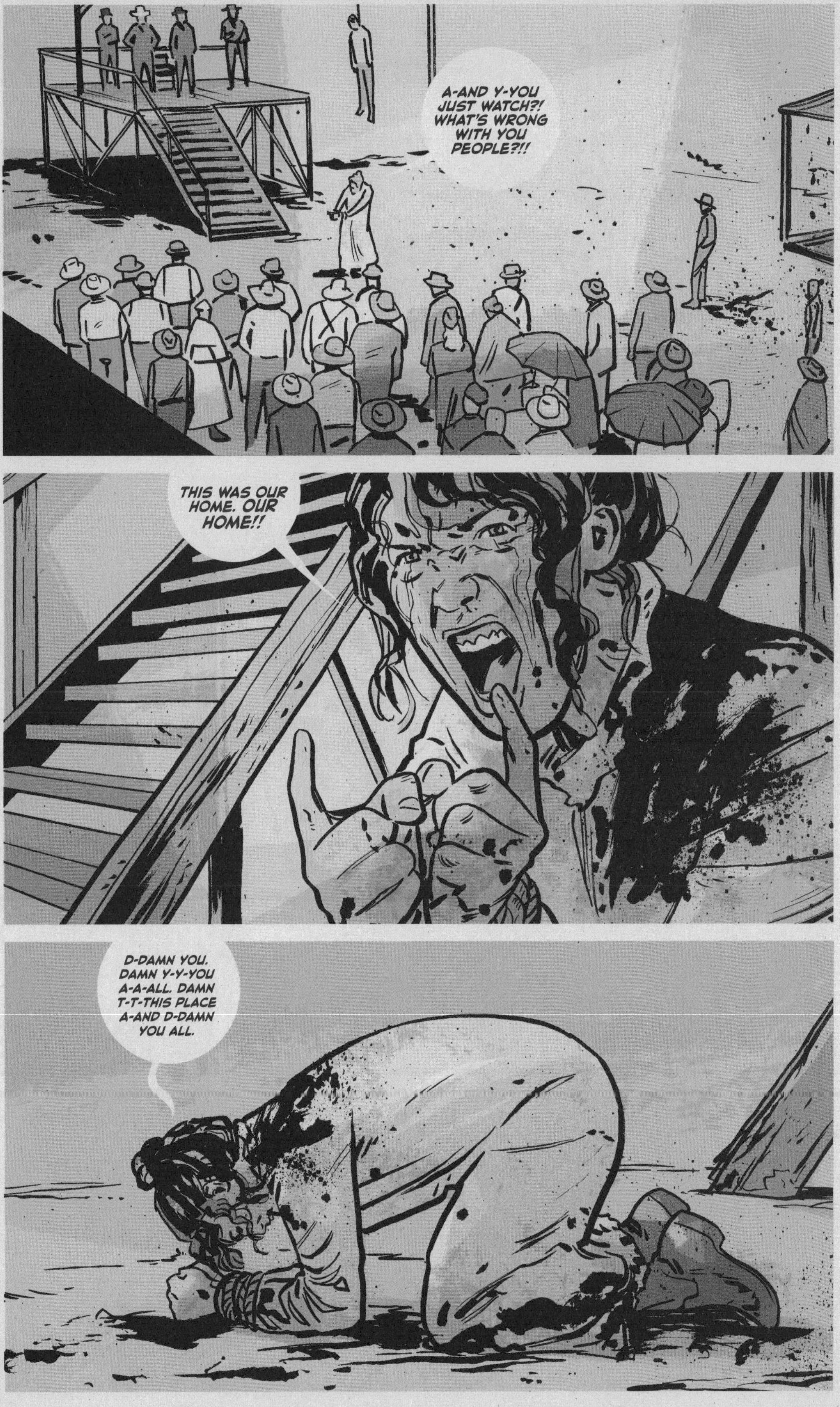
A-AND Y-YOU JUST WATCH?! WHAT'S WRONG WITH YOU PEOPLE?!!
THIS WAS OUR HOME. OUR HOME!!
D-DAMN YOU. DAMN Y-Y-YOU A-A-ALL. DAMN T-T-THIS PLACE A-AND D-DAMN YOU ALL.

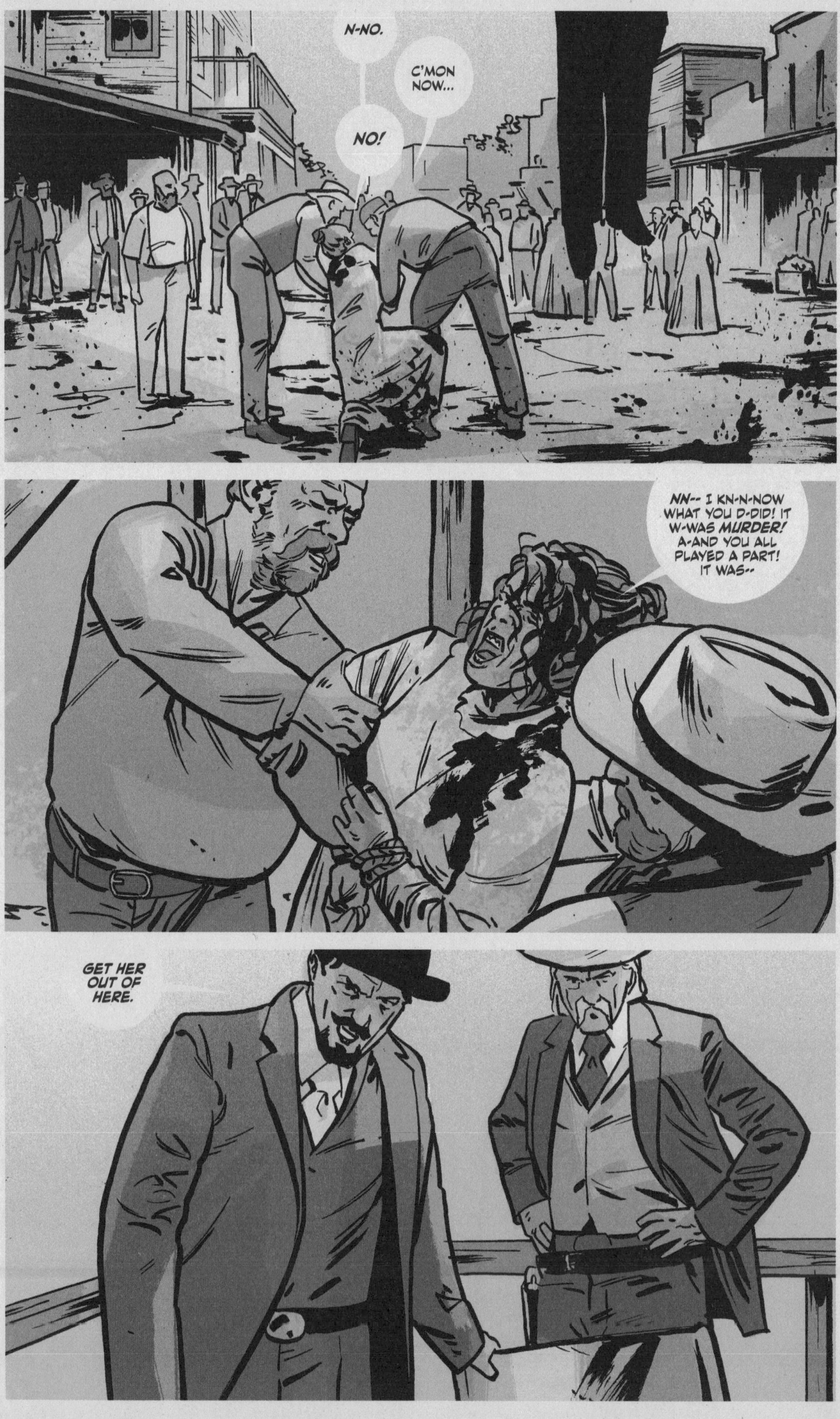
N-NO.
C'MON NOW...
NO!
NN-- I KN-N-NOW WHAT YOU D-DID! IT W-WAS MURDER! A-AND YOU ALL PLAYED A PART! IT WAS--
GET HER OUT OF HERE.

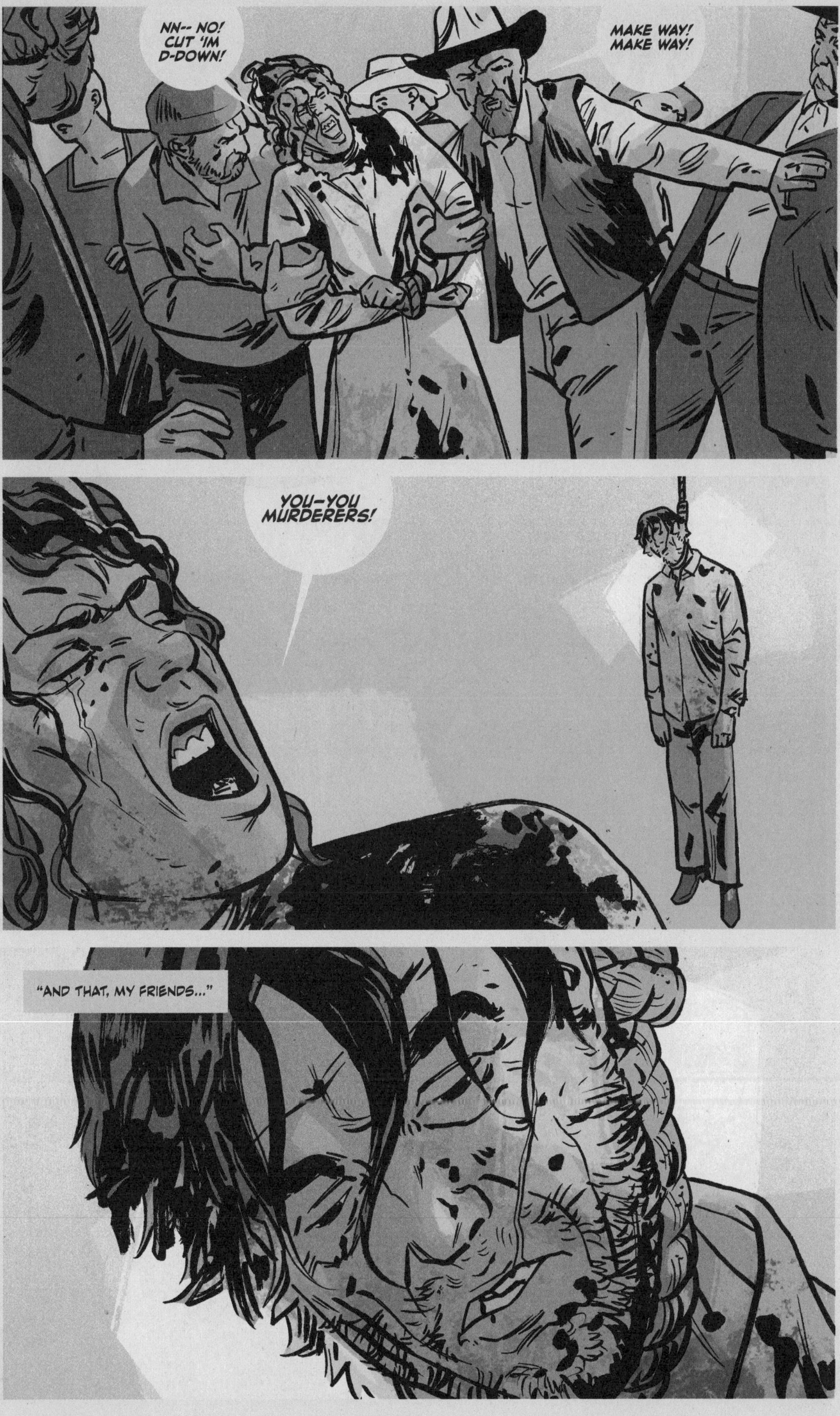
NN-- NO! CUT 'IM D-DOWN!
MAKE WAY! MAKE WAY!
YOU-YOU MURDERERS!
"AND THAT, MY FRIENDS..."

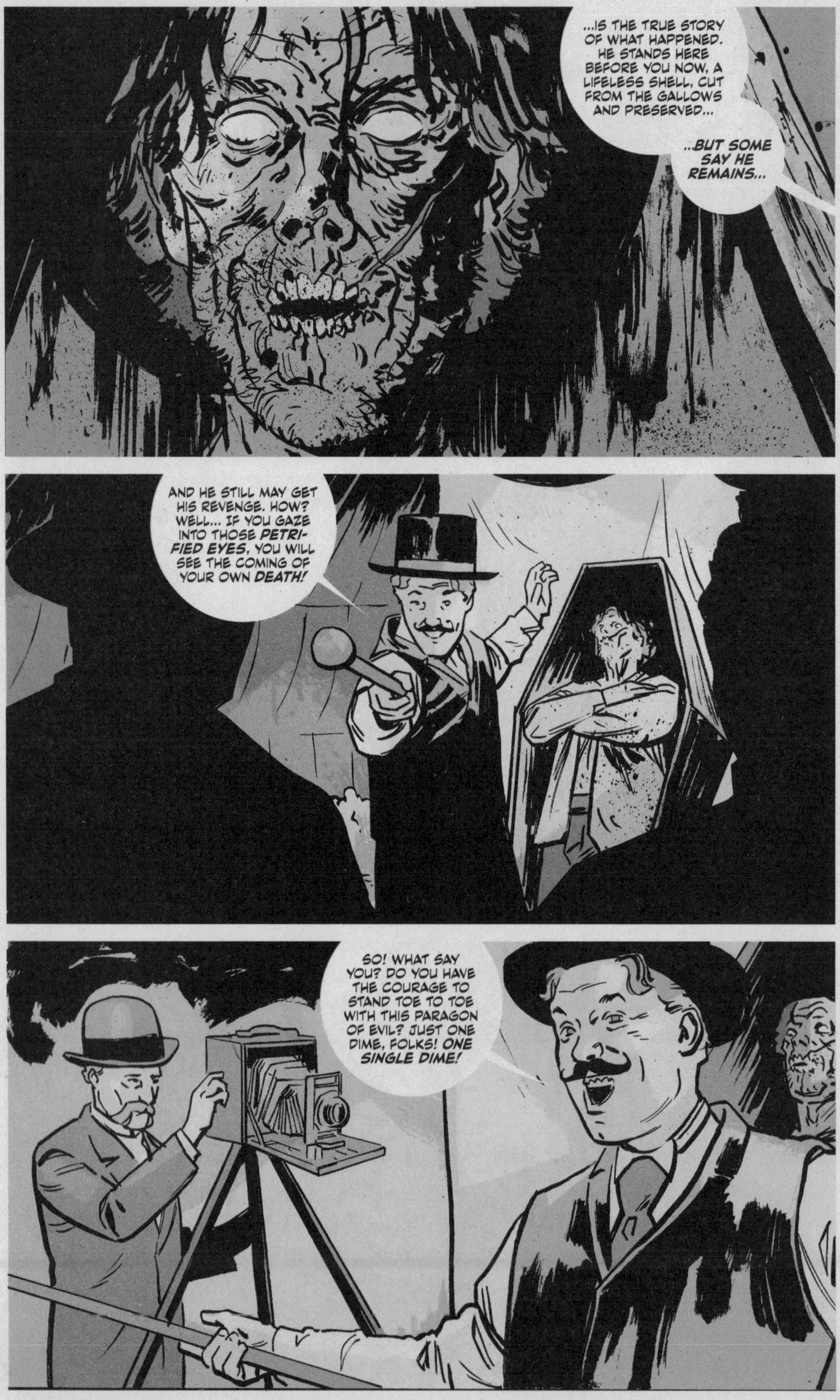
...IS THE TRUE STORY OF WHAT HAPPENED. HE STANDS HERE BEFORE YOU NOW, A LIFELESS SHELL, CUT FROM THE GALLOWS AND PRESERVED...
...BUT SOME SAY HE REMAINS...
AND HE STILL MAY GET HIS REVENGE. HOW? WELL... IF YOU GAZE INTO THOSE PETRI-FIED EYES, YOU WILL SEE THE COMING OF YOUR OWN DEATH!
SO! WHAT SAY YOU? DO YOU HAVE THE COURAGE TO STAND TOE TO TOE WITH THIS PARAGON OF EVIL? JUST ONE DIME, FOLKS! ONE SINGLE DIME!

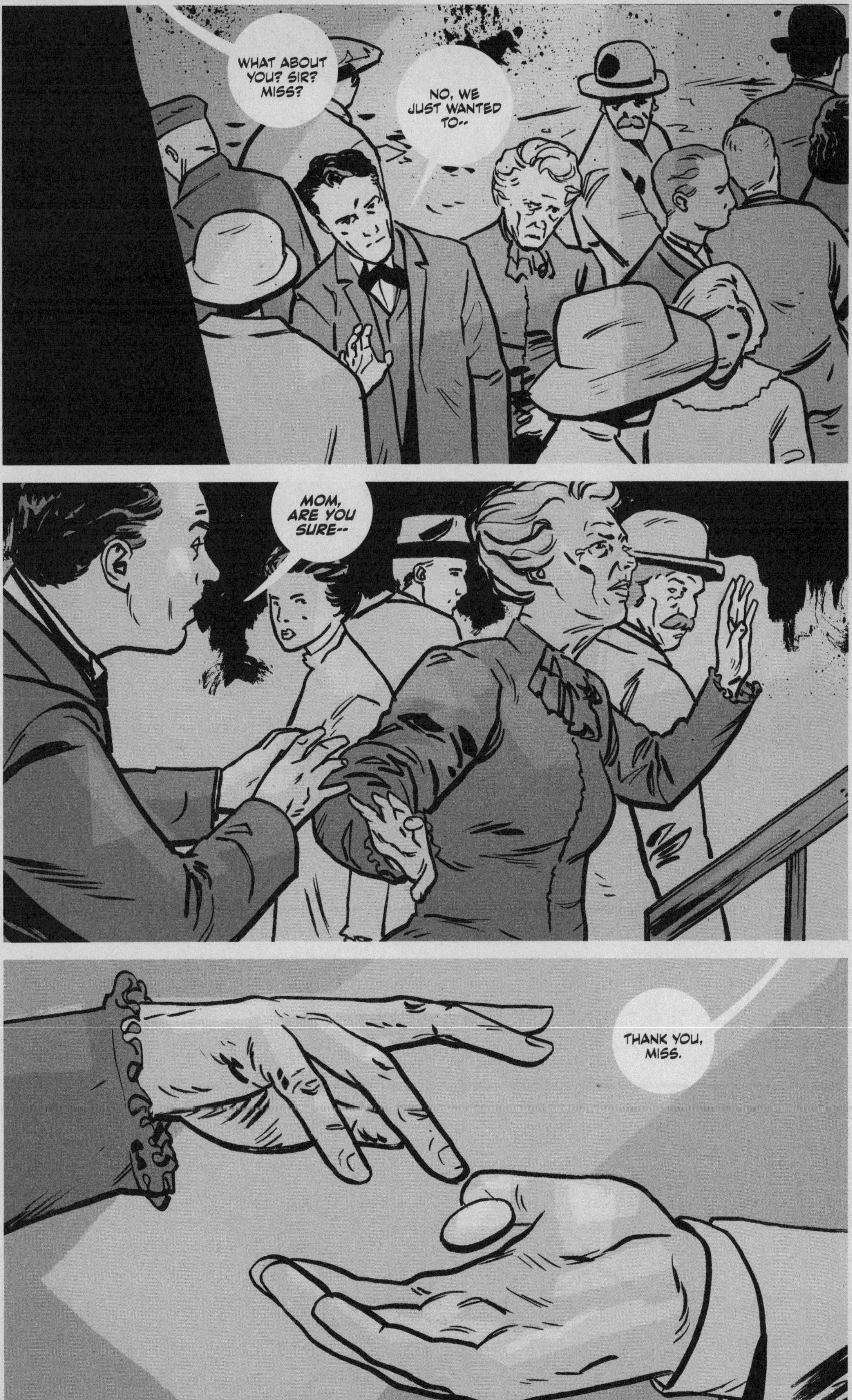
WHAT ABOUT YOU? SIR? MISS?
NO, WE JUST WANTED TO--
MOM, ARE YOU SURE--
THANK YOU, MISS.

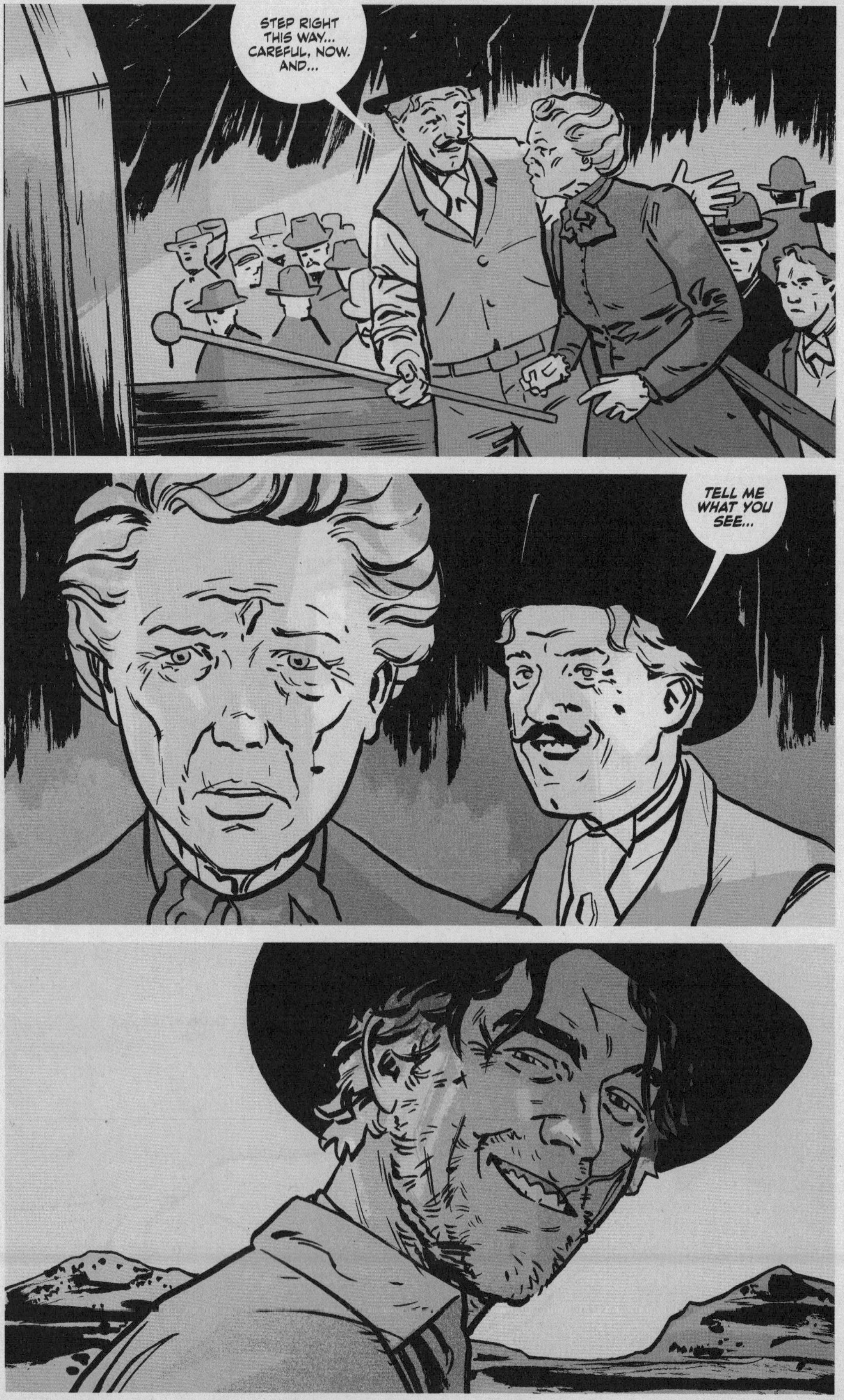
STEP RIGHT THIS WAY... CAREFUL, NOW. AND...
TELL ME WHAT YOU SEE...

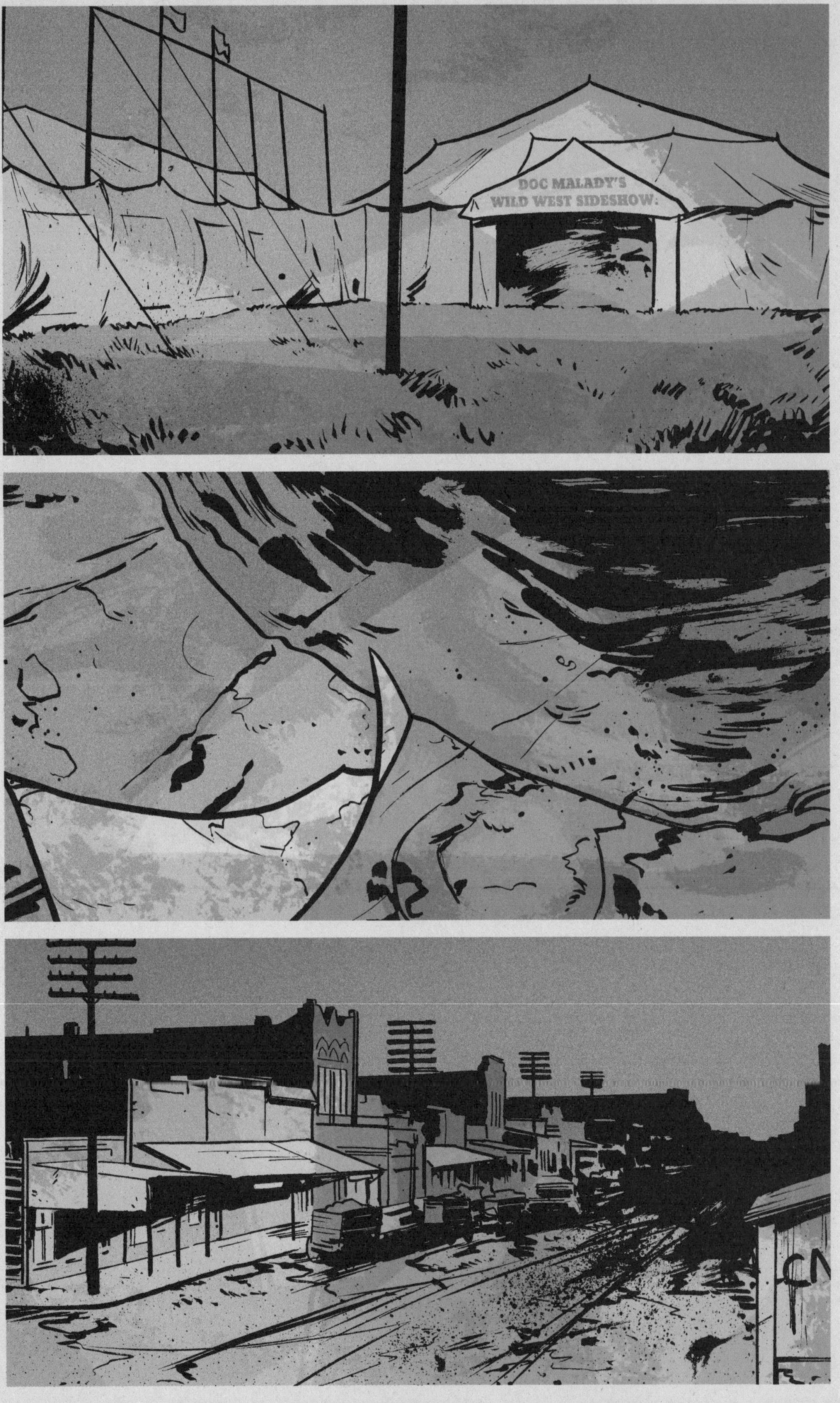
DOC MALADY'S
WILD WEST SIDESHOW:

THE ENFIELD GANG MASSACRE

ont'd.

I landed in Newark, NJ on a crisp spring morning,
New York City skyline visible through the wide win-
ws. I hadn't been to New York in many years, not since
as in my twenties. I felt, briefly, as I imagine those set-
rs that made the trek from the east to the Wild West
y have felt.

A taxicab was waiting outside for me, and I shuf-
d into it. I gave the driver the address I had acquired from
nna and sat back, buzzing with a particular sort of ex-
ement. With the car in motion, traveling along the clut-
ed byways of the New York metropolitan area, I started
ruminate on just who I was going to meet and what the
tential impact of such a meeting could be. It could be
losive or it could be a dud. Either way, I was fascinated
see what I would discover.

The taxi rolled off of route 280 and onto the Gar-
n State Parkway, north, toward Montclair. The ride was
hort jaunt, maybe ten minutes. We soon pulled in front
a Tudor-style home, large, but not oppressive. The lawn
s well-groomed and the landscaping was handsome.
e highlight of the yard was a large oak tree that sat to-
rd the street. A seemingly ancient thing, it reached up
o the sky with its thousand branches, seeking light and

I grabbed my bags from the back of the taxi and
anked the driver. He sped off as I walked the brick path
t cut through the front yard to the three porch steps that
to a red front door. I set my bags down on the top step,
athed in, then knocked. The door swung open and a
man with gray hair, combed neatly into a bun, appeared
ore me. She smiled. Her eyes were blue, strikingly so. I
iled and introduced myself. She took my offered hand
d we shook. She invited me in.

This was Lanna. She sat us down in the living
m, me on the couch, her in an armchair. She asked me if
ould like anything to drink but I declined. I didn't want
attack her with my questions about her dead great-
ndfather whom she had never met, so I eased into the
stions after a gentle, cordial back and forth of conver-
ional formalities. I started with her maiden name.

"Enfield," she said. "Which is why you're here, I
w." I nodded my head. I asked her what she knew about
last name.

"I believe it's Old English, originally," she an-
ered. She was right. It translates to 'lamb, open field.' "I
n't know exactly when my ancestors came to America.
elieve it must've been sometime at the turn of the 19th
tury. Not too long after the revolution."

Moving on, I asked her about her grandfather,
yton, who was the one who moved the family from
ahoma to Connecticut.

"My grandfather was an interesting man, yes,"
e smiled. "I didn't know him well. He died when I was
y five or six years old. I remember he used to sit in a
king chair in the corner of the room, a pillow propped
ind his lower back. He was always scowling, a pipe held
he palm of his hand. Always lit. Despite the scowl, he

was actually very playful. And kind. He was fond of telling
jokes. And stories, too."

That was my chance. I seized the opportunity. I
wondered if he had told any tales about his parents from
when they had lived out on the frontier.

"Yes, he told stories about his mother. Her name
was Amy. I never met her, of course. Amy Westley. She
was married to a man named Jonathan Westley, but that
was not my grandfather's paternal father. His father was
named Enfield.

"He would tell stories about him, too, as they
were told to him by his mother. He said that for the first
half of his life, his mother never spoke about his father.
She was afflicted with 'melancholy,' as he'd call it, and any
mention of his father would send her into an anxious state.
So, he avoided the topic. Then one day, she decided to talk.
It was only after Jonathan, her husband, had suffered a
stroke and was bedridden.

"She told him that his father was a man named
Montgomery Enfield. He was apparently an outlaw from
the old Wild West days and was murdered in Texas. My
great-grandmother was, according to my grandfather,
lucky to escape alive."

She wasn't wrong. I asked her if she had ever
heard of the Enfield Gang Massacre. The look on her face
told me she had not–at least not in so many words. I wasn't
relishing the fact that I was the one to inform her that her
great-grandfather was betrayed, his gang and their family
members killed indiscriminately, and that he was hanged
in public before being stuffed and carted around for some
thirty-odd years as a sideshow oddity. The whereabouts
of his body were still unknown. Some said he was buried
somewhere in East Texas, others said that his body was
burned along with other objects deemed obsolete by the
sideshow workers. Lanna, it seems, knew different.

"Oh, no," she shook her head. "He's buried in Connecticut, next to Amy. It was a bit of an odd request, and
apparently it took some convincing to allow it, but he's
buried beside Amy and my grandfather. Jonathan is on the
other side of Amy, too. She didn't exclude him. They're all
up in Connecticut now. I don't often go up there but I've
seen the stone. It was engraved with just the words 'Enfield' and 'Beloved Husband and Father.' It seems that Amy
and my grandfather thought it important that he join her."

I thought that this must have been a fantasy.
Maybe there was a grave there next to Amy, but surely it
was empty. I thanked Lanna profusely and, before I left, I
asked her if she was interested in joining me on a trip to
Connecticut. To my great surprise, she agreed, and even offered to drive.

Over two hours later, we arrived in Windsor, Connecticut, a picturesque town north of Hartford and a few
miles west of the Connecticut River. Our destination was
an old white church along with its connected graveyard.
Once there, we wound through the graves and came upon
a large marker that read 'Westley.' On the marker were
etched several names. On the right side, it said 'Jonathan'
and on the left, it said, simply, 'Amy.' Beside her name, it
said 'Clayton.' I could feel my heart racing in my chest.

Beside the larger marker sat a small plaque to
the left of Amy and Clayton's. It read, as Lanna had stated,
simply, 'Enfield.' I bent at the knee and ran my finger along
the etched letters of the name. I looked up at Lanna, the
only living descendent of this true Western legend.

How Enfield was retrieved by Amy remains
something of a mystery, though my best guess would be
that she plied–likely purchased–his remains from Doc
Malady or one of his cronies after one of their routine stops
in Oklahoma. My assumption is that this coincided with
her travel from Arkansas to Oklahoma, some time in 1906.
But we don't know for certain. What we do know is that
here he is, and here he shall remain. At rest and, hopefully,
at peace. No sign of struggle. No sign of murder, massacre,
or mayhem. No sign of John Mowbray or the guns of Quentin Ely. No conniving or secret conspiracies. Just a family
laid to rest–together.

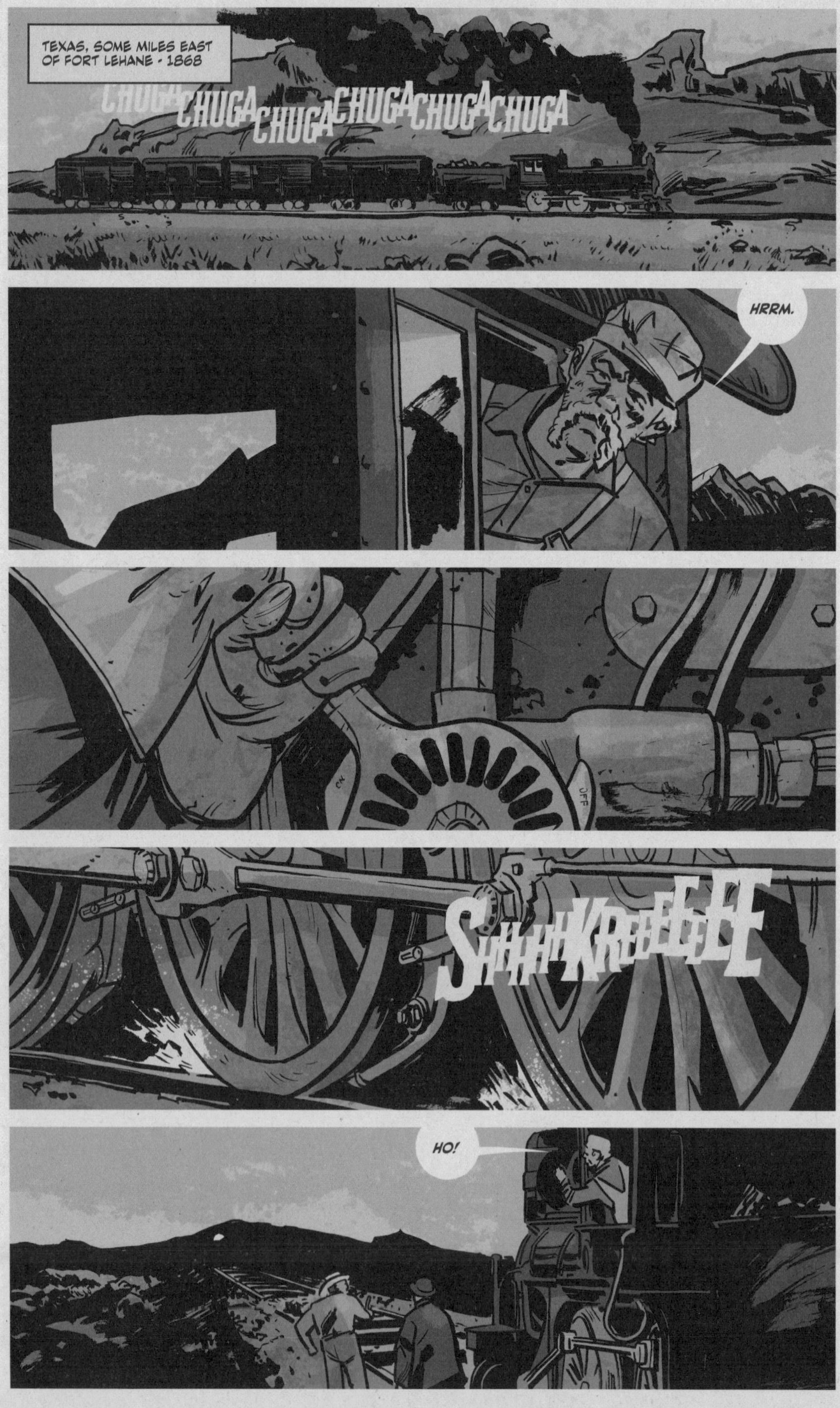
TEXAS, SOME MILES EAST OF FORT LEHANE - 1868
CHUGA CHUGA CHUGA CHUGA CHUGA CHUGA
HRRM.
SHHHHKREEEEEEE
HO!

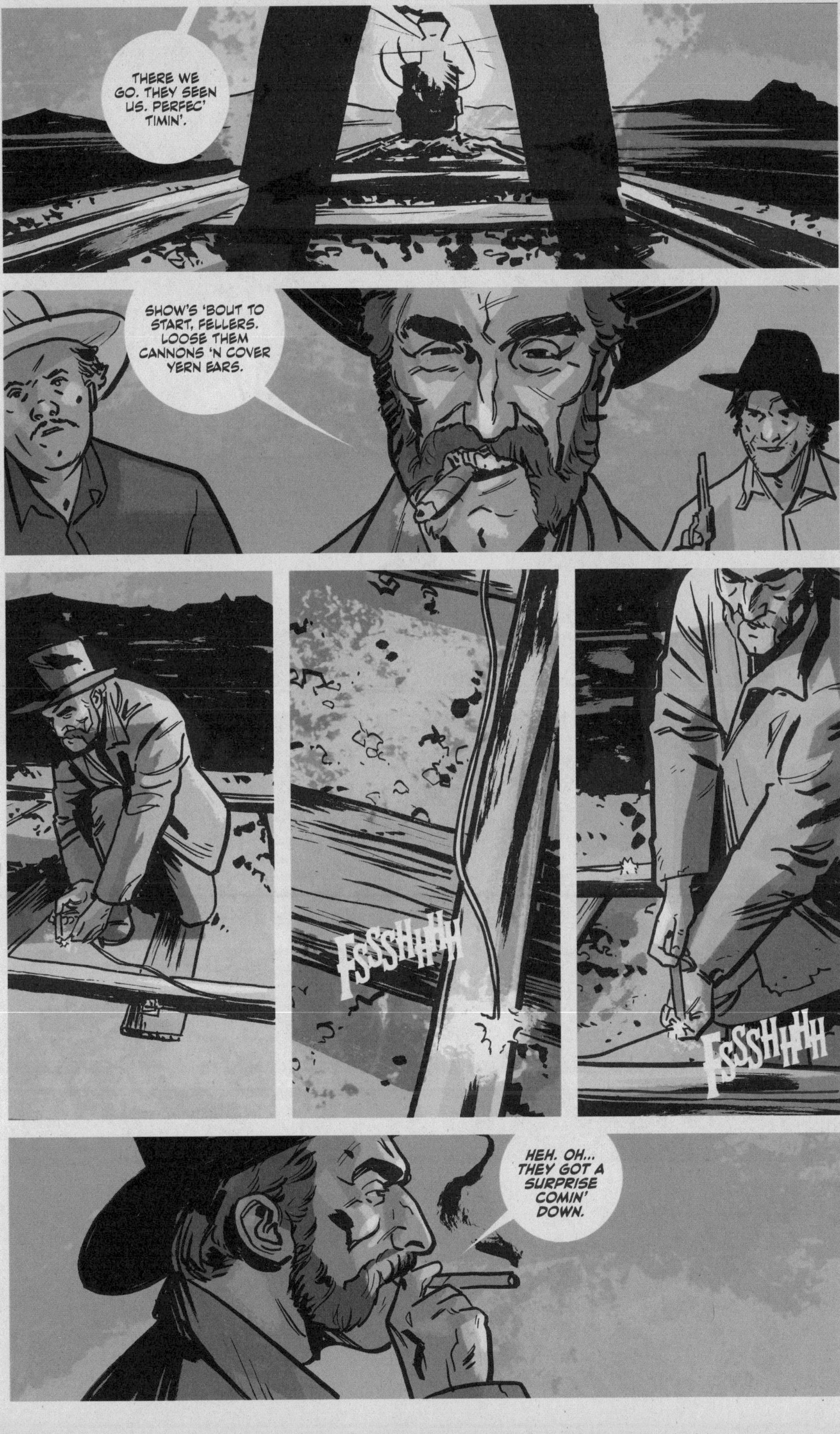
THERE WE GO. THEY SEEN US. PERFEC' TIMIN'.
SHOW'S 'BOUT TO START, FELLERS. LOOSE THEM CANNONS 'N COVER YERN EARS.
FSSSHHHH
FSSSHHHH
HEH. OH... THEY GOT A SURPRISE COMIN' DOWN.

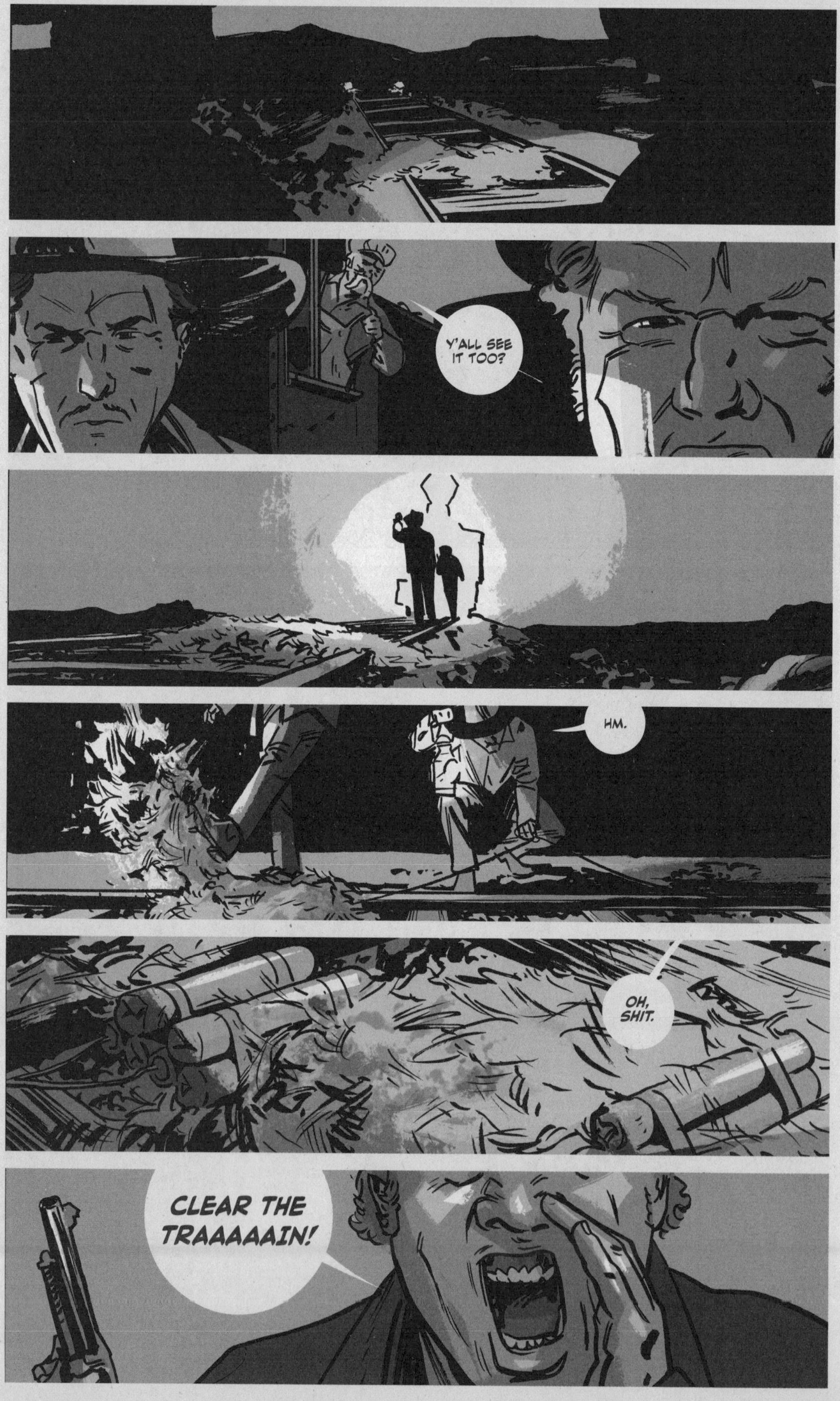
Y'ALL SEE IT TOO?
HM.
OH, SHIT.
CLEAR THE TRAAAAAIN!

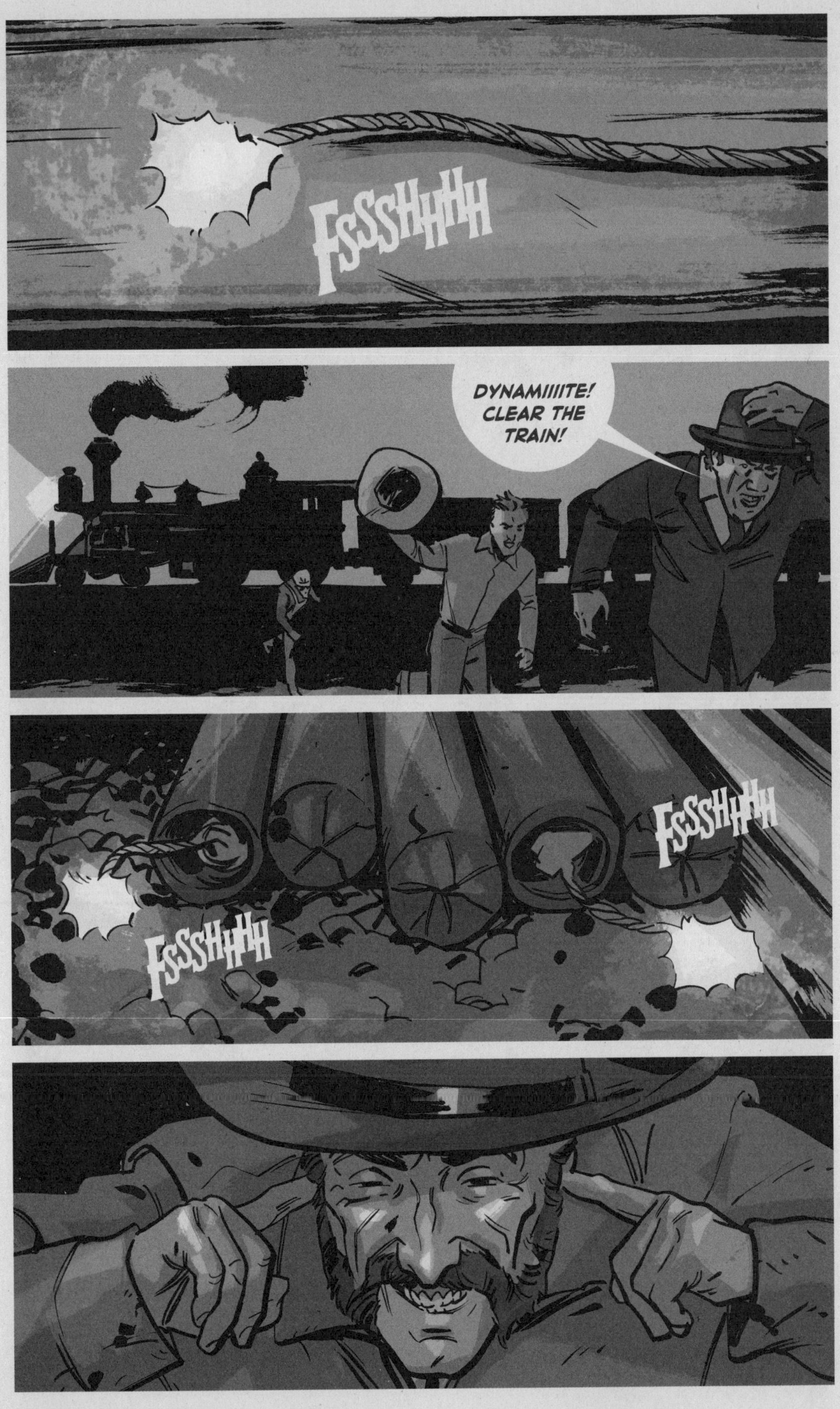
FSSSHHHHH
DYNAMIIIIITE! CLEAR THE TRAIN!
FSSSHHHH
FSSSHHHH

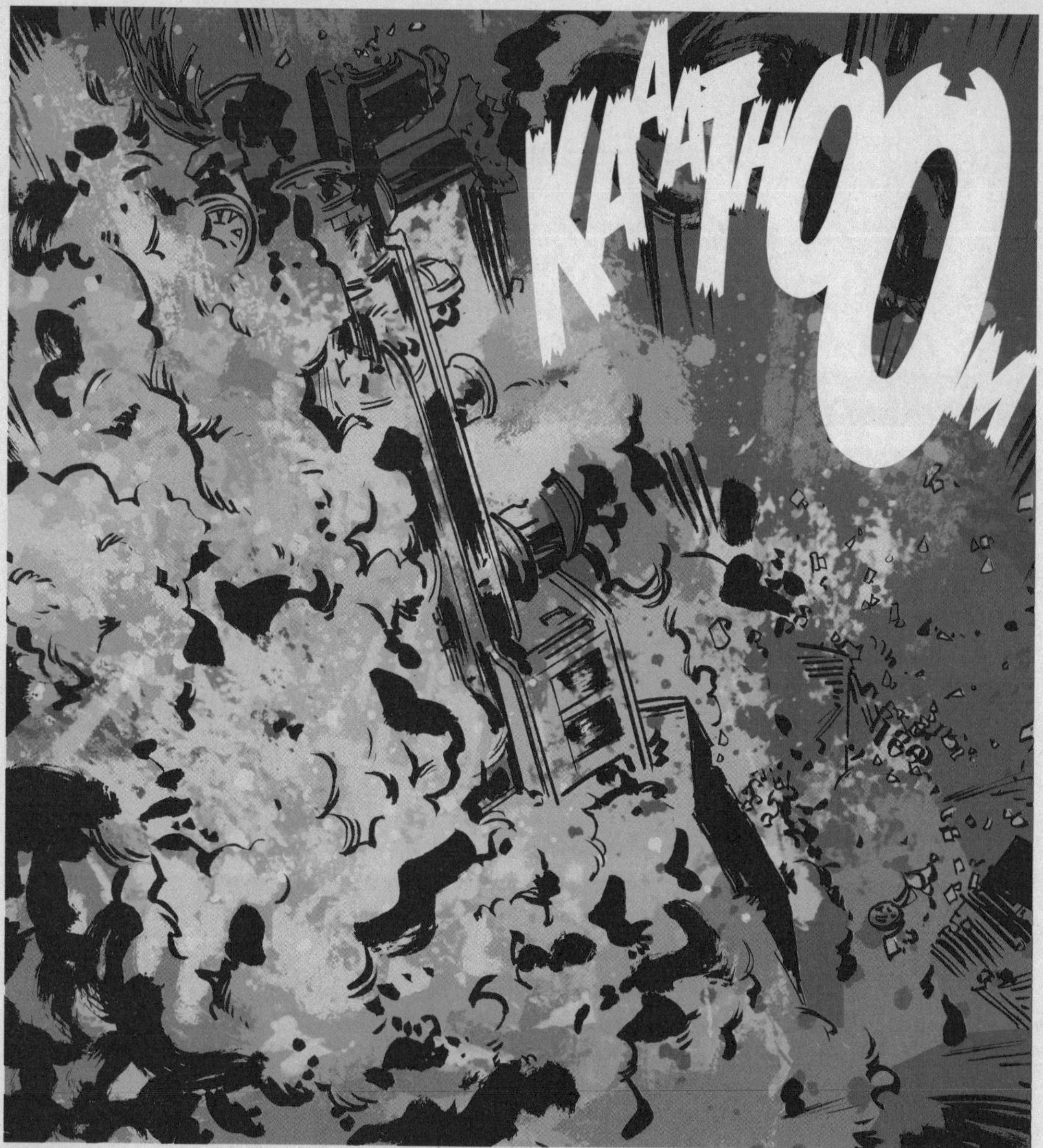
KAATHOOM

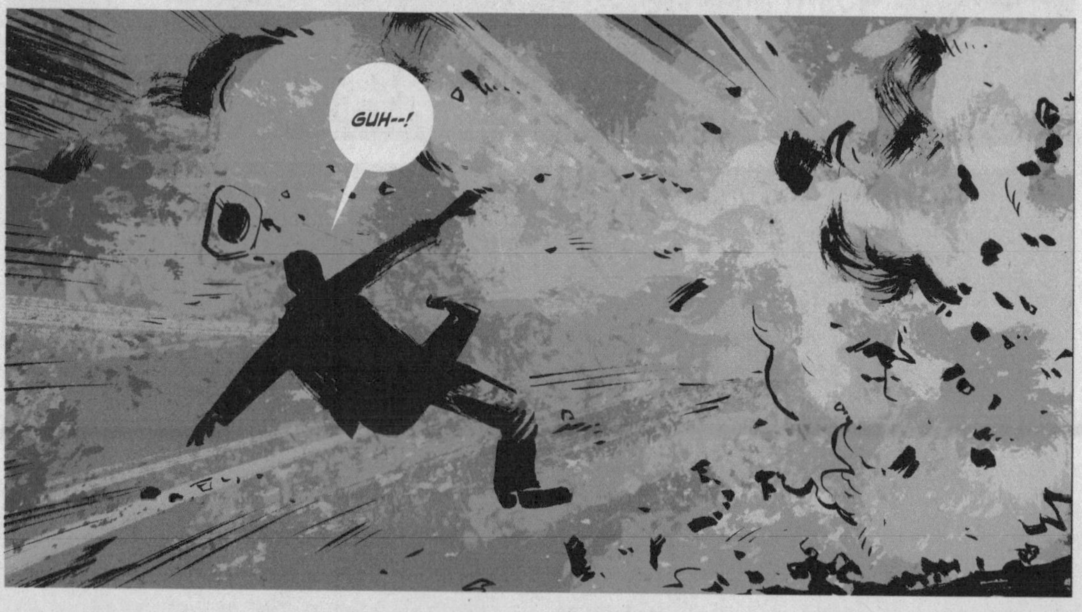
GUH--!

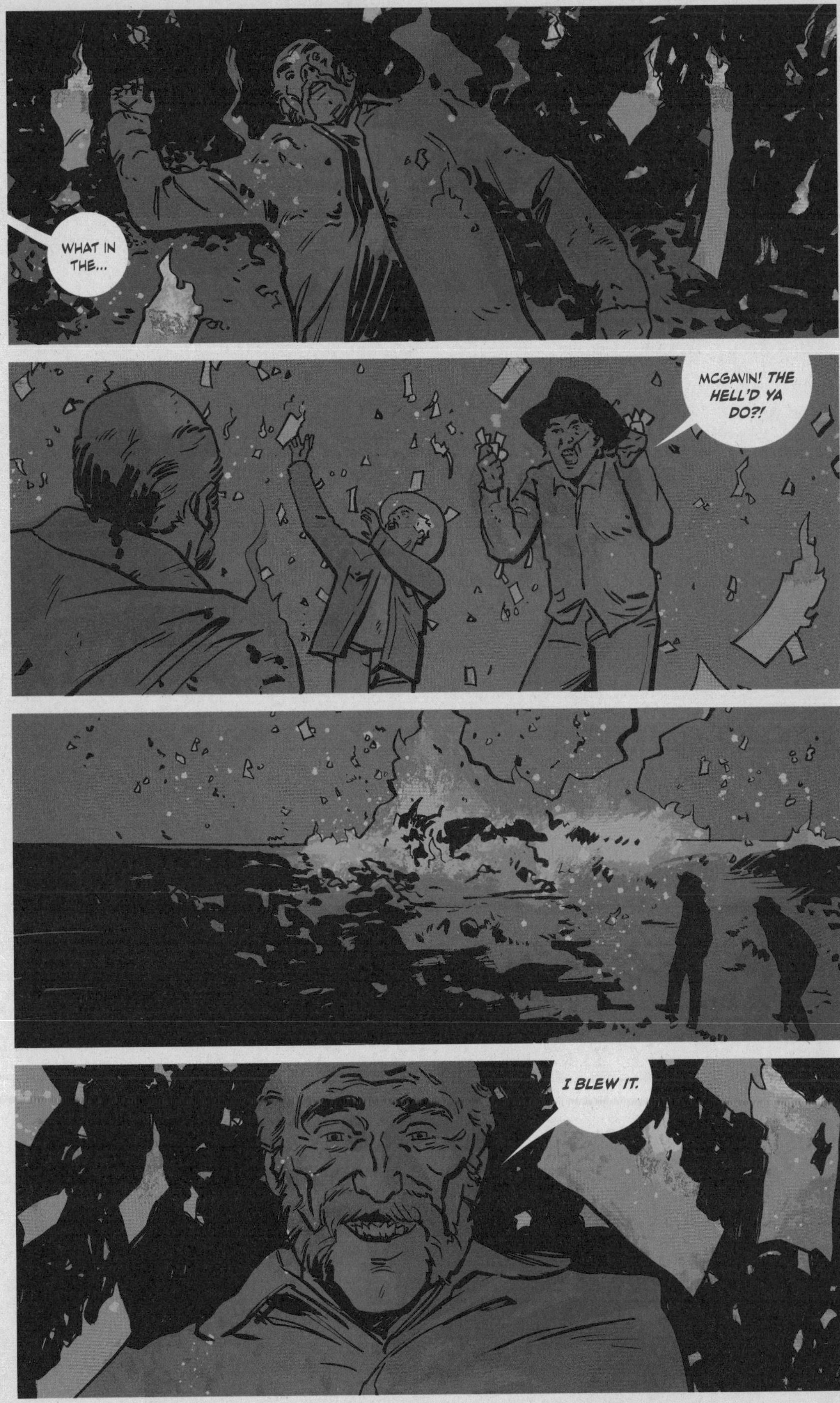
WHAT IN THE...
MCGAVIN! THE HELL'D YA DO?!
I BLEW IT.

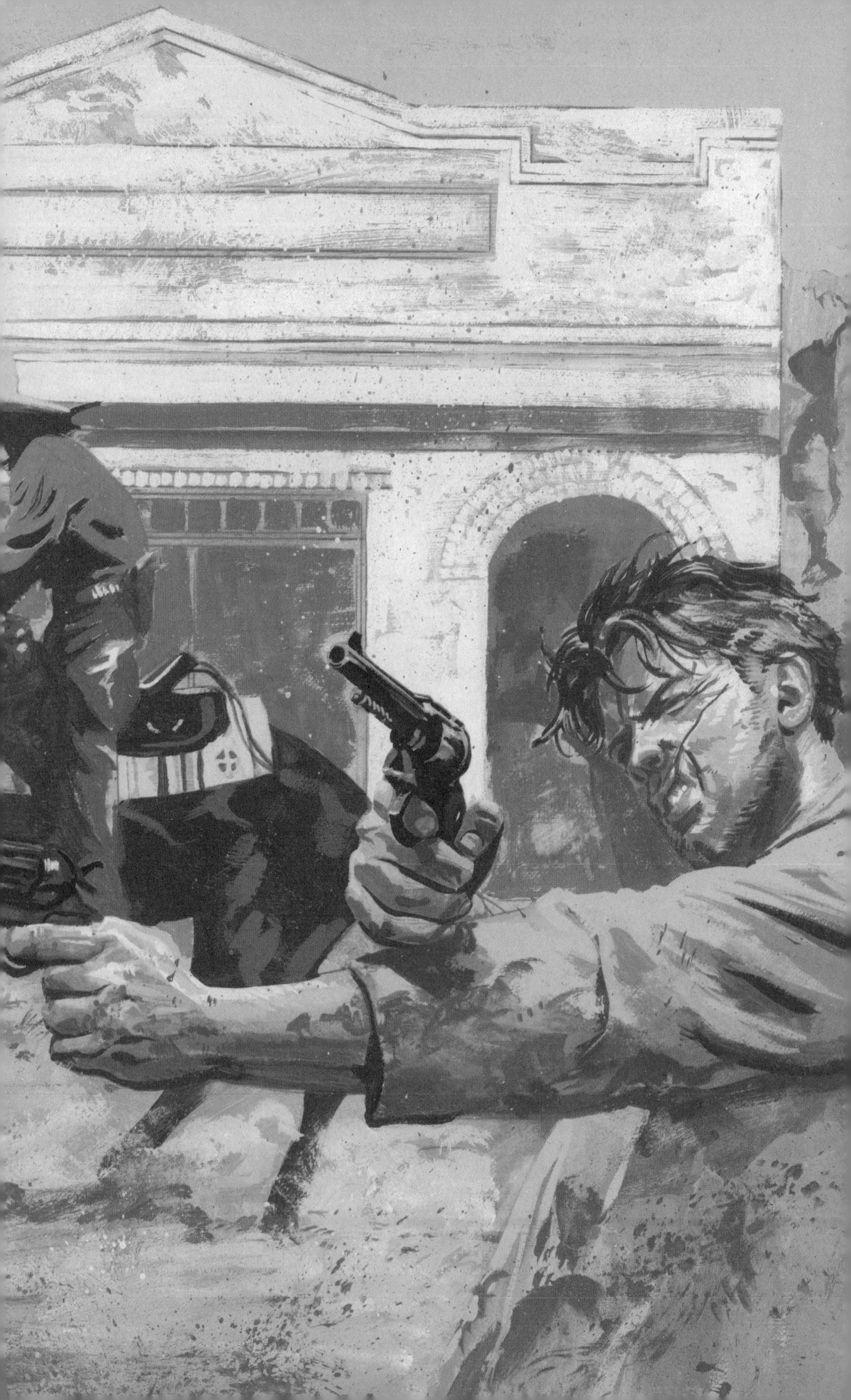

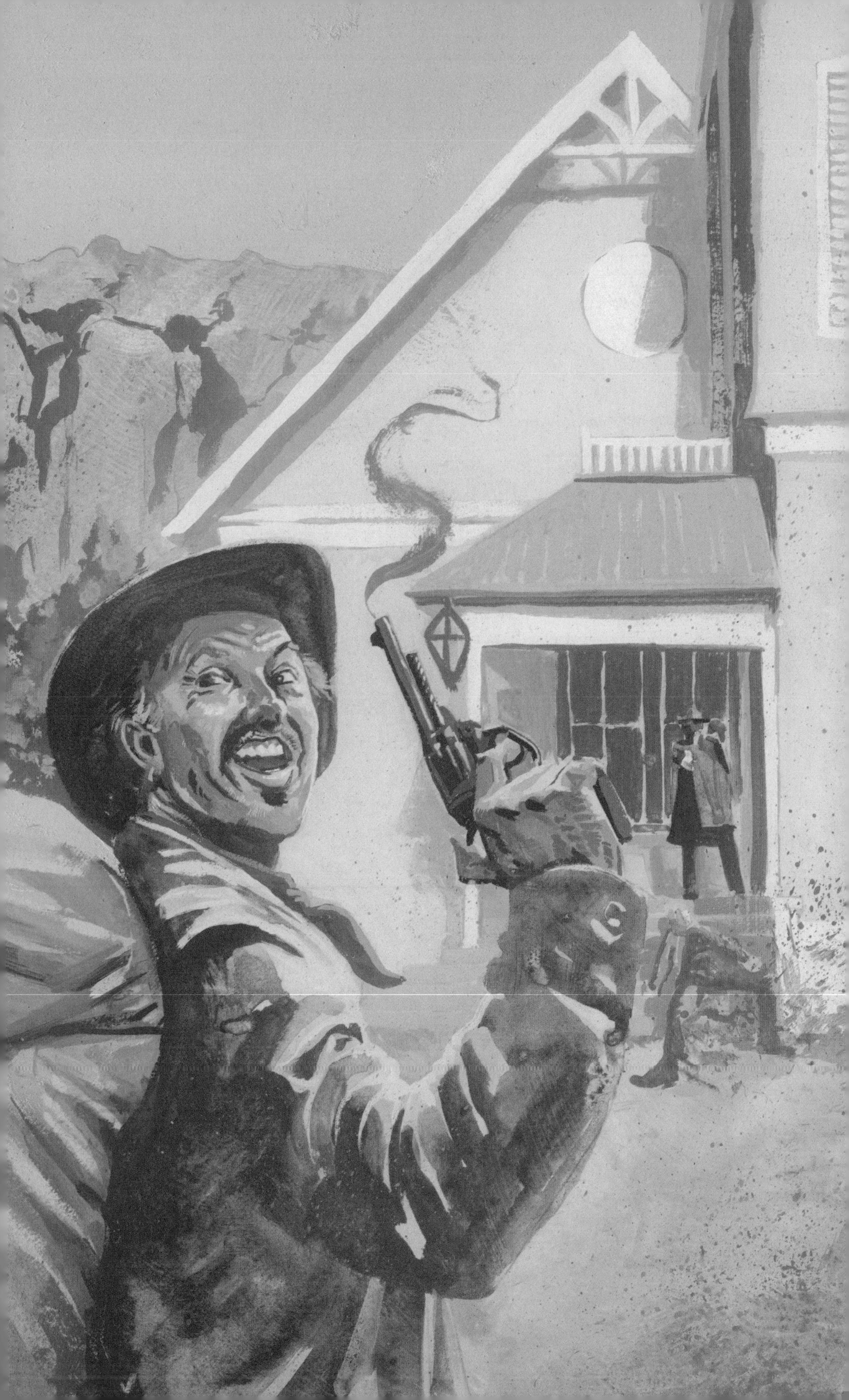

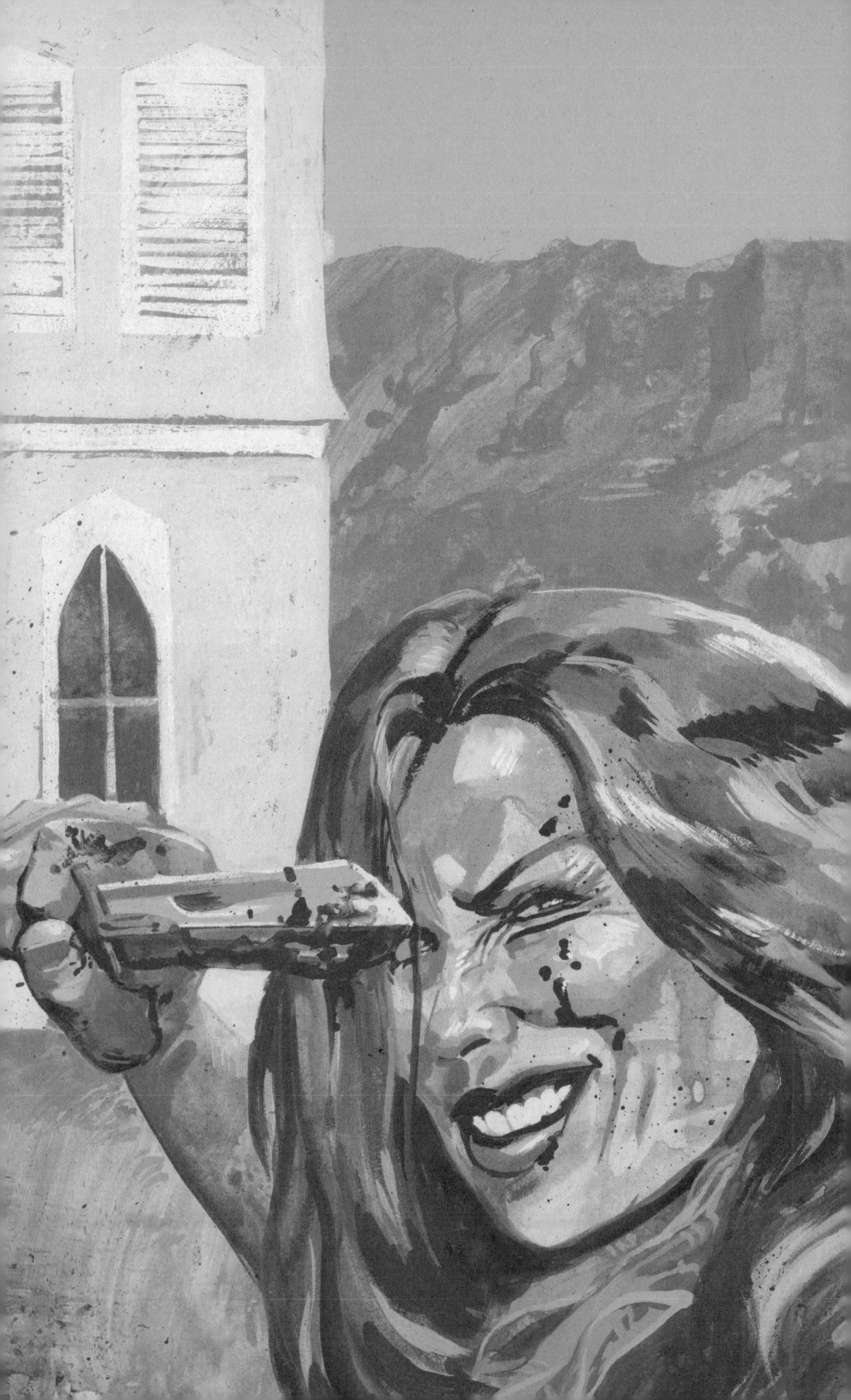

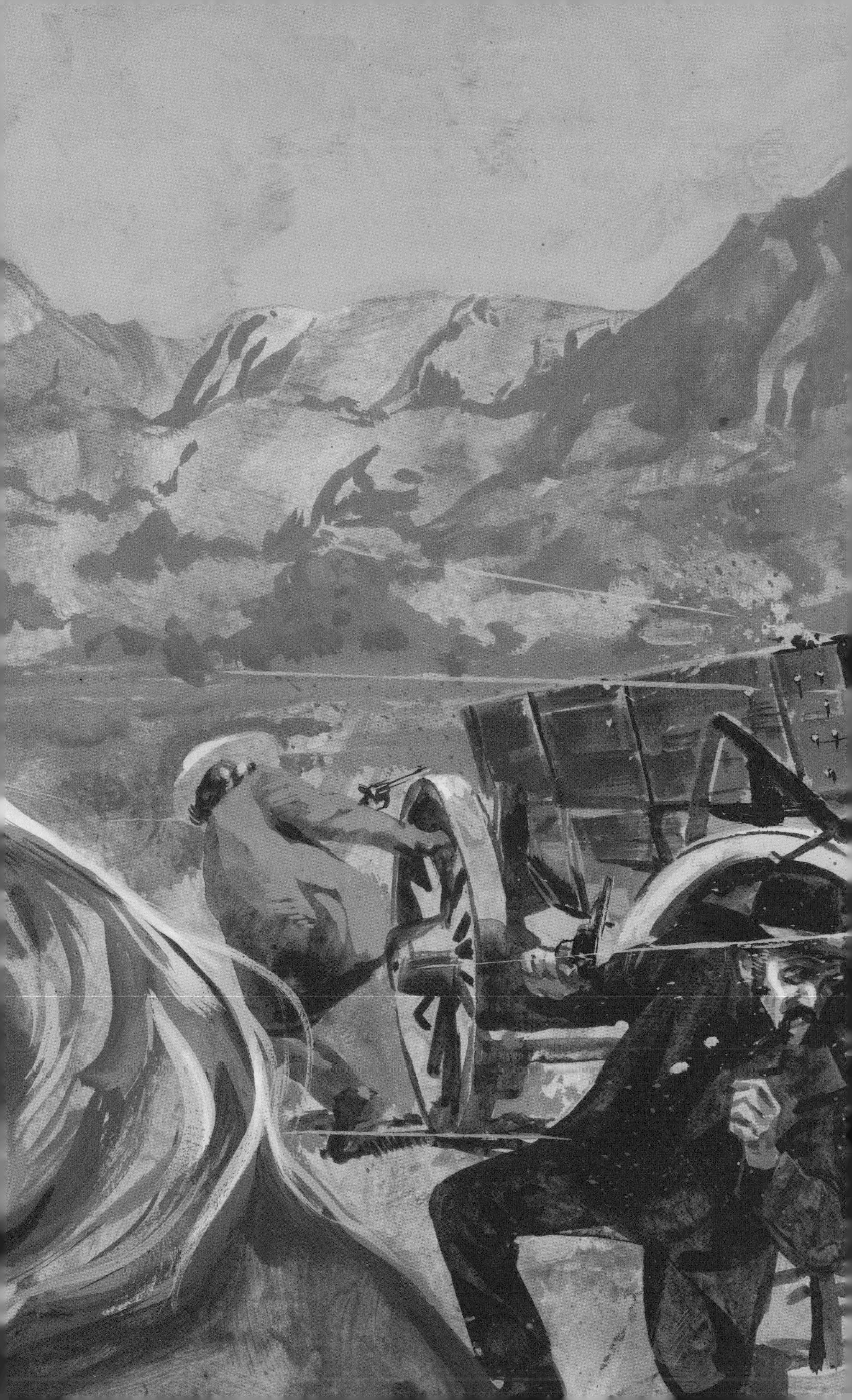

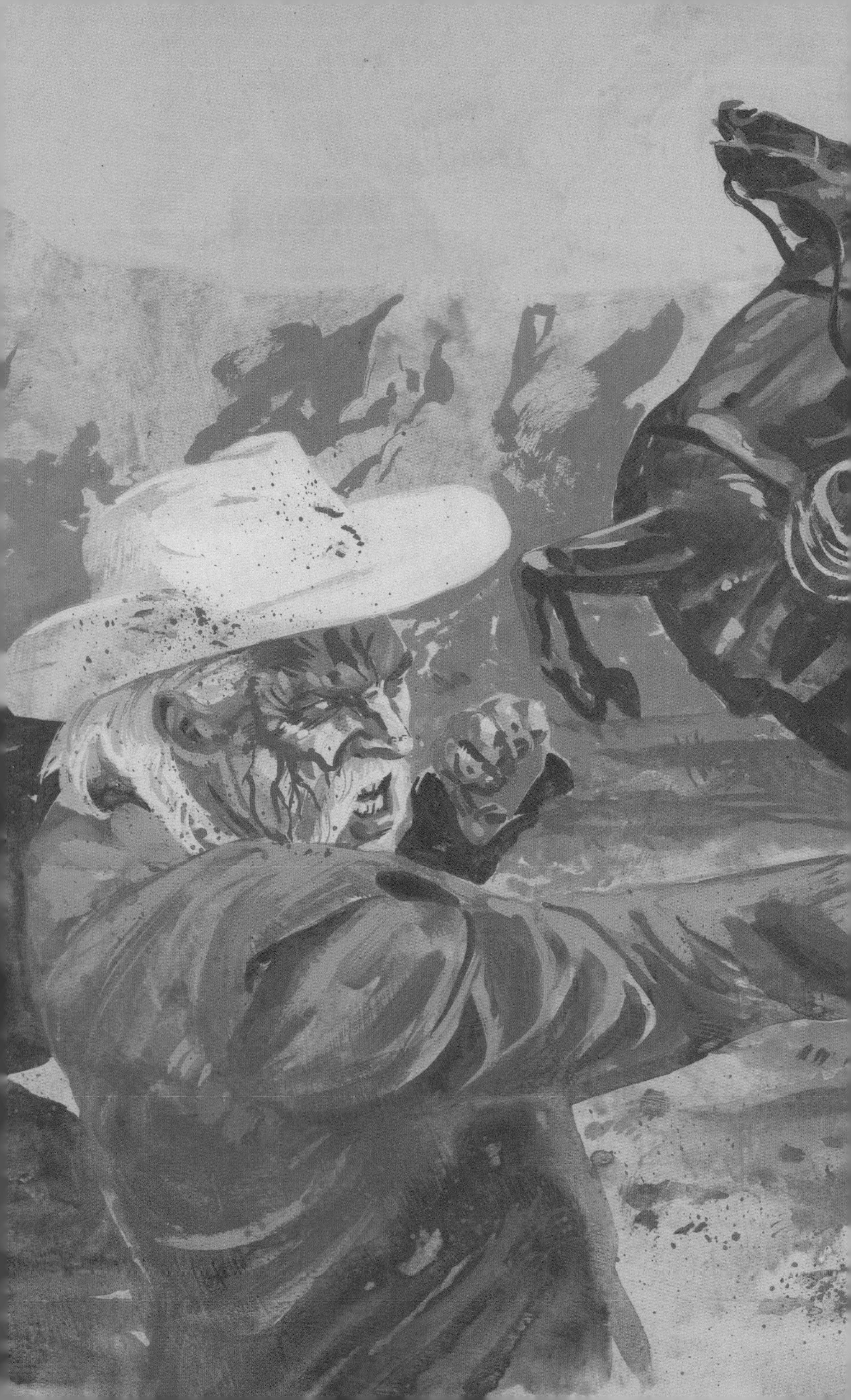

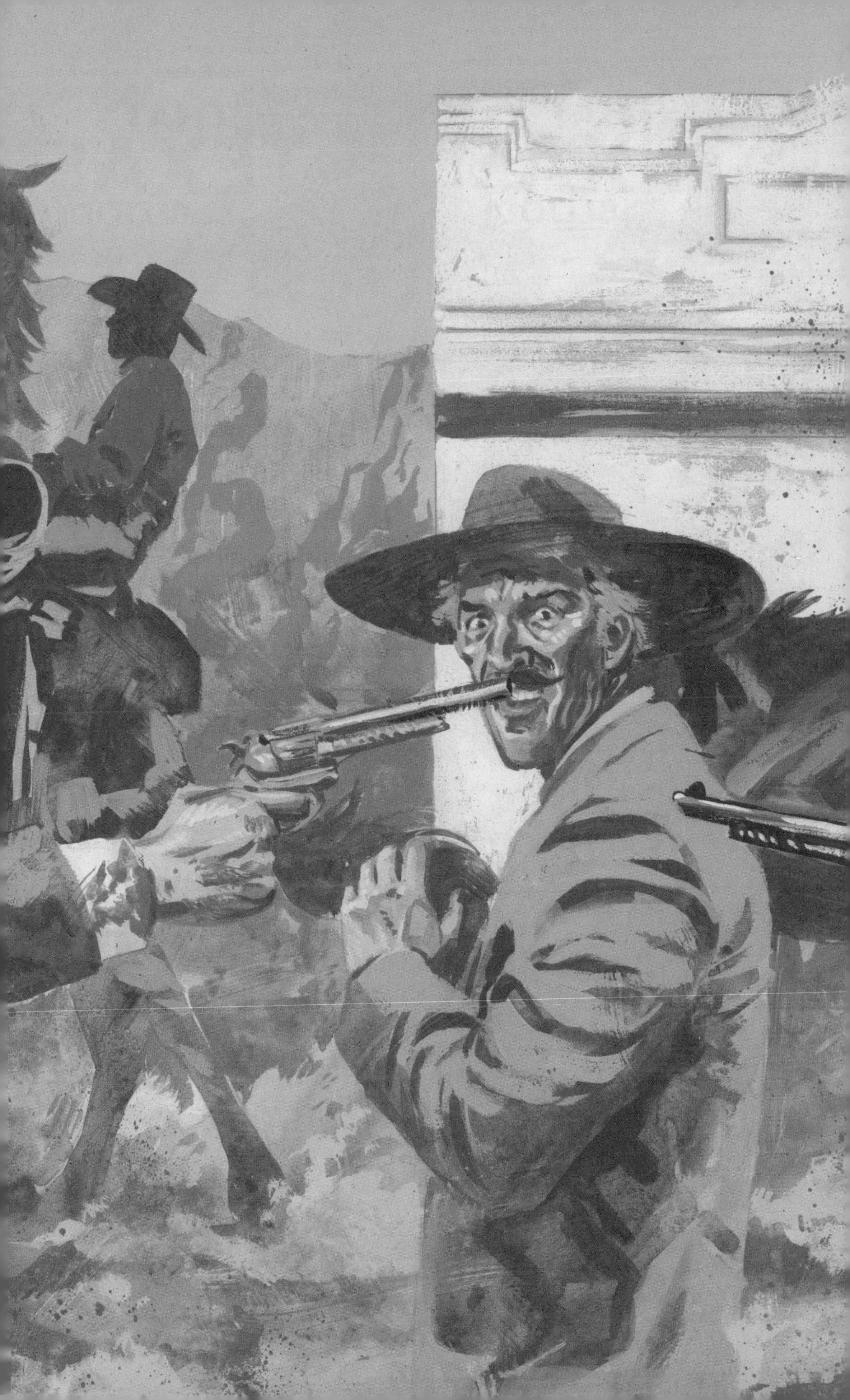

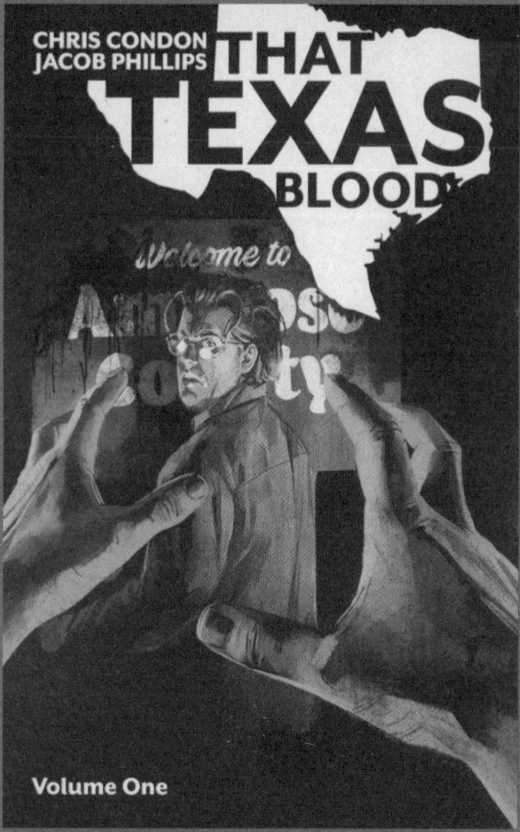
CHRIS CONDON
JACOB PHILLIPS
THAT TEXAS BLOOD
Welcome to
Volume One

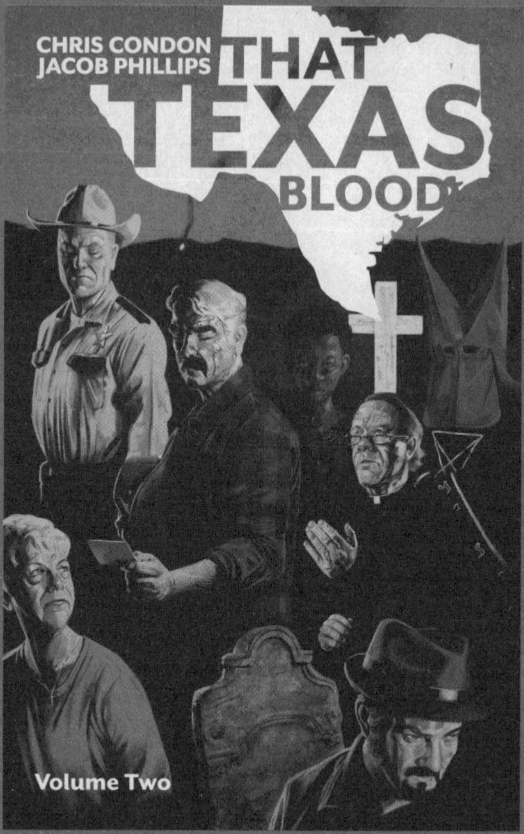
CHRIS CONDON
JACOB PHILLIPS
THAT TEXAS BLOOD
Volume Two

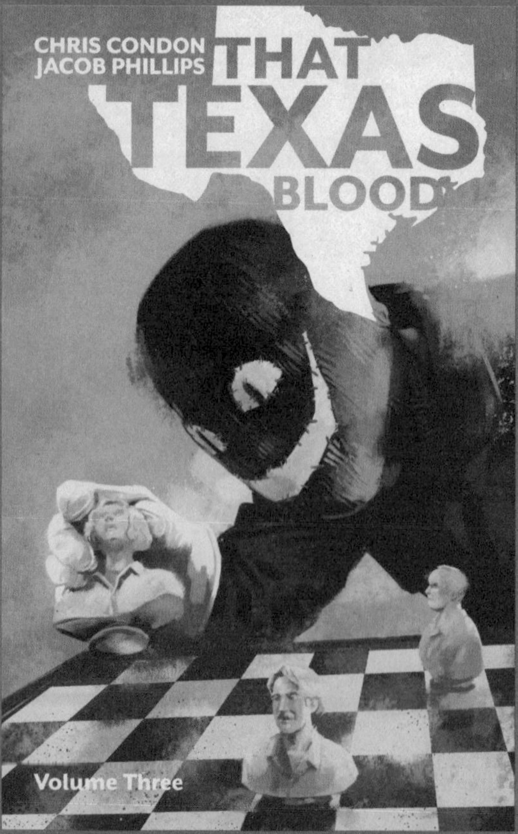
CHRIS CONDON
JACOB PHILLIPS
THAT TEXAS BLOOD
Volume Three